PRAISE FOR DAVID DOWNING

'Outstanding'
Publishers Weekly on *Lehrter Station*

...k Robert Harris and *Fatherland* mixed with a dash of
Le Carré'
Sue Baker, *Publishing News*

...derfully drawn spy novel . . . A very auspicious début,
with more to come'
The Bookseller on *Zoo Station*

...xcellent and evocative . . . Downing's strength is his
...hing out of the tense and often dangerous nature of
everyday life in a totalitarian state'
The Times on *Silesian Station*

...iting and frightening all at once . . . It's got everything
going for it'
Julie Walters

...ne of the brightest lights in the shadowy world of
historical spy fiction'
Birmingham Post

...utstanding thriller . . . This series is a quite remarkable
achievement'
Shots magazine

ALSO BY DAVID DOWNING

Zoo Station
Silesian Station
Stettin Station
Potsdam Station

David Downing is the author of several works of fiction and non-fiction. His first novel in the 'Station' series, *Zoo Station*, was published by Old Street in 2007, followed by *Silesian Station* in 2008, *Stettin Station* in 2009 and *Potsdam Station* in 2010. *Lehrter Station* is the fifth in the series, and the first to be set in the postwar period. David lives in Surrey with his wife and two cats.

LEHRTER STATION

DAVID DOWNING

First published in 2012 by Old Street Publishing Ltd

Trebinshun House, Brecon LD3 7PX

www.oldstreetpublishing.co.uk

ISBN 978-1-906964-75-7

10 9 8 7 6 5 4 3 2 1

A CIP catalogue record for this title is available from the British Library.

Printed and bound by CPI Group (UK) Ltd, Croydon, CR0 4YY

LEHRTER
STATION

14 December 1943

This night train was not like the one that had brought her to Berlin all those years ago. You could walk down that train, stare out of the wide corridor windows, move from carriage to carriage, eat dinner in one set up as a restaurant. This train was just a series of self-contained rooms, each with a pair of long seats and two doors to the outside world.

Their room had been full when they left Berlin. There were herself and Leon, two elderly men wearing old-fashioned collars, a woman and her almost grown-up daughter, and two *Hitlerjugend* on their way home from their annual convention. Baldur von Schirach himself had presented the medals they'd won in a Reich-wide orienteering contest.

So far their papers had only been checked the once, during the long stop at Frankfurt an der Oder. Two drenched officials had come in from the pelting rain, dripped on all the proffered documents, and grumbled their way back again. Hers had survived a dozen inspections in Berlin, but she had still been worried that her face would betray her, that these people really did have a sixth sense when it came to Jews. Sitting back relieved, as the train pulled away, she told herself that she was simply falling for their propaganda, for the lie that Jews were somehow intrinsically different. Her father had always denied this – human beings were human beings, he had always claimed, no matter what faith they chose. The trouble was, he would usually add, some of them didn't know it.

The two *Hitlerjugend* had seemed like nice enough boys. They had admired Leon's tinplate engine, and tried to teach him noughts and crosses. The boy had certainly enjoyed the attention, his eyes wistfully following them when they disappeared down the darkened platform at Glogau. The mother and daughter had also got off there, leaving the two old men to sit behind their newspapers and smoke their foul-smelling cigarettes. 'Victory at Vitebsk!' ran the headline on one, just three words for the whole front page. She wondered how Breslau had fared – would it be as bad as Berlin?

She read to Leon as quietly as she could, aware that even this was irritating the two old men, but reminding herself of Sophie Wilden's oft-repeated advice – 'the more submissive you are, the more they'll wonder why.' When the old men got off at Liegnitz she breathed a sigh a relief – now perhaps she and Leon could lie down and get some sleep. But then, with the whistle already blowing, the door jerked open and a man climbed in.

He was in his forties, she guessed. Quite burly, with a weak chin and gold-rimmed glasses. He was wearing a black uniform, but not *that one* – there were no lightning flashes, only a number on the epaulettes and two stripes on the arms. She could smell the alcohol on his breath and see the animal in his eyes.

He was affable enough at first. He tried to talk to Leon, in much the same way the *Hitlerjugend* had done. But there was nothing genuine in it. Leon was only three, but even he could tell something was wrong, and soon his face was creased with anxiety, the way it had been after the Wildens' house was bombed. And the man kept looking up at her, as if for approval, the glances soon slipping from her face to her breasts.

'I think he should get some sleep,' she said, trying to sound firm but not aggressive.

'Of course,' the man said, leaning back in his corner seat. He took out a silver flask and took a swig. She could feel his eyes on her as she covered Leon with the small blanket she'd brought for that purpose.

'Are you all right, Mama?' the boy asked. He was having trouble keeping his eyes open.

'Of course I am. Now you get some sleep, and I will too.' She kissed him on the head and went back to her corner seat. It was furthest she could get from the man, but perhaps she should have taken Leon's head in her lap – she couldn't decide.

'Where is the boy's father?' the man asked.

'He was killed at Stalingrad,' she said automatically. It was the story she always told, and true as far as Leon knew. But telling it this time had been a mistake – Leon was asleep, and she could have claimed a living protector, one who was waiting on the platform at Breslau. Someone powerful like an SS officer, someone to make this man think twice.

'I'm sorry,' he said, with a palpable lack of sincerity. He took another swig, then offered her the flask.

She politely declined.

'This belonged to a Russian once,' he went on, waving the flask. 'One I killed. Perhaps I avenged your husband – who knows?'

'Are you still in the Army?' she asked.

'No, I work for the General Government in Galicia. We are clearing lands for German settlement,' he explained peevishly, as if someone had challenged his usefulness. 'Your husband, what was his occupation?'

'He was the manager of a department store,' she decided, thinking of Torsten.

'You must miss him,' he said abruptly.

'My husband? Of course.'

'The closeness. The human touch.'

'I have my son,' she said shortly. 'It's been nice talking to you, but now I think I must get some sleep. We have much to do in Breslau tomorrow.'

He nodded but said nothing, just took another swig and stared out into the darkness.

Perhaps he would let her be, she thought; perhaps he'd drink himself to sleep. She closed her eyes, ears alert for any sound of movement. She thought she could feel his stare, but maybe it was just imagination. It wasn't as if she was a great beauty.

She felt weary to the bone herself. It would be so wonderful to fall asleep and wake up in Breslau...

She didn't know how long she was out, but she woke with a start to feel an arm around her neck, a hand roughly squeezing her breast, and waves of schnapps-heavy breath gusting over her face.

'Don't make a fuss,' he said, his arm tightening its grip around her neck. The bulge of an erection was straining at his trousers.

Most of her wanted to scream, to twist and writhe and bite and claw, but she'd had six years to steel herself against this moment, to carve out the composure she would need to thwart the next rapist. 'I won't make a fuss,' she whispered, and was amazed at the steadiness of her own voice. She brushed a finger along the bulge, fighting back nausea. 'If you let me up, I'll take off my blouse.'

He pulled out his arm from behind her neck, and started undoing his belt.

She got to her feet and, standing with her back to him, began unbuttoning the blouse. Leon was fast asleep, his tinplate engine wedged between him and the back of the seat. She'd have just one chance, she thought, and her knees felt weak at the thought.

She reached forward to rearrange the boy's blanket, picked up the engine as if moving it out of his way, then turned and crashed it into the man's face, shattering his glasses and drawing a spurt of blood from his forehead. A gasp of agony came out of his throat as his hands reached up to his eyes.

She stood there for a second, suddenly uncertain, but the moment he tried to rise she hit him again, this time on the side of the head, and down he went between the seats, his head and shoulders against the door.

He was unconscious, maybe even dead.

And Leon, she saw, had slept through it all.

Steeling herself, she stood astride the man's legs and tugged at his armpits until his upper back was also against the door. Then, kneeling on the corner seat, she depressed the door handle until the door sprang open. Head and shoulders dropped into a curtain of rain, but the rest showed no sign of following them out, until she crawled back along the seat, got behind his feet, and started pushing with all her might. For several long moments nothing seemed to move, and then with a rush the body was gone.

It took her longer still to pull the door shut, and the bang when she did was loud enough to wake the boy.

'Mama?' he said anxiously.

'It's nothing,' she said quickly, sitting beside him and stroking his hair. 'Go back to sleep.'

He reached up an arm but obediently closed his eyes. Tomorrow she would need an explanation, she realised. Not for the man, who for all Leon knew had simply got off, but for the damage to his favourite toy.

The men from Moscow

John Russell reached across and rubbed the tea shop window with his sleeve to get a better view of what was happening on the pavement outside. A middle-aged man in uniform was hectoring two boys of around twelve, jabbing his finger at first one and then the other to emphasise his indignation. The boys wore suitably downcast expressions, but one was still clutching a fearsome-looking catapult behind his back. Once the adult had run out of useful advice and stalked haughtily away, the two youngsters raced off in the opposite direction, giggling fit to bust. Russell somehow doubted that they had seen the error of their ways.

He took another sip of the still-scalding tea, and went back to his *News Chronicle*. Like most of the newspapers, it was filled with evidence of Britain's newly split personality. While half the writers explored, with varying degrees of eagerness, the socialist future promised by the new Labour government, the other half was busily lamenting those myriad challenges to Empire that the war's end had conjured into being. Palestine, Java, India, Egypt... the outbreaks of violent disaffection seemed never-ending, and thoroughly inconvenient. The British press, like the British public, might want a new world at home, but they were in no mood to relinquish the old one abroad.

The sports page was still full of the Moscow Dynamo tour, which had begun so inauspiciously the previous weekend. A fellow journalist had told Russell the story of the Football Association reception committee's dash to Croydon Airport, and the subsequent rush back across London when it transpired that the Russians' plane was about to land at Northolt. The FA's choice of Wellington Barracks as a hotel had gone down badly with the tourists, particularly when their arrival coincided with the drilling of a punishment detail. Several of the Soviet players had concluded that they were being imprisoned, and had refused to leave their bus. It seemed as if things had improved since then – yesterday the visitors had been taken to the White City dog-track, where only the Magic Eye photo machine had denied them a rouble-earning win.

Russell looked at his watch – as usual, Effi was late. Clearing a new patch in the condensation he could see the queue outside the cinema already receding up Park Street. He gulped down the rest of his tea and went to join it, hurrying to beat the crowd pouring off a pair of trolley-buses. The visibility on Camden High Street was worse than it had been twenty minutes earlier, and the air seemed twice as cold and damp.

Several people in the queue were stamping their feet and clapping their hands, but most seemed in surprisingly high spirits. Only six months had passed since the end of the war in Europe, and perhaps the novelty of peace had not quite worn off. Or maybe they were just happy to be out of their overcrowded houses. Russell hoped they weren't expecting an uplift from the film they were about to see, which the same journalist friend had warned him was a sure-fire wrist-slitter. But then Effi had chosen it, and it was her turn. She still hadn't forgiven him for *West of the Pecos*.

The queue was beginning to move. He looked at his watch again, and felt the first stirrings of anxiety – Effi's English was improving, but still a long way from fluent, and frustration always seemed to render her German accent even more pronounced. Locals with grudges had no way of knowing that she was a heroine of the anti-Nazi resistance.

He was almost at the door when she appeared at his side. 'The trolley-bus broke down,' she explained in German, leaving Russell conscious of the sudden silence around them.

She noticed it too. 'I have to walk half way,' she added in English. 'How is your day?' she asked, taking his arm.

'Not so bad,' he said, with what had lately become his usual lack of candour. Was she just as reluctant to share her worries with him, he wondered. When they had found each other again in April, after more than three years apart, everything had seemed just like before, but slowly, over the succeeding weeks and months, a gap had opened up. Not a large one, but a gap all the same. He was often aware of it, and knew that she was too. But try to talk about it, as they had on several occasions, and all they ended up doing was re-state the problem.

'Solly has a couple of ideas he's looking into,' he told her, forbearing to add that his agent had seemed even less hopeful than usual. Since the *San Francisco Chronicle* had dispensed with his services in May, Russell had returned to freelancing, but pieces sold had been few and far between, and he sometimes wondered whether he was on some unknown blacklist. He had done enough to warrant inclusion on such a list, but as far as he knew no one else was aware of that fact.

And money was decidedly short, he thought, counting out the three shillings and sixpence for their tickets. Effi and her sister Zarah were earning a little from their needlework, but Paul's job with Solly was their only regular source of income. It was all a far cry from their affluent life in pre-war Germany.

They found two seats in the centre of the back stalls and watched the auditorium slowly fill. For Effi, such moments always brought back memories of her years alone in Berlin, when a darkened cinema was the only place she could meet with her sister. And she was also reminded of evenings with Russell, watching herself up there on the screen, back when she'd been a famous actress. It seemed several lifetimes ago, but lately she'd found herself missing the stage, and wondering if she would ever act again. Not here, of course, not with her English, but back in Germany? Several theatres had already re-opened in Berlin, and sooner or later her country would start making films again.

It would probably be later, she thought, as the Pathé News camera panned across the ruins of her home town. The streets seemed clearer than they had in April, but nothing much else seemed changed. There were no signs of new construction, only military jeeps and haggard-looking women weaving their way through a maze of perforated masonry. British servicemen looked up from their lunches to grin at the camera, but she doubted whether the locals were eating so well.

The 'B' movie had London policemen successfully rounding up a gang of black market spivs, something they seemed incapable of doing in real life. Russell missed the name of the film being trailed, but it involved a man and a woman sharing meaningful expressions in a railway station buffet, and looked likely to end in tears. Another wrist-slitter.

Effi's choice of main feature proved a good one, well-written, well-acted and very atmospheric. Russell found the masculinity of the leading actress somewhat off-putting, but the California-by-night setting was wonderfully evocative, the storyline taut and involving. And something was definitely being said between the lines about a woman's place in the post-war world.

When they finally emerged from the cinema the fog had grown much thicker. They crossed Camden High Street and walked arm in arm past a crowded pub – the beer shortage was clearly less severe than advertised. The interior looked as murky as the streets, blue cigarette smoke merging with greyish fog in the light from the nearest lamppost.

'So how was your day?' Russell asked.

'Good. Rosa had a good day at school. And Zarah had another flirt with the man downstairs.'

They were speaking German now, which won them curious looks from a couple walking in the other direction.

'And you?' Russell asked.

'Oh, I queued for bread, made dinner for everyone. I read this afternoon – three whole pages of *Great Expectations*. But I'm still looking up one word in three, or that's what it seems like. I was never any good at languages.'

'It'll come.'

'I doubt it. But...' Her voice trailed away... 'So what did you think of *Mildred Pierce?*'

'I liked it, I think.'

'You think?'

'I was never bored. It looked good. Though the daughter did seem a bit over the top – would any mother be that blind?'

'Of course. I've known mothers who've put up with much worse. No, it wasn't that...' She paused. They had reached the bus stop on College Street, and a trolleybus was already looming out of the fog. It was crowded with over-exuberant West End revellers, and continuing their conversation in German seemed ill-advised. Effi spent the five-minute bus journey trying to sort out her reaction to the film. The dominant emotion, she decided, was anger, but she wasn't at all sure why.

After alighting on Highgate Road she said as much to Russell.

'The portrayal of women,' he guessed. 'Though the men were just as appalling. The only sympathetic character was the younger sister, and they killed her off.'

'There was also the friend, but she was too smart to attract a good man.'

'True.'

The fog seemed thicker than ever, but perhaps it was the added smoke from the nearby engine sheds.

'But you're right,' Effi went on, as they turned into Lady Somerset Road, 'it was the way the women were written. When the Nazis were portraying them as submissive idiots, it was so wonderful to see someone like Katherine Hepburn show how happy and sexy independent women could be. And now the Nazis are gone, and Hollywood gives us Mildred, who can only have a successful career if she fails as a mother and husband. Goebbels would have loved it.'

'A bit harsh,' Russell murmured.

'Not at all,' she rounded on him. 'You just...'

Two figures suddenly emerged in front of them, silhouettes in the mist. 'Stick 'em up,' one of the two said, in a tone that seemed borrowed from an American gangster movie.

'What?' was Russell's first reaction. The voice sounded young, and both potential robbers seemed unusually short. But it did look like a real gun pointing at them. A Luger, if Russell was not mistaken.

'Stick 'em up,' the voice repeated petulantly. The faces were becoming clearer now – and they belonged to boys, not men. Fourteen perhaps, maybe even younger. The one on the left was wearing trousers too long for his legs. A relation who hadn't come home.

'What do you want?' Russell asked, with what felt like remarkable good humour, given the situation. Only that morning he'd read about two thirteen-year-olds holding up a woman in Highgate. Far too many boys had lost their fathers.

'Your money of course,' the second boy said, almost apologetically.

'We only have a couple of shillings.'

'You Germans are all liars,' the first boy said angrily.

'I'm English,' Russell patiently explained, as he reached inside his coat pocket for the coins in question. He doubted the gun was even loaded, but it didn't seem worth the risk to find out.

Effi had other ideas. 'This is ridiculous,' she muttered in German, as she stepped forward and twisted the gun out of the surprised youth's hand. 'Now go home,' she told them in English.

They glanced at each other, and bolted off into the fog.

Effi just stood there, amazed at what she'd done. She was, she realised, shaking like a leaf. What mad instinct had made her do such a thing?

'Christ almighty,' Russell exclaimed, reaching out for her. 'For a moment there...'

'I didn't think,' she said stupidly. She started to laugh, but there was no humour in the sound, and Russell cradled her head against his shoulder. They stood there for a while, until Effi disentangled herself and offered him the gun.

He put it in his coat pocket. 'I'll hand it in at the police station tomorrow morning.'

They walked the short distance home, and let themselves in to the ground floor flat that Russell had rented. It had two large rooms, a small kitchen and an outside toilet. Russell, Effi and Rosa shared the back room, Paul, Lothar and Zarah the curtain-divided room at the front.

Other families of four and five lived above and below them.

Paul was reading a book on architecture in the kitchen, his English dictionary propped up beside him. 'They're all asleep,' he told them quietly.

Effi went to check on Rosa, the young Jewish orphan who had been her ward since April. Though perhaps not an orphan, as Effi reminded herself. The father Otto had disappeared around 1941, and not been seen or heard of since. He was probably dead, but there was no way of knowing for sure. Effi thought the uncertainty worried Rosa – it certainly worried her.

Sitting down on the side of the bed, she could smell the Vick's Vapo-Rub that Zarah had put on the girl's chest. Effi pulled the blanket up around her neck, and told herself that Rosa was coping better than most with the post-war world. She was doing well at the school that Solly had found for them. Although there were many other refugee pupils, the instruction was wholly in English, and Rosa's command of that language was already better than Effi's own. And Solly seemed more excited by her Berlin drawings than by any of John's ideas. The girl would end up supporting them both.

In the kitchen, Russell was telling his son about the attempted hold-up. Paul's smile vanished when he realised his father wasn't having him on. 'Was the gun loaded?' he asked.

'I haven't looked,' Russell admitted, and pulled it from his pocket. 'It was,' he discovered. 'I'll put it out of harm's way,' he added, reaching up to place it on the highest shelf. 'Anything interesting happen at work?'

'Not really,' Paul said, getting up. 'It's time I went to bed,' he explained. 'Another early start.'

'Of course,' Russell said automatically. His son didn't want to talk to him, which was neither unusual nor intended personally: Paul didn't want to talk to anybody. But he seemed to be functioning like a normal human being – only that lunchtime Solly had confided how pleased he was with the boy – and Russell knew from experience what havoc war could wreak on minds of any age. 'Sleep well,' he said.

'I hope so,' Paul said. 'For everyone's sake,' he added wryly – his nightmares sometimes woke the whole house. 'Oh, I forgot,' he added, stopping in the doorway. 'There was a letter for you. It's on your bed.'

'I've got it,' Effi said, squeezing past him. She gave Paul a goodnight hug before handing the envelope over to Russell.

He tore it open, and extracted the contents – a short handwritten note and a grandstand ticket for the following Tuesday's match between Chelsea and the Moscow Dynamo tourists. 'Your attendance is expected,' the note informed him. It was signed by Yevgeny Shchepkin, his erstwhile guardian angel in Stalin's NKVD.

'So the bill has finally arrived,' Effi said, reading it over his shoulder.

Lying beside her half an hour later, Russell felt strangely pleased that it had. In May he had bought his family's safety from the Soviets with atomic secrets and vague promises of future service, and he had always known that one day they would demand payment on the Faustian bargain. For months he had dreaded that day, but now that it was here, he felt almost relieved.

It wasn't just an end to the suspense. The war in Europe had been over for six months, and the Nazis, who had dominated their lives for a dozen years, were passing into history, but all their lives – his and Effi's in particular – had still seemed stuck in some sort of post-war limbo, the door to their future still locked by their particular past. And Shchepkin's invitation might – might – be the key that would open it.

* * *

Monday morning was unusually crisp and clear, columns of smoke rising from a hundred chimneys into a clear blue sky as Russell walked down Kentish Town Road. There were long lines outside the two bakeries he passed, but most of the queuing women seemed happy to chat while they waited.

It had been a strange weekend. On Saturday morning he had taken the gun to the local police station, and been asked to peruse an alarmingly extensive array of juvenile mug shots. He hadn't recognised his and Effi's would-be robbers, who had presumably just set out on their new career of crime.

That afternoon the whole family had gone for a walk on the nearby

Heath, but their collective mood had matched the grey weather. Paul and Lothar kicked around the latter's new football – one of Zarah's acquisitions from their street's resident spiv – but only the youngster looked like he was enjoying the experience. Effi still seemed subdued by the previous evening's excitement, and Rosa, as usual, responded to her new mother's mood. Only Zarah seemed determined to be cheerful, and after what she'd been through with the Russians – repeatedly raped by a Red Army foursome for three days and nights – Russell could only admire her for that.

Sunday the rain had come down, and they'd tiptoed around each other in the crowded flat, waiting for the weekend to end.

At least today was fine, and the long walk into town could be enjoyed for more than the saving of the bus fare. It took him half an hour to reach the Corner House opposite Tottenham Court Road tube station, where he had lately taken to having his morning coffee. It was a far cry from Kranzler's in Berlin – the decor was dreadful, the coffee worse – but a ritual was a ritual. A journalist had to read the papers somewhere, even one who was out of work, and he had grown used to the Corner House's heady blend of non-stop bustle, sweat and steam.

As usual, he began with the more digestible *News Chronicle*. Remembering he would soon see them play, he sought out the latest news of the Soviet footballers. The Sunday papers had been unimpressed – one witness of a training session at the White City had deemed them 'so slow that you can hear them think' – and the Monday *Chronicle* seemed of similar mind. Russell didn't know what to expect. Stalin's Russia seemed an unlikely source of imaginative football, but the English had a notorious propensity to over-estimate their own prowess. It would be interesting, if nothing more. A nice sugar-coating for whatever pill the Soviets had decided he should swallow.

The rest of the paper held no surprises. There was advice for demobbed husbands returning home – 'be glad to be back, say so as often you can' – and another child drowned in an emergency water tank. In Yorkshire three young women had been sacked from their jobs for refusing to swap their slacks for skirts.

The front page was full of the Prime Minister's visit to Washington. Attlee was apparently asking the Americans to share their atomic secrets with the Russians, and their wealth with an impoverished Britain. The Americans seemed more interested in persuading him to abandon his policy of imposing restrictions on Jewish emigration to Palestine.

There was nothing to match Russell's favourite revelation of the last few days, that Eva Braun's father had written to Hitler before the war, demanding to know the Führer's intentions. Having never received a reply, Herr Braun now believed that his letter had not reached its intended recipient.

What other explanation could there be?

Turning to the weightier *Times*, Russell found some Berlin news. A 'Battle of Winter' had been proclaimed, which sounded rather ominous, and involved cannibalising badly damaged buildings for those with a better chance of being patched up. Meanwhile owners of slightly damaged buildings had been given a year to claim compensation. This would interest Effi, whose building on Carmerstrasse had still been essentially intact when they last saw it.

The Soviets had celebrated the anniversary of Lenin's revolution by handing out gifts: a small sack of coal for each human resident, and extra food for the lions, elephant and hyena who had survived the shelling of the Zoo. And should this seem like small change for raping half the city's women, they had also unveiled a memorial to the liberating army. Anyone expecting a keener sense of irony from the nation of Gogol would be disappointed.

It was almost time for his meeting with Solly. Leaving the Corner House, he walked down Charing Cross Road, checking the windows for any new books. Solly Bernstein's office on Shaftesbury Avenue had survived the Blitz, but the ground floor steam laundry of pre-war days was now an insurance office. Russell walked up the four flights of stairs to the second floor, paused to recover his breath, and let himself in. Solly had a receptionist these days – a waif-like Hungarian refugee named Marisa with dark, frightened eyes and a very basic grasp of English. Told that

Mr Bernstein was 'engage-ed', Russell found his son in the smaller of the two back rooms, bent over what looked like the firm's accounts. Given Paul's emotional state at the time, Solly's offer of a job had been somewhat charitable, but the boy seemed to be managing all right. And *his* English had improved no end.

The two of them talked football while Russell waited for Solly, and Paul expressed an interest in seeing the Russians' second game in London, against the Arsenal. The Gunners' bomb-damaged ground at Highbury was still under repair, so they were hosting the Dynamos at nearby White Hart Lane on the following Wednesday.

He'd try and get some tickets, Russell told his son. He could ask Shchepkin when he saw him at Stamford Bridge.

Marisa put her head round the door, smiled sweetly at Paul, and told Russell he could now see Solly. The agent's news proved as bad as Russell had expected – all his recent ideas for feature articles had been rejected. Solly himself looked older than usual, his hair a little greyer, his eyes a little duller. As usual, he spent ten minutes telling Russell that he should take a break from journalism, and use the time to write a book. His escape from Germany in December 1941, Effi's adventures with the Berlin resistance – either, in Solly's not-so-humble opinion, would sell like fresh bagels. He was probably right, but the idea was still unappealing. Russell was a journalist, not a writer. And while an unsuccessful book would do nothing for his finances, a successful one might raise his profile to a dangerous degree. And what would he live on while he wrote it?

He said goodbye to Paul, walked back down to the street, and stood on the pavement outside wondering what to do with the rest of the day. More walking, he supposed, and set off in the general direction of the river. If the Soviets had no immediate plans for him perhaps he would give the book a try; at least he would be doing something. The world of journalism certainly seemed closed to him. The British nationals and London locals had no vacancies, and should one arise his American citizenship – acquired to allow his continued residence in Germany once Britain and the Reich were at war – was bound to complicate matters.

As were other chunks of his personal history. His time living in Nazi Germany made the left suspicious, and his former membership of both British and German communist parties had a similar effect on those with right-wing sympathies. If editors needed a further excuse for rejecting him, they could always point to his long exile and its obvious corollary, that he was out of touch with British life. Russell always denied this, but without much inner conviction. He did often feel a stranger in the land of his birth and childhood. If he wanted to function as a journalist again, then Berlin was the place to do so.

But Berlin, as *The Times* had told him only that morning, was still on its knees. His extended family had already experienced a stunning variety of traumas in that city, and taking them back for more seemed almost sadistic.

He walked on across Trafalgar Square, down the other side of Charing Cross Station to the Embankment, and slowly up past Cleopatra's Needle and the Savoy Hotel towards the new Waterloo Bridge. He, Paul, Zarah and Lothar had stayed at the Savoy in 1939; they had come to see a well-known Scottish paediatrician, in the hope of allaying Zarah's fears that Lothar was in some way mentally handicapped. Russell had been their chaperone and interpreter, and a tour guide to his eleven year-old son.

It had been a wonderful couple of days. Lothar had been given a clean bill of mental heath; he and Paul had seen a match at Highbury, inspected the streamlined Coronation Scot at Euston, and walked past Bow Street Police Station, where the fictional Saint's sparring partner Chief Inspector Teal had his office. In the bar of the Savoy, an idiot from the War Office had tried to persuade Russell that risking his life for His Majesty's Government was the very least he could do.

And that was the other complicating factor, Russell thought, as he leaned his midriff against the railings and looked down at the swirling brown waters – his mostly unresolved relationships with the world's leading intelligence agencies. Between 1939 and 1941 he had performed, with varying degrees of enthusiasm, services for the Soviets, Americans, British and Germans. Getting into this world had been all too easy, extracting himself wholly beyond him. He had concentrated on surviving the war with a more or less functioning conscience, and just about succeeded. But there was no way of breaking the bond, no way to wipe the slate clean.

The Nazis at least were gone. He had worked for them under duress, and as far as he knew had never done anything actually helpful, but there was always the chance of accusations that only the dead could refute. The British had ignored him since 1939, the Americans since 1942, but Russell doubted whether their indifference would survive a return to Berlin. He was of no use to them in London, but his many contacts in the German capital – on both sides of the new political divide – would make him a valuable asset.

The Soviets, though, were the real danger. In May he had secured his family's exit from Berlin and Germany by leading the NKVD to the cache of German atomic energy documents which he and the young Soviet physicist Varennikov had stolen from the Kaiser Wilhelm Institute. Reasoning that the Soviets might be tempted to ensure his permanent silence on this matter, he had forcibly reminded them that he couldn't tell the Americans anything without incriminating himself. The Soviets had probably already realised as much, and soon made it clear that they would use the threat of revelation to force Russell's cooperation in whatever future ventures seemed appropriate.

It was an effective threat. Neither the Soviets nor Russell knew how the Americans would respond should the story of his theft of the atomic papers become public, but Russell had reason to fear the worst. Another wave of anti-communist hysteria was building in the US, and an American citizen putting family above country when it came to atomic secrets might well end up in the electric chair. At the absolute best, he would never get another job with an American – or British – newspaper.

And now the Soviets had come calling. What would they want this time? Whatever it was, it would probably involve a return to Berlin, and another separation from his son and Effi.

Paul was still in bad shape, but Russell suspected that there was little he could offer in the way of help, that the boy had to find his own road back. And there were signs, every now and then, that he was doing just that. It might be wishful thinking, but he thought his son would eventually work out how best to live with his past.

He was not so certain that he and Effi could survive another long separation. It had been wonderful finding her again, but once the joy of the first few days had passed they had struggled to re-establish the easy loving companionship that they had once taken for granted. It could be a great deal worse – the recently reunited couple upstairs came to mind – but something indefinable had gone missing. What it was, and why it had gone, were still a mystery. Was it just the length of the separation? Three and a half years was a long time, and their lives in that period had been so different: hers fraught with danger, his a relative cakewalk. Had Rosa come between them? Russell felt no resentment – he loved her as much as Effi did – but the girl might have shifted some balance in their relationship. Or was it something simpler, like their both being out of work, or the length of time that they'd been together?

He didn't know, and neither, he guessed, did she. It was probably all those things, and a few more besides.

Maybe time would cure them, but somehow he doubted it. Looking out across the brown river, he felt more than a little scared for the future.

* * *

A light rain began to fall as Effi waited outside the school gates, and she gratefully unfurled the umbrella which Zarah had insisted she take. There had been smiles of recognition from a couple of other women, but frowns of disapproval from a couple more. Her being German had upset some in the beginning, and Effi had hoped that recounting her anti-Nazi exploits in the local paper might reduce any opprobrium which she – and by extension, Rosa – would have to cope with. But while some had probably been mollified, others seemed even more inclined to hold up their noses.

Looking round, she saw another new male face – as the term went by, more and more demobbed fathers were collecting their children. Effi wondered if Rosa had noticed, and thought that she probably had. The girl didn't miss much.

There were other children whose fathers were not coming home, but most of them seemed to know it. Would it be easier for Rosa if she knew that her father was dead?

The young Jewish girl had arrived at the door to Effi's Berlin apartment just weeks before the end of the war. Rosa and her mother Ursel had been hidden by an elderly gentile woman for several years, but first Ursel was killed by an American bomb, and then the woman fell seriously ill. The girl had been left with no one to look after her, and the Swede Erik Aslund, who ran the Jewish escape line that Effi worked for, had begged her to take Rosa in.

She never regretted saying yes – the girl, though obviously and deeply traumatised, was an absolute delight. And now that Effi was thirty-nine, the only child she was ever likely to have.

Effi had asked the girl about her father Otto, but all Rosa could remember was his leaving one day and not coming back. She had been about three, she thought, which would place the man's disappearance sometime around 1941. He was most likely dead, but they couldn't be sure. Up until June of that year, Jews had still been allowed to leave Germany, and even after that date, some had escaped. Of those that stayed, several thousand of the so-called U-boats had survived several years in hiding, mostly in Berlin. So there was more than a fleeting chance that Otto was still alive.

But if he was, no trace had yet been found. Effi had been round all the refugee agencies in London, and each had agreed to pester their Berlin offices, but so far to no avail. Private correspondence between Germany and the outside world was still not allowed, so there was nothing they could do themselves. When a returning British soldier had kindly dropped off a letter from his ex-wife's brother Thomas, Russell had tried and failed to find a carrier for his reply. When the restrictions were lifted,

Effi knew Thomas would conduct a thorough search for Otto, but in the meantime...

The school doors opened, and a host of children swept out to the gate, borne on a tide of laughter and chatter. Such a comforting sound, Effi thought, one of those things you never appreciated until it disappeared, as it had in Berlin during the final years of the war.

Rosa was walking with a blonde girl around her own age. Catching sight of Effi, she almost pulled the other girl across to introduce her. 'This is Marusya,' she said. 'She's from Russia.'

'How do you do?' Effi said carefully in English. She was leaning down to shake the girl's hand when the mother bustled up and seized it instead. 'Yes, thank you,' she almost shouted, and tugged the girl away.

Effi stared after them, feeling more upset for Marusya than herself. Rosa, though, seemed unconcerned. 'Marusya likes drawing too,' she confided.

They started for home, sharing Zarah's umbrella and taking the usual path across the foot of Parliament Hill. Rosa chatted happily about her day at school. If she was thinking about her father, she was keeping it to herself.

Back at the flat Zarah was preparing the evening meal and listening to *The Robinson Family* on the wireless. She was also glancing frequently at the clock, Effi noticed. Lothar had announced the previous week that he was too old to be collected from school by his mother, and the way Zarah's whole body relaxed when she heard him in the hall was almost painful to behold. He gave his mother a dutiful kiss and an 'I told you so' look.

A few minutes later the neighbours upstairs started one of their loud and increasingly frequent arguments. The demobbed husband had been home for several weeks now, and things were clearly building to a climax – the last time Effi had seen the wife she had clumsily tried to conceal the fact that both eyes were blackened. Effi itched to intervene, but knew it wouldn't help. She also had vivid memories of the anti-German outburst that the women had directed at her while complaining about Paul's noisy nightmares.

Listening to them scream at each other in a language she barely understood, she felt a sudden intense yearning for her real home.

'Is John here for dinner?' Zarah asked, interrupting her thoughts.

'I think so.'

'Are you two all right?' her sister inquired in a concerned voice.

'Yes, of course. What makes you ask?' Effi replied, hearing the defensiveness in her own voice.

Zarah didn't push it. 'Oh, nothing. This is a hard time for everyone.'

'How often do you think about Jens?' Effi asked, partly in self-defence. Zarah had last seen her husband, a high-ranking bureaucrat in Hitler's regime, in April. During their final conversation he had proudly announced that he had suicide pills for them both.

'Not as often as I used to. I don't miss him, but I do wonder what happened to him. And I know Lothar does. He has good memories of his father. I don't know. Sometimes I think it's better not to know. Other times... well...'

Through the doorway to the front room Effi could see Rosa drawing. There was so much unfinished business, so many loose ends... She had a sudden mental picture of the blood-soaked operating room in the Potsdam Station bunker, of stumps being tidied up and cauterised. It wasn't so easy with minds.

* * *

Tuesday morning, the fog eventually lifted to reveal a cold and overcast day. Russell caught a Fulham-bound bus in Piccadilly, and was soon glad he had done so. As part of their current dispute, the conductors were still refusing to allow anyone to stand, and the packed bus was soon leaving knots of irate passengers behind. Traffic was heavy in any case, and their conductor's determination to explain himself at every stop rendered their progress even slower than it might have been. When the bus finally ground to a halt halfway down the Fulham Road a large proportion of the male passengers decided to continue on foot.

The hawkers were out in force, and doing a fine trade in toffee apples and oranges. The local children were busy pocketing pennies for storing bicycles in their front gardens and 'looking after' cars in the side streets. There were two programmes on sale – an official blue one and a pirate version in red. Russell bought them both for Paul, more out of habit than anything else. Paul had been an avid collector as a boy, but the urge had obviously faded, at least for the moment. Russell wondered what had happened to the boy's stamp collection. If the albums had been left at the house in Grunewald, someone would have stolen them by now.

Picturing that house brought Paul's mother Ilse to mind. He had met her in Moscow in 1924, at the same conference where his and Shchepkin's paths had first crossed. He still found it hard to believe she was dead.

The crowd grew denser as he approached the ground, with many pushing against the tide. The gates were closed, he heard one man say, but if that was the case it didn't seem much of a deterrent. As Russell crossed the West London Line railway bridge he could see people walking along between the tracks, and others scaling the back of the grandstand. Away in the distance small figures could be seen lining roofs and walls, or precariously clinging to chimney stacks.

He fought his way through to the grandstand entrance, where ticket-holders were still being admitted, and took his place in the fast-moving line. When he passed through the turnstile there was still half an hour before kick-off, so he joined the queue for tea. A party of Russians was ahead of him, happily swapping banter with some of the locals. Watching the exchange, Russell was reminded that most ordinary people still considered the Soviets as friends and allies.

The British press was certainly helping to preserve the illusion. J. B. Priestley had just chronicled a visit to the Soviet Union in a series of articles for the *Sunday Express*, and his impressions had been overwhelmingly favourable. Russell was glad that the popular playwright had noticed some Soviet plusses – particularly in education and culture – but rather more disappointed that he had missed most of the minuses. And Priestley was far from alone. Some descriptions of the Soviet leadership in the British press were naive to the point of idiocy. One journalist had recently compared Stalin to 'a collie panting and eyeing his sheep'; another had announced that his successors would be 'middle-aged Men of Good Will'. Which planet were they living on?

Tea in hand, he followed the signs for the appropriate block and climbed the relevant steps. Emerging above the dull green pitch he found himself looking out across a huge crowd, a large portion of which had already spilled out onto the greyhound track that ringed the playing surface. More to Russell's surprise, the Russian players were already out, passing several balls between them. Their shirts and shorts were different shades of blue, with a old-fashioned white 'D' where British clubs wore their badges. Their socks were a fetching bottle green.

He found his row, and searched the gloom for Shchepkin. The old Comintern operative was a dozen or so seats along, his newly white hair peeking out from under a fur hat. There was an empty seat beside him.

As Russell forced his passage along the row he realised that all those making way were Russians – the whole block was occupied by fur-hatted men smoking strange-smelling cigarettes and conversing in nasal accents. Shchepkin smiled when he saw him coming, and Russell, rather to his own surprise, found himself reciprocating. If a list were made of those ultimately responsible for the mess his life was in, then Shchepkin's name would undoubtedly come close to the top. But so, Russell knew, would his own. And the past was not for changing.

He took the seat beyond Shchepkin, beside a burly blond Russian in a shiny new suit.

'This is Comrade Nemedin,' Shchepkin announced, in a tone which left no doubt of the man's importance.

'Major Nemedin,' the man corrected him. His blue eyes were a definite contender for the coldest that Russell had ever seen. 'Mister Russell,' the Russian said in acknowledgement, before turning his attention back to the pitch.

'We will talk business at half-time,' Shchepkin told Russell.

'Right.'

'How do you like living in London?' Shchepkin asked him in Russian. Nemedin, Russell guessed, did not speak English.

'I've been in better places,' Russell replied in the same language. 'It'll take a lot more than six months to make up for the last six years.'

'Did you grow up here?'

'No, in Guildford. It's about thirty miles away. To the southwest. But my father worked in London, and we used to come up quite often. Before the First War.' He had been thinking about those visits lately. On one occasion he and his parents had been caught up in a suffragette rally. To his father's chagrin and his mother's great amusement.

Down below them the Dynamos were leaving the pitch. The crowd was now over the inner fence of the greyhound track, and, despite the best efforts of the police, creeping towards the touch and goal lines. On the far side a woman was being lifted across a sea of heads towards a posse of waiting St John Ambulancemen.

'How are your family?' Russell asked Shchepkin.

'Oh.' The Russian looked disconcerted for a moment, but soon recovered. 'They are in good health, thank you. Natasha is training to be a teacher.'

'Good,' Russell said. They both knew that Nemedin was listening to every word, but Russell felt childishly intent on not being cowed into silence. 'And how long have you been in London?'

'Since the Sunday before last. We came with the team.'

'Of course.' Russell shifted his attention to Nemedin. 'And how do you like it here, Major?' he asked.

'No,' Nemedin replied, as if he'd heard a different question. 'Are they going to force them back?' he asked, indicating the crowds below.

'I think they'll be happy with keeping them off the pitch,' Russell told him.

'But... is this normal? There is no control.'

Russell shrugged. Where the English were concerned, the controls were internal. 'Do you like football?' he asked the Russian.

'Of course.'

'Will the Dynamos do well, do you think?'

'Yes, I think so. If the referee is fair.'

There was a sound of breaking glass away to their right. Someone had fallen through the grandstand roof, and presumably landed in someone else's lap. It wasn't a long drop, so Russell doubted that anyone had died.

The two teams were filing out now: Chelsea in a change strip of red, the Dynamos carrying bouquets of flowers. They lined up facing each other, and those in the seats rose to their feet as the Royal Marines band launched into the Soviet national anthem. The crowd was respectful to a fault, and the wave of emotion which rolled across the stadium was almost palpable, as minds went back to those months when their two nations were all that stood between the Nazis and global domination. The Americans and their economy had certainly played crucial roles in the Allied victory, but if Britain had broken in 1940, or the Soviet Union in 1941, all their efforts might well have been in vain.

'God Save The King' followed, and the moment it died away the eleven Dynamo players stepped forward and presented the bouquets to their blushing Chelsea counterparts. A storm of laughter engulfed the stadium, leaving most of the Russell's immediate neighbours looking bemused. In the seats below one man shouted that it must be Chelsea's funeral.

A minute later the game was underway, and it was looking as if he'd been right. Far from being 'so slow you could hear them think', the Russian players were soon swarming towards the Chelsea goal, passing their way through their opponents with a deftness and speed which left the crowd gasping. Within minutes shots had hit the goalkeeper, the side netting and the post, and the Russians around Russell were almost purring with pleasure at the lesson their countrymen were teaching the English team.

For twenty minutes they did everything but score. And then, after hitting the post for a second time, they conceded at the other end – Tommy Lawton, much to Nemedin's disgust, forcing the ball from the Dynamo keeper's hands and setting it up on a plate for Len Goulden. When a stupid mistake at the back gifted Chelsea another goal, the sense of injustice was almost too much for Russell's companions to bear. And, rubbing salt into the wound, the Dynamos contrived to miss a penalty just before half time, the left-winger hammering his shot against the post. When the teams disappeared beneath them with the score at two-nil, Russell couldn't recall a less appropriate scoreline.

On his right, Shchepkin seemed less put out that most of his compatriots; on his left, Nemedin was muttering darkly to himself, which probably boded ill. The NKVD were hard enough to deal with when things were going their way.

Nemedin, however, proved able to set aside his disappointment. 'We have two jobs for you,' he told Russell once their mini-conference was underway, the two Russians leaning sideways until all three heads were only inches apart. 'First, you will make contact with several German comrades in Berlin, some of whom you know, some of whom you don't. We want to know where these comrades stand on several crucial issues. There has been a lot of discussion in the German Party about a "German Road to Socialism". This is acceptable, but only insofar as it doesn't become an anti-Soviet road. We want to know how these men feel about this in particular, and where their loyalties lie. Do you understand?'

'Yes,' Russell said. He did. Perfectly.

'You will be supplied with all the relevant information when you reach Berlin.'

'Uh-huh. And the second job?'

'You will offer your services to American Intelligence. They are desperately trying to recruit Berliners, and you will obviously appeal to them. But you will of course be working for us.'

Russell was conscious for a moment of the Russians sitting in the next row down. They were also NKVD, he assumed. He was probably surrounded by a dozen of them. 'You want me to function as a double agent inside American intelligence,' he said.

It wasn't a question, but Nemedin answered it anyway. 'Yes.'

It was no worse than he'd feared, but that was little consolation. 'You expect me to move back to Berlin?'

'Of course.'

Russell risked a slight demurral. 'Moving to Berlin is not a simple matter these days. And I have a family to consider. We would all need somewhere to live.'

'Of course, but we're assuming the Americans will take care of such matters.' Nemedin seemed relieved, as if he'd been expecting more basic objections. 'It would look suspicious if we openly organised your return. But these are details for you and Comrade Shchepkin to discuss.'

'We will take care of you,' Shchepkin interjected, 'but not openly. Fräulein Koenen will soon be offered a job in Berlin – a prominent part in a film. And we will help you with exclusive stories. It is crucial that you remain a credible journalist.'

They were thinking things through, Russell thought. 'And what if the Americans turn me down?' he asked.

'Comrade Shchepkin will discuss contingencies with you,' Nemedin replied, with the slightest hint of impatience. 'Mr Russell, what is your opinion of the current international situation?'

'It's another war waiting to happen.'

'Mmm. And there can only be one winner – you agree?'

'Yes,' seemed the diplomatic answer. 'But it make take a while,' Russell added, hoping to maintain some sort of reputation for realism. 'The Americans have their atomic bomb now.'

'We shall soon have one ourselves,' Nemedin said dismissively, 'and partly thanks to your own efforts. But you have correctly identified the principal enemy of world socialism. The British are finished,' he said contemptuously, his blue eyes scanning the vast crowd. 'The Americans are all that matter now, and you will help us there.'

'I'll do my best,' Russell said, in a resolutely deadpan tone. He wondered who the man was trying to convince – his brand new agent or himself? Nemedin was investing a lot in him, and clearly had mixed feelings about it. The Russian's career might soar as a result, but he clearly resented his dependence on a foreign bourgeois. And if things went wrong, he would show no mercy.

The teams were coming out beneath them. 'Do you have any questions?' Nemedin asked, in a tone that invited none.

Why pick on me, was the one that came to mind, but he already knew the answer.

Nemedin took his silence for acquiescence. 'Then that is all,' he said, leaning back in his seat to watch the game re-start.

Russell decided he might as well enjoy the game and depress himself later. There would be plenty of time to run through the likely consequences of what he'd just been told..

The Dynamos started the second half the way they'd started the first, repeatedly bearing down on the Chelsea goal, only to waste their chances. This time, however, the sustained pressure paid off, and one of their forwards finally scored with a fine shot. The Russians around Russell leapt to their feet, and he found himself doing the same.

The Dynamos had recovered their confidence, and soon scored an equaliser. Chelsea responded, going ahead once more, but as the last fifteen minutes ticked away the Russians looked less tired than their opponents, and another equaliser followed with five minutes remaining. Nemedin thumped the seat in front in his excitement, causing its Russian occupant to swing angrily round, and then do a double-take when he recognised the source of his ire.

The Soviets almost scored a winner, but had to settle for a draw, and the men around Russell seemed happy enough. All the British press experts had been wide of the mark, and the visitors had come away with a clear moral victory. The collie in the Kremlin would be one happy dog.

Nemedin rose and moved away, without so much as a look. 'We all leave for Cardiff tomorrow afternoon,' Shchepkin told Russell, 'so you and I must meet in the morning. We're staying at the Imperial Hotel in Russell Square, and when I looked out of the window this morning I noticed a mobile canteen in the park. Can we meet there, say eleven o'clock?'

He waited only for Russell's nod, then also hurried off.

On the long bus ride home, Russell went over what had been said, and wondered what to tell the others. They all knew why he'd been invited to Stamford Bridge, but he decided to save the inevitable family discussion until after his meeting with Shchepkin. And maybe not until he'd made contact with the Americans. Another meeting he wasn't looking forward to. He sometimes wondered whether he should simply throw in the towel and go into hiding for the rest of his life. If his press contacts could be believed, South America was working for the Nazis.

At home, the women and children were on the floor, playing a board game that Lothar had made in class that day, with Paul watching from an armchair. Russell shook his head in response to Effi's questioning look, and went out to make a pot of tea. Paul joined him in the kitchen to ask about the game, having heard the BBC radio coverage of the second half. It wasn't until eight-thirty, with the children in bed and *It's That Man Again* finished on the radio, that Russell and Effi could walk down to the local pub for a private conversation. It was a clear night, and there was no sign of the local boy gangsters.

The public bar was crowded and full of smoke, the saloon much more sparsely populated. 'So what are their plans for you?' Effi asked, once they'd settled in a secluded corner.

Russell told her everything that Nemedin had told him.

'You're going back,' Effi said, with traces of both resentment and wistfulness. 'For how long?' she asked.

'God knows. I can't see them running out of useful things for me to do.'

'So they're expecting you to finger any independent-minded German comrades, and then spy on the Americans for them?'

'That's about it.'

'Oh, John.'

'I know.'

'And they spelt out what will happen if you say no?'

'They didn't have to.'

'Are you sure of that?' She wasn't quite sure what she'd expected, but it hadn't been as bad as this.

'Ninety-nine per cent. Nemedin made sure to mention my contribution to their atomic research, just in case I'd blocked it out. If he tells the world, my credibility as a journalist will be shot to pieces. And that's the very best I could expect – the Americans might charge me with treason.'

'Okay,' Effi agreed, 'but how would it help the Russians to publicise your involvement? And maybe they don't want the world to know that they've got those German secrets. Perhaps they're bluffing.'

Russell smiled. 'Perhaps. But if they are, and I call them on it, I don't think they'll hold up their hands and say "ah, you've got us there." They'll just find some other way of exerting pressure, and invite me to think again. None of us would be safe. At least while I'm doing their bidding in Berlin, the rest of you will be able to get on with your lives here. And once I'm there, maybe I can find some way out of it all.'

She gave him an exasperated look, and reached for his hand. 'I don't *want* to get on with my life without you.'

'I was hoping you felt that way, because the bastards have invited you too.'

'What do you mean?'

He told her about the imminent offer of a film role.

'What sort of film?' she asked, both pleased and suspicious.

'They didn't give me any details.'

'Oh. But why, do you think?'

'Who knows? Perhaps they think I'll be happier in Berlin with you. Or just more vulnerable. And both would be true.'

Could she leave Rosa with Zarah, Effi wondered. And if not, could they take her with them? She couldn't shake the feeling that Berlin was the last place on earth this girl would want to live.

'And there's another thing,' Russell told her. 'They want me working as a journalist. The Soviets will feed me good stories, and probably the Americans too. And if either of them try to stop me from telling the truth, I can tell them that an independent voice is the best cover a spy could possibly have. So at least I'll get my professional life back. Which is something. Not a lot, but something.'

'Yes,' Effi agreed, though she found herself thinking he was clutching at straws. If so, there were probably worse straws to clutch at. But what did she want herself? To act again? Yes, she did, but more than anything else she wanted some sort of resolution concerning Rosa's father. For the girl of course, but also for herself. And in Berlin she could find out what had happened to him. 'We always knew we'd go back,' she said, trying to cheer him up.

Absent fathers

Russell arrived early at his namesake's Square, and found the mobile canteen. A dozen or so metal tables were spread out across the threadbare grass, and he chose what seemed the most remote. The Imperial Hotel was visible through the trees to his right, but no Dynamos were leaning out of its windows.

The morning papers were full of praise for the Russian tourists. The no-hopers of the previous morning had become 'the greatest side ever to visit this island, playing football as it was meant to be played.' Much was made of the Dynamos' willingness to interchange positions 'without getting in each other's way', a revolutionary tactic which had completely flummoxed their English opponents.

There was other English news of interest – a sweet ration bonus promised for Christmas, and a Parliamentary statement by the Foreign Secretary Ernest Bevin which reaffirmed British opposition to increasing the number of Jewish refugees allowed into Palestine. Those already there were striking in protest.

More to the point, there was news from Berlin. Two political rallies had been held on the previous evening, with both attracting audiences of around four thousand. At one, the German Communist leader Wilhelm Pieck had suggested that his party, the KPD, should share a manifesto and electoral pact with their old rivals, the Social Democrat SPD. At the other meeting, the latter's leader Otto Grotewohl had pledged 'close collaboration' between the two parties, and had declared that 'capitalism no longer existed.'

'In your dreams,' Russell murmured to himself. What was Moscow playing at, and how would it affect his own task in Berlin? If Stalin was encouraging the German left to unite around a moderate line, then the Russians could hardly complain about German comrades who pursued a relatively independent path. Half his job description might already be redundant, which would certainly be good news. Though on reflection it seemed probable that the NKVD would still want the information, if only for future use.

The other news from Berlin was dispiriting - the first snow had fallen, of what promised to be a desperate winter. He put the paper aside and glanced at his watch. It was almost eleven o'clock.

There was no one else waiting at the canteen counter, but he felt reluctant to pay for two teas – the NKVD had called this meeting, and they could supply the bloody refreshments.

There had been several tables occupied when he arrived, but now there were only two. A couple of secretaries had their heads bent over a newspaper, and were giggling at something or other, their heads shaking like a pair of maracas. A few feet away from them, a remarkably smug-looking nanny was staring into space, idly rocking the pram parked beside her.

A flash of white hair caught Russell's attention – Shchepkin was crossing Southampton Row. The Russian was lost from view for several moments, then reappeared inside the park. No one seemed to be following him, but for all Russell knew there were pairs of binoculars trained on them both. Either Nanny was the head of MI5, or she had him hidden in the pram.

Espionage could be dangerous, immoral, even romantic. But it was almost always faintly ridiculous.

Shchepkin smiled as he walked up, and shook Russell's hand. After wiping the seat with his handkerchief, he sat down and viewed their surroundings.

Why are we meeting here?' Russell wondered out loud. 'A bit public, isn't it? Now the people watching you will be checking up on me.'

Shchepkin smiled. 'It's almost as public as a football stadium,' he observed.

'Ah, that's the point, is it?'

'Of course. If the British tell the Americans about your meetings with us, it will increase your credibility as a double agent.'

Russell followed the thought for a few seconds, then let it go. There seemed all sorts of flaws in the reasoning, but then intelligence people used a different form of logic to ordinary human beings. If indeed logic came into it.

'Comrade Nemedin is also a football fan,' Shchepkin added, as if that explained the choice of Stamford Bridge as a meeting place. 'And Dynamo *are* the team of the NKVD.'

'And I expected he wanted to see me in the flesh,' Russell realised. 'See what he was getting for his blackmail.'

'Yes, he did,' Shchepkin agreed, ignoring the flash of bitterness. 'Not that he learnt anything from the encounter. He doesn't understand people like you – or like me, for that matter. People who were there at the beginning, people who knew what it was all for, before the things that mattered were locked away for safekeeping. The Nemedins of this world see themselves as guardians, but they have no real notion of what they're guarding. They find it hard enough to trust each other, let alone people like us.'

'Does it matter?' Russell asked. 'He's got me where he wants me, hasn't he?'

Shchepkin took another look around, as if to reassure himself that no one was within listening distance. 'Yes, it matters. His lack of understanding makes it easier for us to manipulate him, but his lack of trust will make him extremely sensitive to the possibility of betrayal.'

'Is that what we're planning?' Russell asked with a smile.

'I hope so,' Shchepkin said earnestly. 'I'm right in assuming that you haven't changed your mind, that you'll go along with Nemedin's plan?'

'I don't seem to have any choice.'

'No,' Shchepkin agreed, 'not for the moment...'

An ailing bus thundered past them on the nearby road, drowning him out. The windows were still draped with anti-blast netting, Russell noticed.

'But there's no future in it,' Shchepkin went on. 'Double agents, well, they usually end up betraying themselves. Like jugglers – no matter how good they are, sooner or later their arms get tired.'

Russell gave him a wry smile. 'You're not feeling sorry for me, are you?'

'No. Nor for myself, but we're both in trouble, and we're going to need each other's help to have any chance of getting out of it.'

'Why are you in so much trouble?' Russell asked. 'You never told me why you were arrested last year.'

'That's much too long a story. Let's just say I ended up supporting the wrong people. But I was more careful than most of my friends were, and unlike most of them, I survived. Stalin and his Georgian cronies believe I still have some uses, or I wouldn't be here, but like you I'm something of a diminishing asset. And like you, I need to get out before it's too late.'

'Why not take a boat train?' Russell suggested flippantly. 'There's a whole wide world out there, and I find it hard to believe that a man with your experience couldn't lose himself if he really tried.'

It was Shchepkin's turn to smile. 'I'm sure I could, but there are other people to consider. If I disappeared, my wife and daughter would pay the price. I need a way out which includes them.'

Russell gave the Russian a thoughtful look, and then suggested tea. He needed time to think, and a trip to the counter seemed the only way to get it. Through all the years they'd known each other, Shchepkin had never come close to admitting such disaffection with the regime he served. Why now? Was his recent imprisonment the reason, or was that exactly what Russell was supposed to think?

And did the man take sugar? He put several lumps in each saucer and carried them back to the table.

'Have you finally lost your faith?' he asked the Russian in a casual tone, as if they were discussing less weighty matters than the overriding purpose of Shchepkin's adult existence.

'You could say that,' the Russian replied in like manner. 'You may think that only a fool would have carried on believing in the Soviet Union as long as I did. I sometimes think so myself. But then many intelligent men still trust in far less believable gods.' He gave Russell a quizzical look. 'I see you need convincing. Well, let me you tell you when I saw the... I was going to say "light", but darkness seems more appropriate. It was in October 1940...'

'When your people handed the German comrades over to the Nazis...'

'No, that was shameful, but it came a few months later. My moment of truth – believe it or not – came when the leadership decided to abolish scholarships. A less-than-world-shattering measure, you might think, one that killed nobody. But this measure made it impossible for the children of the poor – of the workers and the peasants – to get a higher education, and in doing so it turned the clock back all the way to Tsarism. Almost overnight, power and privilege were hereditary once more. Everyone knew that the sons and daughters of those now in power would automatically take the reins from their parents. We had become what we set out to overthrow.'

'I didn't even know such a measure had been passed,' Russell admitted. He could understand the effect it would have had on someone like Shchepkin.

'We are going to have to trust each other,' Shchepkin told him.

'Okay,' Russell agreed, convinced at least of the need.

'In the short run, we can help each other. As long as you're useful to Nemedin, we'll both be relatively safe, and I think we can make sure you will be. You must go to the Americans, as Nemedin told you to, but you must also tell them everything. Offer yourself to *them* as a double agent – I'm sure you can come up with personal motives, but they'll probably take you whatever you say. They're desperate for people who know Berlin and Berliners, and they won't trust you with any important information, not at first. So what do they have to lose? And soon you'll be able to win them over by getting them stuff they can't get anywhere else.'

'And where will I get that from?' Russell asked. He was beginning to wonder whether all those months in the Lubyanka had weakened Shchepkin's brain.

'From me.'

'You will betray your country?' Russell half-asked, half-stated. He supposed it had been implicit in all that the Russian had said, but he still found it hard to believe.

'It doesn't feel like betrayal,' Shchepkin told him. 'When Vladimir Ilyich told us that the Revolution had no country, I believed him.'

'Okay. So that's how we survive in the short run. But I'm still the juggler with tiring arms, remember? How do we persuade Stalin to leave me alone, and let you and your family go?'

'That's harder. And I can only think of one possibility – we need something on them which trumps everything else. A secret so damaging that we could buy our safety with silence.'

'Is that all?' Russell asked sarcastically. He had found himself hoping that Shchepkin had a plan with some chance of success.

'It won't be easy,' the Russian agreed. 'But we'll be working for people with secrets, and trading them ourselves – we'll have to keep our eyes and ears open, follow any thread that looks promising. It may take years, but I can't see any other way out. Can you?'

'No,' Russell admitted. This one didn't look too promising, but Shchepkin knew his world best, and any hope at all was better than none.

'Then, let us work together. I will see you in Berlin.'

'Okay. When do you expect me to start?'

'As soon as possible. Once you reach Berlin, you will go to the Housing Office at the junction of Neue König and Lietzmann. You know where that is?'

'Of course. But we're counting our chickens a bit – what if the Americans won't take me on?'

'They will. But if by any chance they refuse, then come to our embassy here – I will leave instructions. In the last resort, we will get you there.' He looked at his watch. 'Now I must go – our train is at two.'

'When's the game – Saturday?'

'I think so. The football is nothing to do with me – I check the hotels, arrange excursions, look at the police arrangements.'

It was the first time Russell could remember the Russian actually volunteering information about himself. It seemed a good omen.

Shchepkin made to leave, then abruptly turned back. 'One last thing. I forgot to tell you. Make sure the Americans keep your mutual arrangement from the British – the NKVD have several plants in MI6.' That bombshell dropped, he walked off across the park without a backward look, leaving Russell to ponder his brave new future. He wished he'd had one of those new-fangled recording machines, so that he could listen to Shchepkin's reasoning again. Over the years the Russian had never been less than convincing, but Russell knew from bitter experience that some things were always spelt out better than others. What were the hidden catches in this scheme, he wondered. Other, that is, than the obvious one, that he'd need acting lessons from Effi to pull it off.

He decided to visit the American Embassy that afternoon, while he could still remember the script. Working his way through the streets around the British Museum, he wondered whether Shchepkin declaring war on Nemedin was good news or bad. Letting himself get sucked into a war between competing sections of Soviet intelligence seemed, at first glance, like a poor career move. But it might give him room to manoeuvre, play off one against the other. Or give them both a reason to kill him.

After lunch at his usual Corner House, he walked down Oxford Street and turned left at Selfridges. The American Embassy had moved to Grosvenor Square in 1938, and he had visited it several times since, mostly in connection with his own pragmatic adoption of US citizenship. The welcome had seldom been effusive – Americans might, as they sometimes claimed, be the friendliest people on God's earth, but only when encountered on their home turf.

He opted for the direct approach. 'I need to see the attaché who deals with Intelligence matters,' he told the young man on reception.

'Do you have an appointment?'

'No.'

'Then I suggest...'

'He will want to see me. Tell him John Russell has a proposal for him.'

The man gave him another look, and decided to pass the buck. 'Please take a seat,' he said, and reached for the telephone. Two minutes later another, younger man descended the stairs, and led Russell back up to a small office half full of cardboard boxes, where he laboriously transcribed every detail from Russell's US passport. He then stared at the photograph, as if wondering whether he should sketch a rough copy. Apparently deciding against, he told Russell to wait where he was, and stalked off down the corridor.

A quarter hour went by, and then another. It was getting dark outside, and Russell guessed that the Embassy was now closed for the day. A cursory investigation of the cardboard boxes revealed that each was full of Hershey bars. He pocketed a couple for the children, and, after another fifteen minutes had ticked by, a couple more for the adults to share.

The young man returned, looking pleased with himself. 'Follow me,' he said.

They traipsed down a corridor, and descended several flights of stairs. The unmarked basement room into which Russell was ushered had no ordinary windows, but a deep ceiling well in one corner offered proof there was still some light outside. The colonel behind the neatly-organised desk looked around forty, and none too pleased to see him. His head was as close to shaved as made no difference, and his face seemed equally short on sympathy. The grey eyes, though, were conspicuously alert. Not a fool, Russell decided.

A folder bearing his own name was lying on the desk.

'John Russell,' the colonel said, as if curious to hear how it sounded. His accent was Midwestern.

'And you are?' Russell asked.

'Colonel Lindenberg. The attaché who deals with intelligence matters,' he added wryly. 'I believe you have a proposal for me.'

'Yes. I've worked for your Government before, and I'd like to do so again. In Berlin.'

'Yes? Why now? We asked you to work for us in 1942, but you refused. What's changed your mind?'

Russell considered explaining his earlier refusals and decided there wasn't any point – the reasons he'd given at the time would be in the file. 'I think I have a better appreciation now of what the Russians are capable of.'

'Because of what you saw in Berlin?'

'That, and what I've read and heard about their behaviour in other parts of Europe.'

Lindenberg was looking at the file. 'The Soviets allowed you to accompany the Red Army into Berlin, and then refused to let you report from there,' he said, looking up with a smile of disbelief.

'That's what happened,' Russell lied. 'I tried to tell it the way I'd seen it, and they weren't having it.'

'That I can understand. But they let you go, and you've written nothing about it since.'

'That was the deal,' Russell said with a shrug. 'My family for my silence.'

'If the Soviets know you that well, what good would you be to us?'

'Ah, now we come the interesting part. The Soviets have asked me to work for them, and guess what they want me to do? They want me to offer my services to you.'

Lindenberg smiled at that. 'Okay, I can understand why they'd want a guy of their own in our organization, but why would they choose a journalist who they've just had to gag?'

Had that been a knowing smile, Russell wondered. Did Lindenberg already know of his meeting with the Russians? 'Several reasons,' he answered. 'One, there's hardly a stampede of applicants for a job like that. Two, they think I'm competent. Three, they know I'm having trouble finding work here, and that I want to go back to Berlin. Four, they know from experience that they can buy me off. What they don't know is that my family is the only thing I'd sell myself for, and they'll be safe here in England.'

Lindenberg picked up a pen and started rotating it through the fingers of his right hand. 'Let's go back to the beginning,' he said. 'You're telling me that your reason for joining us is a new-found resentment of the Soviets?'

'I didn't say it was the only reason. My motives are mixed, like most people's. I want to do my bit, maybe not so much for the West as for Berlin. It's my home, and it's been through hell, and it deserves better than a Russian takeover. And I want to help myself. I want to work as a journalist again, and that's not going to happen here.'

'Berlin's no picnic these days.'

'I know. But if I'm on your payroll, I won't have to worry about food and accommodation.'

'You wouldn't be living in luxury.'

'Of course not. But it's hard to do any job well if you're spending most of your time huddled round a fire wondering where the next meal's coming from.'

'True,' the colonel conceded. 'So how do you see yourself being useful? As far as I can tell, your work for us consisted of reporting on the political loyalties of a few Germans and Czechs.'

'And nearly getting killed in Prague for my pains. I don't know, is the honest answer. I don't know what you'll want from me. But I do know Berlin, and I do know a lot of Berliners, quite a few of whom are probably working for the Soviets by now. And I know the Russians, more's the pity. I think you'll find me useful, but if you don't, you can always dispense with my services.'

'And all you want is feeding and housing?'

'I presume you pay your agents.'

'Ah...'

'I only want the going rate. I don't expect to get rich, which is more than you can say for most Americans in Berlin. If you need character references I suggest you contact Joseph Kenyon – I assume he's still at the Embassy in Moscow – or Al Murchison. He was my boss in 1939.'

'Murchison's dead. He was killed in the Pacific.'

'I'm sorry to hear that. He was a good man.'

'I didn't know him.' Lindenberg's finger brought his rotating pen to a stop, and gave Russell a thoughtful look. 'I'll talk to some people,' he said. 'Come back on Monday morning and I'll give you a yes or no.'

Russell stood and offered his hand, which the American took. 'Have long have you been in England?' Russell asked him.

'Too damn long,' was the predictable reply.

* * *

'Do you trust Shchepkin?' Effi asked, after Russell had finished describing his meetings with the Russian and Lindenberg. 'He *was* the one who got you into all this.'

'I don't trust any of them,' was Russell's instinctive response. 'But if I had to choose between him and Nemedin – and I probably will – it would be Shchepkin every time. He's still recognisably human.'

'So we wait,' Effi said. They were whispering in bed, ears cocked for any indication that Rosa was no longer fast asleep.

'We wait for the Americans, but whatever they say I'll be going – the Soviets will still want me there to check up on the comrades.'

'I'm coming with you.'

The feeling of relief was intense, but did nothing to dispel the accompanying anxiety. 'Are you sure that's a good idea?' he asked her.

'Don't you want me to?'

'Of course I do. I just... I just worry. Berlin sounds like hell on earth at the moment, and God knows how difficult the Russians are going to be. At least...'

'But it can't be as bad as the last few weeks of the war. They're not still bombing the place, are they?'

'No, but...'

'The only question in my mind is whether or not we take Rosa,' Effi insisted.

'Well…' Russell thought about offering an opinion, and realised two things. One, that he could see advantages to both options, and two, that this was a decision that Effi would – and should – take on her own.

'The film offer came today,' she told him. 'A motorcycle courier brought it.'

'Did you look through it yet?'

'A quick look, yes. It's not the script, just an outline, but there was a list of the people involved. You remember Ernst Dufring? I always liked his work, and apparently he's back from America. And the storyline seems intelligent – it's about how the members of one family come to terms with what happened under the Nazis, and the various compromises they have to make as individuals. In fact it's more than intelligent. It actually sounds worthwhile.'

'It does, doesn't it?' Russell wished he could say the same for what the Russians had planned for him.

'We need to talk to Zarah and Paul,' Effi went on.

'Together or separately?'

'Together, but without the children. Tomorrow night?'

'Paul's out tomorrow. He's going to see a Bogart film. He didn't actually say so, but I think he's going with Solly's secretary.'

'No!' Effi said, almost leaping up in bed.

'I think so.'

'That's wonderful.'

'Let's hope. But the family conference will have to wait until Friday.'

* * *

The next two days were cold and rainy. Russell went out walking whenever the rain slackened, and read when forced back indoors. No matter how many times he analysed his situation, he came to the same depressing conclusions. And Shchepkin's hope of eventually getting them out from under seemed more fanciful with each day that passed. It would, Russell thought, take another Russian Revolution to set the two of them free.

When Friday evening came round, and he, Effi, Zarah and Paul were wedged knee-to-knee in the small kitchen, he tried for a more positive presentation. The others knew the background to his current predicament, but he went through it again, from Shchepkin's knock on his Danzig hotel room door in the early hours of 1939 to Lindenberg's casual acceptance of his status as an experienced spy. Which he supposed he was – people living ordinary lives didn't find themselves in illicit possession of Baltic naval dispositions, SS pesticide purchases or atomic research documents. He wished he never had, but there it was. He'd signed up to this long game of consequences, and more would surely follow.

'So I have to go back,' he concluded.

'Have to?' Paul asked quietly. 'Couldn't you – you and Effi and Rosa, at least – move out of their reach? America. Australia even. It's not as if anything's holding you here in England.'

Russell shook his head. 'I doubt there's anywhere on earth beyond the reach of the NKVD. And I don't want to spend the rest of my life waiting for them to turn up.'

'Neither do I,' Effi said. 'I'm going back too.'

'Why?' Zarah asked. 'I mean apart from wanting to be with John?'

'I've been offered a movie as well.'

'That doesn't sound like a coincidence,' Paul said.

'It isn't. The Soviets have fixed it up somehow, but the film is being made by Germans, and I know a lot of the people involved. My problem is whether or not to take Rosa. I mean, there'd obviously be practical difficulties – I'll be on set most of the day, and God knows what our living conditions will be like. But even if most of that could be sorted out, I'd still be taking her out of school, and back to a place full of terrible memories. And if I am going to find out what happened to her father, I'll need to visit every Jewish refugee centre I can. Which would mean taking her from one dreadful place to another, raising and dashing her hopes over and over again.'

'You sound like you've already made up your mind,' Zarah said.

'Perhaps, but I'm ready to be told I'm wrong. What do you think, Paul?'

'I think she should stay here. As long as Zarah's happy with that. I'll do all I can, of course, but unless I give up my job most of the burden will fall on Zarah.'

'It's no burden,' Zarah insisted. 'If I had to I could manage on my own, and if Paul's here as well... But I do think you should talk to Rosa,' she told Effi. 'Just in case. She'll be upset, of course, but as long as you make it clear that it's only for a few weeks, I think she'll take it in her stride. If I'm wrong, and she gets hysterical, then perhaps you should think again.'

'I will.'

'And while you're there,' Zarah went on, addressing both of them, 'can you try and find out what happened to Jens? I think he must be dead, but... well, I can live with the uncertainty, but Lothar... I think he needs to know what happened.'

'What if he's alive and we find him?' Russell asked her.

'Tell him... oh, I don't know what to say. I don't want him back, but Lothar does miss him, and we'll be all going back eventually, won't we?'

'Probably,' Russell said. It seemed the likeliest option.

'Then if you see him, tell him Lothar and I are alive, and that when we come back Lothar will want to see him.'

'Okay.'

'But I think he's dead,' Zarah insisted.

'If he isn't, he's probably in prison,' Russell said.

'Yes, of course. Poor Jens.'

Poor Jens, Russell thought. One of the bureaucrats who had organised the deliberate starvation of Soviet cities and Soviet POWs. A mass murderer by any other name. And yet, somehow, 'poor Jens' seemed apt.

'And then, being practical,' Zarah added, 'there's the house in Schmargendorf. If it's still standing, we should reclaim it. It is ours, after all. Mine, if Jens is dead.'

'And my flat on Carmerstrasse,' Effi said. 'Thank God I only rented the one in Wedding. That's just rubble now.' She was, she realised with some surprise, beginning to feel excited at the prospect of seeing Berlin again.

'And you must try and see Papa and Muti,' Zarah told her.

'I'm not sure I want to,' was Effi's retort. Both their parents had behaved appallingly when told of Zarah's ordeal at Soviet hands, and Effi still found it hard to forgive them.

'We have to try and set things right,' Zarah told her sternly. 'They're old. And they don't know any better.'

* * *

Russell and Effi's imminent departure cast a shadow across the weekend, which cold wet weather did nothing to dispel. On Saturday morning Effi took Rosa aside, and told her, in as matter-of-fact a manner as she could manage, that she and John were going away for a few weeks. Rosa looked alarmed, but only for a few seconds, and once Effi assured her that Paul, Zarah and Lothar would be staying, the girl seemed almost eager to show how unconcerned she was. She was being brave, Effi realised, and wished with all her heart that there was no need. 'We can write to each other,' Effi told her, 'and perhaps even talk on the telephone. And it won't be long.'

Russell scoured the newspapers for news of Berlin, but the only stories on offer concerned the Nazis and their offspring. There were pieces on the trial of Hitler's surviving henchmen in Nuremberg, which was due to open on the coming Tuesday, and what seemed a highly imaginative story about a young girl named Uschi, whom the Führer had allegedly sired with Eva Braun. News of ordinary Germans, and of conditions in Germany, were conspicuous by their absence.

On Monday morning he kept his appointment at the American Embassy, and Lindenberg took him for a stroll round the sunlit Grosvenor Square. It was, the American said, the first blue sky he'd seen in more than a week.

Russell's offer had been accepted, and a seat on Friday's boat train provisionally booked.

'I'll need two,' Russell told him, and explained about Effi. He expected objections, but the American seemed pleased that they were going together. Maybe he was a romantic. Or perhaps he thought Effi was a good influence.

'Okay,' Lindenberg said. 'Once you reach Ostend, you'll take the train to Frankfurt. From there, I don't know. Maybe a plane into Tempelhof, maybe another train – the Russians keep changing their minds about which routes they want to obstruct. But you'll be briefed in Frankfurt.' He gave Russell a name and address. 'And you can pick up your tickets here on Thursday.'

Russell thought of pointing out that the Soviets employed couriers, but decided against it. He didn't think Lindenberg had a sense of humour, or at least not where his country and work were concerned.

After they parted, Russell walked west towards Park Lane, and then across Hyde Park towards Kensington Palace Gardens. There were several horsemen exercising their mounts on Rotten Row, and the park seemed chock-full of nannies and their infant charges – the newspapers might decry the government's lurch towards socialism, but power and privilege seemed less than ruffled.

At the Soviet Embassy he was given ample time to study the prominently placed accounts of Dynamo's astonishing 10-1 win over Cardiff at the weekend. When the cultural attaché finally appeared, Russell informed him that Effi would be accepting the Berlin film role, and that the two of them would be arriving in the German capital towards the end of the week. He also suggested – unnecessarily, from the look on the attaché's face – that Comrade Nemedin should be apprised of this fact.

* * *

When Effi met Rosa at the school gates she was still wondering whether to mention the girl's father, and her own intention of searching for traces once she reached Berlin. In the event, Rosa raised the subject herself. Another child in her class – a Jewish boy from Hungary – had only just heard that his father was still alive, and on his way to England. Which was wonderful, Rosa added, in a tone that almost suggested the opposite.

It took Effi a while to coax out the reason for this contradiction: they were half the way home when the girl stopped and anxiously asked her, 'If my father comes back, will you still be my mama?'

Wednesday dawned wet and foggy, and though the drizzle soon turned to mist, visibility remained poor. When Russell and Paul took a train from Kentish Town shortly before noon, they were still hoping that conditions would improve, but the world further east was every bit as murky, and they made the long trek up Tottenham High Road expecting disappointment.

The game was still on. The queues were shorter than Russell had expected, but he soon discovered the reason – most of the fans were already inside. The crowd seemed thinner higher up, but as Paul pointed out, the further they were from the action the less they would probably see. Even close to the touchline the opposite grandstand was only a blur.

They squeezed in behind two school truants waving hammer and sickle flags, and sat themselves down on the damp concrete. There were still almost two hours until kick-off. Russell had initially hoped they would talk during the wait, but Paul had come armed with a book, and he was left alone with his newspapers.

The game in prospect got plenty of coverage, and a win was expected from Arsenal, particularly as several 'guests' – including Blackpool's formidable Stanleys, Matthews and Mortensen – had been drafted in for the day. This was an England XI in everything but name, and national pride was clearly at stake.

Away from the back pages, nothing much caught his attention until an item in *The Times* almost took his breath away. He read the piece twice to be sure, then stared straight ahead for several seconds, stunned by the enormity of what had been decided. Over the next six months, six and a half million Germans would be taken from their homes in the eastern regions of the old Reich, and forcibly relocated in the newly shrunken Germany. Six and half million! How were they going to be fed and sheltered? Or weren't they? Stupid or callous, it beggared belief.

What sort of Germany were he and Effi going back to?

As he sat there, the local brass band began playing on the far side of the pitch. Drifting out of the fog, the tunes sounded even more mournful than usual.

At 1.45 the Dynamos emerged for their strange warm-up ritual. The conditions might be improving, Russell thought – the players on the far touchline were clearly visible, and the welcoming red flags on the West Stand roof occasionally fluttered into view. The Dynamos went back in, more minutes dragged by, before at last the two teams walked out together, the Russians surveying their surroundings with a breezy confidence, the Arsenal players looking grimly introspective.

The latter's apprehension soon proved justified, the Russians scoring in the very first minute, and threatening another only seconds later. Soon the fog grew denser again, and the opposite stand faded from sight. The furthest players were vague apparitions at best, the linesman's luminous flag an almost spectral presence. Stanley Matthews was playing on that side, and playing well if the roars from the opposite stand were anything to go by. But there seemed no end-product until the still-visible Dynamo keeper was suddenly seen diving in vain. 1-1.

The play surged from end to end, the action moving in and out of focus as the fog swirled across the pitch. Unlike the last match, the spirit seemed anything but friendly. Tackles were flying in from all directions, one savage lunge theatrically lit by the blaze of a magnesium flash bulb. Arsenal gradually got on top, and as half time approached they scored twice in as many minutes. There was an almost instant reply from the Russians, but Dynamo were still 3-2 down when the teams went in.

Intervals usually lasted five minutes, but this one had stretched to fifteen before the players re-emerged. The fog had thinned during the break, but now thickened with a vengeance, leaving Russell and his son with only the faintest view of Dynamo's equaliser. They could see that the Arsenal players were livid, but had no idea why. Tempers frayed further, and a fist-fight erupted in the Dynamo penalty area. The referee seemed to send off an Arsenal player, but the man in question just ambled off into a dense patch of fog.

The fog thickened further, until only a quarter of the pitch was visible.

Why the game had not been abandoned was anyone's guess, but there was something highly satisfying about the whole business. It felt almost magical. Glancing sideways, Russell saw a look of utter enchantment on Paul's face, the same one he'd seen at the boy's first Hertha game, all those years ago.

Dynamo went ahead with another invisible goal, and Arsenal finally wilted. Much of the crowd was already heading for the exits by this time, but Russell and Paul hung on until the final whistle blew, and the last of the players had been swallowed by the mist.

'That was incredible,' Paul said, as they emerged onto the High Road. The buses and trolleybuses were all stuck in the stationary traffic, so they joined the stream heading south, stopping halfway down for a bag of soggy chips.

A train steamed out across the road bridge as they neared the station, and their platform was almost empty when they reached it. Russell expected Paul to pull out his book, but he didn't. 'Do you want to go back home?' he asked his son. 'Eventually, I mean.'

Paul stared out into the fog for several moments. 'I don't know,' he said at last. 'I like it here,' he added almost reluctantly after another long pause, 'but perhaps that's only because it's easier to hide from the past here. I don't know. What would I do in Berlin? There's no work there. No paid work anyway. Here I can fill up my day, and earn some money.' He looked at his father. 'I'm happy here,' he said, sounding almost surprised that he was.

'I don't know how long I'll be gone,' Russell told him.

Paul smiled. 'You don't have to worry about me, Dad. Really. I only had one nightmare this last week – did you notice?'

'Yes,' Russell said. Effi had pointed it out.

'It's like a poison,' Paul said. 'It has to work its way out of your system – that's the way I see it. And you have to let it. But not by pretending that everything's fine. Do you remember telling me once how important it was to keep your mind and your emotions turned on?'

'I remember.' He'd been trying to explain what he'd learnt fighting in the First War.

'Well I've tried to do that, and I think it works. It's like an antidote.'

Russell winced inside as he thought of the pain his son had been through, was still going through. 'You don't think talking helps?'

'I do talk to people,' Paul said. 'Just not the family.'

'Who then?' Russell asked, feeling hurt and knowing he shouldn't be.

'Solly's a great listener. And Marisa is too. It would be hard talking to you, Dad. Or to Effi.'

'I suppose it would,' Russell conceded reluctantly. He had never been able to talk to his own parents about the trenches.

A train was audible in the distance, and two fuzzy lights soon swam into view. 'And the talking does help,' Paul said.

'Good,' Russell told him. Crammed inside the suburban carriage compartment for the journey home, he felt a huge sense of relief. He might be going back into hell, but his son was going to be all right.

* * *

On Thursday afternoon Russell collected their tickets from Embassy reception, and had a long talk with Solly Bernstein about the sort of freelance articles which the latter would be able to sell, always assuming that Russell could find some way of getting them back to London. According to Solly, no one was interested in the hardships of ordinary Germans, and not many more in the fate of Europe's surviving Jews. Though there might be some mileage in the growing number of those intent on breaching the British wall around Palestine.

Arriving home around six, Russell walked into a wonderful aroma – Zarah had used all their newly surplus rations for a farewell family dinner. But the cheerful mood seemed forced, and he and Effi were relieved to escape for a few minutes' packing. There was, in truth, not much to take – they had left Germany with next to nothing, and had bought little in London. 'I'm sure actresses are supposed to have more clothes than this,' was Effi's conclusion as she closed her battered suitcase.

In the morning she walked Rosa to school for the last time. When they said their goodbyes the girl seemed determined not to cry, but Effi's tears broke down her resistance. Walking back to the flat alone, Effi couldn't remember when she'd last felt so wretched.

An hour or so later, she and Russell climbed into a taxi and waved goodbye to Zarah. Sitting in the back, they watched London slide by, all the drab buildings and overgrown bombsites, faces still etched by the hardship of war. Berlin, they knew, would be a hundred times worse.

Their boat train left on time, rattling out across the dark grey Thames, and over the long brick viaducts beyond. They might be going home, but they were not returning to anything familiar, and as the misty English countryside slipped past, Russell was assailed by the feeling that, for all their careful calculation, they were simply walking off a cliff, in the hope that some unknown net would catch them.

Death of a swan

That afternoon the Channel was cold and grey, a bitter northerly wind driving everyone off the decks and into the overcrowded seating areas. The passengers were overwhelmingly male, some in uniform, rather more bound for Germany in the civilian dress of an increasingly post-military occupation. Listening to the young soldiers' banter, Russell was reminded of similar voyages in the years of the First War, and experienced what was, for him, a rare awareness of being English. He hadn't felt at home in London, and despite all the apprehension and uncertainty surrounding their German future, he still found it hard to regret their departure.

Beside him on the crowded bench, Effi also had mixed feelings. Though still not convinced that she'd been right to leave Rosa behind, she couldn't escape a sense of satisfaction at the prospect of returning home, even if Berlin was largely in ruins. And, almost despite herself, she felt excited at the prospect of working again. A life spent acting was something she'd taken for granted until 1941, and she had missed it much more than she expected.

Night had fallen by the time they reached Ostend, and their American-supplied papers saw them almost whisked through the entry procedures. Someone at the US Embassy in London had decided that a fictional marriage was the simplest option, and Effi was now travelling as Mrs Russell, with her own American passport. She had initially objected – 'I'm a German,' she had told Russell indignantly. 'Of course you are,' he had told her with a smile, relieved that she'd been given the potential protection. 'Someone else's piece of paper is not going to change that, is it? Think of it as a part, and the passport as a prop.'

Now, seeing the problems that other returning Germans were having, she had to admit the practicality of the arrangement. But she still meant to get a new German passport at the earliest opportunity. The old one had been left in the Carmerstrasse flat when they both fled Berlin in December 1941, and had presumably been scooped up by the Gestapo. If the stories in the British papers could be believed, it had probably been put to use by some fleeing Nazi's wife or mistress.

Their train was waiting on the other side of the arrivals shed, a long line of *wagons-lit* which had somehow survived the ravages of the last few years. A two-berth compartment was better than Russell had expected, but the bedding was sparse and there was, as yet, no heating. He tried closing the door, and found it almost cut out the noise of the soldiers in the next carriage. 'We might even get some sleep,' he muttered.

'It's scary, isn't it?' Effi said.

'What is?'

'We're going back but we're not really going home. When people say they're going home they usually mean they're going back to the familiar, the known, and we're not doing that, are we? We have no idea what we're letting ourselves in for.'

'We have some idea. We're going back to a city in ruins, and we know it'll be difficult. But we have food and shelter guaranteed, and you have a movie to make. If that falls through, you can always go back to London.'

'And leave you in Berlin.'

'I'll fix it so I get back to London on a regular basis. I can always offer to spy on the English as well.'

'John!'

'I know. This is not good. But we'll get through it somehow. We were in a much worse situation than this four years ago.'

'That's not saying much.'

'True, but we'll think of something.' He gave her what he hoped was an encouraging smile.

'I know the flat was crowded, but I loved having everyone around – the children and Zarah and Paul. Didn't you?'

'I did, most of the time.'

'I want a big house in Berlin. Not now, of course, but eventually. Like Thomas's, with lots of bedrooms and a big garden.'

'That would be good,' he agreed, though how they would ever afford one was something else again. He doubted whether double agents and actresses approaching forty were paid that much.

The carriage seemed to be heating up, which suggested an attached locomotive. Russell stepped down onto the platform for a better view, and was promptly told to get back aboard – they were leaving.

The train picked its way through the sparsely lit town and out onto the darkened Flanders plain. Russell waited for it to gather speed, but twenty-five miles an hour seemed the limit of the driver's ambition. They took to their respective bunks, and Effi was soon sleeping soundly, despite noisy stops in Bruges and Brussels. Russell lay there feeling every kink in the war-worn tracks, and woke with surprise to find light shining through the crack in the curtains.

He climbed down as quietly as he could, and slipped out into the corridor just as the train rattled its way through a succession of points. Through the window he saw gutted buildings stretching into the distance, row upon serrated row. And then, as the train began to slow, Cologne Cathedral loomed above him, barely touched by the calamity which had engulfed the surrounding city. 'There must be a God,' he murmured to himself.

'There must,' Effi agreed, appearing beside him and taking his arm. In such a sea of debris the cathedral's survival had all the appearance of a miracle.

In a cleared space beside it, people were laying out items for sale on sheets and blankets. There were household objects of all kinds, and Russell thought he detected the glint of cameras, but there was no sign of food.

The railway bridge across the Rhine was still under reconstruction, and the train could go no further. They joined the scrum on the platform, and followed signs to the pontoon bridge for motor traffic and pedestrians. There was little of the former – only a couple of British Army jeeps – but steady streams of the latter were moving in both directions. A cold wind from the north was rippling the water and the Union Jacks that adorned each bank. The wide river was empty of shipping, and the broken skyline of the city behind them made it hard to believe that hundreds of thousands still called it home.

The morning's journey did nothing to raise their spirits. Town after town seemed sunk in post-war gloom, many with the same desperate outdoor market, hordes of people glancing glumly up at the passing train as they sought to barter their way out of hunger and cold. The chimneys that were issuing smoke were vastly outnumbered by those that were not.

They reached Frankfurt early in the afternoon, and eventually tracked down the station's US Army office. A Colonel Merritt should have been waiting for them, but all they found was a captain. The Soviets had been causing trouble, Merritt had been called away, and a Colonel Dallin would now conduct the briefing in Berlin. Russell groaned inwardly – he had known and disliked Dallin during the war, when the Californian had been attached to the American Embassy.

And there were no flights to Berlin, the captain added cheerfully. They would have to continue their journey by train.

There were no sleeping berths on this train, only a motley collection of pre-First War vintage carriages. Groups of GIs were flooding the compartment coach to Russell's right, and the crates of bottles being ferried aboard suggested a rowdy journey. He went the other way, into a mostly German-populated saloon, and found two rear-facing seats opposite an oldish couple in their sixties. The man wore a pince-nez and clothes that Bismarck would have liked; the woman had an unusually long neck and a face that would once have been beautiful. Neither looked in good health, but she seemed determined to be cheerful.

They were going to visit their daughter-in-law and grandchildren, she told them – their son had been killed in Russia. 'The schools are open again,' she said with evident satisfaction. 'I've brought the children some apples,' she added, patting her bag. 'I don't suppose they have any fruit in Berlin.'

Her husband didn't say much, but obviously doted on her. Russell had the feeling that he'd recognised Effi, but was too well-mannered to say anything.

They fell asleep soon after the train got underway, her head sliding slowly down until it rested on his shoulder. This encouraged Effi to arrange herself in similar fashion, and soon she was sleeping too, despite the growing cacophony of drunken voices emanating from the next carriage. Russell tried closing his own eyes, but to no avail.

Shortly after ten they stopped in Gotha, where Red Army soldiers lined a surprisingly well-lit platform. But there was no onboard inspection, and the train was soon moving again. Russell found himself slipping in and out of dozes, awakened by the frequent stops and lulled back to sleep during each brief episode of forward motion. It was almost one in the morning when a just discernible station name told him they were around fifty kilometres from their destination, and only a few minutes later when the train inexplicably slowed to a halt in what looked like the middle of a forest. A flutter of movement in the darkness outside was probably the wind in the trees, but a sudden loud report from back down the train sounded like the slam of an outside door. A passenger across the aisle pressed his shielded eyes up against the window, then turned back to his partner with a shrug of incomprehension.

Was something happening?

Apparently not. The train started moving again, and Russell sank back in his seat, feeling an exaggerated sense of relief. He was still reflecting on all those unexplained little mysteries that punctuate life when the sound of a shot cut across the rhythmic clatter of the wheels. Effi's head jerked off his shoulder, and the eyes of the old couple opposite were suddenly wide open.

There was shouting in the next carriage now, but no more shots. In their own, some people were halfway to their feet, others almost cringing in their seats. And then a young man with a machine pistol came through the vestibule door, swiftly followed by a boy of about twelve and two other men carrying submachine guns. All four had Slavic faces, and faded patches on two of the jackets bore witness to vanished Foreign Workers badges.

One of the men walked swiftly down the aisle to the door at the other end, disappearing through it for a moment, then returning to stand sentry. While the other man with a submachine-gun held his position at the opposite end, the man with the machine pistol suggested, in heavily Russian-accented German, that the occupants of the first two bays deposit any valuables in the old Reichspost sack that the boy was helpfully holding open.

The operation went remarkably smoothly, once the man with the pistol had clarified what he meant by valuables. Cigarettes, canned food and fresh vegetables joined a few items of jewellery and even fewer watches in the swastika-stencilled sack. Would anyone resist? There were two American officers further down the carriage, but neither seemed armed. Most of the Germans seemed more resigned than angry, as if such robberies were just one more aspect of post-war life that had to be endured.

And what, Russell wondered, was happening elsewhere in the train? Much the same, he assumed, which suggested a gang of considerable size.

The sack was drawing nearer, the Russian with the machine pistol working his way through suitcases and pockets with the sort of professional efficiency that suggested previous experience. The boy looked bored.

Their turn arrived. There was no treasure in the old couple's suitcase, and only the apples in the bag. The woman stifled a protest as these was taken, but there were tears in her eyes. Feeling Effi stiffen beside him, Russell was suddenly afraid that she'd react as she had in London, and this time get shot for her pains. He leapt up to get their suitcase from the rack, which put him between her and the Russian, and then sought to hold the man's attention by telling him in his own language that they weren't carrying any valuables. The Russian disagreed, adding Lord Peter Wimsey and their spare shoes to the bulging sack before demanding Effi's handbag.

She handed it over, much to Russell's relief, with no more demur than a contemptuous look. The man removed her vanity case, handed back the bag, and offered a slight bow, as if recognising royalty. She had played a Russian princess once, Russell remembered, so some sort of obeisance was only fitting.

'Rosa helped me choose that compact,' Effi angrily hissed in his ear.

'I know. And she wouldn't want you getting shot over it.'

The sack moved on. The train rumbled across several bridges in quick succession, and two surprisingly well-lit streets and a straight stretch of dark water briefly showed in the window. The latter had to be the Tel-towkanal. Anhalter Station couldn't be more than fifteen minutes away.

Obviously aware of this, the robbers were working even faster. The train was on the final viaduct approaches when the man standing sentry at the rear vestibule door started down the aisle, waving his weapon to deter any last minute resistance. Turning in his seat, Russell watched all four of them disappear through the door at the other end. There was a silence lasting several moments, then everyone seemed to start talking. But no one left their seat.

The two American soldiers were both grinning, as if they'd just seen an excellent review sketch.

The train was slowing down, and Russell thought he heard gunfire in the distance. He and Effi exchanged questioning looks, but there was no rep-etition. One of the passengers said something that made the others laugh.

They were drawing into the station, and Russell could see lines of boxcars stabled in the other platforms, some in the process of being unloaded. He remembered reading that the Americans were using Anhal-ter Station as their main entry point for supplies.

Where were the Russians? He supposed they might have jumped off, but surely the train had been going too fast. They were probably just waiting by the doors, secure in the knowledge that most of their victims would sit tight until they were sure it was safe. The Russians would just step down from the train, load up their sacks on porters' trolleys, and wheel them down to their getaway lorries. Welcome to Berlin.

The train stopped. A minute went by, and another, without any sounds of commotion outside. In fact people from further down the train were walking past the window, apparently oblivious to any danger. The passengers in their carriage began gathering their things together, and the first brave soul inched his way out of the vestibule door. Russell took their suitcase down again and led the way to the outside world, standing in the doorway for a long moment, listening to the murmurs of conversation, the slap of feet on concrete. Hearing nothing suspicious, he stepped down onto the dimly lit platform. The sky was clear, stars winking down through the skeletal remains of the station roof.

Effi had just joined him when the windows of their carriage exploded inwards, the sound of falling glass chiming through the boom of the offending gun.

Russell dropped to the platform, pulling Effi down after him. 'Flat as you can,' he urged her, remembering the sergeant who'd given him the exact same advice twenty-seven years earlier, in a patch of no man's land a few miles from Ypres.

Raising his eyes, he saw that others had done the same. Most, however, were hopelessly milling.

Another burst of machine gun fire produced screams of pain or alarm.

Who was firing? And at whom?

Feet were pounding towards them, and he did his best to shelter Effi's body with his own. The owners of the feet ran past, and squinting upwards Russell recognised one of the men from their carriage. The boy was there too, mouth pursed with effort as he hauled the heavy sack along the uneven platform.

There were shouts and whistles, and a last burst of gunfire from those in flight. Russell turned to see the old man from the opposite seat crumple silently to the ground. His wife sank down beside him, and a keening cry seemed to slip from her throat. She raised her head on its long pale neck, and the thought crossed Russell's mind that swans always mated for life.

* * *

'It was probably the Lehrter Station Gang,' the American major told them. Once it was safe to do so, they had sought and found his office in what remained of the old ticket hall. As they waited for transport Russell had asked him about the battle on the platform.

'The what?' Russell asked. The 'Lehrter Station Gang' sounded like something out of a Hollywood Western.

'They're mostly Russians,' the major explained, 'prisoners who don't want to go home. They've realised that crime pays much better here than real work does back in Russia. Particularly when the chance of getting caught is close to zero. Unlike the police, they're armed.'

'Why Lehrter Station?'

'It's where the biggest gang is based. Most of the refugees from the east arrive there, and the whole area's just one big camp. Ideal for hiding out.'

'Did they get away with anything?' Russell asked. He hadn't seen anyone carrying booty.

'A few thousand cigarettes.'

'And they kill men for that?' Effi said disbelievingly. She still felt shocked by what she had witnessed. She had seen death in many forms during the war years, from bodies mangled beyond recognition to bodies lacking only that unmissable spark of life, but she had never seen a man killed, or a woman widowed, at such close quarters.

The major smiled. 'You must have just got off the boat. Cigarettes are money here. Better than money.'

'We know,' Russell said. It was why they were carrying a dozen cartons in their suitcases. But an economy that used cigarettes for currency still took getting used to.

The door opened to admit a US Army corporal, a lanky young man of around twenty with a ready smile and hopeful eyes.

'Here's your ride,' the major said.

On the walk to the jeep the corporal told them that his name was Leacock, that his hometown was Cincinnati, Ohio, and that he'd been in Berlin since July. Despite the late hour and the freezing temperature, he seemed more than happy in his work. After ushering Russell and Effi into the back and piling their suitcases next to his own seat, he turned and asked if they'd like to 'see some of the sights.'

'Like what?' Russell asked.

'The Ku'damm's still busy at this time of night. Worth a look, and it'll only add a few minutes to the ride. And you'd be doing me a favour. I need to pick something up there.'

'No, I...' Russell began, but Effi intervened. 'I'd like to see it,' she said in German.

'Have you been here before?' Leacock asked.

'Once or twice,' Russell said drily. He had to admit, he was curious himself. 'Okay, let's go via the Ku'damm.'

Leacock needed no second bidding, and soon they were circling the vast, rubble-ringed Potsdamer Platz and heading up a wide avenue of perforated buildings towards the southern perimeter of the Tiergarten. 'We're in the British zone now,' Leacock shouted over his shoulder.

'Are there no checkpoints between the zones?' Russell asked him, leaning forward.

'None. Not even with the Russians. There are patrols, and you need to stop when they tell you to, but that's it. You can go where you like until someone tells otherwise.'

The Tiergarten was shrouded in darkness, but the damage to Lützow-platz was all too visible – one of Berlin's loveliest squares, it had been virtually demolished. Tauentzienstrasse had fared slightly better, but here too the familiar landmarks were outnumbered by those that were missing. Beyond the sundered remains of the Memorial Church Russell glimpsed a pile of rubble where the Eden Hotel had stood.

The Ku'damm had been hard-hit too, but life had clearly returned to those buildings still standing. There were lights here, and more traffic, both human and motor. Russell had just registered the survival of the Hotel am Zoo when Leacock swung the jeep across the wide avenue and brought it to a halt outside a nightclub. 'I'll just be a minute,' he said, taking the key and vaulting out onto the pavement.

He had only gone a few steps when second thoughts turned him round. 'You don't have anything you want trading?' he asked Russell. 'Cigarettes, maybe? I'll get you a good deal.'

Russell shook his head, vaguely amused.

There were three British soldiers smoking by the entrance, and five German women apparently awaiting their attention. A jazz band was playing inside; the music swelling as Leacock opened the door, subsiding as it shut behind him. Russell noticed one of the women slip her hand inside a soldier's pockets for a casual fondle. The soldier gave her a quick grin, and said something to one of his friends.

The corporal returned, looking less than happy. 'Goddamn limeys,' he muttered under his breath as he let in the clutch and almost jumped the jeep back into motion.

They drove past several more flourishing establishments before turning south through Schmargendorf and on into Dahlem, eventually pulling up in a sea of other jeeps beside a large building on Kronprinzenallee. They were, Russell realised, only a ten-minute walk from Thomas's old home on Vogelsangstrasse.

Leacock led them inside, carrying Effi's suitcase. 'Anything you need, come to me,' he told them *en route* to the duty office. 'Any of the drivers will know how to reach me.'

The duty officer checked through his list, and eventually found their names. A bed was waiting two buildings down, in Room 7. They walked the required hundred metres, found their allotted room, and collapsed onto the double bed that virtually filled it. The last thing Russell remembered was wondering whether or not to take off his shoes.

* * *

Given all they had heard about the difficulties the Americans were having in supplying their Berlin garrison, breakfast came as a very pleasant surprise. Bacon, eggs, pancakes and drinkable coffee, all in quantities which the average Londoner could only dream about. The staff, they noticed, were mostly German, and almost pitiably eager to please. There was no mistaking who had won the war.

Back at the duty office, another baby-faced lieutenant searched his records for some sign of their military relevance. When Russell explained that he was a journalist, the man suggested that a visit to the Press Camp on nearby Argentinischeallee was in order. 'They'll have your ration cards and press credentials there.'

'What about my wife?' Russell asked, rather savouring the phrase.

'What? Ah...' He examined the document he had just discovered. 'There's no mention of a wife here. But a Colonel Dallin wants to see you. Do you know what that's about?'

'Yes, but my wife...'

'I am in Berlin to make film,' Effi interjected in English.

'Ah. Well I don't know about that. Why don't you both have a coffee while I give someone a call, okay? The canteen's in the basement.'

'We were also promised permanent accommodation,' Russell told him.

'Okay, leave it with me.'

They did as they were told, returning twenty minutes later to find the officer looking more than a little pleased with himself. 'You have to report to the *Reichskulturkammer* at 45 Schlüterstrasse,' he told Effi. 'It's in the British zone, off...'

'I know where it is,' she said. It was only a short walk from her old apartment.

'You'll get your ration card from them.'

'Yes.'

'Accommodation... I spoke to someone in Colonel Dallin's office, and apparently they've got something lined up. He's out somewhere, but they think he'll be back soon, so if you could just hang on here...'

'Okay,' Russell concurred without enthusiasm.

They had been sitting there for more than an hour, reading month-old copies of *Stars and Stripes*, when Russell had an idea. 'Are the telephones working – in the city I mean?' he asked the duty officer.

'Some are, some aren't.'

'Could I try a number?'

'Sure. Be my guest.'

Russell dialled Thomas' number, which had worked in April. It still did.

'Dahlem 367,' the familiar voice answered.

'Thomas, it's John.'

'What? John? Where are you?'

'Just down the road. At the American HQ on Kronprinzenallee. Effi's here too. Are Hanna and Lotte with you?'

'They're still in the country. But this is wonderful. Are you coming over?'

'Of course. I was hoping we could stay with you.'

'Yes, yes, I'll find some room somewhere. The Americans dumped three other families on me after requisitioning their houses, so it's a bit... but we'll find a way, please, come. As soon as you can.'

'We'll come now,' Russell told him. It felt so good to hear Thomas' voice.

The officer looked surprised, and Russell realised it was the first time he'd spoken German in the man's presence. 'We're not going to wait any longer,' he said in English. He reached out for one of the man's pencils and wrote out Thomas' number. 'I'll be back tomorrow,' he said, 'but if Colonel Dallin can't wait he can reach me on this.'

'He won't be pleased to find you gone.'

'Tell him how upset I was to miss him,' Russell said, drawing a smile. 'Thanks for your help.'

* * *

Sundays in Dahlem had never been noted for excitement, but the quiet streets offered a welcome corrective to their nightmare arrival at Anhalter

Station. It should have been a cold, clear day, but the sun was muted by hanging dust, the freshness of the air compromised by faint odours of damp, decay and human remains. Russell found himself wondering how many bodies still lay unclaimed beneath the rubble.

Walking beside him, Effi noticed how little the population had changed since April. There were hardly any men on the street, and even fewer children. The only youths they had seen that morning had been begging outside the American mess hall.

Turning off Königin-Luise-Strasse, they could see Thomas waiting by his gate. He hurried to meet them, engulfing first Effi, then Russell, in ferocious hugs. They had last been together in May, when Russell had bought their releases from the Soviet zone with the atomic documents that he and Varennikov had buried in Thomas's garden. But Thomas had soon set off for the country home of his parents-in-law, where his wife Hanna and daughter Lotte had been living for almost eighteen months. Since that day Russell had only received one letter, confirming that all were alive and well.

The house looked much the same as in April – in sore need of attention. Thomas looked fit enough, but Russell couldn't help noticing how much the war – and the death of an only son – had aged his friend.

'When did you arrive?' Thomas asked, leading them in through the front door.

'Late last night,' Russell said. 'We arrived at Anhalter Station in the middle of a gun battle.'

Thomas was not surprised. 'That's a place to avoid after dark. The occupiers don't have the men to police the city, and they won't arm Germans. So...' He shrugged and continued on into the kitchen-dining room. 'This is the only communal room,' he told them, pulling out chairs from under the table. 'You'll sleep in my bedroom,' he added; 'I can use the camp bed in my study.'

'We can't turn you out of your bed,' Russell protested, knowing full well that his ex-brother-in-law would insist. The Americans might offer better accommodation, but Thomas's company seemed infinitely preferable.

'Thank you,' Effi said.

'You're welcome. It's so good to see you both. How is everyone?'

They gave him the news from London – Paul's possible romance, Rosa's excellent reports, Zarah's flirtation with the man downstairs. 'It seemed wiser to leave them there,' Russell said, 'at least until we knew what was happening here.'

'That was probably the right thing to do. Hanna wants to come back, but I'm not sure it's a good idea. I want them back, but I can't help feeling they're better off where they are. And I wouldn't have any time to spend with them if they were here – if the Soviets aren't demanding my presence, then the Americans are.'

'Your printing works are in the Soviet zone,' Russell guessed.

'One street away from the boundary line,' Thomas said bitterly.

'Ouch.'

'Ouch indeed.'

'So who else is living here?' Effi asked.

Thomas grunted and shook his head. 'In the living room,' he began, ticking off one finger, 'an old couple named Fermaier. They're decent enough, but in shock – they've survived and their family hasn't. Their son was killed in the Dresden bombing, their daughter by a Russian shell in Schmargendorf. Two grandsons died in Russia. There's only a granddaughter left, but she's joined the communist party, and they can't decide whether to disown her. I tried to reassure them – I told them that my sister was in the Party once – and they gave me sympathetic looks, as if I'd just admitted a family history of mental illness.

'In Lotte's room,' he continued, ticking off a second finger, 'there's a younger couple named Schrumpf – about your age. How he survived the war is unknown – a civil servant of some sort I'd guess, and there's that tell-tale fading of his jacket lapel where the swastika used to be. They don't go out much, which might be because he doesn't want anyone to recognise him. Or he just can't bear seeing what happened to the thousand-year Reich. She wanders round in her dressing-gown at night, like someone auditioning for Hamlet's ghost.

'But it's the couple in Joachim's old room who give me the most trouble. A mother and her grown-up daughter. They're not very nice, though perhaps they have cause. They both seem incredibly angry, and I'd guess that the daughter at least was abused by the Russians. But God knows it's hard to feel any sympathy. They are so...'

Voices were audible in the hall.

'Speak of the devil,' Thomas half-whispered.

Two women came into the kitchen, one around fifty with pinched features and hair in a tight bun, the other in her twenties with blonde hair cut short and the sort of face a smile might transform.

'Frau Niebel. Fräulein...' Thomas said, getting to his feet. 'How are you this morning?'

The woman sighed. 'That woman kept us awake with her sobbing for half of the night,' she said. 'Again. She may be a "Victim of Fascism"' – a heavy hint of sarcasm here – 'but we ordinary Germans need our sleep. I've been to the Re-housing Office, and they have no record of her, so I assume she's your personal guest...'

'She is.'

'Well, can you talk to her?'

'I can indeed. But her husband is very ill, so she does have something to cry about.' He gestured towards Russell and Effi. 'These are old friends, who'll also be staying for a while, Herr Russell and Fräulein Koenen.'

Russell and Effi got up to shake hands.

'Have we met before?' Frau Niebel asked Effi.

'You're the actress, aren't you?' the daughter said.

'I am.'

'Oh,' her mother said, bewilderment in her eyes. Effi guessed that Frau Niebel was remembering the newspaper pictures from December 1941, and the story that she'd been kidnapped by her English spy of a boyfriend. The woman's involuntary glance at Russell seemed to confirm as much.

But the woman quickly recovered. 'We all have our crosses to bear,' she said, turning back to Thomas. 'I lost a husband myself, and not that long ago. But some of us bear those crosses in silence.'

Thomas merely nodded, but it proved enough.

'What a dreadful woman,' Effi murmured once the door had closed behind her.

'Indeed,' Thomas agreed. 'But you'll never guess who she was complaining about.'

'Who?'

'Esther Rosenfeld.'

'Miriam's mother?' Russell was astonished.

'No!' Effi added disbelievingly.

'The same,' Thomas told them.

Six years earlier, in the last summer of peace, two Jewish Silesian farmers named Leon and Esther Rosenfeld had put their seventeen year-old daughter Miriam on a train to Berlin, where a job was waiting for her at Thomas's printing works. Abducted on arrival, the girl had been in terrible emotional and physical shape by the time Russell and Effi tracked her down. A Jewish family in Berlin had offered care and a bed while she recovered, but when Russell travelled back to Silesia with the news of her survival, he had found the farm in ruins, both parents gone. He had, until this moment, assumed they were dead.

Their survival was wonderful news.

'What's Esther doing here?' he wanted to know. 'Where have she and Leon been all this time?'

'A long story. That summer, they were threatened, and they decided to flee. They walked across the mountains, which must have been hard, even in August. Leon had an old friend in Pilsen, a Jew, and he had a Czech friend who was willing to shelter them all. They spent the whole war on a farm in Moravia, and when it was over they decided to go back home.'

'But by then their home was in Poland,' Russell guessed.

'Yes. And as we know, an awful lot of Poles share the Nazis' fondness for the Jews. The family that had taken their land refused point-blank to give it back, and when Leon tried to get official help he was beaten up. Badly as it turned out, though according to Esther they both thought he was well on the way to recovery. They set out for Berlin, partly to look for

Miriam, partly because they had nowhere else to go, but by the time they got here Leon was having trouble breathing. The two of them turned up at the works – it was the only address they had in Berlin – and I got him admitted to hospital.' He smiled wryly. 'As Frau Niebel pointed out, Victims of Fascism get special treatment these days.'

He gave them a troubled look. 'I also told them everything I know about Miriam, which was probably a mistake. I wanted them to know that she was alive in September 1939, but of course that entailed explaining why she hadn't contacted them. Leon took it all very much to heart – quite literally, I'm afraid – and Esther is convinced he won't recover until he knows what's happened to her. So I've promised to start looking again. Some of the Jewish survivors must know what happened to her.'

Russell sighed. 'I was going to say "she must be dead," but that's what I thought about her parents. Maybe she is alive somewhere. Where would you start to look? We've got Rosa's father to look for.'

'We can look for Miriam while we look for him,' Effi interjected. 'We'll be looking in the same places, won't we?'

'I was actually compiling a list this morning,' Thomas said. 'DP camps, of course – there's probably twenty or more in and around Berlin, some big, some small. Some of the Jews are in camps of their own, but not all of them. It seems the Americans believe they deserve special treatment, while the British think separating them out is too reminiscent of the Nazis. The old hospital on Iranische Strasse where you and Rosa were held is one of them, and there are a couple of others. And then there are the old Jewish neighbourhoods. There are messages pinned wherever you look, telling where people have gone, or asking for news of others. Almost everyone seems to be looking for someone.'

'We'll start tomorrow,' Effi said, looking at Russell. 'I'll go to Schlüterstrasse in the morning, and meet you both somewhere for lunch.'

'Not me, I'm afraid,' Thomas said. 'I have another meeting with the Russians.'

'How is business?' Russell asked.

'A nightmare,' Thomas said cheerfully. 'Living in the American zone, working in the Russian – it's a recipe for trouble. The Russians brought me plenty of work right from the outset, but most of it was propaganda, which didn't please the Americans. So they told the Russians that I had a suspect past, and that they'd be bringing me up before a Denazification tribunal. They haven't yet, but they probably will.'

'You're joking,' Effi said.

'I wish I was. As you both know, I did cosy up to some pretty disgusting people during the war – it seemed the only way to protect our Jewish staff, not that it worked in the end. If it comes to it, I could probably find some Jewish survivors to testify on my behalf, but what a waste of time and energy that would be.'

And embarrassing, Russell thought. Thomas was not someone who liked to publicise his good deeds.

'Business has become politics, I'm afraid,' Thomas concluded. 'But then I suppose it always was.'

'How did the Russians reply to the Americans?' Russell asked.

'Oh, they wouldn't care if I turned out to be Hitler's long-lost brother. They shot all the Nazis they came across in the first few months, and then drew a line under it. Now all they care about is how useful anyone might be. It's almost refreshing, especially when you see the contortions the Americans are going through. But I shouldn't complain,' he added with a sudden smile, 'most Berliners are having a much worse time than I am. You know what the basic ration card is called? The death card, because it doesn't give you enough calories to live on. That's the one everyone in this house has, save me and Esther. I get more for running a business, and Esther for being a 'Victim'. But we both put what we get in the house kitty, not that you'd think so from Frau Niebel's attitude.'

'Well, you'll have two more for the pot now,' Effi said.

'And yours will be the most welcome,' Thomas told her. 'Artists get the highest-grade card, thanks to the Russians. What a strange people they are. Their soldiers rape half the women in the city, and then they sponsor an artistic renaissance.'

'Different Russians,' Russell told him. 'Think Beethoven and the storm troopers.'

Thomas laughed. 'I suppose so. Do you know much about your new film?' he asked Effi.

'Not a great deal. It seems well-meaning, which will make a change in itself. I'm hoping there's a script waiting for me at Schlüterstrasse.'

'And you're back as a journalist?' he asked Russell.

'Yes. Sort of.'

'The Soviets have come back with the bill?'

'Yes, but we can talk about that some other time. Esther Rosenfeld isn't here, is she?'

'No, she spends her days at the hospital. She usually comes back here to sleep, so you might see her tonight.' He smiled at them both. 'Now, how about some lunch? There's a community canteen on Im Dol where the food's just about passable. And then we can go for a walk in the Grunewald. Just like old times.'

'That sounds good,' Russell said, with rather more enthusiasm than he felt. He had last walked the Grunewald at night, in the company of three Russians. Two had died before dawn, the third a few days later. It would be nice to see the forest again, but 'just like old times' seemed a trifle optimistic.

* * *

Through lunch and a long stroll through the winter trees, through dinner and drinks at a local restaurant half-full of American officers, the three of them talked and talked, catching each other up on four years spent apart. Their time together in April had been short, and Thomas had only scant knowledge of Effi's years alone in Berlin and of Russell's long exile in America and Britain. And they knew next to nothing of Thomas's long losing battle to save his Jewish workers, or the months he had spent back in uniform.

It wasn't all reminiscences, but Russell couldn't help noticing that whenever the future cropped up, their conversation soon slipped backwards, as if the pull of the past was still too strong to escape. Later that night, lying, somewhat guiltily, in Thomas' unusually comfortable bed, he tried to explain this thought to Effi.

She was ahead of him. 'In London it felt like people were only thinking of the future, that they wanted to put the war behind them. But it's not like that here. The fighting's over, but not the war. That poor girl in Joachim's room – if she started weeping she'd never stop. The fight we saw at the station, Miriam's father half-killed by Poles, not to mention the Russians' plans for you. I know the Nazis are gone, but...'

'The leaders, maybe. But the small fry are still out there, and from everything Thomas was saying, there's no real acceptance of what happened here. Most ordinary Germans seem to think that the Allies' concentration camp films were faked. Maybe a few thousand Jews were killed, but millions? And most of those who do accept it claim that there was no way of knowing, that only a few people were involved.'

Effi sighed. 'At least no one in our family helped them.'

'Jens?'

'Oh, Jens.'

'We sat at his dinner table, we listened to him explain how hard it was condemning millions of Russians to starvation, and we said nothing because we didn't want to upset Zarah.'

'Yes, but...'

'I spent Hitler's early years writing stories about schnauzers, for God's sake.'

'But you did end up risking your life to expose them.'

'Only when I had to.'

'And I made movies for Goebbels,' she said.

'And you saved a lot of Jewish lives. We both have reasons for pride and shame, like most Germans. And I don't blame us or them. When it's your life or somebody else's it takes a certain kind of bravery – or foolishness – to deliberately put yourself second. And I feel a lot easier praising those that do put themselves second than condemning those that can't. I don't envy the Allies' judges. Those bastards on trial at Nuremberg may deserve all they get, but they're special cases. And there are an awful lot of Germans – communists, Jews, homosexuals, victims and resisters of all descriptions – who deserve both praise and sympathy. And between those two extremes there are about sixty million Germans who deserve neither reward nor punishment.'

'When we were at the restaurant,' Effi said, 'I couldn't help overhearing the conversation at the next table. One man was ranting away about the hypocrisy of the Americans and the British in not trying their own war criminals. I imagine a lot of Germans would agree with him.'

'So do I,' Russell admitted. 'People should end up in the dock for Hiroshima and Dresden and a whole lot else. But they won't. So we have to ask ourselves – hypocrisy or not, do we want Germany's crimes to go unpunished? And I have to say, I don't.'

'Neither do I,' Effi agreed. 'But the condemnation would feel more just if it seemed less partial.'

'I wouldn't argue with that.'

'You know, it seems so strange. Yesterday, today, seeing foreign soldiers in control all over Berlin. They should be, of course they should, but it does feel strange. Imagine how you would feel if Germans were riding up and down Regent Street in their jeeps.'

'With Italian generals running London's opera. Yes, I know what you mean.'

She raised herself on an elbow to look him in the face. 'This is the end of Germany, isn't it?'

He was surprised. 'Depends what you mean by Germany. The people won't disappear. Or the towns or the farms. But the state will probably be divided.'

'Divided!?' She didn't know why, but the thought had never occurred to her. Shrunken, yes, even broken into the old small pieces, but divided?

'It'll have to be. There's no halfway house between free enterprise and the Soviet system – a society has to be one or the other. And since I can't see either Washington or Moscow conceding the whole country to the other, there'll have to be partition.'

'And Berlin?'

'That's where it gets interesting. The Soviets will try and force the others out – the city *is* in the middle of their zone – and who knows how determined the Western allies will prove when the crunch comes.'

'But they all seemed so chummy at Potsdam.'

'If they really were, it won't last.' He gave her a wry smile. 'Not the best place to raise a family, eh?'

She smiled back. 'Oh I don't know. It won't be dull.'

Russell laughed. 'It's never dull where you are.'

'What a nice thing to say. These last few months I've been afraid you were getting bored with me.'

'Never.'

'Well, that's good. It has been twelve years, you know.'

'We missed out on three of them, and this is the first time we've been alone in a proper bedroom for months.'

'True.' Snuggling closer, she felt his response. 'We'll have to be quiet,' she murmured. 'We wouldn't want to wake Frau Niebel.'

A world without cats or birds

Russell was awake early, and took the opportunity to visit the Press Camp on Argentinischeallee. After picking up his new credentials and ration card, he registered his address and talked to the few journalists who had so far put in an appearance. All were very young, but most seemed to recognise his name, albeit with expressions which ranged from the awestruck to the downright suspicious. Reading between the lines, he gathered that his work was appreciated, but that his murky personal history – his tangled relationships with the Nazis and Soviets in particular – told against him.

Would American Intelligence try to re-burnish his reputation now that he was working for them? He would ask Dallin when he saw him.

Back at their room in Thomas' house, he found Effi looking every inch the film actress. The dress she'd brought from England had been ironed, and she was wearing heels for the first time in months.

'You look gorgeous,' Russell told her. And she did. When they'd met again in April, she'd been so much thinner and paler than he remembered, but several months of British rations had restored her normal weight and colour. She'd let her hair grow past her shoulders again, but refused to disguise the streaks of grey. Now the sparkle was back in the dark brown eyes, the smile as dazzling as ever.

'I don't suppose they've sent a limousine for me?' she asked.

'Surprisingly not.'

'Well, at least I've got you to carry my bag as far as the Ku'damm.'

'Yes, ma'am. May I ask what's in it?'

'A change of clothes. I don't think I should turn up at the Jewish Hospital in this outfit. Oh, and I met Esther Rosenfeld...'

'Is she here?'

'She's gone already. But she's hoping to see you this evening.'

'Good.'

Effi took one last look in the mirror. 'Where are *you* going?' she asked. 'And where will we meet? I know it sounds silly, but I'd rather not arrive at the Jewish Hospital on my own.'

'It doesn't sound silly at all,' Russell said. In the spring she and Rosa had spent almost a week there under threat of summary execution. 'I'm going out to Moabit – there's a DP camp there on Thomas' list. So let's meet back at Zoo Station. In the buffet if it's still there, outside if it isn't. You choose the time.'

'Two o'clock?'

'Okay. But I'm coming with you as far as the Ku'damm. Maybe we can grab a quick coffee.'

'Just like old times,' Effi said, echoing Thomas from the previous day.

The roads between Dahlem and the West End were clear, but no trams seemed to be running. Another would-be passenger explained that several stretches of track had been torn up and taken by the Russians in June, and that buses were the only option until the Americans got around to re-laying them. One crowded double-decker eventually arrived, and thirty-five uncomfortable minutes later they found themselves in their old stamping ground at the eastern end of the Ku'damm. Several cafés were open for business, their clientele sitting in coats and mufflers at the outside tables, watching the steam from their coffees coalesce with their own exhalations. It was indeed like old times, but for the facing view, of ruins seen through ruins.

A succession of British jeeps raced by, tiny Union Jacks flapping on their bonnets, soldiers with cigarettes dangling carelessly from their lips at the wheel. When one cast a butt out onto the asphalt, half a dozen children miraculously emerged to contest its possession.

The two of them sipped at the dreadful coffee and ran through Thomas' list of places to check. It seemed lengthy, but Effi thought a couple of weeks should suffice if they all took a hand. 'And we might get lucky long before that,' she added hopefully.

'We might,' Russell agreed. 'Whatever lucky might be. I'm still not sure about this. Do we want to find Rosa's father?'

Effi looked at him. 'Yes and no,' she admitted, 'but we have to try. You could say that the news will be bad either way – if he's dead then Rosa's an orphan, and if he isn't then we'll probably lose her. But I've decided to look on the bright side – if he's dead, we get to keep her, and if he isn't, then she won't be an orphan.'

Russell smiled. It didn't seem worth pointing out the flaw in her logic – Rosa might win either way, but only one outcome would give Effi what she wanted. And there was always the chance of worse – if it turned out that Otto had deserted his family to save his own skin, they would still have to give the bastard his daughter back. Sometimes, Russell thought, it paid to leave stones unturned.

Not that he or Effi had ever knowingly done such a thing.

* * *

Effi walked the short distance to 45 Schlüterstrasse. It was not her first visit – in pre-war days, when the elegant six-storey building had hosted Goebbels' *Reichskulturkammer*, she had attended several publicity parties there. The little runt had drooled all over her on one occasion, and one of his lackeys had telephoned her several times a day for almost a week. The calls had only stopped when Russell answered one, and had them both in stitches with his outraged father act.

Better not to mention such things, she thought, as she pushed her way in through the heavy double doors. In the space where the reception desk had been, an old man in a porter's uniform was sitting on a upright chair.

'Certification?' he suggested, as he got to his feet. 'You'll...'

'I've come to see Lothar Kuhnert,' she interrupted him. 'If he's here today. He's expecting me at some point, but if...'

'He's here. Third floor, room 17.' He led her to the apparently functional lift, and pulled back the gate.

The lift lurched into motion, but only rose to the first floor, where a young man with floppy blond hair and round-rimmed glasses joined her. She noticed the jolt of recognition in his eyes, and the barely-veiled hostility which followed. All those years with an agent she didn't really need, she thought, and now that she might actually need one... A few carefully placed stories in the press extolling her virtues as a heroine of the resistance would surely do the trick. Or maybe not – disloyalty was always frowned on, even if the object was beyond redemption. And the German public would probably still find her screen portrayals more memorable than her real life. The wonder of movies!

As she walked down the third floor corridor, sounds of conversation and laughter behind several closed doors gave her a frisson of pleasure. Something was happening here, some antidote to the deadness outside.

She knocked on the door of Room 17, and received a gruff summons to enter. Inside, a man in his late fifties or early sixties rose from a dusty-looking sofa with a smile and outstretched hand. He still had all his hair, but it was almost white, and the face below was deeply lined. 'Fräulein Koenen, welcome back to Berlin.'

'Thank you,' she said.

He moved a pile of papers from an armchair, and made room for them on an already overcrowded desk. 'Please...' he said.

She sat down and smiled at him. She didn't think she'd ever met him, but there was something familiar about his face.

'We did meet once,' he said. 'In this building, in the summer of 1934. August the 6th – I remember the date because that was the day that I quit. I was the original producer for *Storm over Berlin*, but they didn't like what I had in mind, and I refused to make the changes they asked for. Someone else took over, of course, but, well...'

It had been Effi's third film, and her biggest part to date. Her portrayal of the wife of a storm trooper beaten to death by communists had done wonders for her career; when fans approached her in succeeding years it was almost always that role which they remembered.

She looked at Kuhnert, wondering if the producer was expecting some sort of *mea culpa*.

He wasn't. 'I'm aware of your work during the war, your resistance work, I mean.'

'Oh, how?'

'I'm a Party member,' he said, as if that explained it.

If the Soviets were behind the movie, she supposed it did. 'Is this...' She hesitated, uncertain how to phrase the question. 'This film – are the Russians sponsoring it? Or the KPD?'

'No, no, no,' he insisted. 'There are comrades involved – beside myself, I mean – but this is a commercial project. My own company is financing it. And we are based in the British sector. All the outside filming will be done here, only the interiors at Babelsberg.'

'The studios are still standing?'

'They were hardly damaged. Although most of the equipment was stolen.'

'Who by?'

'Ah, who knows?' He waved a hand in the air as if to dismiss the matter, which told Effi that the Russians must have been responsible.

'Who else is involved?' she asked him. 'Who's directing?'

'We're still hoping that Ernst Dufring will be available.'

'Only hoping?'

'He wants to do it – he really likes the script. And he says he's keen to work with you. A week ago everything seemed fine, but the British authorities asked him in for a second interview – since we're based in their sector we need their permission to hire anyone – and now they're looking into whatever he told them. We don't know why they called him back – the Americans may have asked them to, or another German may have denounced him. We should know in a few days, and if the news is bad, we'll just have to go with someone else.'

'But there is a finished script?'

'Oh yes. And it's good. Have you heard of Ute Faeder?'

'Yes, a long time ago. She had a good reputation.' Another who had dropped from sight soon after the Nazi takeover.

'And most of the casting has been done,' Kuhnert went on. He reeled off a list of names, and all those that Effi recognised were good actors.

'Do we have a title yet?' she asked. She knew it was silly, but her films had never felt real until they had a proper title.

'Nothing definite. "The Man I Shall Kill" is the current favourite.'

'Mmm. And no date for shooting yet?'

'No, I'm sorry. It's frustrating for everyone,' he went on, correctly interpreting her expression. 'So many of us have been waiting for this moment, here and in exile, waiting for the chance to start again, to reclaim German cinema, to make it what it was, a world leader. But the obstacles are still enormous. The war's been over for six months, and not a single film has gone into production.'

'Why?'

Kuhnert shrugged. 'No one knows for sure. The Americans are the main problem, and the cynical among us think that Hollywood fears the competition. There's certainly plenty of their product on show here. But the Americans authorities say it's all about cleaning up the German industry, that after Goebbels and Promi they have to be sure that anyone with the slightest smudge on their record is banned from working in it.'

'That sounds a bit unrealistic.'

'Doesn't it? And that's why most people agree with the cynics. Either way, there's nothing we can do but press ahead, jump through all the hoops they put in front of us, and make sure we're ready when the time ever comes. And we're going ahead with some informal rehearsals, starting tomorrow. I've got a script for you somewhere.' He rummaged around in one of the desk drawers and brought out a string-bound manuscript. 'You're Lilli, of course.'

'Will the rehearsals be here?'

'No, at Dufring's house in Schmargendorf. Tomorrow's starts at ten. I'll write down the address for you,' he added, reaching for a pen. 'If you're desperate for other work in the meantime, the Russians are hiring German actors to dub their own films out at Babelsberg. And there are quite a few theatre companies putting on plays. I could ask around for you.'

'Thanks, but I'm not desperate. And I have some lost relatives to look for, which will probably take a while.'

'Okay. Here's the contract,' he said, passing it over. 'I know the money's terrible, but it'll be worthless in a few weeks anyway. The ration card is what matters, and yours is the highest grade. You won't go hungry.'

Effi skimmed her way through the two-sheet contract. Neuefilm, the name of Kuhnert's production company, rang no bells, but that was hardly surprising. The money was indeed derisory by her past standards, but, as he'd said, the ration card was what mattered. That and the chance to work again.

She borrowed his pen to sign it.

Kuhnert seemed pleased. He reached for a small pile of cards on his desk, riffled through them, and handed her a ration card. Her name and 'Actor: leading roles' had been typed in the appropriate spaces. He also passed across two sheets of paper. 'Here's Dufring's address, and this is your certification from the *Spruchkammer*.'

'The what?'

'It's the committee which examines each artist's political background, before granting permission to work. It's based in this building.'

'Who set it up?'

Kuhnert shrugged. 'Its own members, initially. But the Russians accepted them, and so did the Western allies when they arrived. No one wants the Nazis back.'

'Of course not,' Effi agreed.

'But you will need clearance from the British. I'm assuming that you never joined the National Socialist Party.'

'God no, but I was a member of the *Reichskulturkammer*.'

'All working actors were – that shouldn't be a problem.'

'All right. So where do I go for British clearance?'

'Oh, upstairs. One floor up. They're at the back of the building. Just show them the *Spruchkammer* certificate.' He offered his hand again, and gave her a reassuring smile. 'Until tomorrow.'

She decided she rather liked him, and wondered how he'd spent the last ten years. A question for another day.

Up in the British office waiting room, she found herself fourth in the queue, behind three much younger women seeking the conquerors' permission to work in the arts. None seemed to recognise her, and all were dealt with quickly, a consequence, she assumed, of the obvious fact that all qualified for the amnesty granted anyone born after 1918.

She unfortunately did not.

The fair-haired English major who interviewed her was either tired, bored or badly hung over – perhaps all three. He did, however, speak perfect German. He gave the *Spruchkammer* certificate a cursory glance, took down her name and personal details, and then asked for a list of her film and stage credits. Having completed this, he reached for what looked like a prescribed set of questions. 'Were you ever a member of the National Socialist Party?' he began, finally making eye contact.

'No.'

'Were you a member of the *Reichskulturkammer*?'

'Yes, everyone was.'

'Not everyone. Some of your colleagues went into exile. Others stopped working.'

There was no satisfactory answer to that, or none that would sound so after all that had happened in the last twelve years.

He laid an accusatory finger on her list of credits. 'And these,' he went on in the same self-righteous tone, 'were all Nazi productions.'

He couldn't be that naive, she thought. 'They were produced by different companies, all of them licensed by Promi.'

'The Nazi Propaganda Ministry.'

'Yes.'

'So they were Nazi productions. And to all intents and purposes, Nazi propaganda?'

'Some were pro-Nazi, some had nothing to do with politics.'

'And how many were anti-Nazi? Or spoke out against the persecution of the Jews?'

'None.' She felt like asking him how many pre-war British or American films had taken their governments to task, but decided against it.

He looked at the list again, and shook his head. 'There's nothing after 1941,' he noticed.

'My... my boyfriend is an English journalist. He got in trouble with the Gestapo – it was just before the Americans came into the war – anyway, he had to flee the country. I was going to leave with him, but in the end I didn't. He escaped to Sweden, and I stayed in Berlin, in hiding, for the rest of the war.'

The major looked vaguely interested for the first time. 'His name?'

'John Russell. We were living in London until three days ago.'

He wrote something down. 'So you didn't work again after 1941.'

He wasn't so much naive as stupid, she thought. 'Of course not,' she said with as little asperity as she could muster.

'So how did you support yourself?'

'I still had some money hidden away. I had help from my sister. And I was part of a resistance network.'

'So many people were,' he said wryly.

'Have I done something to make you dislike me?' Effi asked him.

He ignored the question, but she detected a slight colouring in his cheeks. 'Do you have any proof of your involvement in resistance activities?' he asked.

'Not with me, no. I worked with Erik Aslund, the Swedish diplomat, and I imagine you could reach him through your embassy in Stockholm. Some of the Jews I helped to escape may have returned to Berlin, but I assume most of them will never want to see the place again. Do you want names?'

'That won't be necessary. Not yet, at least.' He looked up at her, and the first hint of uncertainty crossed his face, taking several years off his age. It was only a moment; the mask of boredom soon slipped back into place. 'You will be contacted when our investigation is complete,' he told her, 'or if we need to ask you further questions.'

She nodded, rose, and walked out through the waiting room, feeling more dejected than angry. After all they had been through...

She stopped at the head of the stairs and admonished herself. After all they had been through, things *should* be difficult.

Walking down, she heard more laughter and conversation, and what sounded like the clatter of crockery. Advancing down a likely-looking corridor she found herself outside a small cafeteria. The menu was limited to hot soup and drinks, but there was no shortage of customers, and several tables were hosting intense discussions, each ring of heads crowned by a halo of expensive cigarette smoke. She didn't recognise any of the faces.

Effi used her new ration card to procure a cup of tea, and took an empty seat in the corner. Most people there were old enough to recognise her, but the woman who actually approached her was one of the youngest, slightly-built, with dark hair, prominent eyebrows and a very sweet smile.

'You're Effi Koenen, aren't you?' she asked in almost a whisper, as if she doubted whether Effi wanted her identity known.

'I am.'

'I remember your picture from the newspapers, when the police said you'd been kidnapped. And later you helped a friend of mine – another Jew. My name is Ellen, by the way. Ellen Grynszpan. My friend loved movies, and she recognised you, but she never told anyone who you really were, not until after the war, when she came back from Sweden. Inge Lewinsky – do you remember her?'

The name was unfamiliar. 'No, I'm sorry. There were a lot of people. But please, join me.'

Ellen took a seat. 'I just wanted to thank you. For my friend. And all the others, of course.'

Effi shook her head. 'I didn't have much to lose,' she said. 'How about you? How did you survive?'

'Oh, I had an easy time of it. A Christian friend took me in and, well, I could never go out, but apart from that... it was like being in a really comfortable prison. I'm a painter, and I could paint, so I was happy most of the time.'

'And now?'

'I'm still painting, but I was persuaded to organise the exhibition here.'

'I didn't know there was one.'

'Oh, it's in the basement. It's the Berlin Jewish community's collection of paintings.'

'Paintings by Jewish artists?'

'Only a few of them are actually painted by Jews. Most of the richer patrons were more interested in a sound investment than racial provenance.'

Effi laughed. 'I suppose so.'

'Would you like to come down and have a look?'

Effi looked her watch. It might make her late, but Russell was used to that. 'I'd love to.'

The basement gallery was empty of people, but the paintings were well-lit, the room surprisingly warm. There seemed no coherent theme to the collection, and only the sign on the door offered any connection between the paintings on display and a particular community. There were landscapes, still-lifes, portraits of people and cats. The one exhibit which brought Jews to mind was a futuristic painting of a famous Berlin department store, and only because prominent Jews had owned it. If someone had told Effi that all the paintings were German, she would have taken their word for it.

And that, she supposed, was the point.

'They're not that good, are they?' Ellen said.

'They're not bad. I suppose the fact that they're here is what matters.'

'Exactly.'

They both gazed at a Cubist rendition of the Memorial Church. 'Have any of the synagogues re-opened?' Effi asked.

'Oh, at least two. There's one out in Weissensee and one in Charlotten-burg. And someone told me they're using part of the one on Rykestrasse to house Jewish refugees from Poland. Why do you ask?'

'I don't know. Like buds in the spring, I suppose. Signs of life returning – something like that. But I am looking for two Jews, and if the synagogues are housing refugees I shall need to visit them.'

'Who are the people you're looking for?'

'Their names are Otto Pappenheim and Miriam Rosenfeld.'

Ellen searched her memory, but came up empty. 'Sorry, no. But I can ask around. If I hear anything I'll leave you a message on the board outside the canteen.'

They walked back up to the lobby, and stood in silence for several moments, looking out through the open doorway at the mountain of rubble beyond. 'Do you think many of the survivors will want to stay here?' Effi asked. 'The Jewish survivors, I mean.'

'I don't know. Some will, but most would rather go to America. Or Palestine, if the British weren't making it so difficult.'

'And you?'

'I haven't decided yet.'

And neither have I, Effi thought, as she walked back up to the Ku'damm. Her interviews with Kuhnert and the British Major had been more than a little depressing, but Ellen and the crowd in the cafeteria had lifted her spirits. And if Berlin could be resurrected, there was nowhere else she would rather be.

* * *

After leaving Effi, Russell walked east along the rapidly wakening Ku'damm and up Joachimstaler Strasse to Zoo Station. The first DP camp he intended visiting was in Moabit, a walkable distance to the north, but laziness and the sight of a local train rumbling west across the Hardenbergstrasse bridge persuaded him to make use of the Stadtbahn. Walking up to the platform he noticed that most of the signs were also in Russian.

The next train was tightly packed, its passengers almost bursting out through the opening doors. Shoving his way on board, Russell found himself standing with his face almost pressed to the glass, and forced to confront Berlin's ruin. The gouged and pitted flak towers were still there, and beyond them the deforested Tiergarten, a sea of stumps in which small islands of cultivation were now sprouting.

The air on the train offered stark proof of the continuing soap shortage, and once decanted on the Bellevue platform, Russell took several deep breaths of purer air. It was all relative, of course, and his nose was soon under renewed assault, this time from the River Spree. There were no floating bodies as far as he could see, but the scum floating on the stagnant surface was an uncomfortable melange of yellows and browns, and the smell rising up was suitably disgusting. The bridge he had intended to cross lay broken in the water.

A passer-by told him that the next one up was open, but that proved something of an exaggeration – a makeshift wooden walkway offered pedestrian access to the other bank, but the original bridge was still in the river. He crossed and continued northwards, down a street still lined with piles of broken masonry. A team of women was stacking bricks – *die Trümmerfrauen*, Thomas had called them, 'the rubble women' – their breath forming plumes in the cold morning air.

It was time he got to work, Russell thought. Tomorrow he would spend some time at the Press Camp, talk to his fellow journalists, get the lay of the land. The occupiers would be imposing restrictions on reporting, but he had no idea what they were, or whether the different occupation authorities had different rules. And the current mechanics of sending out copy were also a mystery. With civil communications in tatters, were they using military channels?

All of which would sort itself out soon enough. But what was he going to write about? The story that interested him, but apparently not many others, was what had happened to the Jewish survivors. It seemed as if the Nazi crimes against the Jews were still being undersold, almost lost in the general shuffle of European misery. Perhaps he was still seeking atonement for 1942, when he'd been unable to get the story the prominence and urgency it deserved, but he didn't think so. Over the last few months all four occupation powers had forced Jewish refugees to share camps with their persecutors, but there'd been no cries of outrage, or none from anyone with the power to make changes.

His and Effi's search for Rosa's father would make a good story, or provide a good narrative on which to hang the wider theme. He would have to change the names, of course – Rosa had traumas enough to work through without becoming a poster child for orphans.

And then there was Miriam. It would really be a miracle if she was still alive.

He had reached the southern edge of the Little Tiergarten, which looked in no better shape than its bigger brother. He walked diagonally across the bare expanse, past a scorched and trackless Tiger tank with the words 'Siberia or Death' still emblazoned on one side. Two children eyed him warily from the open turret, and he wondered if the tank was only a place to play, or what they now called home.

As he passed the cemetery behind the old municipal baths he noticed several long lines of freshly dug graves, and what looked like a team of prisoners digging more. It was several seconds before he realised who they were probably meant for – the victims of the coming winter.

The old barracks loomed in front of him. There was a wall around the compound and British soldiers at the gate, who checked his papers and gave him directions for the camp administration office. En route, he noticed that one barracks door was slightly open, and took a quick look inside. The large open space had been divided up by the simple expedient of using lockers to form waist-high walls, inside which double-decker bunks were arranged in squares, enclosing a small private space. The barracks were cold and surprisingly quiet, a fact that Russell first attributed to a lack of residents. But as his eyes grew used to the gloom he realised that almost every bunk had one or more silent owner. The sense of hopelessness was almost overwhelming.

He continued on to the office, where three young Englishmen were lording it over three elderly German assistants. Once Russell had explained the reason for his visit, a sergeant with a Yorkshire accent interrupted his game of patience to instruct one of the latter, who reached for the pile of exercise books that contained the camp records, and began working his way through them. He was halfway through the last but one when he found an Otto Pappenheim.

Russell could hardly believe it. Nor did he really want to – he knew what losing Rosa would mean to Effi. As the German checked the final book for Miriam Rosenfeld, he reminded himself that Otto and Pappenheim were both fairly common names.

'Can you tell me anything about him?' Russell asked the man in German, once the search for Miriam had ended in failure.

'No, but maybe Gerd can. Wait a minute.' He walked stiffly across to the doorway of the adjoining room and asked a colleague to join them.

Gerd, a wafer-thin man in his sixties, was still wearing his Volkssturm jacket, albeit without the insignia. When he heard the name 'Otto Pappenheim' he made a face, which worried Russell even more. 'Yes, I remember him,' he said. 'He turned up in the summer, the beginning of August, I think. He had his Jewish identity card, which was unusual – most destroyed them when they went into hiding. I didn't like him, but I couldn't really tell you why. He didn't stay long. He soon found a job and somewhere else to live, which was also unusual, but we can always use the extra bed.'

'So you don't know where he went?'

'Oh, he had to give us an address, or his ration card wouldn't have been re-issued. It'll be in there,' he added, pointing out one of his colleague's desk drawers. And it was, Solinger Strasse 47. 'That's not far from here,' the first German told him. 'It's one of the streets off Levetzowstrasse. On the south side.'

Fifteen minutes later, Russell was walking down Solinger Strasse, trying to deduce which of the still-standing buildings was number 47. An elderly man sitting in a doorway pointed it out. 'The one at the end,' he said, 'thanks to the Reichsmarschal.' Russell saw what he meant – the original end of the block had been destroyed by Allied bombers, which Goering had famously promised would never reach Berlin. Now a wall boasting seven empty grates and seven different wallpapers rose towards the sky.

A woman he met in the lobby gave him Otto Pappenheim's room number. Rather reluctantly, Russell thought, as if she wanted nothing to do with Otto, or anyone looking for him.

Russell climbed three storeys, and knocked on the appropriate door. There were no sounds of life within, either then or after a second hammering, but another woman emerged from a flat across the landing. 'He's hardly ever there,' she told Russell in response to his question. She had no idea where Otto worked, if indeed he did, but he only used the room for sleeping. 'He's a Jew,' she added with barely concealed disgust. 'That's how he got the flat.'

Back out on the street, Russell started walking towards the river. He wouldn't tell Effi, he decided, not till he knew whether this was the Otto they sought.

He was ten minutes late reaching Zoo Station, but there was no sign of Effi in the crowded buffet. He went back out for a newspaper – the American-produced *Allgemeine Zeitung* looked more promising than the British *Der Berliner* – and scanned the front page while he queued for a cup of tea. The main story was the communists' humiliating defeat in the previous weekend's Austrian elections, a result that the editorial attributed to the Russians' behaviour back in the spring. Given that the Russians had behaved ten times worse in Berlin, Russell wondered what the Soviets would deduce from this setback. And what lesson would the German communists take from it? A need to distance themselves from their allies and sponsors? He was beginning to appreciate the importance of the task that Nemedin and Shchepkin had given him – testing the loyalty of the German comrades. And they would not be happy if he kept them waiting. Tomorrow he would follow Shchepkin's instructions and present himself at the Housing Office on Neue Königstrasse.

Effi swept in, still in her glamorous outfit, causing more than a few heads to turn.

She looked more animated than she had for a while, Russell thought.

'I forgot to change at Schlüterstrasse,' she announced, 'and the station toilets are "closed for refurbishment". I'll have to ask here.'

She was back in five minutes, looking more like an ordinary citizen, and the two of them made their way down to the U-Bahn platforms.

'Remember taxis?' Effi murmured wistfully, after they'd waited twenty minutes for an eastbound train.

One eventually arrived, and they squeezed aboard a crowded carriage. The smell of unwashed bodies was bad enough, and Russell dreaded to think what it would have been like if half the windows hadn't been broken.

They changed at Friedrichstrasse, and this time a train came quickly. The lifts weren't working at Leopoldplatz, and the long ascent to the booking hall left them both short of breath. Outside on Müllerstrasse the usual broken facades stretched away in both directions, a single double-decker bus the only thing moving on the once-busy boulevard. The tricolour fluttering above one of the surviving buildings told them they were now in the French sector.

They started up the long Schulstrasse, and were soon passing one of the recently reopened schools. Several of the rooms were still unfit for occupation, but teachers and children were working in the others, and the view through the few unboarded windows was almost surreal in its ordinariness.

The local dogs seemed more in tune with their surroundings. There seemed an awful lot of them, each staring angrily out from his own small patch of ruin. Humans had destroyed their homes, cut off their food supply, and left them nothing to do but snarl at passers-by. Several started slowly towards Russell and Effi, but were easily deterred by the miming of a thrown stone. Most looked too weak to sustain an attack.

At least they were alive, Russell thought. He hadn't seen a single cat since their return. Or a bird.

A sudden ear-splitting roar sounded overhead, causing them both to jump. It was an American Dakota, flying just above the few remaining rooftops, and presumably headed for Tempelhof. Russell wondered why it was flying so low. Because the pilot enjoyed scaring Germans?

Turning to Effi, he saw momentary panic in her eyes, beads of sweat breaking out on her forehead. He found himself wondering whether those Berliners who had survived the years of bombing would ever hear a plane without flinching.

He took her in his arms, and she let out a couple of sobs. For the first time, he fully appreciated how hard all this must be for her, and how extreme her emotional reactions might be. And most of their fellow Berliners would be riding the same emotional see-saw, he thought. A city full of unexploded bombs, in more ways than one.

'I'm okay,' she said at last.

'Are you sure you want to do this today?' he asked.

'Oh yes. What doesn't kill you makes you stronger. What idiot said that?' She was looking back down the street, remembering the view through the barred window of the Black Maria that had brought Rosa from the Frankfurter Allee police station.

Russell laughed and took her arm.

A few minutes later they reached the iron archway entrance. It was unguarded. Passing through, they found the rooms of the old Pathology Department deserted. 'This is where we slept,' Effi told him, pointing out a corner of the first one. It was empty, save for a table with two broken legs which seemed to be kneeling in the middle of the floor. 'And that's where Dobberke signed our release certificates,' she added, gesturing towards it.

When Russell glanced at her, she was angrily wiping tears from her eyes.

'I'm okay,' she said again. 'Can you see anything out of those windows?' she asked, pointing to the row on one side.

Raising himself on tiptoe, he reported movement in the distance.

'That's the main hospital,' she explained. 'All the half- and quarter-Jews lived there. There's a connecting tunnel.'

This had been guarded in April, but now stretched emptily away, lit only by a fortuitous rent in its ceiling almost halfway down. A ladder leant against the rim of the opening, and Russell had a mental picture of Nazi guards slipping out into the Berlin darkness as Russian troops stormed the main entrance.

At the far end of the tunnel, they emerged into a different world, one that was tidy, well-lit and obviously populated. After passing a couple of almost empty dormitories, they climbed the stairs to the ground floor. Here, they found rooms where people were sitting and reading, and one with rows of desks that was clearly in use as a classroom. The first person they asked for directions shrugged and offered a few words in Yiddish, the second informed them in Polish-accented German that the offices were on the next floor. Halfway up the stairs a rabbi passed them on his way down.

In the administration office a young woman was laboriously pushing down keys on an antique-looking typewriter. She smiled up at them, revealing warm brown eyes, and seemed relieved to abandon the task. At Russell's request she explained the current set-up. The hospital was run by an *ad hoc* committee, which had representatives from all the parties involved. There were reps from the American Jewish organisations, and from international refugee organisations like UNRRA and the Red Cross; there were members of the hospital staff and, of course, liaison officers from the French garrison. New refugees were arriving all the time: survivors of the camps, returnees from voluntary exile, people who'd spent the last few years hiding in barns or cellars or garden sheds. There were ex-partisan fighters, who'd made their way west across Poland from the Russian and Lithuanian forests. The hospital fed, clothed and sheltered them all, and did its best to help each individual reach his or her destination of choice. In most cases this was the American Occupation Zone beyond the Elbe, where purely Jewish DP camps were now up and running, staging posts *en route* to the promised lands of Palestine and America.

In the meantime the refugees waited, and often for a great deal longer than they wanted to. But at least they were waiting for something better, and the mood was generally good.

Effi asked the woman whether records were kept of all who passed through.

'Of course. Who are you looking for?'

Effi gave her the names, and watched as she worked her way through the relevant boxes of index cards. The woman was a Berliner from her accent, no more than twenty-five, and almost certainly Jewish. Her whole adult life would have been shot through with fear, Russell thought, but there was nothing downcast about her, no apparent edge of bitterness or well of grief. On the contrary, she seemed full of life. Someone looking forward rather than back.

'No, I'm sorry,' she said, coming back to her desk. 'The only Pappenheim is Greta, and all three Rosenfelds are men. Where else have you looked?'

Effi explained that they'd only just started on their list of possible locations, whereupon the woman insisted on comparing that list with another, which one of the American Jewish organisations had compiled. Three more sites were identified, one of them a recently opened agricultural training camp for Zionists.

They were crossing the downstairs lobby when a familiar face came in through the main doors. Effi had met and befriended Johanna – she had never learnt her surname – during her and Rosa's week-long confinement in the Pathology department, but once Dobberke had signed their releases Johanna had opted to spend the last few days of the war where she was, rather than risk the streets outside. Now a huge smile engulfed her face, and she enfolded Effi in a fierce hug. 'Where have you been? I've often wondered what happened to you when you left. You and Rosa.'

'You're looking well,' Effi said, and Johanna was. In April she'd been painfully thin, but in her case the 'Victim of Fascism' ration card was obviously serving its intended purpose – she looked several stones heavier and ten years younger. 'We ended up in the Potsdam Station,' Effi said. 'It was a nightmare. We should have stayed here with you and Nina.'

Johanna's smile disappeared. 'No, you made the right decision. You remember – Nina thought the Russians would behave themselves because we were Jews and because there were so many of us. She couldn't have been more wrong. I got off quite lightly, but Nina was young and pretty and...' Johanna sighed. 'Well, she killed herself...'

Effi closed her eyes for a few seconds.

'But is Rosa all right?' Johanna asked anxiously.

'She's fine. She's in England, in London. Which is where we were until last week. This is John, by the way. I must have told you about him.'

'Yes, you did.' She gave Russell a knowing look, then turned back to Effi. 'I met another friend of yours a couple of months ago,' she told Effi. 'I work in the hospital, but I was in the office when she came looking for you. Her name was Ali something...'

'Ali Blumenthal!' Ali was the daughter of two Jews whom Russell and Effi had befriended in the first years of the war. They had agreed to 'resettlement' in the East, but Ali, like Effi, had opted for an underground existence. When they ran into each other in 1942, Ali had put Effi in touch with the identity forger Schönhaus, which had probably saved her life. She and Ali had shared a flat, a business and a life of resistance for most of the next three years.

'Yes, that was the name,' Johanna confirmed. 'I told her I'd met you in April, and she told me who you really were. I was surprised, I can tell you. I must have seen some of your films, but I never recognised you.'

'Did Ali leave an address?'

'Not here, but most people leave their contact details on the boards outside. Come, I'll show you where.'

They walked out onto Iranische Strasse, where a line of boarded-up windows were plastered with scraps of paper and card, some neatly cut and printed, others simple scrawls on scraps. It was Effi who recognised Ali's elegant handwriting. 'Hufelandstrasse 27,' she said excitedly. 'In Wilmersdorf. I think I know where that is. We must go there.'

Russell smiled. 'Of course.'

Effi thanked Johanna, and gave her Thomas's address. 'Wherever we eventually end up living, he'll know.'

Johanna was reluctant to let them go. 'Remember how we all agreed to meet on August 1st, in the Zoo Cafeteria. Well, I went to the Zoo, but there was no sign of you and Rosa, and no cafeteria. I wasn't surprised, but...'

'Rosa remembered,' Effi told her. 'She was upset. But we were in England, and even if we'd known where you were, we had no way of making contact.'

'I'm glad you both made it.'

'And you,' Effi said with feeling. With so many gone, each survivor seemed doubly precious.

* * *

Before the war the trip would have taken forty minutes, but more than two hours had passed when they finally reached Ali's apartment building. Hufelandstrasse seemed almost untouched by the war, as if some higher power had intervened to protect its residents from the bombs and shells that rained down on the neighbouring streets.

Ali herself opened the apartment door, and let out a whoop of pure delight when she saw who it was. The two women threw themselves into each other's arms, and shared an excited hug, their feet almost dancing as they twirled each other round. The young man behind Ali smiled and shook his head.

'This is my husband Fritz,' she told them. 'And this is Effi,' she told him.

'I thought it might be,' he said with a grin.

'And Herr Russell,' Ali said, giving him a hug too. They hadn't seen each other since 1941, when she was still living with her parents. In those days she had worn her dark hair long – now it barely reached her shoulder.

She ushered them into a large and cosy living room. There were two desks with typewriters, books and newspapers everywhere. 'So everything turned out for the best,' Ali said, still smiling. 'You always said it would.'

Effi sighed. 'I did, didn't I?' It sounded like a strange thing to say in November 1945, but she knew what Ali meant.

'Look,' Ali said, 'we have a meeting to go to soon, but can you come for dinner tomorrow? Where are you living? Where have you *been* all this time?'

She looked terrific, Effi thought. 'England,' she said. 'We only just got back. We're staying at our friend Thomas's house in Dahlem. It's not that far from here. What have you been doing? How did you get this flat?'

'Oh, the flat's part of the guilt package. We Jews get priority now. It used to belong to a Nazi official, and he's either dead or in a camp...'

'Or in South America,' Fritz added wryly.

'Whatever. We burned his books,' she added with a giggle. 'He had three copies of *Mein Kampf*, one for here, one in the bedroom, and one beside the toilet.' She shook her head. 'They kept us warm for a couple of hours while we worked.'

Russell had noticed the stacks of SPD leaflets. 'Are you working for the Social Democrats?'

'Yes, there's a committee tonight.'

'Ah, I'd be interested in talking to you both about that. Off the record, of course.'

Ali looked surprised, as if she'd forgotten that he was a journalist. 'But if you were both safe in England, why have you come back? Life in Berlin is pretty dreadful, and I can't see it getting any better before the spring.'

'We're here to work,' Effi said. 'I'm doing a film. Well, probably. If it ever gets started. And you remember Rosa?'

'Of course. The girl the Swede sent us. I always felt bad about leaving you then.'

'You shouldn't have. We survived, and I fell in love with her. She's in England with my sister. We know her mother's dead, but I need to find out what happened to her father.'

'Oh. Well, I can probably help you there. There must be someone I know in every Jewish organisation in Berlin. I'll give you a list of names and addresses. And you should leave notices wherever you go. And in the papers. They're even reading messages out on the Russian radio station now. These days Berlin's like a huge missing persons bureau.' She grinned at Effi. 'It's so good to see you again. When we were living together on Bismarckstrasse, I used to dream about this moment – when the war was over, and there was nothing to fear, and people to love and laugh with.'

'She talked a lot about you,' Fritz volunteered. 'And you too,' he added, including Russell. 'You must have known the family.'

'I did. They really are dead then?'

'Oh yes,' Ali said, almost matter-of-factly. 'I found their names on one of the Auschwitz lists last summer. But I'd known for years, ever since the first stories reached Berlin.'

'I'm sorry,' Russell said. 'They were wonderful people.'

'Yes, they were. For a long time I was really angry with them. With my father for being so stupidly optimistic, with my mother for indulging him. But then those were the things I loved about them.' She sighed. 'And now they're gone.' She smiled at Fritz. 'And we have our lives to live. Three of them soon – I'm four months pregnant.'

'Oh, that's wonderful,' Effi burst out, and the two women embraced again. Both were in tears, Russell noticed. He felt like crying himself.

New textbooks

'We need more clothes,' Effi said plaintively. 'I'm wearing almost everything I brought with me.'

A wintry sun was shining in through the window, but the air inside the bedroom was cold enough to show their breath, and leaving the nest of blankets was a deeply uninviting prospect.

Soon after waking, Russell had shivered his way downstairs to brew some tea, and they'd spent the last hour reading through Effi's new script. It was a ritual they'd shared in pre-war days – making a mockery of the Nazi-inspired storylines had been amusing in itself, and, as Russell later came to realise, a way of rendering Effi's participation in the whole process more palatable than it might otherwise have been. But those days, as 'The Man I Shall Kill' made abundantly clear, were over. This storyline was far too apposite to mock, and no apologies were needed for turning it into a film.

The story itself was simple enough – an army surgeon returns to Berlin after service in the East, and seeks refuge in alcohol from the many terrible things he has seen. His own apartment has been destroyed in the bombing, so he moves into one that hasn't, little knowing that the female owner – Effi's character – is on her way home after years of imprisonment in a concentration camp. When she arrives back, he refuses to leave, and they eventually agree to share the space. Their relationship is slowly blossoming into love when he learns that his former CO, the man who ordered their unit to murder over a hundred Polish women and children, is living nearby. And that far from paying for his crimes, the CO has reinvented himself as a successful businessman. Despite the pleas of the woman, the surgeon decides to kill him.

In this script he succeeded, but an additional note said the final section was being re-written. 'Which makes sense,' Russell thought out loud. 'I'd have you stop him. More drama, and a better political message. The civilised way, not the Nazi way. Bring the bastard to trial. And then kill him.'

'Maybe,' Effi said. 'It would certainly help my part. My character's really strong, really interesting, for the first two reels, and then she turns into a helpless bystander.'

'Not your role in life.'

'Not in films. At least, not when I have any say in the matter. But it could be a good film, don't you think?'

'It could. And should be. A good sign, I'd say.'

'Yes.' Effi reached across to look at her watch. 'Oh hell. I have to get up – my script meeting starts at ten. What are you doing today?'

'I'll probably play the journalist for an hour or so. And then I'm off to the Soviet zone.'

'Off to see the wizard?' she asked. They had taken Rosa to *The Wizard of Oz* in London.

'Shchepkin? No. If I sign in at the Housing Office on Neue König-strasse I should see him tomorrow. But while I'm in the neighbourhood I might drop in on Thomas at the printing works. And then see if Uwe Kuzorra's still working at the Alex. I'd like to thank him for saving my life.'

'Thank him for me,' Effi said. 'I think I'd have missed you.'

* * *

After they parted, Russell's first stop-off was at the American Press Camp on Argentinischeallee. Over coffee in the canteen he eavesdropped on several conversations, but the Austrian election results and their sig-nificance for Berlin were not among the topics under discussion – the young journalists seemed focussed on the imminent arrival of a baseball star whom Russell had never heard of. This was depressing, and checking out the mechanics of reporting from Berlin offered little in the way of solace. As far as he could see the current crop of American foreign correspondents were simply appending their by-lines to stories which the occupation authorities had already chosen and virtually written. His old American colleague Jack Slaney would have been appalled.

Filing stories to London was not something the Americans could assist him with. And he didn't think the British authorities would be that eager to help, not now he'd taken out American citizenship. Dallin would have to sort it out, whenever he could bring himself to see the wretched man. There was no hurry. As Slaney had once told him, stories that thrilled or titillated lasted a matter of hours, but news that really mattered usually lasted years.

He took the U-Bahn from Oskar-Helene-Heim to Wittenbergplatz, and changed there for Alexanderplatz. He had a seat on the first train, and managed to read what little there was of the *Allgemeine Zeitung*. Most of the news was foreign, and he found it hard to imagine that Berliners were overly concerned with events beyond their city. His second train was slow, crowded, and extremely pungent. The long unexplained waits in the tunnels were nightmarish, particularly when accompanied by the not-so-distant sounds of explosions.

Alexanderplatz was a relief, even with the giant poster of Stalin and his usual murderous smirk. The Red Army was much in evidence, and the sight of officers and men enjoying each other's company made Russell more conscious of the British and American obsession with hierarchy. As if to correct the impression, a Soviet general drove slowly by in an immaculate Horch 930V, looking this way and that to make sure he was being noticed. The woman beside him looked equally pleased with herself, and was probably his wife. Unlike their British and American counterparts Soviet officers were allowed to bring their spouses with them.

The Alex was still standing, its turrets and roof somewhat the worse for wear, rather in the manner of a prize-fighter proudly exhibiting a badly bruised crown and torn ears. But first he needed to visit the designated Housing Office, which was a couple of hundred metres up Neue König-strasse. He walked up past a troop of women shifting rubble, and a trio of young men in ragged uniforms. Two of the men were on crutches, having each lost a leg. The third was leaning on a blind man's cane.

There was a long queue inside the Housing Office, but it moved faster than Russell expected, and a German official was soon examining the papers that the Soviet embassy in London had given him. The man gave him an almost sympathetic glance, as if he knew what Russell's presence portended. 'You will be hearing from us in due course,' he said eventually, for want of anything more convincing.

Back on the pavement outside, Russell watched as another pathetic clutch of returning POWs straggled by in the middle of the road. As a Soviet jeep approached from the opposite direction, it seemed to take all their energy to step out of its path, and one man proved too slow. Clipped by the front wing of the vehicle, he tumbled to the ground. The Red Army driver shouted abuse over his shoulder and kept going, leaving the man to slowly pick himself up. His comrades plodded on, offering no help.

Russell made his way back to the Alex, and went in through the old No.1 doors on Dircksenstrasse. There was less frenzied activity than he remembered, the faces younger but no less hard. Which was hardly surprising – in Soviet eyes, the German police force would have been irredeemably tarnished by its close association with the Nazi state. Most of the old guard would be gone, replaced by those young or politically reliable enough to satisfy the new masters. The Soviets had their own police HQ in the south-eastern outskirts, but their presence here was no less real for being invisible.

The desk sergeant was one of the few older faces, but denied any knowledge of Kriminalinspecktor Uwe Kuzorra. He suggested a personnel office on the other side of the inner courtyard, but no one there could be of any help. All the police files had disappeared, one young man told Russell. He seemed pleased by the loss, implying that it offered a welcome break with the past.

For the criminals too, Russell thought but didn't say.

He went in search of Kuzorra's old office, where he'd first heard the news that the Gestapo were after him. No one challenged his presence *en route*, but when he reached what seemed the right corridor, all of the likely offices lay empty. There were secretaries in two rooms further along, but neither recalled the detective's name.

Russell traced his way back to the outside world. Kuzorra might have retired soon after their last meeting in 1941. He – and the possibility was chilling – might have been arrested, even executed, for his part in helping Russell escape. Then again, he was more likely to have been killed by a bomb or a shell, like a hundred thousand other Berliners. But whatever his fate, it seemed strange that no one remembered him in the place where he'd spent his working life.

Russell wondered what to do. His main reason for seeking out Kuzorra was to thank him, but he had also nursed a vague hope that the detective would still be working, and in a position to offer him some help. The old Kuzorra could have provided a rundown of what made the new Berlin tick, and what stories were crying out for investigation. He would also have known how best to mount a search for missing Jews.

Maybe he'd retired at the end of the war – he had to be nearly seventy. If so, and if his building had survived, he would probably still be living on Demminer Strasse, which was only a short ride away on the U-Bahn. Or had been in better times. Descending the steps at Alexanderplatz station, he discovered that an unexploded bomb had been found in the tunnels, and the service north suspended.

Back on the surface, he thought about taking a bus, but the first one that came was so tightly packed that only two of the waiting crowd could get on. He supposed he could walk, but what was the point when tomorrow would do just as well?

The problems besetting public transport reminded him he'd once owned a car. Like most private vehicles, it had been forced off the road by war regulations and the acute fuel shortage. Russell had left the Hanomag at the garage where he'd bought it, from Miroslav Zembski's cousin Hunder. And if it hadn't fallen victim to high explosives, the car might still be waiting for him. Ordinary Berliners were still forbidden to drive, and petrol was almost impossible to come by, but he was officially an American, and one of his spymasters might like the idea of motorising their favourite agent. It had to be worth a shot.

This flight of fancy sustained him throughout the S-Bahn ride to Lehrter Station, and down several streets of ruined workshops and small factories. But then came disappointment – Hunder Zembski's yard had not survived its proximity to the nearby railway sheds. The gates were still standing but little else, and the packed lot he remembered from 1941 resembled a wreckers' yard.

Clambering gingerly across a skein of twisted metal, he headed for where he'd parked the Hanomag, but that corner of the yard had obviously taken a direct hit, and all he could find was a jumble of pulverised brick and metal shards. If the car had not been moved beforehand, it never would be now.

He made his way back to Lehrter Station. A train was noisily pulling in, and he used a gap in the fence to get a better view. The locomotive was pulling cattle cars rather than coaches, and the waiting platform was lined with soldiers, nurses and men with armbands who Russell assumed were refugee agency officials. When the doors were opened people burst violently out, as if they'd been held in under pressure. The shoulders of one arrival visibly sagged as he took in the jagged skyline that lay beyond the roofless station. Could this be Berlin?

Around the station a sprawling refugee camp had grown up. There were hundreds, perhaps thousands, of people living in burnt-out offices, overturned wagons and any niche that a sheet of corrugated iron could roof over. As he looked back at the train, the first of many stretchers was lifted down from the cattle cars. Each bore a human load, but none showed signs of life.

Russell remembered the nights in 1941, when he and Gerhard Ströhm had watched trains like these leaving Berlin with their cargo of Jews for 'resettlement'. The cattle cars looked the same, but this time the cargo was German. These families had been driven from the old Junker heartlands in the east by the victorious Russians and Poles. They had paid the bill for Hitler with their loved ones and their homes.

His reporter's instinct told him two things – that this was a huge story, and one that the victors would rather not read. Ninety-nine per cent of these refugees would be innocent of any serious crime, but as far as the world was concerned, being German was guilt enough, and any such suffering thoroughly deserved.

* * *

For Effi, entering Ernst Dufring's house in Schmargendorf was like stepping into a time machine. The hall was plastered with framed movie posters from the golden age of German cinema, the huge living room a shrine to Bauhaus interior design. Even the other actors seemed well-fed, with none of the yellow-grey pallor that characterised most Berliner faces. Only the shell-shattered spire of the church across the street offered proof of the war just fought and lost.

Effi had wondered what sort of reception she would receive, but everyone seemed pleased to have her on board. And more than happy in general, as if they'd just won top prize in a national sweepstake. In a way they had, she supposed. The people in this room were pioneers, the first movie-makers of the new Germany.

The writer Ute Faeder, a tall blonde in her forties with a wry sense of humour, explained some changes she had made in the script, and Dufring then listed the scenes they would run through that morning. He looked much older than Effi remembered, but there was no doubting his enthusiasm for making this particular movie. 'I know you've only just received the script,' he told Effi, 'but do your best.'

Her confidence increased as the morning passed, but nailing this character was going to be hard. She wasn't sure why her character let the man stay on in her flat; she only knew that Lilli's own experiences in the camp had made it impossible for her to evict him. But what experiences, and how could Effi access them? Her week in a cell at the Gestapo's Prinz-Albrecht-Strasse HQ had certainly been frightening, but she hadn't gone hungry, hadn't been physically abused. Lilli, by contrast, had endured years of the worst that the Nazis could offer. How could Effi make sense of her psyche? She needed to talk to people with such experiences, she thought. If she was going to play this role with any conviction, she needed to hear their stories.

It occurred to her that she had never felt this need before – imagination had been enough. Perhaps that was the point – what had happened over the last few years was literally unimaginable. And it would need films like this to make it less so. Movies like this really mattered, unlike most she had made.

This thought had only just crossed her mind when Lothar Kuhnert appeared at her side. 'I'm afraid we have a problem,' were his first upsetting words. 'The British have refused your *Spruchkammer* certification.'

'Oh no. Why, for heaven's sake?'

'A lot of nonsense about you playing "iconic Nazi roles", whatever than means. The real reason is that the Americans have insisted.'

'What in heaven's name have I done to upset them?'

'They're adopting a harder line towards ex-Nazis, and...'

'I wasn't a Nazi!'

'We know that. But some Americans don't understand that it was possible to do well in the Third Reich without being one.'

'Oh God! Doesn't the fact that the Gestapo was hunting me for four years make any difference?'

'It should. It will. Just leave it with me.' He sighed. 'The good news is that there's no urgency. They're still investigating Ernst, and there'll probably be others. But we'll get this film made, one way or another.'

'We should,' Effi told him. 'It's worth making.'

* * *

It was almost dark when Russell found himself outside Otto Pappenheim's door in the Solinger Strasse apartment block. Again there was no answer to his knock, but this time a different neighbour emerged. Three cigarettes – a gross overpayment, as Russell later discovered – was enough to overcome any reluctance he had about disclosing Otto's place of work. It was a nightclub on the Ku'damm called, suitably enough, *Die Honigfalle*. The Honey Trap.

Outside it was growing dark. He walked south, took the temporary walkway across the foul-smelling Spree, and skirted the western perimeter of the silenced zoo. Feeling hungry, he stopped for a sandwich at the Zoo Station buffet and idly leafed through a newspaper that someone had quite understandably left behind. There was nothing in it, save for sundry do-it-yourself tips for the average Berlin householder circa 1945 – 'how to repair a roof without tiles,' 'how to mend a wall without bricks' – and hundreds of messages from people seeking either long-lost relatives and friends or strangers willing to share their body-heat.

There were neon lights burning on the Ku'damm, but not that many by pre-war standards. There were British soldiers on the pavements, and almost as many German girls, but the night was obviously young. According to Thomas, bus-loads of girls from the Soviet sector – where payment of any kind could rarely be taken for granted – arrived around mid-evening.

The Honey Trap was on the northern side, in the basement of a half-demolished building that Russell vaguely remembered as a music school. The two bouncers guarding the top of the steps looked barely out of their teens, and managed to convey the impression that only their dates of birth had prevented them joining the Nazis.

They eyed Russell with professional suspicion, but relaxed when he mentioned Otto Pappenheim. 'He'll be in the office at the back,' one said, in a tone suggesting surprise that anyone wanted to see him. Walking down the steps, it occurred to Russell that mention of his quarry's name had not yet produced a single positive reaction.

The barely-lit basement room smelt of stale beer, cigarette smoke and sweat. A barman gestured him through to the room at the rear, where another man was seated at a small and rickety-looking table, his head bent over an accounts ledger. As he looked up, Russell saw dark hair, dark eyes, and features sharp enough to invite comparisons with rodents. The man was probably in his thirties, which was about right for Rosa's father, but he bore little resemblance to the Nazi stereotype of a Jew. But then few Jews did. 'Otto Pappenheim?' he asked.

'Yes,' the man replied after only the slightest of hesitations. The eyes were suspicious, but what Jew's eyes wouldn't be after the last twelve years?

'I'm looking for someone of that name,' Russell said, looking round for something to sit on. There was nothing.

'Why? Who are you?'

'My name's John Russell. I'm not with the police or anything like that – I'm just an ordinary citizen.'

'Okay,' the man said almost cheerfully. The news that Russell had no connection to the authorities seemed something of a relief.

'I'm looking for an Otto Pappenheim who left a wife and daughter early in the war, most likely through no choice of his own. His wife's name was Ursel, and they had a daughter name Rosa...'

'I never had a daughter,' the man said. 'And my wife died in a camp. We had no children. Thank God,' he added as an afterthought.

'Ah. I'm sorry.'

'No, it's over.' He smiled thinly. 'We have to live in the present now.'

'Of course. But have you ever run across anyone else with the same name?'

'No. There are such men, I'm sure, but I have never met one.'

Russell could think of nothing else to ask. He thanked the man and walked back towards the front. Passing through the sparsely populated bar, he realised he fancied a drink.

'What are you paying with?' was the barman's first question.

'What do you take?'

'What do you have?'

'US dollars.'

'They'll do.'

'And what else?' Russell asked as his beer was poured.

'Pounds. Cigarettes. There's a list of exchange rates on the wall over there.'

Russell took a first sip and examined the sign. 3 British Woodbines were worth 1 American Pall Mall, and both were listed in their cash dollar equivalents. 'What about German currency?' he asked.

The barman laughed and turned away.

Russell found himself a table, sat down, and surveyed the room. The decor was as minimal as the lighting, and no attempt had been made to disguise the myriad cracks in the ceiling. A small dance floor lay between the sea of closely packed tables and a narrow, curtainless stage.

'John Russell,' a surprised voice exclaimed beside him.

'Irma,' he said, smiling and standing to embrace her. They had met in pre-war days, when she and Effi had been in the same musical. Hardly a highlight of Effi's career, *Barbarossa* had marked a real low for Irma Wocz, who had first earned fame as a cabaret artist in pre-Nazi Berlin. She had to be in her mid-forties, but the dark eyes were still challenging, the full mouth still inviting, and the shining brunette hair would have convinced anyone who hadn't last seen her as a blonde. Her figure, or what Russell could see of it inside the buttoned coat, still had curves to spare. 'Please, join me,' he said. 'Have a drink.'

'I certainly will,' she said, sitting down opposite him. 'But don't think of paying for it. I work here.' She raised a hand to get the barman's attention, and ordered a bourbon on the rocks. 'Where have you been since the shit hit the fan?' she asked. 'Someone showed me your picture in the papers,' she explained. 'After your little disagreement with our late lamented leader.'

Russell laughed. 'We've been in England the last few months.'

'You had the sense to stick with Effi?'

'Yes, she's here too. She's making a movie with some people at the old *Reichskulturkammer.*'

She took her drink from the barman, and halved it in one gulp. 'The comrades? That's a sensible move. Once the Americans get bored and go home, they'll be running everything.'

'You think they will? Get bored, I mean.'

Irma shrugged. 'Once they've fucked every girl in Berlin.'

'You're singing again?'

'You could call it that.' She smiled and emptied her glass. 'I'm certainly getting too old to fuck for a living. Look, you and Effi should come one evening, for old time's sake. We're open every day but Monday. One on the house?' she asked him, waving her own glass at the barman.

'No, thanks. I haven't eaten yet.'

'Now there's an overrated pastime. If there's one thing we can thank the Führer for, it's teaching us how to live with hunger. Ah,' she added, looking Russell's shoulder, 'here comes the boss.'

He turned to see a man walking towards them.

'Good evening, Herr Geruschke,' she said in greeting. He was around Russell's age, the short side of medium height, with dark eyes and thick charcoal-coloured hair that was beginning to recede. He was smartly dressed in a dark grey suit, stiff-collared shirt, jazzy tie and shining brogues.

The smile, Russell noticed, did not extend to the eyes.

'Irma,' he said with the slightest of bows. He watched the barman replace her empty glass with a full one, and looked enquiringly at Russell.

'This is an old friend,' she explained. 'John Russell. He lived in Berlin before the war.'

'Are you English?' Geruschke asked with a smile.

'I am,' Russell said. It was simpler than explaining his official pedigree as an American.

'We have many English customers,' Geruschke said. 'But few are here by choice. In Berlin, that is.'

'I'm just here for a visit,' Russell told him. 'Seeing old friends, that sort of thing.' Something about the man gave him the creeps.

'His girlfriend's Effi Koenen,' Irma volunteered. 'She's here to make a movie for the comrades.'

'An actress? I haven't heard the name, but then I never go to films.' He turned back to Irma, whose second glass was almost empty. 'Try not to get drunk before you perform,' he told her sharply. 'Herr Russell,' he added, taking his leave with a slight nod and the faintest clicking of heels. As he walked away Russell found himself wondering what the man had been doing for the last twelve years. A question you could ask of any prosperous survivor.

'He's a real charmer, isn't he?' Irma muttered. 'But he pays well.'

'What's his first name?'

'Rudolf, but I've never heard anyone use it.'

The club was slowly filling up. Three British soldiers had just come in with four young girls, and a good-natured dispute about exchange rates was underway at the bar. On the stage a musician had removed his shining saxophone from its case, and was busy replacing its reed.

'Do you know Otto Pappenheim?' Russell asked Irma.

'The accountant?' I know him well enough to ignore him.'

Russell laughed. 'What's wrong with him?'

'Oh nothing, I suppose. He's one of Geruschke's Jews. He says he likes to help them get back on their feet, which is fair enough. He could be a bit choosier, though. I mean, the Jews have their quota of low-lifes, just like everyone else. And in my experience, being persecuted rarely turns people into saints. Turns them into shits as often as not.'

'You could be right,' Russell agreed. It was beginning to seem that post-war Berlin – indeed, the whole damn post-war world – was hell-bent on meeting his worst expectations.

* * *

Back at the house, he found Thomas and Effi sitting on either side of the kitchen table. They both looked less than happy. 'Has something happened?' he asked. 'Is Leon all right?'

'He's fine,' Effi said, raising a smile.

'We've just had what passes for a normal day in Berlin,' Thomas said wryly. 'The Russians have been obstructing me, and the Americans have been obstructing Effi.'

'How so?'

Effi told him what Kuhnert had told her.

'What's it do with the Americans?' Russell wanted to know.

'Who knows? But anyway, Kuhnert thinks he can sort it out. It's just left a sour taste, that's all.'

'I'm not surprised, after all you went through. It must be really upsetting.'

'It is,' Effi agreed. But not just for those reasons, she thought. Part of her dismay came from recognising the grain of truth in the accusations against her. She *had* played the storm trooper's widow. She *had* played the proud Nazi mother.

Russell put an arm around her shoulder. 'And what have the Russians been doing to you?' he asked Thomas.

'Oh, just making life difficult. They don't understand business. They don't like business. I think they believe deep down that business is like some fast-growing weed, that if they leave it alone it'll grow so fast that they'll never get rid of it.'

'Couldn't you relocate to one of the Western zones? There's certainly no shortage of land for development.'

'I've thought about it. Trouble is, if I set a move in motion the Russians will just confiscate my machinery. And if I could somehow persuade them not to, who knows how welcoming the Americans would be? One of the Soviet officials took me aside today, and warned me again how seriously the Americans would take my hobnobbing with Nazis during the war. And if he was right – if the Americans really are intent on giving me a hard time – then I'm better off staying where I am. At least the Russians let me work.' He stood up. 'But enough. I'm hungry, and Effi tells me you two have a dinner date.'

'God yes,' Russell said. He'd completely forgotten about Ali's invitation.

'And we should be going,' Effi said, looking at her watch. She ducked out from under Russell's arm. 'And you can tell me whose perfume you're wearing on the way.'

* * *

Outside the streets were a lot darker than Russell remembered from pre-war days, but brighter than they had been in the blackout. The sky seemed to be clearing, and the moon's occasional appearances lent the ruins an aura of ghostly beauty.

He told Effi about his meeting with Irma, and the reason he'd been at the night club. When he let slip that he'd known about Otto since the previous day she gave him an exasperated look. 'Don't keep me in the dark,' she said. 'I know you mean well, but I'd rather know. All right?'

'All right.'

'And how was Irma?'

'The same as ever. If not more so.'

Effi laughed. 'We must go and see her perform.'

They reached Hufelandstrasse, and climbed the stairs to Ali's door. A wonderful aroma was waiting inside, and the dinner that Ali served up a few minutes later offered ample proof of the culinary skills she'd learnt from her mother. And, as she herself was quick to point out, of the extra rations they received as Jews.

Fritz seemed increasingly relaxed with his wife's friends, and did most of the talking. His thoughts on the pros and cons of the prospective merger between the KPD and SPD were perceptive for a young man, Russell thought, then silently admonished himself for being patronising.

After dinner, Effi and Ali told tales of their time together. Both Russell and Fritz – who had also survived several years in hiding – had heard the stories before, but only from their own partners. Hearing the tales from them both added another dimension, and made them all the more extraordinary. Yet again, Russell was reminded of how easy his war had been compared to theirs. They'd all been living on their wits, but that was where the comparisons ended – each day for years on end these three had woken with the knowledge that any loss of vigilance, any stroke of bad luck, would likely prove fatal. He didn't know how they'd managed it.

He asked Ali and Fritz if they planned to stay in Berlin. If he'd had their experiences of the city and its citizens he wasn't at all sure that he would.

'For the moment,' Fritz answered him.

'How about Palestine?' Russell asked.

'No,' Fritz replied curtly. 'We want to be human beings first, not Jews.'

'Sometimes we think about America,' Ali admitted. 'A completely fresh start and all that. But...' She shrugged.

'People say they want to leave it all behind,' Fritz said. 'But I don't think they'll find it that easy.'

He was probably right, Russell thought. The world was a lot smaller than it used to be.

Before they left Ali handed Effi a list of possible contacts. Some were people they had known during the war, others were Jews that Ali had met in the last six months.

'Oh to be young again,' was Russell's first comment as they started for home down Hufelandstrasse.

'Would you like to be twenty-one again?' was Effi's more serious response.

He thought about it. 'I'd like that body back – the joints didn't ache in wet weather. And my youthful innocence... no, maybe not.'

'Innocence is overrated,' Effi told him.

It was such an un–Effi-like thing to say that he almost stopped in his tracks.

'I miss Rosa,' she added.

It sounded like a *non sequitur*, but probably wasn't.

* * *

Wednesday morning was as grey as its predecessor. As Russell went through his things prior to leaving the house, he noticed the letter that Paul had given him for the mother and sister of Werner Redlich, the boy soldier his son had met in the final days of the war. Perhaps he would have time to visit them that afternoon. He couldn't say he was looking forward to it.

Or his meeting with Shchepkin, come to that. Riding a tram up the old Herman-Göring-Strasse, Russell thought it a joke when the tram conductor named the next stop 'Black Market', but no one seemed to be laughing. As he left the tram, he noticed that others alighting were all carrying suitcases or bags of some sort, and heading in the same direction as himself, into the adjacent Tiergarten.

He followed them in. Away to his left, allotments gave way to stump-studded wastelands and the shell-pitted flak towers. To his right, in the lee of the dog-eared Brandenburg Gate, an area the size of a football pitch played host to a milling crowd. This market had no stalls, only perambulant sellers whispering their wares. Almost all of them were Germans – women, children and a few old men. The buyers by contrast were mostly soldiers, and most of them were Russian.

Rather to his surprise, he felt more sanguine about his new espionage career than he had when the Soviets first came to call. Wondering why, he realised what had changed. While the Nazis had flourished, he'd had no ethical room for manoeuvre. Helping them, or hindering their enemies, were not things he could live with. Or not with any sense of self-worth. But that black-and-white world had vanished with Hitler, and the new one really was in shifting shades of grey. He could make arguments for and against any of the major players; in helping one or the other he had no sense of supporting good against evil, or evil against good. If, in personal terms, Yevgeny Shchepkin was almost a kindred spirit, and Scott Dallin someone from a distant unfriendly planet, he had no illusions about Stalin's Russia. And though American help was his only way out of the Soviet embrace, that didn't mean he wanted a world run by money and big business.

His instructions were to stay on the edge of the crowd, and wait for contact to be made. He started around the perimeter, looking out for Shchepkin, and trying to ignore the repeated offers of items for sale. In less than a minute he was obliged to decline nylons, butter, soap powder and an Iron Cross First Class, all at allegedly once-only prices.

He saw Shchepkin before the Russian saw him, which had to be a first – in the past the other man had made a habit of appearing at Russell's shoulder with almost magical abruptness. He had half-expected to see

Nemedin too, and was relieved to see Shchepkin alone. 'I see they've let you out on your own,' he greeted the Russian.

Shchepkin smiled. He looked better than he had in London, the skin less stretched, the eyes less darkened. He was wearing a worn dark suit, with a patterned black scarf and grey trilby. 'Let's find somewhere to sit down,' he said. 'My knees are killing me.'

They found an overturned bench which seemed sound, and which still bore traces of the legend denying its use to Jews. Sitting down, Russell felt somewhat exposed, but then he didn't suppose it mattered if they were seen together. The Russians knew he was working for them, and so did the Americans.

'I should give you a brief who's who of the local NKVD,' Shchepkin began.

'Why?'

'Because you should know who you're dealing with,' the Russian said with some asperity. 'The boss here in Berlin is Pavel Shimansky. He's not a bad man all told, and he's a survivor – he's already outlasted Yagoda and Yezhov, and Beria's made no move against him yet. That may be because Shimansky has friends I don't know about, or it may be because he lets his deputy – Anatoly Tsvetkov – do what he likes. Tsvetkov is one of Beria's Georgians, and he *is* a nasty piece of work. Nemedin is his deputy, and you've met him.'

'How is Comrade Nemedin?'

'He's hopeful. And very watchful. My room has been searched twice since I got here.'

'Did they find anything?'

'Of course not,' Shchepkin said, as if his professionalism had been brought into question.

'Where are you living?'

'Out in Köpenick. There's a hotel by the river which we've taken over.'

'I know it. We went boating there before the war. But I don't suppose your people do that.'

'You'd be surprised. But let's get to business.' Shchepkin placed a folded newspaper on the bench between them. 'The list of the men we need vetting is inside. They're all Party members. And there's a couple more that Fräulein Koenen is working with. We'd like her opinion on them.'

Russell bristled. 'That wasn't part of the deal.'

'No, but ask her anyway. She only has to deal in generalities. We just want a sense of where their loyalties lie.'

'She'll refuse.'

'Perhaps. If she does, then we may have to think again. But I presume you've explained the situation to her – your situation, I mean.'

'Of course.'

'Then she may surprise you. In my experience women are more hard-headed about such things than men.'

He might be right, Russell thought, as an emaciated dog sniffed round his shoes. 'I'll ask her.'

The dog gave them both a reproachful look, and trotted off across the allotments.

'Good. Now, your list. There are five comrades on it. Two of them you know – Gerhard Ströhm and Stefan Leissner...'

'He survived?' Leissner was the Reichsbahn official who'd given him and the young Soviet scientist Varennikov a hiding-place back in April. After the latter's death Russell had come upon Leissner lying just outside his bombed office with his right leg almost severed. He'd loosened and re-tightened the unconscious man's tourniquet, but there'd been no time to do anything more.

'Leissner? He lost a leg, but he's alive. And he has an important job – he's virtually running the railways in our zone.'

'He didn't strike me as the disloyal type.'

'Maybe not. But he's certainly being tested – orders keep arriving from Moscow to tear up his tracks and ship them east as reparations.'

'Ah.'

'Yes. Two of the others should provide no problem, but Manfred Haferkamp – have you met him?'

'Never heard of him.'

'He was a Party convenor in the Hamburg docks. In 1933 he escaped to Finland, and eventually turned up in Moscow. He taught at the International School for several years, but was arrested during the *Yezhovshchina* and sent to a labour camp in the North. In 1940 he was one of the German comrades that Stalin handed over to Hitler as part of the Pact. He managed to survive almost five years in Buchenwald, and after his release he chose to live here in Berlin rather than return to Hamburg. We don't know why.'

'Has anyone asked him?'

'He claims this is where Germany's future will be decided.'

'Hard to argue with that.'

'No, but it tells us nothing of how he envisages that future.'

'With or without a Russian hand on every German shoulder? With his history, he's hardly likely to have a framed portrait of the Great Leader on his bedroom wall.'

'Probably not, though stranger things have happened. But we're expecting you to find out.'

Russell made a face.

'And you must do a thorough job,' Shchepkin insisted. 'I know you. You're already sympathising with this man, and wondering how you'll be able to satisfy both Nemedin and your own conscience. Perhaps by reporting enough to demonstrate doubts, but not enough to get the man shot. And yes, that may be possible. But be careful. Nemedin is a clever bastard, and he enjoys catching people out. He and Tsvetkov need this information, but sometimes I get the feeling that Nemedin would get more satisfaction out of skewering us.'

'What's he got against me?'

'Everything. You're an ex-communist with a bourgeois lifestyle and a film star wife. None of which you seem to be ashamed of.'

'I *was* on my best behaviour.'

'Then God help us. Look, he's dangerous. To both of us. Don't underestimate him.'

'Okay, okay, I've got the message.' And he had. His earlier thoughts on pain-free espionage already seemed dated. He couldn't imagine betraying someone as decent as Ströhm, but who knew what the price of refusal might be. And who might have to pay it. Effi's film and Thomas's business would certainly be among the casualties.

Shchepkin was asking him whether he'd seen the Americans.

'I left a message for their man – Dallin, do you know him?'

'Of him. He's not one of their brightest.'

'No. Anyway, I left my address with them on Sunday, and he still hasn't got back to me.'

Shchepkin shook his head. 'Amateurs,' he muttered disapprovingly.

'I suppose I should remind him I'm here, Russell said. 'When do we meet again?'

'Fridays, if that's all right with you.'

'One day's as good as another.'

'What about your work as a journalist? It's important that you establish a good cover.'

'I'm doing a story on the Jews. The survivors. How they're finding each other, how they're being treated, where they want to live.'

Shchepkin nodded. 'That sounds safe enough. And Fräulein Koenen's film?'

'The Americans are being obstructive. But maybe Dallin can help out with that.'

'I expect so. Now that the war's over, the intelligence agencies are more or less running things.'

'So we've fallen on our feet,' Russell said wryly.

Shchepkin managed a thin smile. 'Ah, the British sense of humour.'

* * *

Effi was a quarter of an hour late for the morning's script rehearsal. An expired tram on Hohenzollerndamm was the cause, but she apologised profusely, worried that her new co-workers would be inwardly accusing her of the big star affectations she had always despised. She thought of repeating what her mother, with quite uncharacteristic humour, had once said – that she'd arrived late as a baby, and had been repeating the experience ever since – but the moment didn't seem right.

Everyone seemed more subdued than the day before, but it wasn't until after the session was over, and the director took her into his study, that she found out why. 'The Americans have asked for further checks on three more members of the cast,' Dufring told her. 'They're taking this much further than we expected,' he added, leaving Effi wondering who exactly he meant by 'we'. 'And I think you need to start compiling a dossier of affidavits from those you helped in the war.'

'Really?' Effi exclaimed. Gathering testaments to her own political virtue was not an appealing prospect.

'Really,' Dufring insisted. 'And you'll have to fill out one of these,' he added, lifting a sheaf of papers from the desk.

Effi looked through the document with increasing dismay. There were pages and pages of questions. One hundred and thirty-one of them. 'Who did you vote for in 1932?' she read aloud. 'How am I supposed to remember that? I probably didn't bother.'

'I know,' Dufring said. 'It's absurd. But do your best.'

'They've called it a *Fragebogen*,' Effi noticed. 'Don't they know that's what the Nazis called their form proving aryan descent?'

Dufring smiled. 'Probably not.'

'Why are they doing this?' Effi asked. 'To us in particular, I mean.'

'It's hard to know. There are Jews in the American administration who'd happily string up all the ex-Nazis, let alone bar them from making movies. And there are other, more powerful Americans who are worried about movies like ours, movies that ask real questions and support progressive ideas.'

Effi wasn't Russell's partner for nothing. 'So we've become one of the battlefields between the Americans and the Russians?'

Dufring gave her an appreciative look. 'Something like that, yes.'

* * *

After leaving Shchepkin Russell took a look at the new Soviet Memorial. It was in the form of a stoa, with six columns bearing the names of the fallen, and a statue of a Red Army soldier atop the centre of the colonnade's roof. A tank and howitzer had been placed on each side. The context made it moving, but like most Soviet architecture, it seemed firmly rooted in the past.

He walked on past the Brandenburg Gate and into an almost unrecognisable Pariser Platz. Stretching out ahead, the once stately Unter den Linden was a corridor of ruins. The Adlon Hotel, which had still been there in April, had obviously succumbed in the final days, and was now little more than a shell. The American Embassy wasn't even that.

Wilhelmstrasse had been virtually levelled. The buildings that had housed the Nazi government and its predecessors – the Foreign Ministry, the Justice Ministry, Promi – had all but vanished. Hitler's new Chancellery, whose ceremonial opening Russell had attended in 1939, was a field of broken stone. The street itself was still lined with rubble, with barely room for two cars to pass each other.

Further up Unter den Linden, his favourite coffee house had disappeared. He knew it was ridiculous, but he'd spent so many mornings at Kranzler's drinking their wonderful coffee and reading the newspapers, and he'd hoped against hope that it might have survived. On the opposite corner, the Café Bauer had suffered the same fate.

He eventually found a functioning canteen in the bowels of Friedrichstrasse Station, and a quiet corner in which to examine Shchepkin's missive. Rather to his surprise, it was only a pair of lists. There was one for him with five names, each with a personal and work-place address. Effi's had just two names, Ernst Dufring and Harald Koll.

There were no suggestions at to how these Party members should be approached, and no reiteration of what Shchepkin's superiors wanted to know. The latter, he supposed, was clear enough. If push came to shove, as it probably would, did these German communists feel that they owed their primary loyalty to their own party or to Moscow, to Germany or to the Soviet Union?

What weren't so clear were the consequences of a bad report. A word of comradely admonishment? Summary expulsion from the Party? Incarceration? Or even a bullet in the back of the head? He should have asked Shchepkin, Russell realised. He might have received a straight answer.

After everything that had happened in the last twelve years the current members of the KPD should have a pretty shrewd idea of what was what. Those who'd returned from Soviet exile would certainly be well aware of Stalin's methods, and of the need to use them. But comrades like Ströhm and Leissner – who'd spent the Nazi years in Germany, out of touch with their Soviet mentors – they might still have their illusions intact. And these were the men he might have to condemn.

He couldn't betray Gerhart Ströhm, a man he liked, respected and owed. They had first met in the autumn of 1941, when Ströhm had contacted him, and asked if he was interested, as a journalist, in the first expulsions of Jews from Berlin. Between then and Russell's precipitate flight in December, the two of them had borne witness to several departures from different railway yards. It had been a bitter, frustrating experience, but at least they had got to know each other.

Ströhm had been born in California to German emigrants, then sent back to his German grandparents when both parents were killed in a car crash. At university he had immersed himself in left-wing politics, and soon after the Nazis took power had been arrested on a minor charge. After serving his sentence he had found work as a railway dispatcher and, Russell assumed, been part of the splintered communist underground. But it was not as a communist that he'd come to Russell – his Jewish girlfriend had been killed by the Nazis, and the fate of her community was almost an obsession. As a railwayman and a comrade he had access to all the relevant information – where the trains left from, when they were scheduled, where they ended up.

In 1941, Ströhm had helped Russell recover some crucial papers from the left luggage office at Stettin Station, and a week or so later had helped arrange the first leg of his escape from Germany. Few men had done as much for Russell, and without any thought of personal advantage.

He would talk to Ströhm first – find out what the man really thought. If he was head over heels in love with Stalin, then well and good. If he hated the dictator's guts, then no one need know. And if Ströhm seemed oblivious to the perils of an anti-Soviet stance, then a quiet word might not go amiss. The railwayman could do what he wanted with the news that Stalin was watching him.

Russell left the canteen and headed north towards the river. Another temporary walkway allowed him across, and he picked his way east and north through the devastated University Hospital complex. Ströhm's workplace address was on Oranienburger Strasse, only a stone's throw from the old synagogue, and not much further from the flat where Ali and her parents had lived before the latter's deportation.

The address in question housed new education and welfare departments, and Ströhm's office was part of the former. He was surprised and pleased to see Russell, and begged him to wait while he dealt with a delegation of angry teachers. Russell watched Ströhm listen to their complaints – of which a lack of electricity and fresh water were only the most serious – and was impressed by his response. He neither played down the problems nor apologised for those that were clearly beyond his control, and he didn't fob them off with promises he might not be able to keep. Just the sort of politician the country needed, Russell thought.

He had noticed a busy canteen on the ground floor, but once the teachers were gone, Ströhm suggested they go out for lunch – he knew a good café nearby. It was on August Strasse, and reminded Russell of the workers' café Ströhm had frequented when he worked at Stettin Station. The long room was full of steam and conversation, the food basic but surprisingly plentiful.

'So, what have you been doing these last six months?' Ströhm asked him. 'I heard that you found your girlfriend.'

Russell skimmed through his recent life, something he seemed to be doing several times a day. 'I never asked you in April,' he said, 'but what happened to the comrades who helped us escape in 1941? The Ottings and Ernst and Andreas. And the comrades at Stettin Station whose names I never knew.'

Ströhm grimaced. 'The Ottings were murdered by the Gestapo, and so were the two men who sent you to Stettin. I have no knowledge of the other two. Do you know their surnames?'

'No.'

Ströhm shrugged. 'I'll try and find out, but I can't promise anything. The Poles are in Stettin now...'

'I know.'

'But someone you knew came back from the dead.'

'Who?'

'Miroslav Zembski.'

'The Fat Silesian!' Russell said delightedly. He remembered telling Ströhm about Zembski in 1941, and his reasons for believing the photographer dead.

'The camps had a way of thinning people out – you probably wouldn't recognise him now.'

'Is he working as a photographer?' Zembski had been a well-respected freelance in the 1930s until a brawl at Goering's country lodge cost him his official accreditation. After that he had run a camera shop and studio in Neukölln, while working undercover for the Comintern.

'He works for the Party newspaper. At the office on Klosterstrasse. I was talking to him a couple of months ago, and he seemed to remember you fondly.'

'I'll go and see him when I get the chance.' He felt buoyed by Zembski's survival, though overall it was much as he'd feared. At least four people had died to get him out of Germany. There was only one thing he could do for them – refuse to betray the comrades they had left behind. Comrades like Ströhm. He asked him how things were going.

Ströhm sighed, which was not a good sign. 'Some things are going well,' he said after a pause. He looked at Russell. 'This is off the record?'

'This is between friends.'

'Okay. Well, first the good news. Most of the Soviet administrators in Berlin know what they're doing. Someone said that the Western Allies sent their worst people here and the Soviets sent their best, and that seems about right. It may not look like it, but they made a big difference before the others arrived, and they're still making one in this sector. And they're absolutely determined that we should enjoy their theatre and cinema and poetry and God knows what else. I was hoping for bread but not expecting circuses – they brought both.'

'And the future?' Russell prompted.

'Well, there's some good news in that regard. I don't know how much you know about changes in Party policy, but one of the key debates has been about what sort of socialism we want to build in Germany, whether we want to replicate the Soviet system or develop a distinctive German model. And that debate is still going on. It hasn't been shut down, not yet anyway.'

'You think the Soviets will shut it down.'

'I don't know. To be honest, I'm more worried about the KPD leadership that returned from Moscow – Walter Ulbricht, Wilhelm Pieck, and all the rest of them. They have their own ideas how things should go, and they're not good listeners. They may be following Soviet orders, or just being who they are – it's hard to tell – but if it comes to a choice between their own comrades and Moscow, I can't see them backing the comrades.' He took a quick look around, as if to make sure that no one was listening. 'Look, the Russian soldiers behaved atrociously when they first arrived – the number of rapes was appalling. The situation has improved, but there are still new cases almost every day. And then there's the reparations policy. I understand the reasons – why shouldn't they take our machines and factories to replace what our armies destroyed? – but they're cutting the ground from under our feet. They have to behave like comrades, apologise for their troops' behaviour, and let us stand on our own. The German people will never vote for us if they think we're creatures of the Russians.'

'But Ulbricht, Pieck and the others don't agree?'

'When Party members tried to raise the question of rapes, Ulbricht told them that the matter was not for discussion. When others insisted that the law on abortion should be changed for rape victims, he told them that was out the question, and that he regarded the matter as closed.'

'And the comrades accepted that?'

'They were angry, but yes, discipline prevailed.'

'Perhaps the Austrian election results will give the Russians – and Ulbricht – second thoughts.'

'Perhaps, but I doubt it. It pains me to say it, but these comrades – the ones who came back from Moscow – are not the men I remember. I had to visit the new Party building on Wallstrasse yesterday, and when I went for lunch I discovered that there were four categories of ticket for meals in the dining hall.'

'All for Party members?'

'Oh yes. And that's just the tip of the iceberg. Ulbricht and his friends are living in luxury villas out in Niederschönhausen. The whole complex is fenced off and guarded by the NKVD. And anyone who questions the arrangement – as I foolishly did at one meeting last month – is accused of "starry-eyed idealism".'

There was no humour in Russell's laugh. This presumably was what Nemedin wanted to hear.

'But we've only just begun,' Ströhm added. 'If the merger with the SPD goes through, then Ulbricht's group may find themselves in a minority, and the Soviet may realise that an independent communist Germany is their best bet.'

'It's possible,' Russell said, without really believing it. Stalin didn't seem like a fan of other people's independence.

* * *

After taking Rosa in during the final days of the war, Effi had gone along with the seven-year-old's insistence – inherited, no doubt, from her fugitive mother – that their true histories should remain a secret until after the war was over. In the days and weeks that followed their escape from Berlin and Germany she had tried to make up for lost time, and find out all she could about her ward's past, but Rosa had spent the second half of her life hidden with her mother in Frau Borchers' garden shed, and all she could remember of the neighbourhood was a nearby railway line. She could summon up a few memories of the years before their voluntary incarceration, but none that offered any indication of where the family had lived before Otto's disappearance. And the girl had no idea what, if anything, her father had done for a living. It was probably something manual, Effi thought; by the time of Rosa's birth anything clerical or professional had been forbidden. But before that... well, for all she knew, Otto Pappenheim had been a doctor like Russell's old friend Felix Wiesner.

In 1933 rich and middle-class Jews had lived all over Berlin, but as the Nazi persecution gathered pace most had either left the country or moved into those working-class areas of eastern Berlin where their poorer brethren resided. Friedrichshain had always had a sizable Jewish population, and Effi was not surprised to find that two of the women on Ali's list were now living there. Nor, walking up Neue Königstrasse from Alexanderplatz, was she surprised to see walls and other impromptu notice boards covered with messages from Jews seeking Jews. Some, frayed and faded, had clearly been up for months, and most, Effi knew, would go unanswered – the men and women sought had long since fed the Nazi ovens. Every hundred metres or so she pinned up one of theirs – 'Information sought concerning Otto Pappenheim, (wife of Ursel and father of Rosa) and Miriam Rosenfeld (daughter of Leon and Esther). Contact Thomas Schade at Vogelsangstrasse 27, or telephone Dahlem 367.'

The first woman on her list had narrowly escaped a Gestapo trap in the summer of 1944, and spent several nights with Effi and Ali while the Swede Erik Aslund arranged a more permanent refuge. She now lived in a smart first-floor apartment over what had once been a restaurant. She greeted Effi with a heartfelt hug, and answered her apologetic request for an affidavit with an immediate yes. 'You wouldn't believe how many people have asked me to sign theirs,' she said. 'People who wouldn't have lifted a finger for me if they'd known I was a Jew. Now they all say they knew. So signing a statement for someone who really did help me will be a pleasure.'

She had known one Otto Pappenheim before the war, but he had been in his seventies. And she had known several Rosenfelds, but not a Miriam. She would ask around.

The other woman on Ali's list who lived in Friedrichshain had only stayed one night in the Bismarckstrasse apartment, but Effi remembered her better. Lucie's whole world had collapsed on that one particular evening in 1942. As a Jewish – and therefore unofficial – nurse, she'd been returning from an emergency call when the Gestapo arrived in front of her house. Cowering in a doorway, she'd heard shots inside the building and seen her elderly parents frog-marched into a waiting Black Maria. This had soon sped away, leaving uniformed police standing guard outside the front door. There was no sign of her husband and teenage son, and Lucie of course had feared the worst. Only a friend's determination had got her as far as Bismarckstrasse, and Effi had spent most of the night trying to comfort her. Lucie's face on the following morning, when news arrived of her husband and son's escape, had been a sight to treasure.

And all three had survived, as Effi found when she reached their home. The husband greeted her with obvious suspicion, but Lucie recognised her immediately. 'Frau von Freiwald!' she exclaimed, jumping up from her chair, and rushing to embrace her.

'My real name's Effi Koenen,' Effi said once they were done.

'Not the actress?' Lucie's husband said in surprise.

'The same,' Effi admitted with reluctance.

Many questions followed, and it was almost an hour before Effi could leave with the promise of another signature. Neither Lucie nor her husband had come across an Otto Pappenheim or a Miriam Rosenfeld, but Lucie was doing voluntary shifts as a nurse at Lehrter Station, and said that she would check through what records there were. All their arrivals came from the East, but some at least were returnees, from either hiding or imprisonment. Otto and Miriam might be among them.

Effi enjoyed the time with Lucie and her family, but as she walked back down Neue Königstrasse towards the old city centre a dark cloud of depression seemed to roll across her mind. She missed Rosa, and the search for the girl's father seemed set to be endless. Looking for someone in Berlin reminded her of pyramid schemes, each helping hand seemed to spawn ten more. And the movie... She was loving the involvement, but that too seemed a string without end. When would she ever get back to London? And then there was Russell's problem. Once she had finished her movie, and they'd done all they could to find Otto, she at least could return. But he would still be stuck here.

She wondered again about bringing Rosa back to Berlin, and the ruins around her seemed answer enough. In time, perhaps, but not in winter, not until... what? Until the rubble had been taken away, until all the windows had glass, until the Tiergarten had trees? Her train of thought was interrupted by a cruising jeep full of Red Army soldiers, all of whom seemed to be staring at her. She probably looked too old for sober predators, but she aged her walk just in case.

The jeep sped away.

Until the Russians had gone, she added to her list. But how long would all that take? The war had been over for six months, and Berlin was still in pieces. How many years would it be before a normal life was possible?

It was all so uncertain. She'd always thought of Thomas as a rock, but even he seemed unsure what to do. The way he'd been talking the other night she half-expected him to announce his retirement, and retreat to his in-laws' country farm. But could he afford it? If his money was all tied up in the works, then the Soviets held the whip hand.

She was reminded of her own flat, and decided to see if it was still there. A crowded Stadtbahn train carried her from Alexanderplatz to Zoo, and the old familiar walk brought her to Carmerstrasse as the last light faded in the western sky. The building was still standing, and lights were burning in the first floor flat that her parents had bought her all those years ago. As she stood and watched, the silhouette of a woman cradling a baby appeared on the thin curtains, and Effi thought she heard an infant crying.

Should she walk right in and assert her ownership? No, or at least not now. There were already too many things to do and worry about – for a fleeting moment she felt more overwhelmed than she ever had in the war. Survival had been such a simple ambition.

* * *

Russell spent the early afternoon visiting two more DP camps. Both were in the American zone – one in Neukölln, the other on the edge of Tempelhof aerodrome – but neither had any record of the two they were seeking. At the second camp one of the American administrators told him that all the Jewish inmates had recently been moved to their own exclusive camp in Bavaria. Berlin's other Jewish DPs would probably go the same way, the man thought, and Russell could see why they'd want to. But he couldn't help wishing that they'd put off moving until he found Otto and Miriam.

Realising he wasn't that far from the Redlich address, he decided to get it over with.

Paul had run into fourteen year-old Werner Redlich and his *Hitlerjugend* unit during the final days of the war. Having already lost his father in the North African campaign, the boy fretted about his mother and sister back in Berlin. When a decent Wehrmacht officer discovered how young he was, and suggested that he return home, Werner had offered only token resistance. And then the boy had walked into an SS patrol, which promptly hanged him as a deserter.

Paul had written it all down. He had thought of saying that Werner had died in battle, thereby saving mother and daughter anguish, but if by some chance the body had been returned to them, then the rope burn on the throat would have undermined everything else he said. And he wanted them to know how brave their son and brother had been, and how much the boy had cared for them.

But as Russell now discovered, it was all beside the point. The address was no longer there.

He found a neighbour who had known the family. According to her, Frau Redlich and her daughter had been buried in their basement when a bomb collapsed their building. The son, she added, had not come home.

'He was killed,' Russell told her.

'Maybe a blessing,' the woman murmured.

No, Russell thought as he walked away. A family wiped out could never be that.

Back at the house on Vogelsangstrasse, he found the kitchen occupied by the Fermaiers and Niebels. The old couple were busy preparing a meagre-looking dinner, and Frau Fermaier gave Russell what felt like a warning look, as if she feared his asking to share. Frau Niebel and her daughter were sitting at the table, their rations neatly piled in front of them, waiting their turn at the stove. The mother wished Russell a curt good evening before turning her face away, and the daughter gave him a blank look, as if she'd never seen him before.

The rest of the house seemed empty. He took up residence in Thomas's study, and thought about a stroll to the Press Club for beer and conversation. He was writing a note to leave behind when Thomas came in through the door with – miracle of miracles – three bottles of beer in his briefcase.

'A gift from a Russian major,' his friend announced proudly. He opened two of the bottles with his Swiss Army knife.

'A successful day then,' Russell suggested.

'You could say that. The Soviets have given me a huge job, printing the new schoolbooks for Berlin's lucky children. According to my major the German comrades in Moscow have been hammering out the texts since Stalingrad, and the approved versions have finally arrived.'

Russell was interested. 'What are they like?'

'Oh, what you'd expect. The world through Stalin's eyes. I haven't had time to look them over properly, but the history books are a hoot. Guess how they deal with the Nazi-Soviet Pact?'

'A regrettable necessity?'

'You're joking.'

'You're right – I wasn't thinking. They don't do regrets, do they?'

'They don't. And the Pact, it turns out, was a figment of our imagination. It's not even mentioned. The Germans didn't attack the Soviets in

1939 because the Soviets – all thanks to Comrade Stalin – were much too strong.'

'And 1941?'

'Hitler was desperate, Stalin was ready, but the Generals let him down.'

'Amazing.'

'And deeply depressing. The Nazis feed our children with one set of lies for twelve years, and now the Soviets come along with another set.'

'Wait for the American text books.'

'Oh, don't.'

'Don't what?' Effi said, coming in through the door. She gave them both a kiss and sat down. She looked tired out, Russell thought, but her eyes lit up when Thomas offered her a bottle of beer.

Russell explained about the text books.

'Don't talk to me about Americans,' she said. She reached in her bag for the sheaf of papers. 'This is what they're calling a *Fragebogen*. And I have to fill the whole thing in before they'll even consider letting me work.' She passed it across to Russell, who slowly thumbed through the pages. '"Question 21",' he read out loud. '"Have you ever severed your connection with any church, officially or unofficially? 22: if so, give particulars and reasons."' He looked up. 'Why on earth would they need to know that?' He read on. 'There's a long list of organisations here, everything from the Nazi Party to the German Red Cross. The Teacher's League, the Nurses' League, all the arts bodies. The America Institute! There are almost sixty organisations here – there can't be many Germans who didn't belong to at least one of them. Ah, and that's not all. "Question 101: Have you any relatives who have held office, rank or post of authority in any of the organisations listed?" That should cover just about everybody.'

'If it does, it'll take them years,' Thomas suggested gloomily. 'But maybe we shouldn't complain. We do want them to weed out the real Nazis.'

'But this won't do that,' Russell protested. 'This will just tar every German with the Nazi brush.'

'Okay, they've gone overboard, and they'll probably realise as much in a few months. It'll make them more unpopular than the Russians, and they won't like that.'

'I don't have a few months,' Effi said.

'No, of course not. I'm sorry...'

There was a knock on the door.

'Yes?' Thomas answered.

It was Esther Rosenfeld, whom Russell hadn't seen since the summer of 1939. She had aged a lot, which was hardly surprising, but the smile when she saw him seemed full of genuine warmth. Leon was no better, she said, but no worse either. She wondered if Russell and Effi would like to see him one evening.

'Tomorrow?' Russell asked, looking to Effi for confirmation.

'I'd love to,' she agreed. 'I left a lot of messages this afternoon,' she added. 'And several Jewish friends have promised to spread the word.'

'I can't thank you enough,' Esther said. 'All of you. And Leon thanks you too. He will tell you himself tomorrow.'

After she'd gone they all looked at each other. 'I sometimes think we should make something up,' Russell said quietly, 'just to give them some peace of mind. Miriam must be dead – six years without a single trace – she has to be.'

'Probably,' Thomas agreed, 'but we've only just started looking again. Give it a few more days at least.'

'Of course. It's just...' He left the thought unspoken.

'How was the meeting with your Russian friend?' Effi asked him.

Russell grunted. 'I'd almost forgotten about that.' He told them about Shchepkin's list of comrades for vetting. 'And there are two for you,' he informed Effi, expecting an explosion. 'Ernst Dufring and Harald Koll.'

She took the news calmly, as if she'd half-expected it. 'Dufring's loyal to a fault,' she said. 'I don't think I've even spoken to Harald Koll, but he looks innocent enough. What?' she asked, noticing Russell's expression. 'Am I missing something?'

'What if he isn't? What if he thinks that the Soviets are the KPD's biggest problem?'

'Then I lie to protect him.'

'And later, when they find out what he really thinks.'

'I can always say he lied to me. How could they prove otherwise?'

Russell shook his head. 'They won't even bother to try. This is the Soviets we're talking about. They'll just assume you lied to them, and take whatever action seems appropriate at the time. Darker threats, if they still think you might be useful. A cautionary death if they decide you're too much trouble.'

'Do you have a better idea?' she asked.

'No,' he admitted. 'I'm going to tell Ströhm, but the others... I don't owe them anything. I think I'm just going to pass on whatever they say. I mean, they must know that holding a high position in the KPD involves a level of risk. If they choose to incriminate themselves, then they have to take their chances. I'm not sacrificing myself for a few apparatchiks.'

'What exactly are you going to tell Ströhm?' Effi wanted to know.

'Everything. He can write the report on himself if he wants.'

It was Effi's turn to shake her head. 'You'll be putting him in an impossible position.'

'How?'

'Once you tell him that the Soviets have forced you into this, he'll know that you're talking to other German comrades. And some of them will be his friends. But what can he do? If he warns them, he's betraying you; if he doesn't, he's betraying them.'

She was right, Russell realised. They both were.

Rapists and profiteers

A light drizzle was falling on Thursday morning, washing the air clear of brick dust and reminding Effi of London. Looking out the window of Thomas' study, she imagined Zarah and Rosa walking round the foot of Parliament Hill on their way to the school, and realised she'd forgotten about Jens. Something else to do.

With half the cast filling out American forms, that morning's rehearsal had been cancelled. Effi devoted several hours to the *Fragebogen*, read through her answers, and corrected those that might be considered sarcastic. Her original response to Question 115 – 'have you ever been imprisoned on account or active or passive resistance?' – was brief and truthful – 'I was never caught.' But would the Americans think she was just being cute? She added an explanatory paragraph just in case.

Was it enough? She had no idea, and was tired of second-guessing a bunch of foreign idiots. She forced the papers into her bag and set off for Schlüterstrasse.

Kuhnert wasn't in his office when she arrived, but a secretary she hadn't met before promised to pass on the completed *Fragebogen*. Visiting the cafeteria for tea, she found a message from Ellen Grynszpan on the notice board: 'Something to tell you, come down and see me.'

She reached the basement to find Ellen escorting an American colonel and his wife around the paintings. Ellen gestured for Effi to wait, and two minutes later was wishing her visitors goodbye. 'Her brother was a painter,' she explained. 'He lived in Berlin until 1942. They think he died at Treblinka.'

'Did he paint any of these?' Effi asked, looking round.

'No, all his paintings were burnt by the Nazis.'

Effi sighed. 'I should have guessed.'

'Anyway,' Ellen said, breaking the spell, 'I have news for you. A friend's friend knew an Otto Pappenheim back in early 1941. Otto's brother lived across the street from them, and both men were trying to get to Shanghai, like a lot of other Jews before the Russian war – by that time no one else was letting us in. My friend's friend thinks they succeeded in getting Soviet travel permits. She didn't see him or his brother after that time, so she always assumed they'd gone.'

'Where was this? Where did your friend's friend live?'

'In Friedrichshain.'

'And how old were these brothers?'

'In their late twenties, early thirties. Around that.'

'Did she say anything else?'

'I can't remember anything else. Would you like to talk to her? I'll give you her name and address.'

Effi took them down. 'Have any of the Jews come back from Shanghai?' she asked. 'None that I know of.'

Effi gave Ellen a hug. 'Thank you for this,' she said.

On her way home she found herself wondering about this new Otto. Why had he gone to Shanghai? Had he gone ahead, hoping to send for his wife and daughter? If it was only him the Gestapo were looking for, had his wife insisted he leave to save himself, as Effi had done with Russell? Or had nothing more noble than fear led him to abandon them?

* * *

Uwe Kuzorra's old apartment building on Demminer Strasse was scorched and scarred but still in one piece. But no one answered Russell's knock, and the dust outside the door seemed undisturbed. He tried the neighbours to no avail, but a young boy downstairs said his mother was next door. Russell found her hanging clothes in what had once been someone's parlour, and which now seemed to function as a neighbourhood drying room. Several lengths of rope were strung between jutting bricks across the barely covered space.

'He still lives here,' she said in answer to Russell's query. 'Or he did. They took him away about ten days ago.'

'Who did?'

'French soldiers. We're in their zone.'

'Do you know where they took him? Where's their HQ?'

She shook her head. 'Not a clue.'

Russell thanked her and walked back to the busy Brunnenstrasse, where his chances of meeting a German policeman or French patrol seemed better. He walked north past Voltastrasse U-Bahn station without seeing either, turning west between what was left of the AEG factory complex and Humboldthain Park, where the apparently indestructible flak tower still exuded useless defiance. There were children playing football in the park, their hair slicked back by the drizzle. The schools were open again, but according to Thomas a huge number of parentless children were living almost feral existences in the ruins, playing games by day and working the black market by night.

On Mullerstrasse he found what he was looking for. The French HQ, a shopkeeper told him, was just up the street, in part of the old Wedding Police Station. In Nazi days the building had functioned as a fort, its Gestapo occupants mounting armed forays out into the local streets, where hammers and sickles still plastered the walls. Now the tricolour flew from the battlements, and basement beatings were hopefully a thing of the past.

Once inside, Russell was passed around like an unwelcome parcel, his journey finally ending at the desk of a middle-aged civilian in a beautifully cut suit. He let Russell struggle with his French, and had obvious difficulty containing his lack of interest. 'We don't give out the names of those in our custody,' he eventually replied in perfect English. 'Not to American journalists, in any case,' he added, with something close to a sniff.

Russell wondered whether exceptions were made for scribes of Mongolian or Paraguayan descent. 'I'm not asking as a journalist. I'm here as a friend of the man you arrested.'

'Are you a relative?'

'No....' Russell began, realising his mistake too late. He should have said Kuzorra was a cousin. Or something.

'Then I cannot help you.'

'Can you tell me who can?'

'You could apply to our headquarters at Baden-Baden.'

'That's four hundred miles away.'

The man shrugged. 'I'm sorry,' he said, sounding anything but.

Russell shook his head, walked out, and stomped angrily downstairs to the lobby. He was still seething when a hand slapped him on the shoulder, and a much friendlier French face appeared in front of his own. 'John Russell! What are you doing here? You look like someone just slept with your girlfriend.'

It was Miguel Robier, a French journalist whom he'd met the previous winter, when both were commuting between Eisenhower's Rheims HQ and the Allied front lines. They had enjoyed each other's company, sharing tastes in wine and political cynicism.

Russell explained about Kuzorra, and the interview he'd just had.

'Ah, Jacques Laval. He doesn't like Americans. Or anyone, for that matter. Do you have a few minutes? Let me see what I can do.'

Russell waited and hoped, hugging himself for warmth and watching drizzle drift past the open doorway.

Ten minutes later Robier was back, looking triumphant. 'I have the story. Not from Laval – I know someone in military liaison. He says your friend Kuzorra was arrested for being a member of the SS – is that possible?'

Russell shook his head. 'Anything's possible. In fact I seem to remember that all senior police officers had SS ranks by the end of the war. But that's...'

'It gets more interesting,' Robier interrupted him. 'Our people arrested him at the request of the Americans – which, by the way, might be why Laval was even less helpful than usual. Anyway, it's almost two weeks now, and the Americans still haven't sent anyone to interview him. Our people have already sent them two reminders.'

'Is he here?' Russell asked.

'No. He's out at Camp Cyclop.'

'Where?'

'It's our military base. Out in Wittenau.'

'Okay, thanks. So, how are your family?'

They shared personal news and contact details, and agreed to meet up for a drink before Miguel's return to France. They probably wouldn't, Russell thought, as he headed on up Mullerstrasse to the Ringbahn station, but it wouldn't really matter – their paths were bound to cross again. He had long ago lost count of his chance encounters with other journalists.

One thing seemed clearer with each passing day – who was in charge of western Berlin. The Americans were deciding not only who could work in the British zone, but who should be arrested in the French. And no one seemed to find this strange, let alone feel impelled to protest, unless the sulking of men like Laval was counted as such. The war had only been over six months, but the British and the French were already irrelevant – there were only two real powers in the city, or in the wider continent. And as luck would have it, he was working for both.

If the Americans had arranged Kuzorra's arrest, they could just as easily arrange his release. A meeting with Scott Dallin seemed indicated.

By the time Russell reached the American HQ on Kronprinzenallee, the drizzle had stopped, and there were hints of sunlight in the western sky. After asking for Colonel Dallin he settled down for a long wait, but was only halfway through the lead story in the *Allgemeine Zeitung* when a corporal came to collect him.

Dallin's office was high at the back, with a distant view of the Grunewald. The Californian had grown a moustache since Russell had last seen him, and the golden-brown hair was long enough to flaunt its waves. The visual effect was Gatsby-ish, but this son of privilege had none of that character's easy charm. 'Where have you been?' was his first irritated question.

'I've been waiting for your call,' Russell replied, taking the unoffered seat in front of the other man's desk. 'I left a number and address downstairs.'

Dallin grasped his nose between two fingers and sighed. 'I never received them. But...' He brought both palms down on his desk. 'Let's get on with it.' He gave Russell a cold look. 'You can probably imagine how I felt when London told me they were sending you.'

'Relieved? Ecstatic?'

Dallin grunted. 'You haven't changed. So, please, let's start from the beginning. Give me one good reason why I should believe the story you told Lindenberg.'

'He did.'

'He's in London, and he doesn't know you like I do. You used to be a communist, you flirted with the Nazis. You even worked for us to buy yourself a US passport. Is there any intelligence organisation you haven't worked for?'

'The Japanese. Look, Colonel, I never, as you put it, flirted with the Nazis – every dealing I ever had with the bastards was a matter of necessity. I did used to be a communist, but so did a lot of other people back then. And there are a lot of honourable men still out there who call themselves communists – most of them were fighting Hitler long before Pearl Harbour. But I left the Party almost twenty years ago, mostly because I didn't like what was happening in Russia then, and now it's ten times worse. I'm sure you and I have our differences, but we're on the same side now.'

Dallin looked less than convinced. 'So what made the Soviets think you would work for them?'

'I promised them I would. They had my son in a POW camp, and in return for his release I said I would spy for them. I had no choice if I ever wanted to see him again.'

Dallin steepled his hands as he considered this. 'All right,' he said finally, with almost palpable reluctance.

They really were desperate, Russell thought. Dallin had been told to enlist him, and was either letting off steam or trying to convince himself that he had nothing to lose. Probably both. The American would give Russell enough rope to either hang himself or tie the Soviets in knots. A win-win situation.

'So have you been in contact with the Russians?' Dallin asked.

'Yes. I saw Shchepkin the other day. He's my Soviet contact.'

'How do you spell that,' Dallin asked, reaching for his fountain pen. Like Russell's old boss in Heydrich's *Sicherheitsdienst*, he favoured green ink.

He repeated the name. 'Anyway, the NKVD wants me to check out several high-ranking German comrades. I've seen one already. His name's Gerhard Ströhm – he was a member of the communist underground during the war, and I knew him slightly back in '41. He was actually born in America, but he's lived here since he was about thirteen. He's very disillusioned with the Soviets. And I think he might be recruitable in the long term. I've found out he'll be voted onto the KPD Central Committee next spring, so he'd be an excellent asset.'

'That sounds promising,' Dallin said, placing his hands behind his head. He seemed pleasantly surprised, but was doing his best not to show it.

'It is,' Russell agreed. 'And from what Ströhm told me, there are a quite a few others. The Russians are supporting the German communists who spent the war in Moscow, and they're not giving the ones who stayed in Germany a look-in. The second group are really ticked off. So there's quite an opportunity for us.'

'That sounds good.'

'And there's another friend who could be very useful, but I've run into a problem with him. His name's Uwe Kuzorra,' Russell went on, watching in vain for any sign that the name was familiar. 'He used to be a detective in the criminal police, and he owes me a few favours. But the French have arrested him for some reason or other, and they won't let me visit him. A French friend looked into the matter for me, and he says that we asked for him to be arrested.'

'We?'

'It was an American request.'

'It didn't come from this department.'

'I didn't think it did. But could you look into it? He's not a Nazi. Never was – he actually resigned from the Kripo when the Nazis took over, and set up as a private eye. He only rejoined the police after his wife died, when they were really short of men; he was never in the Gestapo. He could be very useful to us both. He knows Berlin better than anyone I know, and he doesn't like the Russians.'

Dallin reached for the phone on his desk. 'You'd better wait outside,' he said, almost apologetically. Noting the marked change in attitude, Russell closed the door behind him. The way to a spy chief's heart was clearly to offer him spies.

He could hear Dallin's tone through the door, and there was no mistaking the rising anger. Call seemed to follow call, and the voice grew harder, more insistent. Finally Russell was summoned back in.

'I can't get a straight answer from anyone,' Dallin told him. 'No one admits to knowing your friend, let alone demanding his arrest. In the end, I just cut through the crap and phoned the French. You can visit the man on Saturday. 11 a.m., out at their army camp. You know where that is?'

'Roughly. That's great, thanks. Just one more thing', he added, thinking that he might as well push his luck. He explained about Effi, and the problems she was having with other invisible Americans. 'They promised me in London that she'd be able to work,' he told Dallin, neglecting to mention that 'they' were the Soviets. 'She's a heroine of the resistance, for God's sake – you'd think whoever it is would have some real Nazis to chase. If you could have a word with whoever's responsible, I'd take it as a personal favour.'

'I can't promise anything,' Dallin said, 'but I'll look into it.' He got up to shake hands. There was, Russell thought, almost a smile on the American's face.

* * *

They had arranged to meet Esther Rosenfeld just inside the main entrance to the Elisabeth Hospital. Effi had last seen the complex in 1941, when she'd been one of the famous names invited to cheer up the wounded. The last four years of bombs and shells had rendered it almost unrecognisable. Now parts of buildings were supported by iron and wooden struts, with temporary shelters nestling in between.

Esther was waiting for them. 'He's not so good this evening,' she said, 'but I'm sure he'll be pleased to see you.' She led them down a long corridor, across an open space to another building, and up a flight of stairs. Effi suddenly knew where she was – they were passing the office where she and Annaliese Huiskes had often shared a bottle of hospital-brewed alcohol. She wondered what had happened to the blonde nurse. The last time Effi saw her, Annaliese was driving off down Bismarckstrasse in the car they had both 'borrowed', hoping to escape the Russians' pincers as they closed around Berlin.

They passed through one ward and entered another. Leon Rosenfeld was in the penultimate bed, lying on his back with a blank expression in his eyes. He seemed smaller than Russell remembered, and much older – he couldn't be much more than fifty, but he looked about seventy. The marks of the beating he'd received in Silesia were still visible, but only just.

Esther took his hand, and told him who they were. 'This is John Russell,' she said. 'Remember he stayed at the farm?'

There was a slight flicker in the eyes, and a look, both hopeful and dumb, that reminded Russell of the dog he'd had as a child.

'And this is his wife Effi,' Esther was saying. 'They both helped rescue Miriam.'

The eyes found Effi, a slight smile creasing the lips. And then the eyes closed, and he winced as if in pain. 'Thank you,' he whispered.

After sitting in silence for a couple of minutes, it became obvious that Leon had fallen asleep. 'He's not so good in the evenings,' Esther said again. 'He's much livelier in the mornings.'

'Then next time we'll come in the morning,' Effi promised, getting to her feet. 'Are you coming back with us?'

'No, I'll stay a while longer. Thank you for coming.'

The two of them walked back through the wards. At the end of the second Effi noticed a vaguely familiar face. 'Were you working here in 1941?' she asked the nurse in question, an unusually plump woman with short brown hair.

'I feel like I've been here since the First War,' she said. 'Why?'

'I had a friend who worked here – Annaliese Huiskes. I wondered...'

'She's still here. She came back, that is. About two months ago, I think. I saw her earlier – she's on duty this evening.'

It took them five minutes to find the relevant ward, where another joyous reunion took place. Russell smiled at the patients' gawping faces as the two women did a jig in the aisle.

Annaliese was wearing a sister's uniform now. 'I see you found him,' she said, eyeing Russell over Effi's shoulder.

'I'm not so easy to shake off,' Russell said, giving her a kiss on each cheek.

Annaliese just stared at them, a big grin on her face. Her blonde hair was longer than Effi remembered, and tied back with a red ribbon. 'Go wait in the office,' Annaliese said, 'I'll be along in a minute.'

She was back in two. 'No booze, I'm afraid,' she told Effi. 'I'm being good.'

They sat and talked for almost an hour. Effi told Annaliese all about England and Rosa, and the nurse told her what had happened after their nocturnal parting in April. Annaliese had reached her late husband's parents in Spandau, and they had hidden her in their cellar for several weeks while the Russians raped the neighbourhood's women. She had then set out across country, hoping for better from the Western Allies, but had ended up in an American camp at Rheinberg. 'It was more terrible than you could imagine, but I'll tell you about that another time. I have to do my rounds in a few minutes, and I'd like to show John something before you go.'

'Me?' Russell asked, surprised.

'You're still a journalist, aren't you?'

'I sometimes think so.'

'Yes he is,' Effi said, cuffing him round the head.

After finding a nurse to cover for her, Annaliese led them through two large wards to a third, where all the beds were occupied by thin-faced children. Two immediately asked for water, which Annaliese went to fetch. Around twenty pairs of eyes stared dully at Russell and Effi.

'They're all diabetic,' the returning Annaliese explained, 'and we don't have enough insulin.'

'Why not?' Russell asked, though the answer wasn't hard to guess.

'The only suppliers are *Grosschieber* – the big-time black marketeers – and they make sure that supplies are tight. When they do release some, they invite all the hospitals to bid on them, to maximise the price. They do the same with penicillin, and the VD drugs, Pyrimal and Salvarsan. The staff dip into their own pockets, but it's not enough. There was a twelve-year-old in that bed there' – she pointed to the one lying empty – 'but she died this afternoon. When she arrived ten days ago there was nothing wrong with her that an insulin injection wouldn't fix.'

'Where did it come from before?' Russell asked.

'There were two labs in Berlin, but both were bombed out. We did get some from Leipzig for a while, but the supply dried up – we don't know why. One doctor went down there on his day off with some money we'd collected, but he never came back. And no, he wasn't the sort to steal it.' She looked at Russell. 'This would be a story worth telling, don't you think?'

'It would,' he agreed.

It would, he thought, as they walk back through the wards. Trouble was, he'd had the same thought looking at Leon. And watching the dazed refugees tumbling out of their train at Lehrter Station. The victims were different, but there was only one story, and it wasn't the one he wanted to write. He had spent enough time with sadness and evil, and to what useful end? Any fool could shout 'never again', but he might as well change his name to Canute. It *would* happen again. Somewhere, sometime in the not too distant future. Most people were incapable of looking beyond themselves and those they loved – the camp on the other side of the hill was never their business. There was nothing new or surprising about children dying for someone else's greed. As the seventeen-year-old Albert Wiesner had told him six years earlier, the only mystery in this world was kindness.

Effi was asking Annaliese when they could meet again.

'I get Saturday afternoon and Sunday off. I usually go out to see Gerd's parents on Saturday, but if the weather's nice on Sunday we could go for a walk in the Grunewald.'

They agreed to rendezvous at Thomas's house.

'And think about that story,' Annaliese told Russell. 'Anyone here will talk to you.'

'I will,' Russell told her.

Effi said nothing until they were back outside. 'You didn't sound very enthusiastic.'

'I'm not. It's terrible, of course it is. But it won't be news to anyone in Berlin, or anywhere in Germany.'

'What about England and America?'

'No editor would buy it. He'll know his readers, and they won't care about Germans killing Germans.'

* * *

'How long do you think we've been back?' Russell asked as he shaved the next morning.

Effi was still cocooned in their blankets. 'Oh I don't know. It feels like weeks.'

'This time last week we were on our way to Victoria,' he told her.

'I don't believe it!' She sat up against the headboard. 'Your friend Shchepkin – do you think he'd check out the Shanghai Otto for us?'

'He might, if I ask him nicely.'

'The Soviets must keep records of people who travel across their country. And we'd know for certain that he went.'

'True. I'll ask him when I see him, but that won't be till next Friday.'

'Oh... So what about Shanghai? If he did go, how can we find out if he's still there?'

Russell rinsed his face in the bowl. 'I'll ask Dallin. The Americans must have a consulate there.'

'Your spymaster friends are coming in handy.'

Russell shook his head. 'Don't joke about it.'

'All right. So where are you off to this morning?'

'The Soviet sector. I'll try and see a couple of the men on Shchepkin's list.'

'What do you say to them? I'm running a survey for Stalin?'

Russell laughed. 'Something like that.'

'No, seriously.'

'I'll tell them I'm writing an article on reconstruction, and talking to those most responsible. Off the record, of course – no names or direct quotes. If they say yes – and most people do love talking about themselves and what they're doing – then I'll ask how they're getting on, what problems they're having, that sort of thing.'

'Problems like the Russians taking half their zone back to Russia?'

'A failure to mention that could be construed as loyalty. And vice versa, of course. You get the idea. I make up the details as I go along.' He checked his jacket pockets for pen, paper and cigarette currency. 'Are you going out?'

'Yes, Kuhnert left a message – there's a rehearsal at eleven. And this afternoon I thought I'd go over to Lehrter Station, and see if I can find Lucie. She was going to look out the arrival lists.'

'I could meet you there,' Russell said. The arrival he'd witnessed at the station was still fresh in his mind.

'Where?' Effi asked. 'It's probably a sea of rubble.'

'No, it's mostly cleared. The clock's still there – we can meet under that. Say four o'clock?'

* * *

A couple of broken-down trams and another unexploded bomb in the tunnels stretched Russell's journey to almost four times its pre-war duration, but both intended interviewees proved willing to see him without a prior appointment. Kurt Junghaus, a harassed-looking man with prematurely grey hair and a chubby face that ill-suited his skinny figure, worked for the recently-established Propaganda and Censorship Department at the KPD's new Wallstrasse headquarters. The job itself suggested a high degree of trust, and Russell found no reason to doubt him, at least in the short term. If disillusion ever came it would be complete, but this was a man who wanted to believe, and Russell had no qualms about stressing his loyalty.

Uli Trenkel worked in a new Soviet-sponsored planning office further down the street, a long stone's throw from the Spree. The glasses perched halfway down his sharp nose gave him the air of an intellectual, but the rough-skinned hands told a different story – this man had probably worked in one of Berlin's war industries. He seemed much more relaxed when it came to technical issues than he did with politics, and where the latter was concerned Russell guessed he would follow the path of least resistance. He wouldn't be any trouble to the Soviets or their KPD friends.

After talking to him, Russell sat in the building's canteen with a mug of tea. There was no sign here of different grades, and the overwhelming impression was of energy and enthusiasm, of people enjoying their chance to start again. On the other hand, the two interviews he had conducted that afternoon, with men he assumed were important to the Soviets, hadn't exactly left him feeling excited about the future.

He was just getting up to leave when three Soviet officers entered, all wearing the light blue shoulder tabs of the NKVD. One of them was Nemedin.

The sight of Russell induced a slight hesitation in the Georgian's stride but no overt sign of recognition. Russell wondered whether Nemedin and his colleagues had noticed the change in atmosphere that accompanied their entrance, a sense of deflation rather than fear, as if the joy had all been sucked away.

He had to decide about Ströhm, Russell thought, as he stood on the pavement outside. At least he had a week before his next meeting with Shchepkin. Maybe Effi's solution was best after all – he would simply make something up, give Ströhm enough doubts to make him credible, but not enough to cause him problems.

On impulse, he walked the final few metres down to the river. Away to his right the Jannowitz Bridge lay broken in the water, and beyond it, to the south and east, a few surviving buildings stuck out like broken teeth against the blue sky. This area between the Old City and Silesian Station had taken a dreadful hammering.

There was only half an hour before he was due to meet Effi. Rather than trust to public transport, he set off at a brisk pace, heading up Breite Strasse towards the sad wreckage of the Schloss, silently mouthing what lines he could remember of Shelley's 'Ozymandias'. He expected more of the same beyond, but the Lustgarten proved a scene of transformation. On one side a tank was being towed away by Russian horses, on the other, beneath the pocked northern facade of the Schloss, Soviet soldiers and German civilians were erecting three carousels. It was the last day of November, Russell realised – Christmas was less than four weeks away.

The Soviets had obviously sanctioned the Christmas fair, and Russell felt almost sorry for the image that popped into his head – of Soviet Santa Clauses dropping down German chimneys and stealing the presents left under the trees.

As on the previous occasion, his arrival at Lehrter Station coincided with that of a refugee train. This one had old carriages as well as cattle cars, but the people emerging onto the platform looked every bit as lost. Maybe the wind was blowing in a different direction, because this time he could smell the human waste.

What was the number he'd read in that English paper? Was it six million dispossessed Germans on the move? Or seven? How many trains would that involve? And how many passengers would be carried off on boards or stretchers, bound for hospital or the waiting graves down the road?

He aimed for the main terminal building, forcing his way through the anxious crowd. 'Is this Berlin?' one man asked him, as if he couldn't believe it possible. A woman in once-expensive clothes asked directions to the Bristol Hotel, and stood there open-mouthed when he said it no longer existed. When a couple asked him for money, he gave them four cigarettes, knowing that would buy them a meal. But they looked more annoyed than grateful, as if they thought he was trying to cheat them.

Inside the old booking hall things seemed less frantic. He was early, but Effi was already standing under the clock, which the war had stopped at half-past twelve.

'I've already seen Lucie,' she said. 'She's been through what records there are, and there's no Otto Pappenheim. No Miriam Rosenfeld either.'

'She's busy, I take it,' Russell said, as a single woman's wail rose and fell in the tumult outside.

'They're saints, these people,' Effi said. 'And what am I doing? Acting...'

'Not that they'll let you,' Russell ventured in mitigation.

'Oh, I haven't told you yet. The Americans have apparently decided that I'm safe to let out. Maybe your talk with the colonel did the trick.'

'Good. You said this film needed making.'

'I did. But when I see what's happening here... well, I can't see these people queuing up outside a cinema, can you?'

'But that...'

'I know,' she said, taking his hand. 'I'm feeling useless, John. Ever since we got here.'

He opened his mouth to disagree, but thought better of it. He understood where the feeling came from, although 'useless' was not the word he would have chosen for himself. Frustrated, perhaps, or uncertain. Lost, even. And the strange thing was, it had almost come as a shock. Who would have thought that peace would prove more difficult than the war? The diminished danger of a violent death was certainly to be welcomed, but what else had peace brought in its train? Chaos, hunger, and corrupted ideals. Ivan the Rapist and GI Joe the Profiteer.

'We need cheering up,' he decided. 'How about an evening at the Honey Trap? Irma said she'd get us in.'

* * *

When they entered the nightclub that evening, Russell hardly recognised the place. The lighting was dimmer than before, just a few chandeliers with most of the bulbs removed, and the white tablecloths shone like dull spotlights within each circle of patrons. Tuesday's bare brick walls were now festooned with posters from Berlin's pre-Nazi past, along with large portraits of Churchill, Truman and Stalin.

The place was more than full, and they were lucky to be passing a table as a couple stood up to leave. They had barely sat down when a waiter whisked away the empty glasses and demanded to know their order. A bottle of red wine set them back seven cigarettes, the waiter providing change for their pack from a tin case he carried in his inside pocket. The wine proved weak and slightly sour.

Russell and Effi gave their fellow revellers the once over. The male clientele seemed exclusively foreign, and mostly uniformed. The nightclub was in the British Sector, but that hadn't deterred the Americans and Russians, who were both present in large numbers. The Americans were mostly officers or NCOs, but the Russians ranged from general to private, all bedecked in medals and wearing several visible wristwatches. For the moment at least, the room seemed almost awash with international goodwill.

Almost all of the females were German, and most of them were young. There were many low-cut tops and short skirts on display, but the fashions seemed dated to Effi, as if the girls had been raiding their mothers' wardrobes. How many were 'real' prostitutes, how many girls just trying to get by? Or did that distinction no longer apply? She could see three girls happily chattering away as male hands fondled their breasts.

Up on stage a small orchestra of middle-aged men was offering a lively mixture of jazz and popular music. They'd been playing 'In the Mood' when Effi and Russell arrived, but the subsequent tunes had all been around since pre-Nazis days, when these musicians had presumably learnt them. Three couples were dancing on the small floor, two gyrating wildly, the third locked together with almost ferocious insistence.

'It feels like a trip in a time machine,' Russell said between tunes.

'There were German men in those days,' Effi replied. 'This feels...'

'Wrong?'

'Humiliating.'

'Yes,' Russell agreed. There didn't seem any point in stating the obvious, that victors had always humiliated losers, and fucking their women was just one of many means to that end. At least these women were getting something back, which was more than could be said for most of the Red Army's victims.

'Effi!' a voice cried out behind them. It was Irma, floating on a cloud of expensive-smelling perfume. As the two women hugged, Russell grabbed an empty chair from the next table. For the next few minutes, Effi and Irma swapped tales of *Barbarossa*-the-musical and brought each other up to date. They were only silenced by the behaviour of a nearby couple, whose tongue-wrestling and under-table groping became impossible to ignore.

'Where do they go?' Effi asked, half amused and half disgusted. 'As least I assume they're not going to do it here.'

Irma laughed. 'Does it shock you?'

'No. Well, yes, a bit. Is it really the only way to survive?'

'They think so. And to answer your question, there's an alley out back with plenty of darkened doorways. But most girls like to take the soldiers home – if they give them family as well as sex it's more likely to last. The parents lie there listening in the next room – they might disapprove, but they're usually willing to share the spoils.' She looked at her watch, an American Mickey Mouse model. 'I'm on in half an hour; I have to get changed. How long are you staying?'

'What time do the fights usually start?' Russell asked.

'Not for a couple of hours yet. The amount of water Geruschke adds, it takes most of the evening to get drunk.'

'I haven't seen him this evening.'

'He'll be around somewhere – he always is.'

They watched her squeeze her way through the packed tables, responding to each boisterous soldier's greeting with a wave and a smile. The band started playing 'Sentimental Journey'.

'Do you think we'll get our seats back if we have a dance?' Effi asked.

Russell looked around. 'Other people seem to,' he said, noticing several empty tables with half-full glasses and coat-draped chairs.

They had three dances, and were beginning to enjoy themselves when two British soldiers decided to show off their jitterbugging skills. Effi was nearly laid out by a flailing arm, and decided enough was enough. Their seats were still vacant, but another couple had colonised one side of the table – a Russian corporal and a German girl who looked about fifteen. The former asked in stilted German whether they minded sharing their table, and seemed almost ecstatic when Russell responded in Russian. He spent the next ten minutes complaining how much he missed his wife, children and village by the Volga.

Russell sought escape with a trip to the toilet. In the corridor outside, two men were doing some kind of deal. They both gave him a quick once-over, decided he posed no threat, and went back to their business at hand. In the toilet, Russell detected marijuana among the less agreeable odours.

Back at the table, the Russian was ready to resume his life-story. Russell could think of no polite way of stopping him, but the German girl contrived to alleviate her own boredom, and finally shut him up, by the simple expedient of inserting a hand in his trouser pocket.

He grasped her by the arm, pulled her to her feet, and almost dragged her away towards the rear exit.

'A darkened doorway,' Effi murmured.

'If they make it that far.' As he watched them disappear, Russell had the sudden sensation that he was being watched. Turning his head, he found Rudolf Geruschke looking straight at him. The nightclub boss raised a hand by way of hello, and turned away.

A few minutes later two glasses of bourbon were delivered to their table. Unwatered. Compliments of the boss.

Why? Russell wondered. The man only knew him as Irma's friend, and he didn't seem greatly enamoured of her. And he'd never heard of Effi.

The thought was drowned by a drum-roll, and the appearance of a nattily-dressed MC. He treated his audience to a few jokes – all either rich in sexual innuendo or dripping with amused contempt for the no longer dangerous Nazis – and introduced Irma to rapturous applause.

A spotlight revealed her, now wrapped in a metallic-looking sheath of a dress. The voice was slightly huskier than Russell remembered, but she could still hold a note. She sang a couple of songs in English, then switched to German for a version of 'Symphonie' which reduced several of the Russians to tears. One more song in English had the Brits and Americans happily singing along, before she closed the set with a song that Effi knew of but hadn't yet heard – 'Berlin Will Rise Again'. It was stately, sad, defiant:

> *Just as after the dark of night,*
> *The sun always laughs again,*
> *So the lindens will bloom along Unter den Linden,*
> *And Berlin will rise again.*

The lights went out as the applause began to fade. Irma had vanished when they came back on, and Rudolf Geruschke was standing by the side of the stage, deep in conversation with an American colonel.

Kyritz Wood

Russell left early for his trip out to Wittenau, but the buses and trains proved worse on a Saturday, and it was early afternoon before he reached the French military base. The duty officer examined his passport and found his name on the shortlist in front of him, but still felt the need to seek confirmation from a senior officer. The major who emerged reeked of Gauloises, and gave Russell a long stare before examining his documentation.

Russell kept his temper. If they were seeking an excuse to renege on the promised visit, he wasn't going to offer them one.

He wondered sourly why the French were even here in Berlin. The Resistance might have covered itself in glory, but the regular army had played no significant part in the Wehrmacht's defeat. Half the generals had supported Vichy, yet here they were claiming equal shares in the occupation.

The major returned the passport to his subordinate, and walked back into his room without a word to Russell. A few seconds later a lieutenant appeared, and asked Russell to accompany him. They walked down a long line of wooden barracks still bearing *Hitlerjugend* exhortations, and into a large two-storey brick building. In an upstairs room two upright seats faced each other across an open table. The only item of wall decoration was an unframed photograph of General de Gaulle.

After about five minutes the door swung open and a limping Uwe Kuzorra was ushered in by the same lieutenant.

The detective showed surprise and pleasure when he saw who his visitor was. 'John Russell,' he said with a smile, extending his hand.

'Fifteen minutes,' the French lieutenant said, and left them to it.

They sat down. Kuzorra looked in poor health, Russell thought, but then so did most Berliners. 'It's good to see you,' he said, 'but if we have only fifteen minutes we'd better save the small talk for later. I'm here to help, so tell me why you've been arrested.'

'I was denounced as a former member of the SS.'

'But you were never...'

'Not in the usual way, no, but the reorganisations under Heydrich did confuse matters.'

'But there must be colleagues out there who will testify that you were never a Nazi.'

'There might be. But it wouldn't help.'

'Why not? Who denounced you?'

'A man named Martin Ossietsky.'

'Why? Has he got a grudge against you?'

Kuzorra shook his head. 'He was paid to denounce me, and if his accusations prove insufficient then there'll be others.'

'Who paid him?'

'A man I was trying to bring down. His name's Rudolf Geruschke.'

It was Russell's turn to be surprised. 'The owner of the Honey Trap?'

'Among other things. You've met him?'

'In passing. I can't say I liked him.'

Kuzorra grimaced. 'He's one of the *Grosschieber*, the black market kingpins. And probably the worst of them – some draw the line at certain traffics, but not him.'

Russell had a mental picture of Geruschke and the American colonel. 'I've got a friend in the French press – according to his sources, it was the Americans who asked for your arrest. Could they be in bed with him?'

Kuzorra considered. 'It's a thought. I'd assumed they were being over-zealous, but Geruschke might have friends over there. Some Americans have got very rich here, especially in the last few months.'

'I might have some pull in that direction,' Russell told him. 'Maybe not enough, but I can try. What about colleagues? You can't have been handling the investigation on your own.'

'It sometimes felt like it. And I don't imagine any of my colleagues have been eager to pursue matters since my arrest – they know a threat when they see one. I expect the investigation has been abandoned, or put off until "circumstances are more favourable". And there's nothing unusual about that – most black market investigations have ended the same way. They're too damn dangerous. The black marketeers have guns to spare, but the occupation authorities won't let us carry them.'

'Okay,' Russell agreed, 'but it must be worth finding out whether they've given up on Geruschke. Are there any of your colleagues who would talk to me?' Dallin, he knew, would need more than his and Kuzorra's protestations of the latter's innocence to take up the case.

'Gregor would probably talk to you,' the detective decided after some thought. 'Gregor Jentzsch. He still has the makings of a good policeman, despite four years in the East. He works at the station on Mullerstrasse, and lives a few blocks further down – Gerichtstrasse 44.'

'I'll find him. Now what have the French told you? Have they given you a date for a hearing?'

Kuzorra shook his head. 'They've told me nothing.'

'I'll ask,' Russell promised.

'Good luck. I'm surprised you found someone to tell you I'd been arrested.'

'One of your neighbours saw them take you away. I came to thank you for what you did in '41.'

Kuzorra grunted. 'I was glad you got away. Every now and then I got the chance to stick a spoke in the bastards' wheels, and nothing gave me more joy. The one great pleasure I have here is knowing that most of my fellow inmates are Nazis.' He smiled. 'What are you doing now?'

'Effi took in a young Jewish girl near the end of the war, and we've come back to look for her father. Or find out how he died. And Miriam Rosenfeld – remember her, the girl who disappeared at Silesian Station?'

'I saw her,' Kuzorra said unexpectedly. 'Not long after you escaped – just after the New Year, I think. I was walking down Neue Königstrasse, and this young woman was walking in the opposite direction. I looked at her photograph often enough when I was questioning people at Silesian Station. I'm sure it was her. She had a baby in a pram.'

'A baby?'

'A baby, a small child – I didn't get a good look. The mother looked happy, I remember that. She hurried on past when she saw me staring at her, which was no great surprise. She wasn't wearing a star, but of course I knew she was a Jew.'

The French lieutenant reappeared, and indicated that their time was up.

'I'll do what I can,' Russell told the detective.

'Be careful with Geruschke. I was nowhere near nailing the bastard and he got me locked up – I dread to think what would happen to anyone who really threatened him.'

'I'll bear it mind.'

When Russell asked his French escort how long Kuzorra would be held, he got only a Gallic shrug in return. Back at the office, the major had disappeared, and the duty officer might as well have. This particular investigation was not yet complete, he said. If Monsieur Russell wished to testify on the prisoner's behalf, he should leave his address, and someone would be in touch.

With Kuzorra's warning still fresh in his mind, Monsieur Russell declined to leave his address. If the detective was right, the only people who could get him released were the people who had got him locked him up – the Americans. Russell would be waiting at Dallin's door when he arrived on Monday morning.

In the meantime, he had news of Miriam. News that was four years old, but four was better than six. In September 1939 she'd been in terrible shape, and here she was more than two years later with a baby in a pram. And 'looking happy'. She must have found somewhere safe to live, at least until then. So why not the four years that followed? It still felt unlikely, but less so than it had.

Darkness was beginning to fall by the time he reached Wittenau Station. They were dining at Ali's again, but he still had time to visit Gregor Jentzsch. After changing trains at Gesundbrunnen, he took the Ringbahn to Wedding and walked the short distance to Gerichtstrasse.

The street seemed more intact than most. The man who answered the door was around thirty, with short blond hair, gold-rimmed glasses and a boyish face. Hearing the name Kuzorra made him wary, but he agreed to give Russell a few minutes. In the living room his equally blonde wife was sitting on the sofa, cradling a blonde baby. Goebbels would have thought himself in heaven.

Jentzsch was clearly fond of Kuzorra, and seemed more than willing to talk, but Russell could tell from his frequent glances at wife and child that the young policeman had no intention of putting his family at risk.

He and other colleagues had been told of Kuzorra's arrest, and were warned not to involve themselves without specific instructions from the occupation authorities. Their superiors were doing what they could to secure the detective's release.

'Kuzorra thinks that Rudolf Geruschke has set him up.'

'I'm sure he did.'

'Do your superiors think so?'

'I don't know. But we were told to suspend the investigation, at least for the time being.'

'What about the man who denounced him, Martin Ossietsky?'

'He works for Geruschke.'

'At the Honey Trap?'

'No. He's in charge of a warehouse out in Spandau. Geruschke brings a lot of goods into the city, and that's one of his storage depots. There are several others.'

Russell thought for a moment. 'I could confront Ossietsky. As a journalist, I mean. He might give something away.'

Jentzsch shook his head. 'He won't. And you'd be putting yourself in real danger. Geruschke doesn't like people prying into his business.'

'What could he do – kill me?'

'He might.'

'He didn't kill Kuzorra, just moved him out of the way.'

'He's not a psychopath – he doesn't go around killing people for the fun of it. But people who oppose him have turned up dead. Always in circumstances where someone else could be blamed, but that's not hard to arrange, not these days. At least twenty violent deaths are recorded each day across the city, and that's only in the British, French and American zones. The Soviets don't keep records of the ones they bury.'

'So what can I do to help Kuzorra? Do you know anyone in the French administration who would talk to me?'

'Not really. There's a major I deal with sometimes. He seems a reasonable man, but I don't think he works in the right section.'

'What's his name?'

'Jean-Pierre Giraud.'

'Okay. So what have you and your colleagues been doing? Or have you just washed your hands of Kuzorra?'

'Not quite,' Jentzsch said with commendable honesty. 'I keep asking the bosses, just to let them know that we haven't forgotten him. I think our best hope is that they let him retire.'

'Which would mean dropping the investigation.'

'It's already been dropped.'

'But would Kuzorra let it lie?'

Jentzsch sighed. 'Probably not.'

* * *

Russell was an hour late arriving at Ali's, but dinner was still cooking. He was about to tell Effi about Miriam when she announced some news of her own. 'You know you thought Wilhelm Isendahl was too cocky to survive the war?'

'Yes.' When Russell had first met Isendahl in 1939, the blond young Jew had enjoyed dining in restaurants patronised by the SS. He and his gentile wife Freya had helped them rescue Miriam and the other girls from the house on Eisenacher Strasse.

'Well, Ali's found him. And he's here in Berlin.'

'I don't believe it. That's great.' Isendahl had found four families to shelter the rescued girls, but had, at the time, told no one else who they were. But now he could tell them who had taken Miriam. And if any members of the family had survived, they might know what had happened to her, or even where she was.

'What about Freya?' he asked.

'Someone told me that she was in America when Pearl Harbour was attacked,' Ali said. 'She may be back now. I don't know. Anyway, here's his address.'

Russell pocketed the piece of paper, thinking he could go there next day. 'I saw Uwe Kuzorra today,' he announced. 'He's the detective we hired to find Miriam in 1939,' he explained to Ali and Fritz.

'The one who helped you escape in 1941,' Ali added for her husband's benefit.

'The same. Anyway, he swears he saw Miriam early in 1942. Recognised her from the photograph I gave him. She was walking down Neue Königstrasse with a baby in a pram.'

'A baby,' Effi echoed. 'How old was it?'

'Kuzorra couldn't tell.'

Effi did a quick calculation. 'If the child was less than eighteen months old, then the father was someone she met after we rescued her. But if it was older than that...'

'Then the father was one of those SS bastards who visited the house on Eisenacher Strasse,' Russell said, completing the unwelcome thought. 'Kuzorra thought she looked happy,' he added in mitigation.

'Motherhood can do that,' Effi told him. 'It makes no difference who the father is.'

* * *

Sunday morning, Effi and Russell went their separate ways. Annaliese expressed disappointment that Russell wouldn't be sharing their walk, but he suspected she was being polite, and set out for Friedrichshain with a clear conscience.

Isendahl had lived there in 1939, and Russell found himself wondering whether the man had managed to bluff his way through the entire war without even moving apartments. It seemed unlikely – by the end of the war, few adult males of any race had been able to evade the call of the state – but he wouldn't have put it past him. As it turned out, this apartment was two streets away from the old one, which he and Effi had visited in 1939. Isendahl lived alone in two large rooms, with a panoramic view across the ruins.

His blond hair was longer than Russell remembered, and the old resemblance to Hitler's security chief Reinhard Heydrich was less marked. 'We Victims of Fascism are doing well,' he told Russell, as he ushered him into the spacious book-lined living room. It had taken Isendahl a few seconds to recognise his visitor, but he seemed genuinely pleased to see him. Wilhelm was still a young man; he'd been a prominent member of the KPD youth wing when Hitler first came to power, so he couldn't be much more than thirty.

What a way to spend your twenties, Russell thought. But then he'd spent most of his own following Lenin's illusory star.

Isendahl reclaimed the bottle of beer that stood beside his typewriter, and opened one for his guest. After filling each other in on their respective wars – Isendahl had, in his own words, 'settled for mere survival' in 1943, and spent almost two years cooped up in a comrade's roof-space – Russell asked what his host was doing now. Isendahl was happy to tell him, or at least to keep talking, but his answers were somewhat vague. He was working for a local Jewish group which helped survivors get where they wanted to go. He was also liaising with the Soviet occupation authorities, but in what capacity and on whose behalf was less than clear. When Russell asked after his wife Freya, Isendahl looked uncharacteristically sheepish, and mumbled something about this not seeming the right time to send for her. A further question elicited a reluctant admission that she'd been living in New York with her parents since 1941.

Back in 1939, Isendahl had scorned the notion of a Jewish homeland in Palestine – 'you don't fight race hatred by creating states based on race' Russell remembered him saying – but the six years since had modified his stance. Now he was keen to stress the distinction between right and left-wing Zionists, rather than condemn Zionism *per se*. Without being asked, he rattled off a long list of different groups, ending, somewhat dramatically, with one called the Nokmim, or Jewish Avengers. These followers of a Lithuanian partisan named Abba Kovner were, as their name suggested, determined on vengeance. They believed that six million Nazi deaths were necessary before the Jewish survivors could learn to live with themselves.

Isendahl smiled at the conceit. His view of the Nokmim seemed a mix of amusement and awe.

Russell had never heard of the group, but he recognised the makings of a story. He asked Isendahl if he was in contact with them.

He wasn't, but he promised to ask around. He was thinking of becoming a journalist himself – or a writer of some sort – once Europe was put back together.

'Do you remember Miriam Rosenfeld?' Russell asked abruptly.

'The mute one.'

'Do you know what happened to her?'

'Not in the end, no.'

'Did she get better?'

'Yes, she did. I remember now – she had a baby, and that changed everything. Or so I heard.'

'Did she stay with the same family?'

'The Wildens? Yes, but later they were killed in the bombing. Someone told me that Miriam hadn't been hurt, but I don't know what happened to her after that – we all got more isolated as the war went on. But I can ask around.'

'Thanks. I don't suppose you know any Otto Pappenheims?' He explained about Rosa, and their search for her father.

'I do know one Otto Pappenheim. Not well – I only met him once.'

'When was this? How old would he be now?'

'I only met him a few weeks ago. I should think he's about thirty-five.'

'Did he ever have a wife and daughter?'

'I've no idea.'

'How would I find him?'

'Good question. He's not in Berlin, anymore. He and a friend of mine went off to Poland last month. They're on their way to Palestine.'

'Through Poland?'

'The road begins there, in Silesia. Do you know about this?'

Russell shook his head. He had assumed that Palestine-bound Jews were following well-beaten paths, but had seen no reports of their actual location.

'A group called Brichah started organising things in Poland,' Isendahl explained. 'Then the Haganah – the army of the Palestinian Jews – did the same at their end, and eventually the two of them met in the middle. There are people right along the route now, in Czechoslovakia and Austria, across the mountains and down through Italy to the ports and the ships. The ships that the British try to intercept and send back.' He noticed the gleam in Russell's eyes. 'Another good story, yes? And I am in contact with these people. I could arrange a meeting if you want. They won't talk to many Western journalists, but I think they would talk to you.'

'I'd like that,' Russell admitted. It did sound like a great story, and he might get news of this third Otto Pappenheim.

* * *

Walking in the Grunewald was like walking through the past. Some damage had been done by stray bombs or shells, but nature was rapidly repairing all but the deepest scars, and the smell of the pines reminded Effi of Sunday strolls before the war. It was only when they reached the Kaiser-Wilhelm-Turm, and looked back across the treetops at the lacerated skyline in the distance, that the present again became real.

It was a cold day, and seemed to get colder as Annaliese told her story.

'When I was picked up by American soldiers I felt really pleased with myself. I'd done it – I'd got away from the Russians. The GIs were pretty free with their suggestions, but the ones I met took no for an answer – I wasn't raped, and neither were any of the other women I came across during those first few days. I was put on a truck with other refugees and some soldiers they'd found hiding in a village, and we were driven west. We were told that there were camps waiting for us, which sounded a little ominous, but just letting us loose didn't sound so wonderful either – there had to be some sort of organisation, and we thought that was why they were keeping us together.'

Annaliese shook her head. 'We couldn't have been more wrong. The camp was called Rheinberg – it can't have been far from the river – and it was hell on earth. You wouldn't believe how bad it was. There were thousands of us: mostly men, but families as well, and far too many children. When we got there it was just a huge field surrounded by barbed wire – there were no buildings, no tents, no shelter of any kind. And there was hardly any food. Teething troubles, I thought, but things got worse rather than better. Any food that arrived was rotten, and there was hardly any water. Before too long we were eating grass, and getting sick.'

'People started digging holes for shelter – the soil was sandy so it wasn't too hard – but the walls would collapse and those inside were covered in sand, and too weak to fight their way out. Almost everyone had dysentery, and the toilets were just poles strung across pits. People who didn't have the strength to hold on would fall in and drown.'

'Did the people higher up know about this?' Effi asked. 'Was it just this one camp?'

Annaliese shook her head. 'I don't know who knew, but it wasn't just Rheinberg. I've met people since from several other camps, and they all sounded much the same. It was policy – it had to be. How should I say this? The guards didn't beat people up or torture them with irons – they just killed them with neglect. We found out later that there was enough food and water – but they'd deliberately withheld it. During the weeks the Americans were in charge about a hundred bodies a day were carried out. They stacked them in quicklime outside the fence.

'There were a few doctors in the camp, and several nurses like me. We did what we could, but it wasn't much. We were all so weak ourselves. I'm still thinner than I was in the Bunker last spring.'

'How did you get out?'

'The camp was in the British zone, and in June the Americans handed it over. The British couldn't believe what they found, and some of their officers talked to the press, but it was all hushed up. One officer told me that a few dead Germans weren't worth a big row with the Americans, not with the Russians to worry about.'

'I expected better of the Americans,' Effi said.

'So did I. But most of them seem so angry. When the British arrived they were much more sympathetic – they seem to get it that we weren't all Nazis. The Americans hate us, or at least a lot of them do. The ones at Rheinberg blamed every last one of us for the war, and all the horrors that were done in our name. And they were quite prepared to let us all die.'

They were both silent for a few moments, listening to the breeze stirring the pines. 'Why did you come back here?' Effi eventually asked.

Annaliese smiled. 'I missed the place. And I felt guilty about leaving Gerd's parents to fend for themselves. I persuaded the British to let me go – one officer took a bit of a shine to me, I think – and I managed to get on a train. What a journey that was! I've never seen anything like it – every place we stopped there were other trains full of people, and huge camps by the side of the tracks, with everyone hungry and begging for food. It felt like the whole world was on the move.

'It took me four days to get here. I needn't have worried about Gerd's parents – their staying was a damn sight more sensible than my going. They were surprised to see me, but pleased, I think. And I got my old job back. I took a trip in to the Elisabeth Hospital, partly to see if it was still there, and hoping to find old friends if it was. And of course they were short-staffed.'

'But you're a sister now.'

'Impressive, isn't it? The pay's better too, or would be if the money ever showed up. And if you could buy anything with it. But it's all so frustrating, Effi. Without medicines, we're just a half-wrecked hotel with nurses. We know the medicine's out there, but most of the time we can't afford it. I ask you, what sort of bastard wants to get rich on the backs of dying children? After all we've been through, it's still pieces of shit like that who are running things. Why don't the occupation authorities do something about it?'

'I think you already answered that – because, consciously or not, they want to see us suffer. And because they're up to their ears in shit themselves.'

Annaliese gave her a look, part surprise, part admiration.

'We've all lost our innocence,' Effi said. 'Even the children.'

* * *

That evening Russell told Esther what he'd learned from Kuzorra and Isendahl, that Miriam had given birth to a child in either 1940 or 1941, and that both had been alive in early 1942. Esther had listened with her usual composure, made sure that she had understood him correctly, and then sat in thoughtful silence, as if carefully weighing what it did and didn't mean.

* * *

First thing on Monday morning, Russell arrived at the French administrative HQ on Müllerstrasse. Major Giraud proved willing to see him, but, as Jentzsch had feared, knew nothing of Kuzorra or the reasons for his arrest. Thinking he was being helpful, he took Russell upstairs and introduced him to Jacques Laval, the man who'd been so singularly obstructive on his last visit.

Russell refused to be daunted. He told the cold-eyed Frenchman that he'd been to see Uwe Kuzorra at the detention centre in Wittenau, and was pleased to note the momentary look of surprise in the other man's eyes. 'I'm writing a story about his arrest,' he lied glibly, 'and the treatment he's receiving at French hands. As far as I can tell, no date has been set for a hearing or trial.'

'That is quite usual,' Laval replied. 'We only have the people to conduct a few cases at a time. Even the Americans have this problem. Your friend will just have to wait his turn. Now...'

Russell noticed the slight sneer in Laval's voice when he mentioned the Americans. 'You arrested Kuzorra because the Americans told you to,' he said coldly. 'Are you holding onto him out of spite?'

'Don't be ridiculous.'

'Then why? Why hasn't he been handed over to them?'

'He will be.'

'When they snap their fingers, perhaps.'

'When they make an official request.'

Russell laughed. 'Monsieur Laval, let me tell you what my story will be. That you are holding a wholly innocent man in custody, with no intention of giving him a fair hearing or trial. And that you're not doing this in the interests of France, but because the Americans have ordered you to. Is that a fair summary of the situation?'

'We don't take orders from the Americans.'

'Then give me the name of the American who wanted Kuzorra arrested, so I can ask him why the man's been left to rot out at Camp Cyclop.'

Laval considered, but only for a second. He had, Russell guessed, no qualms about holding an innocent man for as long as expedience dictated, but a public reputation for sucking up to the Americans was not something he wanted to defend at Parisian dinner parties. 'Colonel Sherman Crosby,' he said, almost biting out the syllables.

'Thank you,' Russell said, and left it at that.

He made the long trip back to Dahlem – he was, he reckoned, covering more miles each day than he had with Patton – and asked for a brief meeting with Dallin. 'I can give you five minutes,' he was told on reaching the intelligence chief's office.

'I've found out who had the French arrest Kuzorra,' Russell began.

'Who's Kuzorra?'

'My detective friend. We agreed he'd be an asset to any Berlin network.'

'Did we? So who was it had him arrested?'

'Colonel Sherman Crosby.'

'Ah.'

The name had made Dallin sit up, Russell noticed. And the look on his face suggested a rival. Had the Americans decided to imitate the Nazis and Soviets, and create their own perpetual feud between competing intelligence services? He sincerely hoped not. Four years earlier he had almost been crushed between Canaris and Heydrich, and was not keen to repeat the experience.

He suggested that Dallin talk to Crosby. 'Ask him why him why he wanted Kuzorra arrested. And whether the name Rudolf Geruschke means anything to him. He's a black marketeer that Kuzorra was investigating, and one of the letters denouncing Kuzorra came from one of his employees.'

'I can ask,' Dallin agreed, almost too readily. 'Come back this evening. Say five 'o'clock.'

It was now almost two. Russell walked round to the Press Club on Argentinischeallee in search of lunch and some news of the local journalists. The former met all expectations, but the latter was harder to come by. In pre-war days Berlin's foreign press corps had shared watering holes with its German counterpart, but under the occupation there seemed little in the way of mixing. Fortunately for Russell, one of the older American scribes had run into a German colleague, Wilhelm Fritsche, whom they both knew from pre-war days. Fritsche was keeping 'office' in one of the re-opened coffee shops at the eastern end of the Ku'damm.

Russell took to the buses again, wondering where he could find a bicycle. According to Thomas, the Russians had stolen most of the city's supply in the spring, and broken them learning to ride.

He found the coffee shop without too much trouble, and saw Fritsche and another man right at the back. Fritsche had never been a Nazi, but, like any German journalist who wanted to work in the Thirties, had kept his true political opinions to himself.

He was surprised to see Russell. 'I thought you'd escaped from Berlin.'

'I had.' For about the twentieth time since his return, Russell went over his and Effi's recent history. Fritsche had heard of Effi's film, and seemed encouraged by the fact that it was being made. So did his younger companion, who introduced himself as Erich Luders. He was also a journalist, and exactly the one that Russell was seeking. Luders, as Fritsche announced with a mentor's pride, was investigating Berlin's black marketeers.

Most of the big operators were Germans, the young journalist told Russell, but they all had powerful friends in one or more of the occupation authorities. Rudolf Geruschke was one of the most successful. He used muscle when he had to, but generally preferred a more discreet approach, buying people off rather than burying them. He had businesses in all four sectors, but none of the occupation authorities seemed inclined to interfere with his activities, and neither did the German police.

Russell asked if Luders had heard of Kuzorra.

'He was an exception, and Geruschke managed to get him arrested. Why? Do you know him?'

'He's an old friend,' Russell admitted. 'I went to see him on Saturday at the French camp in Wittenau.' He told Luders what Kuzorra had told him.

'Off the record?' Luders asked.

'On,' Russell decided. He didn't think Kuzorra would mind a little publicity. 'When are you planning to file?'

'Too soon to say. When I've got enough dirt, I guess. Maybe I'll give Kuzorra a visit myself.'

Russell was reminded of Tyler McKinley, the young American journalist killed by the Gestapo in 1939 for digging up dirt on their political masters. Seeing the eagerness in Luders' eyes, he worried for the young man. Things had changed since 1939, but not that much.

Delayed by another disabled tram on the way back to Dahlem, he had time to reflect on the paucity of his own journalistic output – personal matters, an all-too-active espionage career and Berlin's convalescent public transport were taking up every hour he had. He needed to get something written, but when? He had to complete the interviews for Shchepkin, and he couldn't just abandon Kuzorra. But then maybe Dallin would have something for him.

When he reached the American's office he found him about to leave, bound for some formal function in what looked like a borrowed monkey suit. 'I talked to Crosby,' Dallin said, hustling Russell towards the stairs. 'He says they asked the French to pick up Kuzorra after several people denounced him. And that the only reason he hasn't been interviewed is the backlog of cases they're having to deal with.'

'Did you tell him that at least one of the denouncers was an employee of the man Kuzorra was investigating?'

'I did. He said he'd look into it. When I asked him what he knew about Geruschke, he said he knew the man was a black marketeer, but that Berlin was full of them. Which sounds fair enough. And apparently this one has a habit of helping Jews.'

Russell was sceptical. 'Do you trust him? Crosby, I mean.'

They had reached the main entrance. 'No,' Dallin said eventually, 'but there's nothing more I can do. Your friend will have to wait his turn.'

'That's not good,' Russell said, following him out.

'That's the way it is.' Dallin stopped and raised both hands to close the subject. 'And we have something else to talk about,' he added, lowering his voice. 'I have a job for you. There's a man in the Soviet sector who we need to bring out. Theodor Schreier.'

'Why can't he just take a bus?' was the first question that came to mind.

'Because he's being watched by the Russians. And if he tries to come over they'll probably arrest him, and ship him off to Moscow.'

'Who is he? What does he do?'

'He's a research chemist – something to do with polymers, whatever they are. They're important apparently, and this man was the best in his field. He worked for I.G. Farben.'

'So why haven't they whisked him off already?'

'We don't know, which is one good reason for haste. What I need from you – from your man Shchepkin, that is – is whatever he knows about the surveillance operation. We're going to bring Schreier out, but we'd rather not do it in a hail of bullets.'

'That's all you want from me?'

'We'll also need you for the actual extraction.'

It sounded like a trip to the dentist's, and might prove a lot more painful – the 'hail of bullets' reference was hardly encouraging. But Dallin was looking steadily at him – this was a test, Russell realised, and one that he had to pass. 'I'm not seeing Shchepkin until Friday,' he said, 'and I've no way of contacting him before then.'

'When on Friday?'

'In the morning.'

'That's okay. We're looking to bring Schreier out on Saturday evening.'

'What if Shchepkin doesn't know anything?'

'Then you'll have to wing it.'

Russell smiled. 'Say I succeed – will you have another go at Crosby for me?'

'If we succeed,' Dallin said slowly, 'then I'll be able to argue the case for taking on more locals, whatever their crimes in the past.'

'Sounds fair,' Russell said. It wasn't much, but it was the best he was likely to get.

* * *

As he reached home, Effi was seeing off a smiling British sergeant. 'And what have you been doing in my absence?' he asked her.

'Entertaining the British Army,' she told him, leading the way back in. 'He brought a letter from Rosa and Zarah,' she said happily over her shoulder, 'and I had to give him something in return.'

'A biscuit, I hope.'

'Twenty cigarettes, actually.'

'What's in the letter?'

'You can read it,' she said, passing it over.

Zarah's handwriting was almost florid, Rosa's small and fastidious. The latter stressed how hard she was working at school, described London's recent weather in enormous detail, and listed the meals that Zarah had taught her to cook. A long line of kisses was addressed to them both. Zarah reported that Rosa had cried for two nights following their departure, but seemed much better since, and was still doing well at school. A letter from Berlin would help, she added pointedly. Lothar had come down with a cold, but seemed to be on the mend, and Paul had taken Marisa to the theatre. He was, Zarah thought, very much in love. And he was also taking his 'man of the house' responsibilities seriously, constantly asking if there was anything he could do to help.

'She says nothing about herself,' Russell noted.

'I know. It reminded me that I've done nothing about Jens.'

Russell grunted his agreement. It all seemed so wonderfully ordinary in London. He wondered if Paul would ever come back to Berlin, because he doubted the Soviets would ever let him leave. He sighed and put the letters put back in their envelope. 'How was your day?' he asked Effi.

'It was good,' she said, picking up the envelope and holding it across her chest. Hearing from London had clearly made her day. 'We had another rehearsal this morning, and filming starts next week – Dufring has been cleared by the Americans.'

'Fantastic.'

'Isn't it, especially after last week, when everything seemed against us. Oh, and this afternoon I visited the two synagogues Ellen told me were open. No sign of Miriam, and no more Ottos.'

'Shanghai Otto and Palestine Otto are probably enough to be getting on with.'

'Oh, we can't have too many Ottos.'

'Maybe not.'

'And the English Tommy turned up just after I got here. He was a nice boy. What about you?'

Russell detailed his failure to advance Kuzorra's cause, and the task which Dallin had dumped in his lap. He was well on the way to dampening Effi's high spirits when Thomas arrived home, triumphantly bearing a radio. They spent most of the evening listening to the BBC, enjoying the music and reminding themselves of all those nights they'd broken Hitler's law, with one ear tuned to London, the other cocked for sounds outside. But these days the Gestapo was just a bad memory, and the men in long leather coats wouldn't be coming to drag them away.

* * *

Next morning, Russell was in Thomas's study trying to get something written when the telephone rang. Out of service for the last two days, the line had apparently been repaired.

It was Miguel Robier. 'John, I've got some bad news. Your friend Kuzorra is dead. He was killed last night.'

'What?' Russell said stupidly. 'Who by?'

'By another prisoner, or at least that's what they're saying. I got the news from my friend at Müllerstrasse, the one who told us where Kuzorra was being held. I'm going up there now – there's something wrong here, I can smell it. Do you want to come with me?'

Russell was still in shock. 'Yes,' he said eventually. 'Yes, I do.'

'How long will it take you to reach Stettin Station?'

'An hour,' he said optimistically.

'I'll be waiting.'

Russell fumbled the earpiece back onto its hook, and stood staring at the floor. The man he owed his life to was dead. And he was terribly afraid that he himself had been the cause.

For once the buses cooperated. Robier was waiting on the concourse of the half-ruined station, a newspaper under his arm. 'Ah, *bien*,' he said. 'There's a train in a few minutes.'

Soon they were rattling out past the yards, where the remnants of shattered wagons and coaches had been raised into piles, looking like anthills on an African plain.

'I'm glad I'm with you,' Russell told Robier. 'If I turned up on my own they'd just tell me to get lost.'

Robier warned him not to be too optimistic. 'The people at Müller-strasse are politicians – they like having friends in the press. The Army couldn't care less.'

In the event, the authorities at Camp Cyclop seemed eager to display a reasonable front. The major seemed inclined to ignore Russell's existence, but answered Robier's questions readily enough. Kuzorra had been found dead in his room that morning – someone had cut the detective's throat while he slept.

It would have been mercifully quick, Russell thought – a few split seconds of consciousness at most.

The perpetrator was not known, and, if the major's demeanour was any guide, never would be. They were interrogating other inmates, of course, but there were no fingerprints on the razor blade.

When Russell asked to see the body the major seemed set to refuse, but nodded his acquiescence when Robier demanded the same. They were taken to what looked like an empty storeroom. Kuzorra's body was laid out on a table, still dressed in his underwear, still wearing an apron of congealed blood. His eyes, still open, looked surprisingly at peace.

Russell suspected that much of Kuzorra's will to live had died along with his wife Katrin, back in the early years of the war. His own death would probably have worried the old detective less than the fear that Geruschke might profit from it.

He won't, Russell silently promised the corpse. He didn't suppose he would ever connect the nightclub owner to this particular murder, but there had to be some way of bringing the bastard down.

He and Robier thanked the still nervous major and talked things over on the Wittenau platform. The Frenchman said he'd try and dig a little deeper into the circumstances surrounding the original arrest, but warned Russell not to expect too much. 'I know what the line will be – Kuzorra was about to be handed over when he fell victim to some deranged fellow prisoner. Who could we find to prove otherwise?'

Robier got off at Wedding, leaving Russell to travel the last lap alone. As he walked across the Stettin Station concourse he noticed two British military policemen – 'Red Caps' they were called – striding towards him.

'John Russell?' the shorter of the two asked him.

'Yes.'

'Come this way please?' the man said, shepherding Russell with one arm towards a nearby archway. The other man was at his other shoulder, funnelling him towards the same objective.

Russell went where he was told. 'What's this about?'

They were through the archway now, in a part of the station that Russell remembered had once been used by taxis. Now it was empty, save for two men in civilian clothes and a scruffy-looking two-seater Mercedes with its trunk wide open.

'He's all yours,' the shorter MP told the two men, one of whom, almost casually, slid a revolver out of his pocket.

Russell realised why the car's trunk was open.

'In' the man said in English, confirming his guess. The MPs had vanished.

'No,' Russell said, playing for time. He could hear other people close by – surely someone else would come through the archway. Or were the MPs making sure that they didn't?

The man brought the muzzle level with Russell's head and seemed inclined to pull the trigger. One blast of a locomotive whistle would certainly drown out the noise.

'All right,' Russell agreed. The man smiled, and gestured him into the trunk. He was about thirty, Russell guessed, with a long scar on the back of his gun hand and what looked like ancient burns down one side of his face. A veteran of something nasty.

Russell took his time getting into the trunk, and was still arranging his body to fit the space when the lid slammed down, plunging him into darkness. A few more seconds and the car lurched into motion, running straight for a while and then taking what seemed a right turn, presumably onto Gartenstrasse. Maybe they'd be stopped at a military checkpoint, Russell thought – there were few enough cars on the road. If so, he'd make a racket that no one could ignore.

'Johann's buried there,' Scarred Man said as they took another turn. They must be on the street which bisected Wedding cemetery.

'He was an unlucky bastard,' the other man said. It was the first Russell had heard his voice, which sounded unusually shrill.

He had no trouble hearing their conversation – the trunk's inner wall was much thinner than the outer. He wondered if they realised he could hear them, and whether they would care.

They'd been silent for several minutes when Shrill Voice came out with a question: 'When are you going to do it – when we get to the factory?'

Scarred Man's laugh was derisive. 'We'd have to carry the body, wouldn't we? I'll wait until Kyritz Wood.'

'I see what you mean.'

So did Russell, who suddenly felt cold all over. And his bowels were feeling loose – it was Ypres all over again.

They were going to kill him. Why? It had to be Rudolf Geruschke, but why? All he'd done was take an interest in an old friend. He hadn't even kicked up a real fuss. Not yet anyway, and certainly not with Geruschke. So why?

And then he realised. He had turned up at the man's nightclub. He hadn't even heard of Geruschke until that evening, let alone known of his connection with Kuzorra. But Geruschke didn't know that. And someone – Irma most likely – must have told him that Russell was a journalist.

Even so.

How had they known where to find him? Had someone at Camp Cyclop put in a call, and told them he was heading back into town?

But what the hell did that matter? They had found him, and now they were going to kill him. In Kyritz Wood, wherever the hell that was. But first they would stop at a factory. He might get a chance there. If they ever let him out of the trunk.

He had a sudden memory of the Saint in similar circumstances. *The Saint in New York* was the book, one of Paul's childhood favourites. Two of Dutch Kuhlmann's hoodlums had driven the Saint to a wood in New Jersey – it was amazing how much he remembered of the story. The Saint got away of course, but only because the love interest showed up in the nick of time to distract his would-be killers.

That wouldn't happen this time. No one else knew where was. No one except Geruschke.

How far had they gone? He couldn't see his watch, but reckoned they'd been driving about twenty-five minutes. They were still in the city.

He'd been dicing with disaster for six years now, but the thought of surviving the best that Hitler and Stalin could throw at him, and then falling victim to some jumped-up profiteer, was more than a little galling.

And they would bury him in the wood, he realised. From Effi's point of view, he would simply have vanished. She might guess who was responsible for his disappearance, but she could never be sure, of either his death or his probable killer. At the very least, he had to find some way of reporting his own demise. A message of some sort.

Searching his pockets he realised how much of a rush he'd left in that morning. His pen was still on Thomas's desk. Some reporter.

His abductors were conversing again. He could hardly credit it – they were not only talking football, but both seemed to be fellow-Hertha supporters.

The car made another turn, and was suddenly bumping over less even ground. Had they reached the factory?

He told himself he had to be ready, to take a chance if it came, to make himself one if none did. Easy words. The phrase 'hanging by a thread' had never carried more weight. He needed some sort of plan, but his mind was a raging blank.

The car stopped, bouncing a little as the two men got out. The lid of the trunk lifted up, revealing a row of far-away skylights. 'Raus,' the gun-man said. 'Out,' he added in translation, looking pleased with himself.

They had no idea he spoke German, Russell realised – they'd been ordered to kill an American, and had made the assumption that he only spoke English. Was there any way of using the mistake against them? He couldn't think of one.

Back on his feet, he felt more than a little unsteady. If he tried to run he'd only get about two metres. Not that there was anywhere to run to.

Shrill Voice was sliding shut the door they'd come through, and there was no other obvious exit.

The car had drawn up in one of four loading docks, and a lorry with US Army markings occupied another. Crates and other containers were stacked along the side walls of the platform, and a long, glassed-in office space lined the back.

Scarred Man gestured him towards the open rear of the lorry.

'I need a piss before we go,' Shrill Voice told his partner.

'Okay.'

Shrill Voice was halfway to the office when a telephone started to ring. 'Should I answer it?' he shouted back.

Scarface grimaced. 'I suppose so.'

Russell could hear the high-pitched voice from thirty metres away, but not what was being said. Was this the moment to throw himself at the other man? If the bastard had any reflexes at all, he would empty the gun before Russell reached him, but would there be a better chance?

There might.

There might not.

And Shrill Voice was on his way back. 'Change of plan,' he told his partner, three short words that almost caused Russell's heart to explode. 'We've got to take him back to town.'

'And do what with him?'

'Let him go.'

'What! Why for fuck's sake? That's another hour's driving. We won't get back from Rostock until God knows when.'

'He didn't give me his reasons,' Shrill Voice said sarcastically.

'Why didn't you say we'd already killed him?'

'I didn't think of it.'

Scarred Man looked angrily at Russell. 'Well, it's too late now.' He waved the gun towards the Mercedes. 'I thought the fucking phone was out of order,' he added, apparently to himself.

'What's happening?' Russell asked in English, as if he had no idea.

Scarred Man lifted his gun, and for a second Russell thought he might use it. But the man just shook his head. 'You one lucky bozo,' he said in English, a quote no doubt from a Hollywood movie.

Russell climbed back into the trunk, trying to look bemused. Once the lid was down it was all he could do not to cry out with joy. He felt almost hysterical. If the phone had rung ten minutes later – or if some sweetheart of a Telefunken engineer hadn't got their line working – he'd been halfway to Kyritz Wood. Some day he'd have to drive out there. The place he hadn't been shot and buried.

He couldn't remember a nicer trip in a trunk.

The return journey seemed shorter, but that didn't surprise him. When the car eventually stopped, there was a long wait before the trunk was opened. Clambering out, he discovered why – they were parked at the side of the Chaussee, in the middle of the Tiergarten. His abductors had been waiting for an empty road.

He thought he should say something, but couldn't think what, so he just started walking. He heard the slam of the door, and the purr of the motor as the Mercedes pulled away. He felt like falling to his knees and kissing the bare earth, but wasn't sure how he'd ever get back to his feet.

A last game of chess

Russell was still wondering why as he worked his way round the flak towers and down past the Zoo. Why had Geruschke – or someone else – decided he needed killing? And what had changed his mind?

He was waiting for a bus on the Ku'damm when he remembered Fritsche's young colleague. Luders might have useful things to say about the way these people operated, and Fritsche should have his address. The café he used as an office was only a short walk away.

Fritsche was sitting in his usual seat, hands resting intertwined on the table, staring into space. He looked up with a jerk when Russell loomed over him, and the momentary flash of fear was hard to miss.

'Has something happened?' Russell asked.

'It's Luders. He was beaten up in the street last night. Badly. An arm and a leg broken. He's in the hospital.'

'Christ. Does he know who it was?'

'No, but he can guess.'

'Has he – has anyone – brought the police in?'

Fritsche managed a wan smile. 'The hospital doctor insisted, but he needn't have bothered. There's nothing to go on, and even if there was...' He shrugged.

'How is he?'

'In a lot of pain. They're low on morphine at the Elisabeth – only the very worst cases are given any. Half the ward seemed to be screaming when

I went in this morning – it sounded like the end of a battle.' Fritsch seemed to take in Russell's appearance for the first time. 'You look like you've seen a ghost yourself.'

'My own.' He told Fritsche what had had happened that morning: the news of Kuzorra's death, his own abduction and unlikely reprieve.

Fritsch shook his head in wonder. 'Someone up there likes you. But the men who took you – they sound like American gangsters. They take people for "rides", don't they?'

'So did the Gestapo.'

'True. So who have you annoyed?' Fritsche wondered out loud.

Russell felt reluctant to name him. 'The same bastard as Luders, I think. Maybe I should go and see the boy in hospital, compare notes.'

Fritsche grunted. 'I don't think that's a good idea. If anyone's watching it'll look like a council of war, and Luders can't even sit up in bed, let alone defend himself. Once he's back on his feet I'm sure the young idiot will be happy to join forces. The two of you can sign a mutual suicide pact.'

'I'd rather not.'

'Good. Walk away, that's my advice. Situations like this, all sorts of diseases are bound to be rife. And there's precious little you can do about it until the situation changes. As long as you have a black market you'll have people like Rudolf Geruschke. Once it disappears, so will he.'

'And in the meantime?'

'In the meantime, we live with the guilt of watching better men go down in flames.'

Russell admired the clarity, but not the world-view.

Back on the pavement, he found his knees were still shaky, and spent a few moments leaning against a convenient lamp post, wondering what to do next. Was there any point in going to the police or the occupation authorities? The pair who'd marched him out of the station were probably genuine soldiers, but was it worth looking for them? There were upward of ten thousand British troops in Berlin, and even if he found this particular duo it would only be his word against theirs.

There was certainly no point in openly declaring war on Geruschke –

the man would hang him out for the crows. But he couldn't just let him get away with it – he owed Kuzorra too much for that. He would stay out of the ring for a while, let Geruschke believe he'd been scared – not difficult, that – and then, very quietly and carefully, start amassing evidence. It might take a while, but he and maybe Luders would take the bastard down with good old-fashioned journalism.

A communal canteen offered itself, and he exchanged some ration stamps for a bowl of surprisingly tasty vegetable soup. 'I'm alive,' he told his reflection in the washroom mirror. 'But Kuzorra isn't,' the reflection retorted.

A bus dropped him off on Dahlem's Kronprinzenallee, and he walked back through the suburban streets to Thomas's house, eyes peeled for any sign that he was being followed. Berlin felt less safe than it had that morning.

Once home, he shut himself up in his and Effi's room. Feeling suddenly cold, he lay down under the blankets. He began to shiver, and realised that the shock was wearing off. An hour later, when Effi came in, he was more or less recovered, but she immediately knew that something had happened.

She listened aghast as he told her what. 'And this was the man who had Kuzorra killed?' she asked, after holding him tight for a minute or more.

'I don't know for certain. It could have been someone with a personal grudge that we don't know about – Kuzorra must have made enough enemies in his years at the Alex. But Geruschke was the one he was after.'

'And you weren't?'

'No, I just visited Kuzorra. All I can think is, I went to the Honey Trap before I knew Kuzorra had been arrested – I was looking for Otto, but Geruschke might think that was a cover story, that I was already investigating him when I heard about Kuzorra, and that I went to see Kuzorra because I hoped he could tell me more. So first he killed Kuzorra and then he came for me.'

'But changed his mind,' Effi said doubtfully.

'Yes. It doesn't make sense.'

'Perhaps they were only trying to scare you,' she suggested hopefully.

'If they were, it worked. But no, they were really annoyed when someone told them to bring me back.'

'Were they wearing masks or anything? Would you know them again?'

'Oh yes.'

'The police could watch the nightclub for them.'

Russell shook his head. 'The police are a broken reed at the moment. Even if they wanted to help, I don't think there's anything they could do. I think my best bet is to lay low for a while.'

She gave him a who-are-you-kidding look. 'Really?'

'For a while – yes, really. I'm sure Kuzorra wouldn't want me to throw myself on his pyre.'

'No, he wouldn't. And if you change your mind I want to hear about it before you do anything risky, all right?'

'Okay,' Russell said, taking her into his arms. They held each other so tightly that the phrase 'like there's no tomorrow' popped into his head. 'So what have you been doing?' he eventually asked her.

'Rushing around. We're actually starting filming tomorrow. At Babelsberg, believe it or not.'

'That's great.'

'Yes, yes it is.' She heard the lack of conviction in her own voice, and wondered why that was. It *was* wonderful to be in at the beginning of something so important. She was so lucky. She'd had an extraordinary life, with and without him. But now she wanted something else for the two of them, something that seemed more impossible each day – an ordinary life.

'But?' he asked.

She shook her head. 'John, what are we going to do?'

'I don't know. Something'll come up – it always has.'

There was a knock on the door. It was Thomas, come to tell Russell that he had a visitor.

'Who?'

'A British soldier.'

'I'll come down.'

Frau Niebel was guarding the hall, the visitor still poised on the stoop. He was wearing a Jewish Brigade uniform. 'You are John Russell?' he asked in English. 'Wilhelm Isendahl gave me your name and address, and since I was leaving Berlin this evening, I thought I would take a chance on finding you at home.'

'I'm glad you did. Please, come in.'

The visitor watched Frau Niebel scuttle away. 'Is there somewhere private we can talk?'

'Use my study,' Thomas suggested.

Russell ushered the man in and shut the door behind them.

'My name is Hersch,' the man began. He was about thirty, Russell guessed, with deeply tanned skin and dark, almost racoon-like eyes. 'As you can see, I'm an officer in the British Army' – he allowed himself a wry smile – 'but I'm here on behalf of the Haganah. I assume you know who we are?'

'The defence force of the Palestinian Jews.'

'Yes. And you, I believe, have proved yourself a friend of the Jews.'

It seemed easiest just to nod.

'We have a proposition for you. You know about the flight route to Palestine?'

'Isendahl gave me a primer.'

'Would you like to write about it?'

'Very much, but why would you want the publicity?'

Hersch smiled for the first time, and looked about ten years younger. 'To give the survivors hope. To encourage them to join us. To tell the world that the Jews have seized control of their own lives, and that we're no longer willing to submit.'

'All good reasons. But won't you also be making it easier for the authorities to stop you?'

'We will expect you to keep some secrets, to change the names of people and places.'

'I can do that.'

'Then I think we have a deal.' He reached inside his tunic pocket for a crumpled piece of paper, and handed it across. 'You must reach Vienna by Monday if you want to be sure of joining the next group. If you arrive any later, then you may have to wait for the one after that. If you contact that person at that address, then everything will be arranged for you.'

* * *

It was almost light next morning when he watched Effi walk out to the waiting single-decker. According to her, the Russians had provided the vehicle to carry the film cast and crew to and fro, but Russell recognised the familiar outline of an American school bus. It chugged off down the otherwise silent street, spewing dark clouds of exhaust into the grey dawn.

No one seemed to be watching the house, neither then nor later, when he walked to the Press Club for an American breakfast. He picked up his allowance of cigarettes before leaving, and handed out a few to the feral-looking urchins who loitered outside the gates. The first word of the 'No Germans Allowed' sign had been obliterated with a wodge of something brown.

Back in Thomas's study, he wrote accounts of his conversations with the three KPD men. He couldn't actually remember whether Shchepkin had asked for written reports, but a material record seemed less prone to distortion than some NKVD version of Chinese Whispers. He gave Kurt Junghaus and Uli Trenkel the clean bills of political health that their loyalty undoubtedly warranted, and felt slightly worried that the NKVD would find such trust suspicious. His report on Ströhm was more nuanced, admitting the man's support for a 'German path to socialism' while stressing his belief in party discipline. Ströhm, he said, would argue his case with intelligence, but accept those decisions that went against him.

'Neither yes-man nor no-man,' Russell murmured to himself. A comrade of the old sort.

He had abandoned the notion of telling Ströhm about his vetting job, deciding instead on a more generic warning. He would say that a Soviet acquaintance had been asking questions, and that he had told this fictitious character what he was in fact reporting to Nemedin. This would warn Ströhm that he was being watched, yet leave Russell's own role looking peripheral.

He put the reports to one side, and leafed through his notes on the DP camps and their Jewish inmates. He had enough for a thoroughly depressing feature – the Western Allies seemed lost for a plan where the surviving Jews were concerned, and the Poles were making matters worse by driving their survivors out. The uplifting news would have to come later, if Hersch and his colleagues proved suitably inspirational.

After two hours at the typewriter, he went back to the Press Club for lunch, and sat listening to a bunch of young journalists at the next table discussing the new United Nations. The Senate in Washington had just voted to join the organisation, and most of the journalists seemed less than impressed. 'United Nations, my arse,' as one man elegantly phrased it.

Another two hours and he had fifteen hundred words for Solly to sell. It was just like the old days, he thought – him at a typewriter, Effi out on set. He walked to Kronprinzenallee for a third time, and left the finished article for Dallin to forward. With any luck it might reach London before Christmas.

He hadn't been home long when the Soviet bus dropped Effi off. In the old days they would have walked down to one of their favourite restaurants on the Ku'damm, window-shopping on the way. Now they had to settle for Thomas's favourite communal canteen, with only ruins to inspect. So many buildings had been hollowed out, their walls left scorched but standing, their blown-out windows like eyeless sockets.

Effi had enjoyed her day's work, but it was hard to stay cheerful in such surroundings.

Russell asked if she knew how long the filming would take.

'Four weeks is what they're saying, but I can't see it – it takes half the day to pick everyone up.'

'Oh for the days of the studio limo.'

'It had its uses. And anyway, four weeks will take us up to Christmas. I was hoping to spend that with Rosa.'

'Has she ever celebrated Christmas?'

'I don't know. Now you mention it, I don't suppose she has.'

'So will you go back in January?' Russell asked.

She gave him a look. 'For a few days at least. I wish we both could. Do spies get holidays?'

'Who knows? Sometimes I feel like telling them all to do their worst. They *might* agree to let me go.'

'They might not. And I'd rather be visiting Rosa in London than you in prison. Or putting flowers on your grave.'

* * *

Thursday morning, Russell was back in the Soviet zone, hoping to see the last two comrades before his meeting with Shchepkin the following day. Leissner's office was at Silesian Station, but the man himself was in Dresden, dealing with some undefined railway emergency, and wouldn't be back until the weekend. Manfred Haferkamp, the only man on his list without an administrative job, was at his desk in the newspaper office, but too busy to see Russell before the afternoon.

It was a reasonable morning for December, bright but not too chilly, and after scrounging a coffee in the office canteen Russell walked on up Neue Königstrasse towards Friedrichshain, checking the various notice boards for any mention of Otto or Miriam. He came across several of Effi's messages, but no one had added anything useful.

He walked past several 'antique stores' selling salvage from bombed-out apartments. A couple of trackless tank hulks faced each other across the next junction, and a group of Soviet soldiers were taking turns having their picture taken in front of one, arm in arm with a young German woman. She was either enjoying herself or putting on a good act. On the other side of the street two white-haired German men were staring stony-faced at the changing tableaux, almost pulsing with repressed rage.

Realising Isendahl's flat was nearby, Russell decided on a visit. He doubted he'd find anyone better informed when it came to the local Jews and communists, and a journalist should cultivate his sources.

Isendahl had obviously been writing – a cigarette was burning in the ashtray by the typewriter – but seemed pleased to be interrupted. 'I tried to call you,' was the first thing he said after bringing Russell in. 'Is your telephone out of order?'

'It comes and goes.'

'Well there's someone to meet you.'

'Hersch? He came round a couple of evenings ago.'

Isendahl picked up his cigarette. 'No, not Hersch. You remember the group I told you about – the Nokmim?'

'Who could forget?'

'There are two of them in Berlin. And they'd like to talk to an American journalist.'

'It seems to be catching,' Russell said wryly.

Isendahl smiled. 'It's a propaganda war for the Jewish soul. Revenge, Palestine or the good life in America.'

'I know which I'd choose.'

'You're not Jewish.'

'True. You didn't include remaining in Berlin on your list of options.'

'No. A few may stay, but...' He shook his head. 'Would you?'

'Probably not, but Berlin will be the poorer.'

'Without doubt.'

Something suddenly occurred to Russell. 'Why are the Nokmim here? Are they planning some spectacular act of vengeance?'

'You'll have to ask them that. If you want to meet them, that is.'

Russell knew an ethical minefield when he saw one, but it was too good an opportunity to turn down. 'I do,' he told Isendahl.

'There'll be restrictions, of course. This has to be a secret meeting – they don't want the authorities to know they're here in Berlin.'

'Of course,' Russell agreed. It would, he realised, depend on what they intended. If the Nokmim told him they had plans to execute some deserving Nazi, then he could probably live with keeping it off the record. But if they outlined plans to poison the city's water supply, then they could hardly expect him to hold his tongue. Anything in between, he would play it by ear. 'When do they want to meet?'

'Tonight's a possibility.'

'They're not far away then?'

'No.'

'Where do they want to meet?'

Isendahl shrugged. 'Here?'

'Suits me.' He gave Isendahl a quizzical look. 'You haven't made up your mind about these people, have you?'

'No. At first I thought they were crazy, but I'm not so sure any more. Or maybe their craziness just seems more appropriate than other people's sanity.'

Russell looked at him. 'How about you? Have you ruled out any of the options on your list?'

'Not really. I'm beginning to think certainty died with the Nazis.'

* * *

Manfred Haferkamp would not have agreed. He looked younger than his thirty-five years, which spoke well of his constitution after spending the last seven in Soviet and Nazi prison camps. He had light brown hair and bright blue eyes, and an air of absolute certainty that Lenin's buddies would have found familiar.

The other interviewees had all mentally poked and prodded at Russell's cover story, but Haferkamp just took it for granted that the world would be interested in what he was thinking. Russell had tried and failed to find some innocent means of introducing the subject of Stalin's betrayal – the handing over to Hitler in 1941 of some fifty KPD victims of the Great Purges, Haferkamp included – but he needn't have bothered. The German brought it up himself, and the ironic nature of the disclosure failed to conceal the residual bitterness.

He was nothing if not consistent in his view of the Soviets. The task of German communists was the same as it always had been – to mount a real revolution and build a communist Germany. And who was standing in their way? Their supposed allies. The Soviets wanted the Party in charge but no real change; what was needed was the people in charge and a real transformation. The Anti-Fascist committees which had sprung up all over Germany were communist-inclined and truly popular, which was why the Soviets were trying to squash them.

Russell played devil's advocate – surely no one expected the Soviets to grant the KPD free rein, or not this soon at any rate? Not after the Germans had killed twenty million Soviet citizens.

'I don't expect them to ever do so of their own accord,' was Haferkamp's reply. 'We have a real fight on our hands.'

'Do other comrades share this view?'

'Most of them, I'd say.'

'And the leadership?'

Haferkamp made a disdainful noise. 'The ones who came back from Moscow are just stooges.'

'All right, but they still have to counter your arguments. And haven't they said that they support a German road to socialism?'

'They give it lip service, nothing more. And they don't counter our arguments, or not in any constructive sense. They just throw insults about. The last piece I wrote, they accused me of "left-wing infantilism". There was no discussion of the real issues.'

Russell noted with relief that Haferkamp had already aired his views in public. His report wouldn't tell the NKVD anything they didn't already know.

He asked if there was any chance of a home-grown challenge to the KPD's current pro-Soviet leadership.

'It's bound to happen eventually. These people have been away too long. Listen, this is the German Communist Party, not some provincial branch of the CPSU. We fought against Hitler and, if we have to, we'll fight against Stalin.'

Russell couldn't resist one more question. 'A statement like that would get you arrested in Moscow. Aren't you worried that the same will happen here?'

Haferkamp's blue eyes were cold and determined. 'I've spent half my life in prison or exile. I'm not afraid of either.'

Russell thanked him for his time, and walked out into the night. He couldn't fault the sense of anything Haferkamp had said, but he still hadn't liked him. The man might be sincere in his political convictions, but they weren't what drove him on. He might have been a good comrade once, but the Nazis and Soviets had taken their toll, and his heart was running on empty.

He was also backing the losing side. Russell wondered what an old communist like Brecht would find to admire in the current KPD leadership. Maybe nothing. It would explain why he hadn't come back from America.

It was still only five – he had two hours to kill before his meeting with Isendahl's 'Jewish Avengers'. The name made him smile, which was probably not the effect they were hoping for.

He found a small bar behind the wreckage of the old Reich Statistical Office – the pre-war press corps had called it Fiction Central – and exchanged a pack of cigarettes for a glass of alleged bourbon. The only other customers were two Red Army soldiers, and they were engrossed in a game of chess. The barman disappeared out back in response to a woman's summons, leaving Russell to idly skim through the Soviet-sponsored *Tägliche Rundschau* that someone had left on the bar. It was full of poems and short stories, and almost devoid of politics. A reader from Mars might reasonably conclude that sponsoring the arts was the Russians' main reason for being in Berlin.

Well, no one could make that mistake with the British or Americans.

Two 'bourbons' and two excellent short stories later, he was ready for the Nokmim.

When he reached Isendahl's building, the man himself was standing in the doorway, smoking a cigarette. 'We're meeting in a café,' he announced, crushing the stub under his foot. 'It's not far.'

It was three streets away, in the candlelit basement of a bombed-out house, and felt more like somebody's kitchen than a commercial establishment. There were two Nokmim waiting for them, and rather to Russell's surprise one was a young woman. She seemed to have blonde hair – it was hard to be sure in the gloom – and probably blue eyes too.

Her companion, a man of similar age, had a mass of frizzy hair which stuck out at the sides, and gave him the look of a wind-blown cedar. His piercing stare reminded Russell – somewhat inappropriately – of the happily departed Führer.

Isendahl introduced them – the man's name was Yeichel, the woman's Cesia – and then sat off to one side, rather in the manner of an umpire.

'What would you like to tell me?' Russell asked the two of them.

'You ask the questions,' Yeichel said. 'Isn't that how it works?'

'Okay. Tell me about the Nokmim? Who are you? What are your aims?'

Yeichel man smiled for the first time, and it lit up his face. 'Do you know Psalm 94?' he asked.

'Not that I remember.'

'He will repay them for their iniquity, and wipe them out for their wickedness; the Lord our God will wipe them out.'

'The Nazis, I assume. So if God has them in his sights, where do you come in? Are you God's instruments?

'Not at all. If there is a God, he has clearly abandoned the Jews. We will do the work that he should have done.'

'And wipe out the Nazis.'

'That is the intention.'

Cesia seemed about to add something, but apparently thought better of the idea.

'Have many of you are there?' Russell asked.

'A hundred or so. Perhaps more by now.'

'And you have a leader?'

'Our leader's name is Abba Kovner. He is from Vilna. He was the leader of the ghetto uprising there, and the commander of the partisan army in Rudnicki Forest.'

'Where is he now?'

'We cannot tell you that.'

'And the rest of the group?'

'All across Europe. Wherever Nazis or their friends can be found.'

'And you plan to wipe them out?'

'We plan to kill as many as possible.'

Russell found himself imagining an army of 19th-century Russian anarchists carrying out coordinated bombings. 'How?' he asked.

'However we can.' Yeichel made a face. 'And when we strike, you will have the answer to your question.'

Russell paused to marshal his thoughts. 'Why are you telling me this?' he asked. The answer seemed obvious, but he wanted to hear it from them.

'The world must know who was responsible, and why.'

'You want me to explain your actions after the event. Like a spokesman. But I can't promise to dress it up the way you want me to. I understand your desire for vengeance, but that doesn't make it a good idea. Some might accuse you of acting like Nazis.'

'So we should turn the other cheek?' Cesia asked, speaking for the first time. 'We are not Christians,' she added contemptuously.

'No,' Russell agreed.

'Look around this city,' Yeichel said calmly. 'Everywhere you turn, there are Nazis resuming their old lives as if nothing had happened. No one is going to punish them.'

'We are living in the ruins of their capital.'

'Oh, the Germans have been punished for invading other countries. But not for what they did to us. Read the reports from Nuremberg – the Jews are hardly mentioned.'

'We are the lucky ones,' Cesia said bitterly. 'We survived when millions didn't, and we owe them a debt. One day we will have homes and families and jobs again, but our war will not be over until that debt is paid. Until then we belong to the dead.'

'And when do you think that might be?'

'Soon,' Yeichel told him. 'We have a homeland to build in Palestine, so our business here cannot take long.'

Russell could think of other questions, but he wanted away from the two of them, from her burning resentment and his chilling self-righteousness. Haferkamp would have fitted right in.

Three corroded souls.

Interview over, he and Isendahl walked back down to Neue Königstrasse. 'What do you think they're planning?' Russell asked his companion, not really expecting an answer.

'I don't know. But... I have a Jewish friend – this is off the record, all right?'

'Okay.'

'This friend is also in a group – they call themselves the Ghosts of Treblinka. Or just the Ghosts. And they look for ex-Nazis. Not the sort who just joined the Party out of greed or fear, but men who killed Jews, or sought profit from their deaths. Men they could turn over to the Occupation authorities with a reasonable expectation of punishment.'

'Sounds admirable.'

'But they don't turn them over,' Isendahl continued. 'They dress up as British soldiers, tell these men they're arresting them, and then drive them out into the countryside. When they reach their destination, they tell the Nazi that they're Jews, and execute him.'

'Ah.' Russell found himself wondering whether the Ghosts made use of Kyritz Wood. 'You think the Nokmim are planning something similar?'

'No. I told Cesia about these people, and she hated what they were doing. She said they were treating the Nazis as individuals, which was not how the Nazis had treated the Jews. She said the Nazis should be killed the way the Jews were killed. Anonymously, impersonally. On an industrial scale.'

'Of course,' Russell murmured. 'Gas?' he wondered out loud. 'Poison in the water? But where would they find that many Nazis?'

'In a prison camp.'

'Did they tell you that?'

'No, it just seems logical.'

It did. And almost just. Almost. 'And you're happy to let them get on with it?'

'Happy overstates it,' Isendahl admitted, 'but then again, I'm not in the business of rescuing Nazis. Are you?'

It was a fair enough question. And the answer, Russell realised, was no.

* * *

Effi was already asleep by the time he got home, and already gone when he woke in the morning. In the old days he would have made his leisurely way down to Kranzler's on Unter den Linden, read the papers, sipped his way through at least one cup of excellent coffee, and basked in the life of a freelance journalist in Europe's most exciting city. But that was then – he was, he realised, dwelling more in the past than was healthy. Maybe ruins encouraged nostalgia.

He was not looking forward to meeting Shchepkin, and realised that was unusual. Asking himself why, he decided that he'd always seen himself as a self-employed, independent sort of spy. A permanent place on Stalin's payroll evoked very different feelings.

The sun was shining as he emerged from the Potsdamerplatz U-Bahn station, but the chill in the air was appreciably sharper than on the previous day. The home of Europe's first traffic lights was still a wreck, but several reconstruction gangs were at work behind the shattered facades of the perimeter, the dust from their efforts hanging red in the bright blue sky.

Russell walked up the old Hermann-Göring-Strasse and into the Tiergarten. The open-air market seemed as popular as ever, and would doubtless remain so until the occupation authorities created the conditions for something more legal. As he arrived, he noticed two women proudly bearing away a precious square of glass. Berliners were only allowed to glaze one room per dwelling, but people were travelling out into the country, removing windows from their own or others' cottages, and bringing them back to the city to sell.

Shchepkin appeared halfway through his second circuit, and the two of them retired to the same bench as last time.

Russell placed his copy of the *Allgemeine Zeitung* between them.

'Your report is inside?'

'Uh-huh.'

'Anything else worth reading?' Shchepkin asked, looking down at the American-sponsored newspaper.

'There's an article about the adoption of orphans. It seems that Germans prefer them blond.'

'That's hardly news.'

'No.' Perhaps the Nokmim were right, Russell thought.

'So have you seen all five men?'

'Not Leissner. He's out of town. He'll be back this weekend, but I'm leaving town myself, so he'll have to wait.'

'Where are you going?'

Russell explained about the Haganah offer. 'You did say you wanted a working journalist.'

'We do. And I'm sure that Leissner can wait. So what about the others?'

Russell went through the list. 'Junghaus and Trenkel – the planner and the propagandist – you won't have any trouble with either of them. Ströhm will argue for what he thinks is right, but only until a decision has been made. He'll always accept Party discipline because he can't imagine life outside the Party. Haferkamp is a bomb waiting to go off, but I assume you know that already – he told me he'd published an article outlining his views.'

'It was only just brought to our attention,' Shchepkin said. 'The German comrades like to keep their disputes to themselves.'

'Even Ulbricht's pro-Soviet bunch?'

'Especially them. They're afraid that opposition in their own ranks reflects badly on themselves.'

'Well Haferkamp's only a journalist. Maybe the Party could find him a job in the sports department.'

'Maybe.' He gave Russell an enigmatic smile. 'I hope you've been completely honest in your appraisals.'

'Of course I have,' Russell lied. 'There seemed no point in anything else. A man like Haferkamp has no future in the KPD – he just hasn't realised it yet. He'll be happier filing football reports.'

'And the names we provided for Fräulein Koenen?'

'She says they're pathetically grateful to your people for the chance to make their film, and that they hardly ever mention politics – just the occasional anti-American gibe. And that when they remember they belong to the Party, no one could be more loyal.'

Shchepkin snorted. 'The worst kind – when people like that wake up, they always get really angry. But thank you, and thank Fräulein Koenen.' He tapped his fingers on the folded newspaper. 'Have you given the Americans a copy?'

'Not yet, but I will.' He would have to give Dallin the same report, just to be on the safe side – he had no idea how much information the Americans shared with the British, and he hadn't forgotten Shchepkin's warning of Soviet moles in MI5 and MI6. He could always give the Californian a fuller verbal report. 'The Americans have found a task for me,' he told Shchepkin. 'Have you ever heard of a chemist named Theodor Schreier?' he asked, half hoping that the Russian would say no.

'Yes,' Shchepkin answered, clearly interested.

'Well the Americans want him, and they've more or less ordered me to go and fetch him.'

'Alone?'

'I doubt it. They're hoping you can find out how well he's being guarded.'

Shchepkin seemed lost in thought for some time.

'Well?' Russell asked eventually.

'Yes, we're sitting on Schreier. He's agreed to work in our country, in Yaroslavl, if I remember correctly. His laboratory is being packed up for moving. I don't know the details, but the procedure is the same in all such cases – two men with him around the clock, in three shifts. For his protection,' the Russian added wryly.

'That doesn't sound good,' Russell observed.

'Mmm, no. But why? – that's the question. The Americans must have a thousand Schreiers. Just to deny us, I suppose. Why are they being so petty?'

Russell let that go. 'I've been wondering whether this has more to do with me – or us – than Schreier. I think they're testing us. Giving us a chance to prove our loyalty.'

'You're learning,' Shchepkin said. 'And speaking of proving our loyalty, I'll have something for them in a few weeks. But in the meantime...'

'Can you help me?'

'I don't see how. And I will have to tell Nemedin about this.'

'Why, for God's sake?'

'Because our lives will be forfeit if he hears it from somebody else. We can't assume you're his only American source.'

Russell supposed not.

'It depends on how important Schreier is,' Shchepkin went on, 'whether we really need his skills or might just find them useful. If he's expendable, then perhaps I can convince Nemedin that it's in our interests to let you take him. Your success will please your American control, and the more he trusts you, the more use you will eventually be to Nemedin. Or so he will think. You must remember,' the Russian said, turning towards him for emphasis, 'we need to keep proving our loyalty to both sides.'

Yes, Russell thought, after you through the looking glass. Shchepkin's world made him feel dizzy.

He reverted to practicalities. 'So Nemedin will remove the guards?'

'Oh no, that would make the Americans suspicious. How many men are you coming with? And when?'

'Saturday evening. No numbers have been mentioned.'

'I would send a four-man team,' Shchepkin said, as if this was the sort of operation he organised every week. 'There shouldn't be any problems, especially if the guards have been told to only offer token resistance.'

It sounded promising, until Russell remembered the original premise. 'What if Schreier *is* vital to the future of the Soviet Union?'

'Then he won't be there when you come to call. Other than that, I don't know. If I was in charge I'd put on some kind of show, and make sure you got marks for trying, but if I suggest that to Nemedin he'll find some reason to do something else. He doesn't trust me any better than he trusts you.'

'That's almost an honour. So let me get this straight – when I arrive at wherever it is I'll either find Schreier and two amenable guards or no Schreier and... what?'

'Whatever Nemedin decides. You'll be safe enough – he may not like you, but you're still his best hope of a career boost. And he's not impulsive – if he ever comes after you it won't be on a whim.'

'That's comforting. So what do I tell Dallin?'

'Just say that I thought there'd be two guards, and that if there's anything I can do to help without raising suspicions then I'll do it.'

'Okay. Now, something personal. Just before the end of the war, here in Berlin, Effi was asked to shelter a Jewish girl whose mother had just died. She's still with us, and we're trying to find out what happened to her father. His name is – or was – Otto Pappenheim, and someone of that name was given a transit visa to Shanghai via Moscow sometime in the six months before Hitler attacked you. Is there any way you could confirm that he actually took the trip? And if he did, whether he ever came back. We're not at all sure he's the right Otto Pappenheim, so knowing his age would be useful – there must have been a date of birth on the visa.'

Shchepkin had a weary look in his eyes. 'I'll do what I can,' he said.

They both got up and surveyed the crowd in front of them, as if reluctant to leave each other's company.

'I don't suppose you've uncovered any useful secrets lately,' Russell said.

'No, not yet.'

* * *

An hour or so later Russell was sitting in Scott Dallin's office. In future, Dallin told him, they would meet in less official surroundings – the Grunewald seemed conveniently close. Two reasons were offered. First, that 'the Russians might know, but we're not supposed to know that they know.' Second, that Crosby had been asking questions about Russell. His interest might be completely innocent – Crosby might simply want to recruit him – but the more separate their two organisations were, the better Dallin liked it.

Why, Russell wondered, did governments delight in creating competing intelligence organisations? They always – always – ended up spending more time fighting each other than the enemy.

'So what did Comrade Shchepkin have to say?' Dallin asked.

Russell trotted out the pre-arranged answer.

'A team of four, then' Dallin said, fulfilling Shchepkin's prophecy. 'Brad Halsey will be in command. I'll get him down here.' He reached for the internal telephone.

'And the other two?' Russell asked once he'd put it down.

'A couple of GIs.'

'Out of uniform, I assume.'

'Of course.'

'Shchepkin said that Schreier has agreed to work in the Soviet Union. What if he refuses to come with us?'

Dallin gave him a disbelieving look. 'He'll jump at the chance. Why wouldn't he?'

A thought occurred to Russell. 'It is just him? There's no wife or girl-friend? No children?'

'Not as far as I know.'

Amateurs was about right, Russell thought. 'What if there are? Should we bring them as well?'

'If he wants them to come, then yes, I suppose so.'

It didn't seem worth a debate. 'So we just bring him back on the U-Bahn, and deposit him where?'

'That'll be up to Brad.'

Russell supposed it would be. He himself was on probation, useful if they got lost, but otherwise only along for the ride. He wondered out loud whether any of the others spoke German.

'No,' Dallin told him, causing Russell to wonder what the powers in Washington had been doing for four years. Had Germany's defeat come as a surprise?

Brad Halsey arrived. He looked and sounded like a typical Midwestern kid – athletic-looking and open-faced, with neat, almost golden brown hair – but there was someone else behind the bright blue eyes, someone the war had shut down. His opening glance was hardly friendly, causing Russell to wonder how much of his chequered past Dallin had passed on.

'I still don't have the address,' Russell told them both.

'It's in Friedrichshain,' Halsey answered. 'Lippehner Strasse 38. Do you know it?'

'I know the street,' Russell told him. 'And it must be almost two kilometres from the nearest U-Bahn station.'

'That won't be a problem. But we need somewhere close by for a rendezvous point. The less time we spend as a group, the less chance the Russians will notice us.'

Halsey might be a cold fish, but he clearly wasn't a fool. 'The western entrance to Friedrichshain Park,' Russell suggested. 'It's about a five minute walk away.'

'Sounds good.'

Dallin also nodded his agreement. 'And the time?'

'Eight o'clock?' Halsey suggested. The eyes glittered at the prospect.

* * *

Effi was still awake when he arrived home, but only just. 'If we stay in, I'll be asleep in an hour,' she told him. 'Let's go out.'

'Okay, but where? Do you have any suggestions?' Russell asked Thomas, who had followed him in.

'The cabaret on Königin-Luise-Platz is pretty good, and it's not that far to walk. The Ulenspiegel is better, but...'

'Where's that?' Effi asked.

'On Nürnberger Strasse.'

'Too far,' Russell said. 'Will you come with us?' he asked Thomas.

'Yes, why not? I was going to write to Hanna, but I can do that in the morning.'

'Have you heard from her?' Effi said. 'How are they?'

'Fine. Well, fed up with the country. And... other things. Hanna and her mother, really. They always got on well enough for a few days, but after a year... I think the strain is beginning to tell. She wants to come home, and so does Lotte.'

'That's good news,' Russell said.

'You'll need us to move out,' Effi realised.

'It won't be for weeks but, yes, I was going to talk to you about that. None of the others have anywhere to go, and I thought, well, with your connections, you won't have any trouble finding somewhere else.'

'I'm sure we won't,' Russell reassured him. 'In fact I think it's time Effi reclaimed her flat.'

'If I ever have the energy. But of course you have to make room for them. I'll look into it while you're away. Now let's go out before I keel over.'

The walk took twenty minutes. The food in the next-door café was good, the cabaret just what they needed. Some of the sketches were funnier than others, but all seemed infused with the spirit of a newer Berlin. There was little sentimentality – the new Berliner was a fourteen-year-old with her pram, explaining in verse how she'd come by her baby – exchanging sex for a Hershey bar. And there was little respect for the victors – one sketch lampooned the American decision not to screen the movie *Ninotchka* in Berlin for fear of upsetting the Russians.

The one group spared ridicule were the Nazis, which Russell found surprisingly pleasing. Some Germans at least were putting the past behind them. Walking home, he realised that he'd needed an evening like that. One with a future.

* * *

Effi was working on Saturday, and Russell found it hard not to dwell on the evening ahead. Writing anything decent proved beyond his powers of concentration, so he had a long lunch at the Press Club, and headed into the city centre. He spent a couple of hours watching Bing and Bob's *Road to Morocco* at a recently re-opened cinema off Alexanderplatz, and another couple nursing two weak beers at a bar close by. By seven-thirty he was walking slowly up the southern side of Lippehner Strasse, examining the buildings opposite.

The street had fared better than most in Friedrichshain, and No. 38 was one of five adjoining buildings spared by bombs and shells. According to Dallin, Schreier's apartment was on the third floor, the one at the front on the right. A faint light was gleaming round the edge of the windows.

Walking on, he noticed a boy of around fifteen watching him from a nearby stoop. The house behind it was a field of rubble. Keeping his eyes on the curtained windows, Russell sat down beside him. 'Would you like to earn some cigarettes?'

'Doing what? Are you some kind of pervert?'

Russell couldn't help smiling. 'I want to know about the man who lives in that apartment over there.'

'The one with the Ivans?'

'Yes.'

'What about him?'

'Is he there now?'

'How many cigarettes are we talking about?'

'A pack.'

'A whole pack?' the boy exclaimed in surprise.

Russell felt like offering a short lesson in bargaining tactics, but decided against. 'A whole pack,' he confirmed.

'So what do you want to know about him?'

'Is he there?'

'They came back about an hour ago. Him and the Ivans.'

So Nemedin had been told that Schreier was expendable, Russell thought. Which meant they were expected. He asked how many Russians there were.

'Two. It's always two. They swap over later.'

'When exactly?'

The boy shrugged. 'Who knows what the time is? The Ivans have all of the watches.'

'How do they get here? Do they walk?'

'No, they come in a jeep. They drive up, blow their horn, and wait for the two upstairs to come down. Then they go up, and the other two drive off.'

Russell took a pack of Chesterfields from his pocket and handed it over. 'Now go home,' he said.

The boy stared at his prize with glowing eyes, like a prospector finding a golden nugget. 'This is my home,' he said, and skipped away across the rubble.

By the time Russell reached the meeting point it was almost eight o'clock. The park stretched away into darkness, and would have been closed if it still had gates. He had met Wilhelm and Freya Isendahl at this entrance in the summer of 1939, and Albert Wiesner six months earlier. Albert was still in Palestine, as far as he knew.

A little way from the entrance, two men were lurking in the shadows. They looked uncomfortable in their German clothes – Dallin been obviously been shopping at one of the black markets – and grinned with relief when Russell gave them the pre-arranged password, a request for directions to Braunsberger Strasse. They introduced themselves: Vinny had the face and accent of an Italian-American from New York City, George the sort of earnest face and broad 'a's that Russell associated with Boston.

Halsey appeared out of the gloom a few seconds later, as if he'd been waiting to make his entrance. He was wearing the kind of long coat that gangsters wore in movies, and was presumably trying to look like a black marketeer. Which was fitting, Russell thought – what else were they doing that evening but trying to boost American business prospects? White marketeering, the respectable kind.

Halsey took a gun and silencer from his left coat pocket and offered it to Russell.

He only hesitated for a second – he had seen nothing to alarm him on Lippehner Strasse, but if his companions and the Russians were all carrying guns it seemed foolish to be the odd man out. If all hell did break loose he wanted to be more than a sitting duck.

He told Halsey and the two GIs what he'd discovered in the last half-hour. Halsey looked annoyed at being upstaged, but only for a moment. 'Let's get it over with before the next shift arrives. We'll walk in pairs. You two' – he indicated Vinny and George – 'keep about fifty yards behind us.'

They set off. In the old days it would have been three in the morning before the streets were this empty, but post-war Berlin went early to bed. Many dim lights were visible in the obviously habitable buildings, a few in some that looked mere shells. There was no traffic in sight, but every now and then Russell could hear a vehicle on the nearby Greifswalder Strasse. Two pedestrians passed by on the other side, both half-running, as if pursued by a curfew.

They turned into Lippehner Strasse. Halsey hadn't said a word since they started walking, but Russell could almost feel the young man's eagerness. The glitter in his eyes suggested something more, and Russell found himself wondering whether Dallin's favourite had been sampling the cocaine now readily available on Berlin's black market.

There didn't seem much point in asking.

They stopped outside Schreier's building, and waited for Vinny and George to catch up. Staring across the street, Russell thought he saw movement in the ruins, but couldn't be sure. Maybe his informer had put two and two together, and come to see the show.

The four of them went in through the front door. There were no working lamps in the hall or on the stairs, but enough light was seeping round the edges of doors to offer a modicum of visibility. The building smelled of cabbage, sweat and human waste, like most of the rest of Berlin. Music was playing somewhere up above – the sort of sultry jazz that Goebbels had found so repellent.

The stairs creaked alarmingly, causing Russell to wonder whether the house was as solid as it looked. According to Annaliese, half the people arriving at emergency rooms were the victims of collapsing walls, floors and staircases. The other half were simply starving.

They reached the third floor without mishap. A ribbon of light shone under Schreier's door, and the music was playing behind it.

'You knock,' Halsey told Russell in an exaggerated whisper. 'Pretend to be a resident complaining about the music. We need to know the situation – where Schreier is, where the Russians have their guns. Okay?'

Russell felt like asking 'why me?' but unfortunately knew the answer –

none of the others spoke German. He waited until they had disappeared up the stairs, took a deep breath, and knocked.

The music abruptly ceased.

'Who is it?' a voice asked in Russian.

'Herr Hirth,' Russell improvised. Hauptsturmführer Hirth had been his SS spymaster in the good old days.

There was no reply.

He knocked again and took a quick step sideways, just in case. Drunken Russians had a habit of shooting doors which annoyed them.

These two proved to be sober. The uniformed man who opened the door was holding a machine pistol half aloft, like someone intent on starting a race. Another slightly older man was sitting at a chessboard on the other side of the room. Both sported the pale blue shoulder insignia of the NKVD.

They looked confused, as if they'd been expecting someone else.

'Herr Schreier?' Russell said tentatively.

The Russian at the table leant back in his chair and called into the adjoining room. A few seconds later a tall thin German emerged, and gave Russell an enquiring look.

The complaining resident act seemed unconvincing, but he couldn't think of anything else. 'I was just wondering if you could turn the music down,' he said. 'My wife is sick, and she needs her sleep.'

Schreier walked across to the radio and mimed Russell's request to the watching guards, both of whom smiled their assent. The one who had answered the door was still holding the machine pistol, but its barrel was now pointed at the floor. The other man's gun was sitting on the table, beside a clutch of sacrificed pawns.

Russell made gestures of thanks and withdrew. The door closed behind him, and the music resumed at a lower volume. An accommodating NKVD – what next?

Halsey was waiting a few steps up.

Russell reported what he'd seen, and watched with alarm as Halsey screwed the silencer onto his gun. Vinny was taking position on the flight of stairs below, George holding his on the flight above.

It occurred to Russell that Halsey might not know that they were expected. 'You won't need to use that...'

'I will,' Halsey contradicted him, and the look in his eyes told Russell much more than he wanted to know.

The young American slipped away down the stairs and applied his own fist to Schreier's door. When it opened seconds later a few Russian words were abruptly cut off by the 'phhhtt' of the silenced revolver. There was a sound of tumbling furniture, another 'phhhtt', a cry of fear.

Halsey had disappeared into the apartment, and Russell reluctantly followed. The younger Russian was lying on the ragged carpet behind the door, a bloody hole where his left eye had been. His comrade was on the ground behind the table. As he struggled to get up, Halsey administered the coup de grace, a bullet in the back of the head. He was clearly a fan of the NKVD.

Russell was aghast, and obviously showed it.

'What did you think we were going to do?' Halsey asked. 'Tie them to chairs?

Something like that, Russell thought. He looked from one corpse to the other. Another two families in mourning. He hoped that neither were Nemedin favourites.

Schreier also looked in shock. 'Tell him he's coming with us,' Halsey told Russell.

He did so.

Schreier didn't look eager, which was hardly surprising. 'Where are you taking me?' he asked in a tremulous voice.

'To the American sector,' Russell told him.

Schreier shook his head, more in disbelief than refusal.

'Get whatever you want to take,' Russell said. 'You won't be coming back.'

The German went into the bedroom, and reappeared moments later with a framed photograph of a woman. 'My late wife,' he explained.

A horn sounded in the street below.

'Who the fuck's that?' Halsey asked, heading for the window. He peeled the curtain back a few inches and looked down. 'It's two Ivans in a jeep. An American jeep,' he added, as if that made their appearance even less welcome.

'The changing of the guard,' Russell guessed. He'd forgotten to tell Halsey about the horn routine, and there didn't seem much point now.

'It looks like we won't need the U-Bahn,' Halsey said. 'We'll wait for them to come up, then take the jeep.' He walked to the door and softly called the other two in. They hardly looked at the two corpses.

'What if they don't come up?' Russell asked. He didn't want two more Russians to die, but short of shooting Halsey could see no way around it. 'They won't want to leave the jeep unattended, so they'll probably wait for these two to come down.'

Halsey smiled. 'Then I guess we'll have to take their places.'

A hail of bullets was about right. 'How many Russians are you going to kill?' Russell asked. 'I thought Dallin sent us to fetch Schreier, not start World War Three.'

The horn sounded again, a touch more impatiently.

'Well they're down there, we're up here, and we have to get past them somehow. Have you got a better idea?'

'Yes. You three take Schreier down to the ground floor, and find somewhere out of sight. I'll lean out of the window, tell them there's a problem, and that I need them up here.'

'Do you speak Russian as well?' Halsey asked. It was almost an accusation.

'Enough.'

'Hmm. What if only one of them comes?'

'Then you'll have one less to deal with.' And one life saved was better than none, Russell thought but didn't say.

'And what'll you do?'

'Once they start up I'll head down a flight or two, and stay out of sight until they've gone past.'

Halsey nodded. 'Okay. Give us a couple of minutes.' He took one last look at his victims and led the others out through the door, Vinny and George clutching their guns, Schreier his photograph.

Russell was still wondering about the jeep. They'd be more exposed above ground, but it would certainly be quicker than walking to the nearest U-Bahn and waiting for a train. They'd be out of the Soviet sector in fifteen minutes, provided they weren't stopped.

He found himself looking at the dead Russians again. How were the American authorities going to explain this? He supposed they could simply deny all knowledge, but who else would have a motive for snatching Schreier and killing two NKVD men? Schreier himself was the only credible scapegoat, and if the Americans blamed him they could hardly put him to work in one of their laboratories. Or not without giving him a new identity.

The two minutes were up. He reached for the window latch just as the horn sounded again, and after a struggle managed to disengage it. He stuck out his head just as a Russian stepped out of the jeep. 'You must come up,' he shouted down, hoping that an unfamiliar voice wouldn't alert them. 'There's a problem. I'll need you both,' he added, then swiftly withdrew his head.

Please, he silently advised them, save your lives.

He closed the door behind him and hurried down the stairs, alert for the sound of feet below. Reaching the first floor, he ducked back along the passageway that led to the flats at the rear, and was just flattening himself against a wall when torchlight flickered across the ceiling. The Russians were lighting their own way up.

There were footfalls on the stairs now, so the others had not been spotted. And there were – thank the Lord – two pairs of feet ascending. Russell crouched in the darkness, and prayed no beam would shine his way.

It played on the walls in front of him, but then vanished upwards along with the feet. He waited until these reached the next landing, then descended, as swiftly and quietly as he could, to the ground floor, door and street.

The others were already on board, with Halsey and George sandwiching Schreier in the back, and Vinny at the wheel. Russell scrambled into the empty front seat, wondering why Halsey had forsaken the honour.

He soon found out. The engine burst into life, and Vinny accelerated off down Lippehner Strasse, shouting 'which way?' at him over the roar of the motor.

'Left,' he said automatically as they roared up towards the intersection with Greifswalder Strasse. Which was the best way to go? The American sector was closest, but how would they get across the Spree? When he'd walked to that stretch of the river the other day, all the bridges had still been down. The simplest route was straight along Neue Königstrasse to Alexanderplatz, crossing the Spree and Spreekanal by the Old City bridges – he knew that they were open. Then down Unter den Linden to the Brandenburg Gate, where the British zone began. The British might stop them and make a fuss, but they wouldn't shoot anybody.

Neue Königstrasse was almost empty, a late night tram brimming with passengers striking sparks in the other direction.

A nasty thought occurred to Russell. He turned to Schreier, and asked him in German whether there'd been a telephone in the apartment.

'Yes.'

'Was it working?'

'Sometimes.'

'There was a telephone,' Russell told Halsey, in response to the latter's quizzical look.

They were passing between the remains of the Statistical and Tax Offices, Vinny driving the jeep at a steady forty as they approached the brighter lights of Alexanderplatz. Back in the spring Russell had done a day's involuntary labour on this stretch of road, helping dig gun emplacements for the defence of the city.

After Neue Königstrasse, Alexanderplatz and the streets leading into it seemed almost brimming with life. Several strands of music were audible and the square itself was awash with people. Some of the men looked German, but most were wearing uniforms, and clinging on to a local girl. Judging by the high-pitched screams of delight, almost everyone was drunk, and the only thing waved at their passing jeep was a clearly empty bottle.

They swung round under the Stadtbahn bridge, drove down König-strasse's rubble-lined canyon, and crossed the Spree on the makeshift replacement for the old Kurfürsten Bridge. On the other side of the Schloss the Christmas fair in the Lustgarten offered a second oasis of life and light, the carousels gaily circling against a backdrop of ruptured stone.

Another makeshift bridge and they were slaloming down Unter den Linden, twisting this way and that through the gathered piles of rubble. A mile in the distance, the silhouette of the Brandenburg gate was hardening against the night sky. As they crossed the almost deserted Friedrichstrasse, Russell began to believe they would make it.

His confidence was short–lived. There was something up ahead, something involving movement and vehicles, between Pariserplatz and the site of the vanished Adlon Hotel. Was it a checkpoint, or just some Soviet unit doing God knows what? He could see a brazier aflame by the side of the road, several soldiers warming their hands. Two jeeps and a truck were lined up beyond.

An officer had noticed them coming, and was striding out into the road, clearly intent on pulling them over.

Russell took in the scene. The brazier suggested the Russians had been here for a while, and there was no sign that they were expecting a gang of murderous American abductors – none of the soldiers were taking cover or reaching for rifles. 'It's just a routine check,' Russell told Halsey. 'Let me handle it.'

They were about a hundred metres away now, and Vinny's foot was easing down on the brake.

'No,' Halsey said suddenly. 'Don't stop. Drive on through.'

There was no time to argue the pros and cons. Vinny did the best job he could, slowing down enough to lull the Soviet officer into a false sense of security, then ramming his foot through the accelerator. The Russian jumped aside a second too late, and cried out in pain as the wing struck his trailing leg.

The soldiers were lunging for their rifles now, and Russell hunched himself down in his seat, waiting for the first whining bullet, blessing the fate which had put him in front. It seemed an age, but then there was a sudden volley of shots, and a cry of pain from behind him. They were crossing Pariserplatz now – another hundred metres and they'd be in the British sector.

More single shots rang out, and then a burst of automatic fire. A spray of liquid bathed the back of Russell's neck, and something heavy dropped onto his shoulder. He felt the slight shift of light as they ran under the Brandenburg Gate and into the Tiergarten. The shooting had stopped.

Vinnie pulled the jeep to a halt a few hundred metres down the Chaussee, and helped Russell get out from under the body. Halsey had taken a bullet through the nose, and bits of his brain were everywhere.

Schreier was dead as well, still clutching his photograph. He had taken two bullets in the centre of the back.

A heartfelt 'fuck' was Vinny's comment on the situation. He lit a cigarette and stood there gazing out across the darkened Tiergarten.

George just shrugged, like he'd seen it all before.

Looking at the dead Halsey, Russell realised he couldn't care less. Which was a sobering thought.

The face in the cab

Russell stared out at the city below. It was probably Leipzig, which from this height looked deceptively intact. He remembered Goebbels going there and giving one of his pep talks, spouting off amidst suitably Wagnerian ruins. Victory or Siberia! It hadn't taken a genius to work that one out, even then.

He still felt worried about leaving Effi, despite all her protestations. In the war she'd learned to take care of herself – that was what she'd told him. And he knew it was true, up to a point; these days she took time to consider, rather than jump straight in. But there were a lot of careful people pushing up daisies.

The plane lurched again, and he told himself he'd be better advised worrying about his own safety. The way the DC3 rattled, it was easy to imagine the plane shaking itself to pieces on the ground, let alone in the winds now raging over Germany. The Soviet fighters which had shadowed the early part of the American flight had long since scurried back to base.

Their pilot announced that they were crossing the zonal border, and the turbulence abruptly vanished, as if it had been a Russian trick. Or perhaps the Americans had found a way of calming the winds. They had to be good at something.

He closed his eyes and re-ran his last meeting with Scott Dallin. The American had been furious. A dead chemist, a dead operative, the Soviets already raising merry hell with his superiors. All of which had been bad enough, but what apparently galled him most was the fact that he couldn't blame Russell. Vinny and George had obviously corroborated his own version of the events, and correctly identified Halsey as the author of his own demise.

'I think you'll find he was on something,' Russell had told Dallin. 'If you bother to look.'

'*On* something,' Dallin had echoed, as if Russell had chosen the wrong preposition.

'Drugs. Uppers of some sort. Cocaine would be my guess. You can get it at any nightclub.'

'We should close them all down.'

Russell had let that pass – if Dallin had his way, he'd have razed what was left of the city. His hero was probably Tamerlane. *He* had never bothered with occupations.

He smiled at the thought. At least Dallin had raised no objection to his trip. On the contrary, he had seemed only too pleased to have him out of the way.

Russell wondered how the Americans would placate the Soviets. By giving them Halsey's head on a plate, most likely. Metaphorically speaking. If the boy had parents they were in for a shock. Death *and* disgrace.

He closed his eyes again, and let the throb of the engines lull him to sleep. He was only expecting a nap, but when he finally woke more Soviet fighters were riding shotgun on either side of the Dakota, patrolling the skies above their Austrian occupation zone.

Half an hour later they were down, and taxiing to a halt outside the Schwechat Airport terminal building. Austria and Vienna, like Germany and Berlin, had been divided into four occupation zones, and Schwechat had fallen inside the capital's British sector, but civilian planes of all four powers were using the runway and other facilities.

The entry formalities were just that, and Russell's progress was only halted by the lack of a taxi or bus. On Sundays, it seemed, arriving civilians were expected to walk the eight kilometres to the city centre, and it was more than an hour before he managed to cadge a lift in a British Army jeep.

After a twenty-minute drive along mostly empty roads the driver dropped him off in the Stephansplatz, at the heart of the inner city. Russell had made several trips to Vienna in pre-Anschluss days, but the current city bore little resemblance to the one he remembered. Many of the hotels had been destroyed, and rooms were at a definite premium. It took him an hour to find one that was empty, and half an hour more to find one he could afford. This hotel was on Johannesgasse, and almost in one piece, the staircase climbing past a boarded-over rip in the wall, through which the cold wind literally whistled. His room was fine, apart from the lack of hot water.

Feeling peckish, he went out looking for a café. Vienna's centre looked in better shape than Berlin's, but not by much. There were the same, precarious-looking, lattice-like facades, the same inner walls with their scorched decorations exposed to the world. Fewer of them, perhaps, but more than Russell had expected. Either the Austrians had been daft enough to put up a real fight or the Russians had just felt like breaking things. Or both.

He eventually found a small bar. The interior reminded him of days gone by, but the same wasn't true of the coffee. There was no heating, so at least the windows were clear of steam. He sat there for half an hour, watching well-wrapped people trudge past, all looking grim as the weather.

As he walked back down Kärntner Strasse towards his hotel a jeep drove by in the opposite direction. It was flying the flags of the occupying powers, and carrying soldiers in all four uniforms. Russell had read about these international patrols in the English papers, and he wondered again how the French and Russians could bear it. A soldier's life, as he knew from the trenches, was one long stream of banter, and here they were spending their days with no one they could talk to.

* * *

Waking alone on Monday morning, Effi had the momentary sensation of being back in the house on Bismarckstrasse, with the war still underway.

The sense of relief when she realised it wasn't caused her to laugh out loud.

The Russians had announced the closure of the Babelsberg studios until Tuesday. The reason given was 'refurbishment', but what this amounted to was left unspecified – one joker among the prop boys had put his money on the installation of hidden microphones and cameras. Whatever the reason, Effi had the day off, and a chance to question the authorities about her flat on Carmerstrasse.

She was relieved that Russell had left Berlin. The exodus to Palestine seemed a good story, and few things made him happier than gnawing at one of those. Rather more importantly, it put him – or so she hoped – beyond Geruschke's reach. Russell might have presented the story of his abduction as a bad, semi-comic movie script, but she could tell how badly it had shaken him. And that had scared her. Losing him was not something she wanted to contemplate.

And then there was Otto 3, who seemed, from the little that Wilhelm Isendahl had told them, like a father who might be worth finding. She might not like the consequences, but she had to put Rosa first.

She was pleased that Hanna and Lotte wanted to come home, even though that meant that she and John would need to move out. The sooner normal life was resumed, the sooner Rosa could come home.

Though of course it would be different for her. Rosa was Jewish – that was why Effi had needed to take her in. But what did that mean for the future? Sometimes the girl's Jewishness seemed easy to ignore. Rosa had never mentioned, let alone requested, any sort of religious or cultural observance, and she had, on one or two occasions, displayed an unusually virulent atheism for a seven year-old. Though after what she and her family had been through, perhaps nothing should seem surprising.

But still. Could she and John just ignore the girl's background? Didn't it help people to know where they came from? The girl's life had been shaped by the catastrophe that the Nazis had inflicted on her people, and one day she would want to know why. If her father was found, he would raise her as a Jewish daughter.

A second pang of prospective loss was enough to drive Effi from the bed. She threw on some winter clothes and went downstairs in search of breakfast. If they did bring Rosa back, she would have the highest-grade ration card, just like herself and John. The leading actor, the journalist-spy, the 'Victim of Fascism' – Berlin's privileged few.

Half an hour later she was boarding a bus at the stop on Kronprinzenallee. Riding northward, she realised that her own doubts were gone – she wanted to stay. The filming was going well, and it felt wonderful, not just to be working again, but to be making a movie that mattered, one that might help her fellow Germans come to terms with what had happened. It felt like atonement of a sort, or the beginnings of such.

And it was good to be around Thomas again, and Ali, and Annaliese.

And John had to be here, at least until he found some way of disentangling himself from the Soviet embrace. Effi remembered him once saying that espionage was like quicksand – the more you struggled, the more you were trapped. But if anyone could wriggle his way free then he could.

The previous evening she had talked to Thomas about the flat on Carmerstrasse, and he had suggested legal help – Berlin might be short of food and housing, but lawyers were springing up like weeds. Effi knew she couldn't cast a family of refugees out onto the street, but that begged the question of who she *would* be willing to eject – whoever the current inhabitants were, they wouldn't have anywhere else to go.

She had hoped Thomas would know how the current system worked, but it seemed to vary from district to district. There had to be tens of thousands of people returning from war or exile, and only a few would be Jews. And, as Thomas had cheerfully reminded her, most of the city's property deeds had fallen victim to explosions or fire. He had advised her to start at the local town hall and see what they had to say.

She seemed to remember that their local *Rathaus* had been reduced to its constituent bricks, but, as she'd expected, enough of the front wall remained for a notice board bearing the new address.

The new offices were a ten-minute walk away, in what had once been an elementary school, and probably would be again. There were about twenty people waiting in the old lobby, but none, as she soon discovered, were there to enquire about housing. She was directed down a long corridor, still lined, somewhat surprisingly, with thematic maps of the vanished Reich, to the classroom now occupied by the Housing Office. This comprised an elderly man and woman, stationed at adjoining tables beyond several neat rows of abandoned desks.

The man made a note of her name and the Carmerstrasse address, and began working his way through the twenty or so cardboard boxes which lined the wall behind him, occasionally pausing to stretch his back. After about five minutes he emitted a grunt of surprise, which Effi rightly assumed meant success.

He brought several pieces of paper back to the table, and skimmed through them. 'This flat was confiscated by the state on February 10th, 1942', he told her. 'Ownership was forfeited following the owner's – your – arraignment for treason.' He looked over his glasses at Effi with rather more interest than he'd initially shown.

'Which means what?' Effi asked him.

He looked confused. 'Which part don't you understand?'

'I understand all of it. Are you telling me that this ruling still holds?'

'As of this moment, yes.'

'Decisions of the Nazi courts are still valid?'

'Most of them, yes. There has to be continuity.'

Effi held on to her temper. 'Are you telling me the apartment is no longer mine?'

'No, not necessarily. But I'm afraid you cannot expect to simply resume possession.'

But it's *mine*, she felt like shouting.

'You will have to apply for repossession,' he said. He was, she realised, actually trying to help.

'So I'll need a lawyer.'

He nodded. 'I would certainly recommend it.'

'Who's living there now?' she asked. 'And how long have they been there?' She would feel much better about ejecting a family who'd been gifted the apartment by the local Nazis than she would a group of refugees from the East.

'The name of the current residents is Puttkammer,' he read from his papers. 'A woman and three children. They moved in earlier this year, in March.'

Well at least they weren't Jews, Effi thought. Not then, and not with a name like that. She asked for advice on how to proceed, and gratefully watched as he wrote out a simple list of steps she needed to take, and where she should go to take them. It sounded straightforward enough, though likely to take every hour God sent. It would all have to wait until filming was over.

She thanked him and made her way back to the street. Schlüterstrasse and its cafeteria were only a short walk away, so she headed that way, hoping for lunch with Ellen Grynszpan. The former was available, the latter not, and after eating Effi started for home. But as she passed the remains of the Schmargendorf *Rathaus* on Hohenzollerndamm, it occurred to her that Zarah's house might be standing empty.

This time it was a woman she eventually spoke to. Effi explained the situation: that she was there on her sister's behalf, that Zarah and her son Lothar were in London, and that her brother-in-law was probably dead.

'Jens Biesinger?' the woman asked, reaching for a file of papers.

'Yes,' Effi agreed, somewhat surprised.

'What makes you think he's dead?'

'The last time Zarah saw him, he told her he had suicide pills for them both. That was in April, just before the Russians entered the city.'

'And she wanted to live,' the woman said drily. 'Apparently he did too.'

'You mean he's still alive?'

She was still looking at the file. 'He is indeed. And would you believe it? – he's working for us.'

'Us?'

'The District Administration. At the Housing Office.'

Effi couldn't believe it. 'And where's that?'

'On Güntzelstrasse. It's only a short walk away.'

'So he's still the legal owner of the house?'

'According to this.'

'Then I suppose I'll have to go round there,' Effi decided. She couldn't honestly say she was eager to see Jens again, but he was Lothar's father.

She walked back outside, and asked a passing boy for directions. Ten minutes later she was outside a door signed 'Jens Biesinger, Director'. Of what, it didn't say.

She knocked and a familiar voice said 'Come in.'

The expression on Jens's face passed through astonishment and pleasure before settling on apprehension. 'Effi!' he said, scrambling out of his chair and advancing for a familial embrace.

She allowed him one kiss on the cheek before shooing him back to his chair. He was wearing a remarkably shabby suit, a far cry from the Nazi uniform which Zarah had ironed about ten times a day. But he looked in better health than most Berliners, and several kilos fatter than when she'd last seen him four years before.

'What are you doing here?' she asked.

'I work here.'

Why haven't you been arrested, she wanted to ask.

'Lothar, is he alive?' There was a quiver in his voice, as if he feared the answer. 'And Zarah, of course.'

'They're both in London.'

'London!?'

'It's a long story. We've all been living there. John and I only came back last week.'

'London,' Jens repeated. 'I spent months looking for them. I never dreamed... Are they coming back too?'

'I expect so. Eventually.'

'How is Lothar? Does he ask about me? And Zarah... why hasn't she...?'

'She assumed you were dead. Or in prison. We all did.'

'Why would I be in prison?'

'Your past allegiances,' she suggested.

He looked a trifle shamefaced, but the justification was clearly well-honed. 'I was in the Party, true, but so were millions of others. I was a civil servant, after all, working for the state, so loyalty was expected. But we civil servants were not responsible for framing policies – we just did what we were told to do.'

Effi shook her head in disbelief, but he didn't seem to notice.

'Will you give me their address in London?'

'No, but I'll give her yours. And I'm sure she will write to you, for Lothar's sake. And I know he will.'

'I'm still at the old house on Taunusstrasse. In the basement, that is – there are families on the other two floors. It *is* good to see you,' he said, as if vaguely surprised by the fact.

Effi smiled, and wished she could say the same. She told herself she was being mean. Lothar, at least, would he happy to hear that his father was alive. Not to mention free as a bird.

* * *

After finding and drinking a better than expected coffee in a café just off the Stephansplatz, Russell set off with his ancient Baedeker in search of the Rothschild Hospital. Beyond Vienna's inner ring road the war damage was less extensive, and several streets seemed almost pristine. There was an obvious dearth of motor traffic – even the jeeps of the occupying forces seemed thin on the ground – and some vistas seemed more redolent of the Habsburg Empire than 1945.

The pavements outside the Rothschild Hospital were crowded with Jews. They were not, as one told Russell, intent on getting in, but were waiting for friends or relatives who might soon arrive from the east. The hospital itself had suffered some damage, but most of it seemed in use. After queuing at one of several reception desks in the old emergency room he was given directions to the Haganah office.

It was in the basement, at the other end of the long building. The corridors were jammed with people, and the rooms on either side offered a wonderful kaleidoscope of activities, from shoe repair through kindergarten lessons to full medical examinations. By the time Russell reached the Haganah office he felt as if he'd travelled through a small country.

The office was not much larger than a cupboard, but its contents seemed admirably organised. The man squeezed behind the desk introduced himself as Yoshi Mizrachi. He was obviously not surprised by Russell's appearance, which was something of a relief. He spoke English with a London accent, and opened proceedings by stressing the restrictions on Russell's reporting – he must not mention real names, of either people or places, if such exposure might compromise the *Aliyah Beth*.

Russell raised an eyebrow at the last phrase.

'It is what we call this emigration. *Aliyah* has no direct English translation, but "moving to a better, or a higher, place" is as close as I can tell you. *Beth* means second – the first emigration is the one allowed by the British – only a few hundred per year.'

Russell wrote it down. 'No names,' he agreed.

Mizrachi passed a folded piece of paper across the desk. 'This says that you are a journalist sympathetic to our cause, one that our people can trust. In some places you may be asked to produce it.'

Russell assumed the writing was in Hebrew. He wasn't so sure about the sympathy – Zionism seemed a pretty mixed bag when it came to rights and wrongs – but Mizrachi's *imprimatur* could hardly hurt. The journalist inside him bristled a little at having to prove his trustworthiness. 'Is this necessary?' he asked mildly.

'It might be. Forgive my bluntness, Mr Russell, but there are many Jews on this road who would be only too happy if they never saw a *goy* again, and they will treat you as an enemy. This letter will persuade at least some of them to give you the benefit of the doubt.'

'That makes sense,' Russell admitted. He asked Mizrachi what his official position was.

'I don't have one. I'm a *sheliakh*, an emissary. There are many of us in Europe now. In all the countries where Jews are living and travelling.'

'Was it the Haganah who got it all started? The *Aliyah Beth*, I mean?'

'Not in Europe, no. It was young men and women from Poland and Lithuania – partisan fighters, most of them. They began establishing routes before the war was even over. They sent the first people south to Romania and the Black Sea, and then others through Hungary and Yugoslavia. Once the war was over it became possible to move people westwards, into the American zones in Germany and Austria.'

'How did the Haganah get involved?'

'We've always been involved in bringing Jews to Palestine – we have a special section called Mossad which is responsible for this. When the war ended the British Jewish Brigade was billeted in north-east Italy, outside Tarvisio. The Mossad people visited the camps in Germany and Austria, and talked to the Jewish DPs about Palestine. Those that expressed an interest were told where to go.'

'So you are running things now?'

'Yes and no. We provide documents – mostly forged, of course. We arrange routes and transport. We negotiate border crossings, usually with bribes. We've created reception areas along the way, with food and shelter for large groups. But we do have a lot of help. The organisations themselves can't openly support us, but there are many individuals in the US Army, UNRRA, the Red Cross, the Italian police – even the Vatican, believe it or not – who do their best to smooth our way. This place is run by UNRRA, the US Army's DP division, the city's Jewish Committee and the DPs themselves. It's often chaotic, but most of the time we all seem to be on the same page.'

'So what's the official position of the occupying powers? The British are obviously hostile, so I don't suppose the Americans can be openly helpful. And what about the Soviets?'

'The Russians don't seem to care. The Americans... well, like you said, they're stuck in the middle. A few weeks ago they intercepted three of our trains at Linz, and sent them straight back here. We organised demonstrations, got publicity in the American press, and they agreed to organise transit camps if we restricted the flow to 5,000 a month, which is more than it's ever been. They want to help us.'

'And the Italian authorities?'

'Much the same. In fact, we had an almost identical situation with them – a trainload of refugees which the British wanted sent back. They forced the Italian police to put our people back on board, which took them half a day and really ticked them off. Ever since then the Italians have turned a blind eye whenever they could.'

'Are there lots of different routes?'

'Usually one or two. They change – one gets closed and another opens up.'

'Does everyone end up in Italy?'

'No, some go to France. We had a boat leave Marseilles not long ago.'

Russell leant back in the chair. 'Why do they want to go to Palestine, rather than America?'

Mizrachi smiled. 'You'll have to ask them that.'

'But how do you feel about the ones who want to go to America? Or the ones who want to stay in Germany? Do you think of them as traitors?'

'Traitors, no.' He shrugged. 'The ones who want to stay in Europe... it's their choice, but I don't believe it's a tenable one, not in the long run. Have you heard what's happening in Poland?'

'What, lately?'

'A lot of Polish Jews thought they'd go home after the war, but they soon discovered what a bad idea that was. There have been anti-Jewish riots in Cracow, Nowy Sącz, Sosnowice... there was one a few weeks ago in Lublin. The murderers may be different, but Polish Jews are still being killed.'

Russell just shook his head – sometimes there seemed no hope for humanity. 'So, what are the arrangements?' he asked after a moment.

'I'm waiting to hear when the next party is crossing the border. If it's soon, you should take the train to Villach – it's the quickest way. If they're waiting for another group from here, then you can travel with that, by the usual route.'

'Which is what?'

'The train to St Valentin, then across the Ems River by boat – the river's the border between the Russian and American zones. Then south to Villach and the Italian frontier. That takes two or three days.'

'Okay,' Russell agreed reluctantly. He told Mizrachi the name of his hotel, and the Haganah man promised to be in touch the moment he heard anything. 'There is one other thing,' Russell added. 'I'm looking for two people, a man and a woman. For personal reasons. And I know a man with the right name was travelling this way from Silesia. Is there anyone here keeping records of the people who pass through?'

Mizrachi smiled. 'Indeed there is. And he's very proud of them. Let me take you to him.'

They walked back through the basement, and up to the reception area, where a door behind the desks led through to several offices. In the last of these a middle-aged man in a yarmulke was bent over a ledger. 'This is Mordechai Landau,' Mizrachi said. He explained what Russell wanted, and left the two of them to it.

Once apprised of the names, Landau began searching the filing cabinets that lined two walls. 'The records are all alphabetised,' he said over his shoulder. 'We have Jews from sixteen countries here,' he added proudly. '8,661 of them since July.'

An indictment in itself, Russell thought.

'Ah, I have an Otto Pappenheim. And you've just missed him – he left for the American zone a week ago.'

'Do you know when he arrived here?'

'A week before that,' Landau said triumphantly.

The date fitted, Russell thought. This had to be Isendahl's Otto. A week ahead of him.

'You don't have any more details?'

'See for yourself,' Landau said, handing him the paper.

He skimmed through it, and found nothing to rule the man in or out.

'But no Miriam,' Landau reluctantly concluded. 'Four Rosenfelds, but no Miriam.'

Not for the first time, Russell wondered if she'd changed her name. If she had, they'd never find her.

He thanked Landau and walked back out to the crowded pavement. Above the broken skyline to the south the sun was trying to break through, but it seemed, if anything, colder than before. He put up the collar of his coat, tied the scarf a little higher round his throat, and started back towards the city centre at a hopefully warming pace. It wasn't yet noon, but he already felt hungry, and when an open restaurant presented itself on Währingerstrasse he took the opportunity to grab some lunch. The proprietor seemed pleased to see his dollars, and he was pleased to see the food, which seemed better than anything Berlin had to offer.

It seemed the Austrians were getting off lightly, which Russell found less than fair. He remembered the scenes after the *Anschluss*, the Viennese Jews forced to clean unflushed toilets by their laughing tormentors. And those had been the lucky ones. No one had filmed the Jewish pensioners' involuntary high-speed ride on the city's scenic railway – an experience that had given several of them fatal heart attacks.

The Austrians were hardly innocents.

But then who were?

He decided he would walk to the Danube. He had always liked big rivers, ever since seeing the Thames as a boy. And the Spree's lack of real width had always seemed a major shortcoming. Though it would make the bombed-out bridges cheaper to replace.

Once a convenient tram had carried him back to the Stephansplatz, he walked north to the Danube Canal, whose crossings seemed mostly intact. He was now moving into the Russian sector, but there were no signs to tell him so, and no obvious military presence on the streets. Praterstrasse offered the straightest route to the river, and he headed on up past the entrance to Prater Park, where the famous Ferris wheel was in the early stages of post-war reconstruction. Russell had written about it once, in an article on European funfairs that some American magazine had commissioned, and he could even remember some of its history. It had been built to celebrate the Habsburg Emperor Franz-Josef's Golden

Jubilee in 1897, and the following year one of his subjects had summed up Franz-Josef's reign in spectacular fashion – hanging by her teeth from a gondola to protest against the treatment of the Empire's poor. Twenty years later another woman had gone full circle while seated on a horse, the latter standing, no doubt nervously, on a gondola roof. That stunt had been staged for an early silent film, and Hollywood had been back on several further occasions. Everyone loved the Vienna Wheel.

Ten minutes later, he was gazing out across the wide Danube. There was nothing blue about it, and no sign of the once busy traffic – the wharves away to his left stood empty and apparently abandoned. The dark, heavy current rolled remorselessly past, like a conveyor belt with nothing on it. Over on the northern shore the hulk of a burnt-out Panzer had its gun barrel dipped in the water, and looked like an animal taking a drink.

Russell stood there for several minutes, stray thoughts hopping in and out of his mind, then turned abruptly on his heels and started back towards the city centre.

Once in his hotel room, he spent a couple of hours sorting through notes and ideas, then closed his eyes for a nap. Awoken by coughing heat-pipes, he was thrilled to find the water running hot, and was only slightly deflated by the absence of soap. A long soak in a full bath might be a luxury in much of post-war Europe, but it still felt like a human necessity. Feeling suitably restored, he sallied out in search of alcohol and food.

There would be an American Press Club, he realised – it was just a question of finding it. The hotel desk clerk thought it was on Josefstädterstrasse, which was only a five-minute walk away. Once there, a convenient passer-by directed him, with rather an envious look, towards a nearby side-street. The Press Club was open, well-lit and warm. As an added bonus, his old friend Jack Slaney was propping up one end of the bar, one hand wrapped round a half-empty stein.

Slaney had come to Berlin for the 1936 Olympics, and stayed on as the resident correspondent of the *Chicago Post* for almost five years. He had sailed pretty close to Goebbels' wind on several occasions, and had finally been asked to leave in the early summer of 1941, allegedly for calling

Barbarossa an overgrown version of the Charge of the Light Brigade. He and Russell had spent many a happy hour trying to out-cynicise each other in the Adlon Bar, contests which Slaney had usually won. Russell hadn't seen him since the summer, when the American had spent a few days in London *en route* to the Potsdam Conference.

'So what are you doing here?' Russell asked, sliding himself onto the neighbouring bar stool and signalling for two more drinks.

'The bar or the country?'

'The continent.'

Slaney considered. 'A valedictory tour, I suspect. A sort of "now that they're gone, was it all worth it?" What brings you to Vienna?'

Russell told him about the illegal Jewish exodus to Palestine, and how he'd been asked to tell the story.

Slaney nodded his appreciation. 'If I wasn't leaving tomorrow, I might follow along at a respectable distance. Not that I have the knees for mountain-climbing anymore.'

'Neither do I. I'm assuming trucks – it must be too late in the year for walking.'

The beers arrived, and tasted as they should.

'Your government won't be too pleased at your dallying with the enemy,' Slaney observed.

'The British Government? No, I don't suppose it will.' This should have occurred to him, with half his family living in London at His Majesty's discretion.

'I can see their point of view,' Slaney went on. 'About the Jews and Palestine, I mean. It was bad enough before the war, when the Jews were a small minority. If they let in every Jew that wants to go they'll have all the Arabs gunning for them.'

'I can't see that worrying anyone else.'

'No, it won't – the Jews will win the propaganda war. They have the two things that matter – lots of money and the biggest sob story in history. They'll get their homeland all right. Though I doubt it'll be the paradise they're hoping for.'

'After the last few years I expect they'll settle for somewhere safe.'

Slaney snorted his disbelief. 'In the middle of an Arab sea?'

Russell sighed. 'Point taken.'

'They've been giving out chunks of Germany to all and sundry – why not give the Jews a piece, make the criminal pay for the crime?'

'Because "Next year in Düsseldorf" doesn't have the same ring to it?'

It was Slaney's turn to sigh. 'I guess.'

'So, "now that they're gone, was it all worth it?" Was it?'

Slaney took a first sip from the new stein and wiped his lips on the back of his hand. 'I really don't know. A year ago I had no doubts. And sometimes I still get that feeling – like the other day, when I was reading that testimony from Nuremberg about camp commandants using Jewish heads as paperweights. You think to yourself, we just had to get rid of those bastards, whatever it took.'

'And yet,' Russell prompted.

'Yeah. And yet. What we did to Hiroshima and Nagasaki, what you limeys did to Dresden. And God only knows what good old Uncle Joe has been getting up to – the Poles are already accusing him of wiping out their entire officer corps.'

'The same Poles who are now persecuting their returning Jews.'

'Exactly. You end up asking yourself – how much better off are we? Enough to justify fifty million dead?'

Russell grunted his agreement. 'And you missed out the French,' he added. 'Last week one of their journalists told me that they murdered around ten thousand Arabs in Algeria. Last spring, a little place called Sétif.'

'Never heard of it.'

'You wouldn't have – nothing appeared in the French papers. You know, there's one thing that really upsets me. Every last idiot in thrall to violence, every last government hoping for some glory that rubs off – they'll be trotting out the Nazi precedent for another hundred years. And even if the war against the bastards actually was worth fighting, I can't help thinking they were the exception that proved the rule.'

'The rule being?'

'That wars sow only death and grief. I thought we'd learned that in 1918, but apparently not.'

Slaney grimaced. 'You know, until I ran into you, I didn't think I could feel any more depressed.'

* * *

Having arranged to meet Annaliese for some sort of supper on Tuesday evening, Effi asked the Russian bus driver to drop her off at the Dahlem-Dorf U-Bahn station. The train that arrived reeked to high heaven, but was mercifully almost empty. Exhausted, she sat with her eyes closed, drifting in and out of sleep, and almost missed her change at Wittenbergplatz.

It was dark when she finally emerged, and some desultory flakes of snow were visible in the dim glow of the few working streetlights. When she reached the Elisabeth there were twenty minutes remaining of Annaliese's shift, so she took the opportunity to look in on the Rosenfelds. Esther had reported an improvement in her husband's condition since the latest news of Miriam and the baby, and Effi was delighted to find him sitting up in bed. He still looked dreadfully weak, but his breathing seemed more regular and the flatness had gone from his eyes. He even looked interested when she told him the story behind Russell's trip to Vienna.

Annaliese looked even tireder than Effi felt, but still insisted on their going out to eat. A new place had opened on nearby Lützowstrasse, and several of the nurses had been astonished by the variety of food on offer.

Word had spread, and they had to queue for a table, but the aromas wafting past them seemed well worth the wait. 'Chicken!' Annaliese almost cried out when they finally got to see the menu. 'Fish!' Effi replied in equal amazement. 'My treat,' she added, pulling out her leading-actor-grade ration coupons. Looking around, she became suddenly aware of the clash between decor and clientele – a café used to serving workers was playing host to Berlin's new rich. 'Someone's making a lot of money,' she noted.

'*Grosschieber* bastards,' Annaliese observed almost cheerfully.

The meal cost the best part of a week's coupons, but was worth it. There was even wine – nothing wonderful of course, but better than either of them expected. As they sat there nursing the last few drops, Annaliese leaned forward in her chair. 'I've got something to ask you,' she said softly. 'I feel guilty about asking, so please, please, don't feel guilty about saying no.'

'All right,' Effi agreed, wondering what was coming. 'I learned to say no in the war,' she added, then laughed. 'That doesn't sound right, does it?'

'No. But here it is. The works committee that runs the hospital has negotiated a deal with a certain supplier for a bulk load of medicines. But the doctor who arranged it has come down with pneumonia, and now he needs the drugs as much as the patients do. No one was willing to take his place – they're all too spooked by what happened to his friend, the one who went looking for insulin.' Annaliese sighed. 'So, like an idiot, I volunteered.'

'Aren't you spooked?'

'Well, yes and no. I mean I know these are not nice people, but the deal has been agreed. The other time was different – that doctor was trying to find a legal source of insulin.'

'Threatening their business.'

'Exactly. This deal *is* their business. Anyway, I was wondering if you'd come along for the ride. Like old times.'

Effi smiled. The memory of their night drive across Berlin the previous April was one of her fondest. Not least because it had ended with her finding Russell half-asleep in her armchair – the first time they'd seen each other for more than three years. 'Where would we be going?' she asked. 'And when?'

'Tomorrow evening. The meeting's scheduled for nine o'clock, out in Teltow. We bring the money, they bring the medicines. Will you come?'

'How could I resist?' She wouldn't get much sleep that night, but her character was supposed to look wasted – she would save the make-up people some work. And, if she was being honest with herself, the prospect excited her. Her work in the war had occasionally been terrifying, but it had thrilled her in ways that acting never could. She had assumed *that* life was over, but maybe it wasn't. She dreaded to think what John would say, but there it was. As long as she remembered to think before she leapt.

One thought occurred straight away. 'How will we get there?'

'A jeep. The British gave four to the hospital.'

Effi grimaced – after Russell's experience in a jeep she would have preferred something a little more bullet-proof. Then again, they would be doing all their driving in the American sector, and would happily stop if so requested. 'What if they try and rob us?' she asked Annaliese.

'Why should they? The *Grosschieber* want regular customers, and the men we meet won't dare cross their bosses.'

That sounded like sense. 'Where does the money come from?' she asked out of curiosity.

Annaliese shrugged. 'The committee gets money from the Occupation authorities and our local administration, and quite a few of us have dipped into our own pockets – doctors, nurses, families of patients who need the medicines.'

'Do the Allies know what their money's being spent on?'

'Of course. They pretend not to, but that's just a joke. They could bring us supplies from the outside, destroy the black market in medicines overnight if they really wanted to.'

'Why don't they?'

'Remember what you said about that camp I was in? It's the same two things. They still think we need to be punished, and more than a few of them are making small fortunes selling official supplies on the black market.'

'I suppose that's it,' Effi agreed. There were free tables now; it was getting late, and she had another six o'clock start. 'I must get home,' she told Annaliese, 'but I'll see you tomorrow. Same time at the hospital?'

'Okay. And thank you,' she added, giving Effi a hug. 'You know, I've almost forgotten what a normal life looks like.'

That said, it couldn't hurt to take precautions. The gun that the dead American had given to Russell was still in the bedside table, and taking it with her would provide some insurance.

* * *

Russell's train left the Südbahnhof at ten past eight on Wednesday morning, and was soon rattling out through the Viennese suburbs. There had been no message waiting for him when he returned, somewhat the worse for wear, from his evening with Slaney, and none when he woke up, feeling very little better, on the following day. He had spent Tuesday morning vainly checking Vienna's DP camps and Red Cross offices for any trace of Otto or Miriam, the afternoon sauntering around the city, wondering how long he'd be stuck there. It might be a great story, but he wouldn't be back before Christmas at this rate, and no matter how often he reminded himself that Effi was well capable of looking after herself, the anxiety persisted. The trip in the Mercedes boot was still fresh in his mind.

Then a message had finally arrived, asking him to come to the Rothschild. There was a group crossing the border on Thursday or Friday, Mizrachi told him when he reached the hospital. If Russell took the morning train, he should reach Villach in plenty of time.

So here he was, staring out across the sun-washed Austrian countryside, the sky only smudged by the smoke from their engine. The landscape grew more mountainous by the minute, and after almost two hours they reached the small town of Semmering, which lay astride the Russo-British zonal border. There was no through service, and those passengers heading further east had to walk three kilometres to the British-sponsored train. There were plenty of soldiers in evidence from both armies, but none seemed keen to spoil their day with work, and only a few travellers' papers were subject to a cursory examination.

The new train puffed its way down the Mürz valley, as the outflung eastern arm of the Alps grew larger in the window. It was almost 250 kilometres from Semmering to Villach, and the scenery was mostly magnificent – the train leaping across torrents and delving through dark forests, skirting pellucid lakes and offering glimpses of distant snow-covered peaks shining in the afternoon sunlight. The towns they stopped in looked untouched by war, but Russell knew that wasn't the case – each would be mourning its quota of men lost on Hitler's battlefields.

Darkness was falling when the train pulled in to Villach. He had bought bread and sausage at one of the stops, but that seemed a long time ago, and an unofficial refugee camp seemed an unlikely place to find a decent dinner. Villach, it turned out, was not that much better, but he did find a reasonable bowl of soup in one of the bars near the station. Suitably fortified, he laid claim to the only apparent taxi and quoted the address that Mizrachi had written. It was only a street and number, but the driver wasn't fooled. 'Where the Jews are,' he said, with only the slightest hint of distaste.

So much for secret camps, Russell thought.

In the event, it wasn't so much a camp as a mansion, a large and rambling house with several outbuildings, set quite a way back from the road leading south, right on the edge of town.

On first impression it felt like a school – the house seemed full of children. 'They're mostly orphans,' his Haganah host explained a few minutes later. His name was Mosher Lidovsky, and like Mizrachi he spoke perfect English. Before perishing in the death camps, a large number of Polish Jews had entrusted their children to Catholic friends, and since the war ended the Haganah had been systematically reclaiming them, and moving them out of Poland. As he looked round the faces, Russell noticed a shortage of smiles.

'Naturally some of the children grew attached to their new parents,' Lidovsky answered the unvoiced question. 'But they are Jews. There is no place in Poland for them. Not now.'

Russell changed the subject. 'Is the group still leaving tomorrow or Friday?'

'At midnight tomorrow. The British patrol the road by day, which is unfortunate – it is harder at night with so many children. But it is only twenty-five miles.'

'Aren't we driving all the way?'

'Most of it. We have to walk round one checkpoint, which takes a couple of hours. We'll be there before dawn. Now, I have things to do. If you have any more questions, ask me tomorrow. You'll sleep in the men's dormitory – anyone will show you where it is – and there's soup in the kitchen.'

'Fine,' Russell said. 'Go.'

'You can talk to anyone you like, but no real names, okay?'

'Okay.'

Lidovsky hurried away, leaving Russell wondering how to spend the evening. He had all the following day to interview the travellers, but this would probably be his last opportunity to meet their would-be interceptors. He found the dormitory, parked his bag on an empty cot, and walked back into Villach.

A bar on the Hauptplatz provided what he wanted – a group of slightly drunken British soldiers. He bought them a round with his US dollars, told them he was a journalist writing a series of articles on how the top brass treated the common soldier, and settled back to hear their complaints.

The war was over and they wanted to go home. The Germans and Austrians were on their knees – anyone could see that. So why not leave them there?

The Jews? They were a bloody nuisance. You couldn't really blame the poor buggers, but the soldiers had better things to do than chase them all over Europe.

'It was like that at the concentration camp,' one man with a Yorkshire accent said. 'We liberated the camp, but we couldn't let the Jews just leave. We had to keep them there to help them – there was nowhere else. Now they're haring all over the place, and we have to round them up again. It's a pain in the arse.'

'What do you do when you catch them?' Russell asked.

'Just take them back where they came from.'

'And a few days later they're off again,' a Welsh boy complained.

'It's a fucking waste of time,' the Yorkshireman concluded, to general murmurs of agreement.

* * *

Effi was ten minutes late reaching the hospital, and Annaliese's face seemed to sag with relief when she saw her. 'I thought you'd changed your mind,' she said, as they walked back down to the entrance. Their jeep was parked in the old ambulance bay, amidst the makeshift collection of horse-drawn carts now used to bring in emergency patients. Effi was pleased to see the canvas roof – since the cloud disappeared that afternoon the temperature had dropped precipitously.

Annaliese rammed the canvas holdall under Effi's seat and plonked herself in the other. She was also wearing a long coat, hat and boots – they looked, Effi thought, like two flappers from the Twenties. 'How much money is there?' she asked Annaliese.

'Three thousand US dollars.'

'My God, that's a fortune.'

'Yes.' Annaliese produced one of her schoolgirl grins. 'Shall we just head for the border?'

They pulled out onto Potsdamer Strasse and headed south.

'Where exactly are we going?' Effi asked at the first opportunity, when a stopping tram blocked the single lane.

'Just off Goerzallee,' Annaliese told her. 'When it turns sharply right we just keep going for a few hundred metres down a dead-end street. It's about twelve kilometres altogether,' she added. 'Half an hour there, half an hour back.'

They motored on through Schöneberg, Potsdamer Strasse turning into Hauptstrasse, Hauptstrasse into Rheinstrasse. A single lane had been cleared in each direction, and more stationary trams were all that slowed their progress. Annaliese kept the jeep moving at a steady thirty – anything faster and the cold wind would have been unbearable.

The further south they got, the higher the proportion of surviving buildings, the lower the ridges of rubble. But the lights grew no brighter –

the suburbs were dim as the centre, as if the city had only one battery, and that was nearing exhaustion. Almost all the people they saw were congregated around a few bars and places of entertainment – American soldiers and German girls enjoying varying degrees of drunkenness and physical togetherness. The girls' mothers and grandparents were seemingly sequestered in their homes, eking out their meagre rations and trying to stay warm on a few bits of wood, while their daughters bought in extra food and fuel with what had once been considered their virtue.

In Steglitz centre they turned left onto the Hindenburgdamm. A drunken melee was underway beneath the railway bridge, but a quarter-moon hung above the straight and empty road ahead. If it hadn't been so cold, it might have been an evening to treasure. Effi pulled the coat tighter around her, and narrowed the gap between hat and collar.

The street lights became sparser, and when the Hindenburgdamm segued into Goerzallee they disappeared altogether. Annaliese slowed the jeep down and followed the headlights into the suburban murk. A few minutes later they came to the sought-after junction, Goerzallee heading off to the right, a smaller road running straight on. Annaliese pulled the jeep to a halt and they both peered forward, down what seemed a factory-lined cul-de-sac.

'It doesn't look very inviting,' Annaliese said, almost indignantly.

'No,' Effi agreed. 'How long have we got?'

'Almost ten minutes. I think I'll drive in and turn round. I'd rather be facing out than in.'

She drove the jeep slowly down between the factory facades, finally emerging in a wide open cobbled space at the head of a long canal basin. A bomb-broken line of factories extended along the northern bank, dimly lit by the sinking quarter-moon. The wind-rippled water lapped against the exposed belly of a half-sunken barge.

Annaliese turned the jeep and brought it to a halt. She left the headlights on for a few seconds, the twin beams vainly searching the road ahead, then thought better of the idea. Staring out along the darkened road Effi had a mental image of cars lined up at the end of the AVUS Speedway, waiting for the starting gun.

Which reminded her of the one in her pocket. She gingerly took it out, and saw the surprise on Annaliese's face. 'Just in case,' she said, placing it down between her feet.

'Maybe we really should rob them,' Annaliese suggested.

'They'd know where to find us.'

'True.'

Two headlights were approaching in the distance, but they eventually swung away.

'How's your love life?' Effi asked Annaliese.

'What love life?'

A luminescent beam filled the intersection, and then two more headlights appeared, turning towards them. Soon they could hear the rumble of a lorry engine above the purr of their idling jeep.

Annaliese flicked their lights off and on again. The lorry slowed to a halt some twenty metres in front of them. If the driver wanted to block their escape he had failed – the street was too wide, and there was still enough space for the jeep to squeeze past.

There were two men in the cab, the driver already opening his door, the other man shielding his eyes with a raised hand.

'Turn your lights off,' the driver shouted as his feet hit the ground. His German was perfect, but the accent suggested another origin. Polish, Effi thought. He didn't sound Russian.

'After you,' Annaliese shouted back with her customary combativeness.

He hesitated for a second, then reached an arm back into the cab to douse the lorry's headlights. The other man instantly raised his hands to shield his face, and it crossed Effi's mind that he feared recognition.

Darkness ensued when Annaliese turned off the jeep's headlights, but only for a second – the lorry driver was now waving a torch in their direction. 'Women!' he exclaimed, as if he couldn't believe it.

Annaliese clicked on her own torch, and shone it straight back at him. In the cab the hands shot up again, but not quite fast enough. The face was familiar, Effi thought.

'We're nurses,' Annaliese told the driver, in a tone that suggested it should have been obvious. Still shining the torch straight at him, she got out of the jeep. 'Shall we point these at the ground?'

He followed her lead. 'Doctors scared of the dark, are they?' He was young, not much more than twenty.

'Something like that. Where are the medicines?'

'Where's the money?'

Annaliese pulled the bag out from under her seat and set it down on the bonnet.

He started forward.

'The medicines first,' Annaliese insisted, laying a protective arm across the bag.

He hesitated for a moment, and Effi reached down a hand for the gun. The butt was cold to the touch, and she had the strange sense of time standing still. Could she shoot him?

She probably could.

She didn't have to. He laughed, turned and walked to the rear of his lorry. They heard the door latch clank open, and a few moments later he was on his way back with two large cardboard boxes piled up in his arms.

'Put them in the back,' Annaliese told him, stepping back a few paces to keep a safe distance. Effi, still grasping the gun, kept one eye on the driver, one on the shadowy figure in the cab.

He placed them on one of the back seats.

'How many are there?' Annaliese asked.

'Six. Another four.'

'Does that sound right?' Effi asked softly as he went for more.

'More or less.' Annaliese was opening the uppermost box with a fearsome-looking pocket knife, then shining her torch at the contents. 'It looks all right,' she muttered.

The driver returned with two more, and placed them on the other seat. 'You don't need to check them,' he said indignantly, as if his integrity as a black marketeer had been called into question.

He collected the last two boxes, and wedged them between the others. He ran his torch up Annaliese, starting with the boots and ending with the blonde curls peeking out from under her hat. 'Maybe next time we can combine business with pleasure.'

'In your dreams,' Annaliese told him contemptuously.

Effi's grip tightened on the gun, but the man just laughed. 'We'll see,' he said, sweeping up the bag and turning away.

Annaliese got in, handed Effi the torch, and turned the headlights back on. As Effi had expected, the man in the cab was ready, his face well covered. But would he lower his guard once the headlights had swung past? As Annaliese aimed the laden jeep through the gap between lorry and factory wall, Effi aimed the torch at the lorry's cab and took her masking hand from the beam. She was treated to a close-up of a furious face, and a clear recollection of where she'd seen it before.

* * *

'It was towards the end of 1943,' she told Thomas. They were alone in the kitchen, the rest of the house having long gone to bed. The Russian bus would be picking her up in about five hours, but after all the evening's excitement she felt far too restless to sleep. 'I collected a Jewish boy from a house in Neukölln – Erik had told me the boy was fourteen, but if so he was big for his age. He was going to stay with us at Bismarckstrasse for a few days while Erik arranged his exit from Berlin. I was carrying the forged papers of an imaginary nephew in case we were stopped on the U-Bahn. I used those papers whenever I had a young man to move.

'Anyway, the boy was nervous. More than nervous – he seemed almost hysterical, in a quiet sort of way. He'd been living in a room not much bigger than a cupboard for almost a year, and he'd lost all his family and friends, so I wasn't surprised to find him in bad shape. But I didn't realise how bad until it was too late.'

'What was his name?' Thomas asked.

'Mannie,' she said after a moment's reflection. 'I don't think I was ever told the family name.'

'Go on.'

'On the walk to the U-Bahn station he kept looking round to see if anyone was following us, and I had to tell him he was making us both conspicuous. That seemed to calm him down, and once we reached the station he managed to sit and wait without drawing attention to himself. He insisted on sitting several seats away from me once we boarded the train, so I wouldn't be implicated if anyone recognised him. He had this horror of running into one of his old non-Jewish schoolmates, and being denounced.

'So we travelled a few seats apart, me reading a paper, him staring rigidly into space. And after we changed at Stadtmitte he kept the same distance on the second train, still looking like a frightened rabbit.

'The Gestapo got on at Potsdamer Platz. Four of them, two through each end door. All in their stupid leather coats. I turned to give the boy a reassuring look – it was only a routine check, and our papers were as good as they got – but it was too late. He was already halfway through the doors.

'And once he was out he had nowhere to go. He just jerked his head this way and that as the four of them closed in.' Effi shook her own head in sympathy. 'And then he just threw himself at one of them. Like I said, he was a big boy. The man went down with the boy half on top of him, and a gun skidded across the platform.

'The boy looked at it. We could all see him – the train was still standing there with its doors open. He looked at the gun. He didn't even reach out a hand, but you could see him thinking about it.

'And then one of the Gestapo shot him. Not just once, but four times, and the boy just slumped down on his side. One of them knelt down beside him and went through his pockets, and I was sitting there thanking God that I'd kept his papers with my own. The other three just stood around making small-talk.

'The one who did the shooting was smiling as he reloaded his gun. He was the man I saw tonight.'

Leon and Esther

Russell watched as the two open lorries were loaded, around twenty people to each. A dozen of them were children, and all but one had left Poland as orphans. All had since been adopted, temporarily at least, by one or more of the adults. Russell had spoken to most of the latter that day, sometimes alone, sometimes with Lidovsky acting as an interpreter. They had all impressed him with their singularity of purpose, some more than others with their outlook on the world. Their Palestine would not lack for solidarity, but it might have trouble loving its neighbour.

The quarter-moon lighting the scene was the reason for their early departure. It was due to set soon after midnight, and without it, as Lidovsky explained, the obligatory detour through the forest would be very dark.

It was five past nine when they set off, the two lorries rolling quietly down towards the River Gail, and drumming their way across the girders. There were sometimes British spot checks at the bridge, but thanks to a Jewish lieutenant at the local British HQ, they knew that none were arranged for that night.

The lorries started climbing, their engines noisy in the clear mountain air. Most of the passengers were standing, hands clutching the sides for balance as they stared out at the moonlit landscape. The phrase 'shining eyes' came to Russell, which sounded romantic but fitted the bill. A night this beautiful would cause most eyes to shine, and these people had a vision to live for. He thanked fate and Isendahl for letting him share their journey.

The lorries rumbled down the cobbled street of a small and almost lightless town, where a swaying drunk sidestepped the leading lorry with a matador's aplomb, then sunk gracelessly back against the kerb. The road was now sharing the valley with a river and railway, the three of them intertwining their southerly course as the slopes above them steepened.

Two more towns followed, each darker than the last. A few minutes after leaving the second, the lorries drew to a halt in a passing place above the noisy river. It felt like the middle of nowhere, but was, as Lidovsky told Russell, just three kilometres from the Italian frontier. 'We used to get nearer, but the British started moving their checkpoints towards us. So now we have a longer walk.'

Once everyone was off the lorries, Lidovsky's partner Kempner gathered them in a circle and stressed the need for silence, before leading them across the road and up the bank beyond. Soon a long column was winding its way up through the trees, grateful for what little illumination the quarter-moon could offer. Behind and below them, the sound of the returning lorries slowly faded into silence.

About fifty metres above the road a parallel path wound through the pines. They followed this for what seemed a long way, with only an occasional whisper disturbing the silence. The valley below was lost in shadow, but they could hear the river rushing over the stones, and the moon still hung above the opposite ridge, threading the forest with a wash of pale light. It was bitterly cold, and despite the risk of stumbling Russell had both hands buried in his sleeves.

They'd been walking about half an hour when Lidovsky appeared, working his way down the column. He was warning everyone to be extra careful – they would soon be passing above a British checkpoint.

Russell heard it before he saw it, the sounds of laughter rising above the ferment of the river. And then he could see the glow of the brazier, and the jeep it illuminated. Four of them stood round the fire, evenly spaced like points of the compass, holding their hands out to warm them, first the palms, then the backs.

The column trekked on in silence, the light of the fire disappearing from view. It was another half an hour before they stopped, and then for no apparent reason. Russell's curiosity got the better of him, and he worked his way up the stationary column to where the trees abruptly ended. About seventy metres in front of him, across a wide stretch of snow-dusted meadow, smoke was drifting from the chimney of a small building. This, he presumed, was the Italian guardhouse that Lidovsky had told him about, one of many built in the mid-1930s, when the Duce still had doubts about Hitler.

And someone had got there before them, someone who soon would get a surprise. As Russell watched, two shadowy figures – presumably Lidovsky and Kempner – arrived beside the door, where they paused for a second before entering in quick succession. There were no sudden shots, which had to be good, but a long couple of minutes elapsed before one man emerged and waved the rest of them forward.

It was Kempner. 'It's a man and his son,' he said. 'They have papers from the Rothschild.'

'But what are they doing out here alone?' one woman asked.

Russell didn't hear the answer. He was staring at the man who'd followed Kempner out. The last time he'd seen that face it had been a good deal chubbier, and the body had been encased in the black cloth and leather of Heydrich's *Sicherheitsdienst* – the SS foreign intelligence service. Hauptsturmführer Hirth had been his handler in the summer of 1939, when the SS had employed him as a double against the Soviets. It had been either that or see Effi dispatched to a concentration camp.

The son had now emerged, a boy of about ten. He held his father's hand and stared at the assembled Jews.

Then Hirth saw Russell. The eyes blinked in disbelief, the lips opened and closed, then mouthed the word *bitte*. Please. And as if to strengthen the plea, he glanced down at the boy beside him.

Hirth's other hand, Russell noticed, was thrust deep in his pocket. Did he have a gun?

Russell hesitated. If he exposed the man now, people might get shot. And there seemed no urgency – Hirth had nowhere to run.

People were squeezing into the guardhouse, drawn by the warmth of the fire. Russell left Hirth hanging, and went in search of Lidovsky. They'd be there for several hours, the Haganah man told him. Until dawn. Then an hour's walk back to the road, where their transport would be waiting.

Russell asked him where the man in the hut was from.

'Danzig originally. His wife was Polish, a *shiksa*. They spent the war on a Polish farm, but she died in the summer. Why do you ask?'

'Just a journalist's curiosity. I thought I'd seen him somewhere before.' He watched Lidovsky disappear inside, and felt Hirth arrive at his shoulder.

'Please,' the former *Hauptsturmführer* pleaded in a whisper, 'don't give me away. For my son's sake. He's already lost his mother. Don't...'

'The *shiksa*,' Russell said sarcastically.

'No, his real mother. She was killed last year in the bombing.'

Which was probably the truth, Russell thought. He asked Hirth where he was going.

'Rome. Then, well, there are people there who will help me. South America, I expect. A new life. Look, if you give us away, they'll turn us over to the authorities. They'll shoot me, and then they'll have to shoot the boy. And he's done nothing to deserve that.'

He probably hadn't. Neither had the millions that Hirth and his kind had sent to their deaths, but Russell had to admit that wreaking vengeance unto the last generation seemed a touch medieval for 1945.

Could he really let Hirth walk away?

What did he actually know that the man had done? Hirth had worked for Heydrich when the death camps were being planned, but Russell had no idea how implicated the *Sicherheitsdienst* had been in the actual slaughter. They hadn't run the camps, driven the trains or fed the ovens. Had Hirth used a Jewish head for a paperweight? He had to have blood on his hands, but how much? Enough to justify killing his son?

The son couldn't have been much more than five when the orders went out – he had nothing to answer for. But Hirth was right – if the Jews didn't kill the boy they would probably leave him to die. At best he'd be an orphan.

There was no justice in letting Hirth go free, and none for the boy in killing his father.

'All right,' Russell agreed reluctantly.

'Thank you,' Hirth said quietly as Lidovsky walked towards them.

'You and your son must come with us,' the Haganah officer insisted.

'We'd be most obliged,' Hirth said, after a quick glance at Russell. 'I must find my son,' he said, after Lidovsky had gone.

There was no need. They were entering the guardhouse by one door when one of the Jews burst in through the other, holding Hirth's son by the scruff of the neck. The boy was screaming, his trousers round his knees. 'See what I saw,' the man said, pushing the boy to the ground. He tried to cover himself, but there was the tell-tale foreskin.

Hirth tried to help his son, but Lidovsky had a gun to his head. He pushed the SS man onto the ground and held him down with a foot on his chest. 'Pull off his trousers,' he told two of the men.

Hirth squirmed and kicked, but all to no avail. First the trousers and then the underpants, and another uncircumcised penis was shrivelling in the cold.

It was the way the Gestapo had checked for Jews, but Russell doubted whether Hirth was relishing the irony.

Kempner was going through the coat and trouser pockets. They had already seen the fake papers, but not the gun. It was a Sauer 38H, with SS lightning rods engraved in the grip.

Russell imagined Hirth taking it from his desk, realising the risk it represented, but bringing it along regardless, because any gun was better than none.

Now Lidovsky and Kempner were discussing his fate – short sentences batted to and fro across the few inches that separated their faces. Russell considered intervening, but to say what? He glanced at the boy, who was firmly held by one of the Jews, trousers still flopping around his ankles. The fear in his face was almost too much to bear.

Kempner and Lidovsky pulled Hirth to his feet, took an upper arm each, and dragged him out through the door. The boy cried out once, a heartfelt wail, and struggled in vain against the arms that were holding him.

The shot came sooner than Russell expected.

Hirth's son screamed and redoubled his efforts to break free; the man held him for a few seconds more, then abruptly released his grip. The boy hitched up his trousers and half-stumbled out through the door, holding one palm raised before him, as if to ward off evil.

Russell sank down to the floor with his back against the wall. He told himself that Hirth had gone to whatever Jew-hating Valhalla Heydrich's finest went to, and that most SS Hauptsturmführers probably deserved shooting. But it was the look on the son's face that he would remember. The dawning of irretrievable loss.

Several hours later, when Lidovsky came round announcing that it was time to go, Russell asked him what they intended doing with the boy.

'We'll leave him here. One of the women tried to talk to him – she told him we would take him to the nearest town, but he just ignored her. He's out there trying to dig a grave with his bare hands.'

'He'll die if we just leave him.'

'Only if he wants to. The path to the road is clear enough.'

Russell walked outside. Hirth's body was lying on its side in the frosty grass, an angry red hole above the ear. The boy was sitting a couple of metres away, staring out at the lightening sky to the east. His assault on the frozen earth had barely scratched the surface.

'Come with us,' Russell said.

'I'd rather die,' the boy replied without turning his head.

* * *

Some days at Babelsberg, after hours inside the skin of camp survivor Lilli Neumann, Effi would stare at the face in the dressing room mirror and wonder whose it was. Sometimes it would take as much as an hour to claw her own self back, but even with Russell away she never doubted the need – this was a character that could take her over, and drag her down to who knew where.

She was more or less herself again when a knock sounded on the door. 'Come in,' she called out, expecting to be told that the bus was waiting.

A man stepped into the room. 'Effi Koenen?' he asked, with only the slightest hint of query.

'Yes.'

'May I have a word?' he asked in more than passable German. The accent was American, but he was in civilian clothes, a smart black coat over a light grey suit. He was about thirty, Effi guessed, with straight brown hair, regular features and unusually white teeth.

'What about?'

'May I sit down?' he asked, indicating the easy chair.

She gestured her acquiescence. 'I can't give you very long,' she said.

'I only need a few minutes.' He put one leg over the other and brushed an imaginary speck of dirt off his knee.

'Who are you?'

'I represent the American Government – your husband's employer. Or one of them at least.'

'Do you have a name?'

'Seymour Exner.'

She went back to the mirror to finish removing her make-up. 'So what can I do for you, Seymour?'

'We have a request to make. Well, to be honest, it's more than a request. Two weeks ago your partner John Russell asked for our help in removing certain obstacles to your participation in this film, and at the time we were happy to oblige....'

'At the time?'

'If you had confined yourself to the job in hand we would have no regrets about helping out. However...'

She turned to face him. 'What on earth are you talking about?'

'The black market.'

'What about it? I don't have time to visit markets, black or otherwise.'

'The other night?'

The penny dropped. 'I was helping a friend buy medicines – she's a sister at the Elisabeth Hospital.'

He brushed that aside with a wave of an arm. 'The black market is a fact of life,' he said. 'You must realise that. People must buy and sell whatever they have to in order to survive, to prevail, and morality doesn't come into it – not for the moment. And the same is true of politics. The Nazis are gone and people would like to think that there's an end to it, but we believe that the new enemy is already here in Berlin. And we will do whatever we have to, use whoever we have to, in order to prevail. Do I make myself clear?'

'You'll do what you have to. It sounds familiar, but I never took much notice of politics. And I still don't understand what all this philosophising has to do with me.'

He breathed a sigh of frustration. 'Nothing, if you confine yourself to what you are good at, and leave crusades to the church.'

Effi smiled inwardly, remembering something Russell had told her weeks ago, that a quarter of the country's Protestant clergy had joined the Nazis before they even came to power.

'We intend talking to Mr Russell when he returns,' Exner said, as if that would make Effi feel better. 'Perhaps the two of you should talk this through before you take any more unconsidered actions.'

That made Effi angry – receiving an incomprehensible telling-off from a brash young idiot was bad enough; hearing him suggest that she wait for the balm of Russell's calming influence was downright insulting. 'So you're telling me I should come to work each day, do my job and go back home, and forget about everything else.'

'A dramatic way of putting it, but yes.'

She shook her head. 'And if I don't? What are you threatening me with?'

'Nothing terrible. You will just find that the difficulties you encountered in getting a work permit – those difficulties that we resolved for you – will rear their ugly heads once more, and the film will need a new leading lady. If it proceeds at all, that is. We help those who are prepared to help us,' he added, his voice turning suddenly colder.

Effi's first and almost overwhelming impulse was defiance, but she bit back her tongue on the words that were forming. 'I understand,' she said, a deal more graciously than she felt. 'No more crusades.'

He smiled at that. 'It's in all our interests,' he said. Job done, he got up to leave. 'Have a good weekend.'

Once the door had closed behind him she went back over the conversation. If their trip out to Teltow had occasioned his visit, then there had to be more to it. Neither she nor Annaliese had done anything to suggest they were anything more than buyers, so where had anyone got the idea they were starting a crusade?

There was only one explanation that fitted. The men they had met must work for Geruschke – hadn't Kuzorra told Russell that the black marketeer included drugs and medicines among his illicit trades? One or both of the men had recognised her as Russell's partner, and reported it to Geruschke. And he had concluded that her presence at the canal basin was part of a continuing 'crusade' on her and Russell's part.

So Geruschke employed the former Gestapo officer. She had been wondering what to do about the latter ever since she recognised him. She had thought of reporting him to the occupation authorities, but what was the point if she didn't know where to find him again?

Now she probably did. She had arranged to meet Irma at the Honey Trap on Saturday – she would see if the singer recognised the man's description.

But – and the realisation brought her up short – she had also learned something else, something much more troubling. If Geruschke was behind it all, how come his envoy was a man from the American Government? Had she just been warned to lay off the black marketeer because he was vital to their war against the 'new enemy'?

That, she realised, could explain why Geruschke had let Russell go. The Americans needed them both, so first they saved Russell from Geruschke, and now Geruschke from Russell and her.

How crazy was that?

The party reached the transit camp at Pontebba early on Tuesday evening. Since reaching the road on the Italian side of the border, they had endured a day of seemingly interminable waits, first for the lorry, and then for the various Italian authorities to decide on what bribes they were willing to accept. The British had been conspicuous by their absence, but that hadn't felt surprising – even up here in the northern foothills, Italy seemed far removed from the war and its hangover, from the bleakness afflicting so much of northern Europe.

It was partly the relative warmth, Russell thought, as he stiffly climbed down from the back of the lorry. It was the first time in a week that he hadn't felt really cold.

The Pontebba site had hosted a munitions dump before the Jewish Brigade arrived, and now that both were gone it look like a half-abandoned POW camp, a few dusty barracks in a sea of discarded packing. Russell headed straight for the office to enquire after Otto Pappenheim.

'He's here,' the Haganah representative confirmed, once Russell had explained why he wanted him. 'But he and a few of the others have driven down to Resiutta – there's a cinema there. And girls.'

Russell walked across to the group's designated barracks and left his suitcase on an empty cot. The room was full of excited chatter – his Jewish companions might still be a long way from their Palestine, but reaching Pontebba obviously felt like a huge step in the right direction.

He went in search of something to eat, and ended up sharing a table with two young men from Breslau. They were happy to describe their escape from Poland – a meet at the abandoned farmhouse, the walk across the mountain border, a long train journey through Czechoslovakia. But what had impressed them most was the warmth of their reception in the small Czech town of Náchod, where two local Jews had created a place of refuge for those heading south and west. This was brave but not surprising – what astonished Russell's companions was the whole-hearted involvement of the town's non-Jews. Náchod, almost alone in Europe, seemed eager to lend a helping hand.

Listening to the two young Zionists, Russell knew he would have to visit the town. Not on this trip perhaps, but soon. Both Poles and Czechs had treated their new German citizens appallingly in the immediate aftermath of the war – like Nazis, as one sad American journalist had told him in London – and if one Czech town was doing well by the Jews it deserved both praise and publicity. In post-war Europe kindness was a story in itself.

He returned to his bunk intent on waiting for Otto, but thirty-six hours without sleep had taken their toll. The next thing he knew a hand was gently shaking his shoulder. He opened his eyes to morning sunlight and someone standing above him.

'You wanted to speak to me,' a male voice said. 'I'm leaving in half an hour so I thought you'd want me to wake you.'

'You must be Otto Pappenheim,' Russell said. He levered himself off the bunk and offered his hand. This Otto was a tall young man in his twenties, with bushy black hair and a friendly smile. 'Where are you going?'

'Palestine, I hope.'

'Thanks for waking me,' Russell said. Looking around, he saw that many others were still asleep. 'We'd better talk outside.'

It was a lovely morning, the sun dousing the distant hills in an almost golden glow. A large bird of prey was drawing circles above the camp, presumably hoping for breakfast. Otto lit a cigarette as Russell launched into his now familiar spiel.

Otto shook his head. 'I have no children,' he said. 'I've never been married,' he added, in apparent explanation.

'Are you sure? I don't mean to question your honesty, but you're a good-looking boy...'

Otto gave him a self-deprecating smile.

'You didn't know a girl, a woman, named Ursel? In the summer of 1937?'

'I had my first real girlfriend in 1938, and she threw me over for a *goy*. I was only sixteen in the summer of 1937.'

'Okay,' Russell said. 'Thanks.'

'Pappenheim is not an unusual name,' Otto remarked, grinding his cigarette out in the dust.

'So I've discovered,' Russell agreed. 'You're our third Otto.'

'Well, good luck with the fourth.'

'And to you,' Russell replied. Watching the young man walk away, he wondered whether Shanghai Otto would prove to be the one. With any luck Shchepkin would have some news the next time he saw him. Whenever that was. He wondered how long an absence from Berlin the Soviets would tolerate.

With no little effort, he worked out what day it was – Saturday the 15th of December. What should he do? If he continued on with the group, he might end up hanging around some South Italian port for weeks on end. Sailing on to Palestine – or a British internment camp on Cyprus – would certainly round off the story, but could he spare the time? And he had the gist – the journey and how it was organised, the people and why they were taking it.

The Soviets might or might not be pining for him, but he was certainly missing Effi. If he started back now he should reach Berlin by the end of the week, in plenty of time for Christmas.

Always assuming he could find some sort of transport. He doubted whether any trains or buses were running into Austria, at least along the road they'd travelled. There might be flights north from Venice or Trieste, but it would be a long journey south to find out. Hitching a lift seemed the best bet. A lorry most probably, though a private car would be nicer.

A car like the one moving northwards along the road that skirted the camp. He thought of waving to attract the driver's attention, but knew he was too far away. And then the need disappeared – as if in response to his silent entreaty, the car turned in through the open gates and drove up to the barracks containing the office.

The young man who got out seemed familiar, but Russell was still trying to work out why when the man caught sight of him. 'Herr Russell!'
he exclaimed with what sounded like pleasure, and walked across to meet
him.

It was Albert Wiesner.

Russell should have been surprised, but he wasn't, not really. In these
circumstances, running across Albert was not such a great coincidence –
there couldn't be many young Palestinian men better versed in the whys
and wherefores of fleeing a hostile Europe.

Almost seven years earlier, in March 1939, Russell had helped smuggle
the seventeen-year-old Albert out of Germany. Originally employed by
Albert's doctor father to teach English to his daughters Ruth and Marthe, Russell had quickly become a friend of the family, and when Frau
Wiesner had begged him to talk to her son – whose angry outbursts were
putting them all in jeopardy – he had reluctantly agreed. Albert was certainly prickly, but few of Berlin's Jews were brimming with good humour
in March 1939. At their meeting in Friedrichshain Park, Albert had
calmly predicted the death camps. 'Who's going to stop them?' was the
question he'd posed to Russell.

Then his father Felix Wiesner had been beaten to death in Sachsenhau-
sen concentration camp, and Albert had gone into hiding after braining
a Gestapo officer with a table lamp. As part of a convoluted deal with
British and Soviet intelligence, Russell had managed to arrange the boy's
escape to Czechoslovakia and the rest of the family's emigration to England. Albert had gone on to Palestine, and had been there ever since.

He was now in his mid-twenties. He looked bigger and healthier than
Russell remembered, with shorter hair, a permanent tan and the same
intelligent eyes. 'It's good to see you,' Albert said. 'The last time Marthe
wrote to me, she said you'd all had dinner together in London.'

'In early November,' Russell confirmed. It seemed months ago. He
explained his and Effi's return to Berlin as best he could, given the need
not to mention spying.

'So what are you doing here?' Albert asked.

'Telling these people's story. Someone thought I'd be a sympathetic witness.'

'And are you?' Albert asked with a disarming smile.

'How could I not be?' Russell replied in kind. 'But what are you doing here?'

'I'm a *sheliakh*. You know what that is?'

'An emissary.'

'Yes. I'm here to find out how things are going – the camps, the transport, all the arrangements. There's more trouble in Poland, and that means more people we have to move. So I'm travelling back up the chain, checking that everything's working smoothly.'

'Do you feel like company?'

'I thought you were travelling south.'

'I don't think so. I have all I need at this end – I'm much more interested in the early stages of the journey. There's a place called Náchod – are you going there?'

'Ah, Náchod.'

'Do you remember, in the car on the way to Görlitz, you said that cruelty was easy to understand but that kindness was becoming a mystery?'

'Did I really say that?'

'You did. I was impressed.'

Albert shook his head. 'How wise I was at seventeen!'

* * *

On Saturday evening, Effi asked Thomas to accompany her to the Honey Trap. 'If I go on my own I'll spend the whole evening fending off drunken Russians – they won't care that I'm almost forty. And you need a break,' she insisted.

He told her he spent his weeks watching Russians behaving badly, and doing so at weekends hardly constituted a break.

'But you'll come anyway?'

'All right. But only because Frau Niebel has invited friends over for dinner.'

The latter were arriving as they left, two women who stared at them with almost indecent interest. Frau Niebel must have been gossiping overtime.

On their walk to the bus Effi asked Thomas exactly how badly the Russians were behaving at the Schade print works.

'Oh, no worse than anywhere else. They've brought in extra presses for the school books, but no one will tell me whether I'm expected to pay for their hire. Sometimes it's hard to tell whose business it is – I sometimes think it would make more sense if they confiscated it, and then hired me to run things. I know it's Lotte's inheritance, but...'

His voice trailed off, and Effi knew he was thinking about his son, who should have inherited the works, but had died in far-off Ukraine.

They didn't have long to wait for a bus, and there were even seats to spare. Across the aisle a woman was sitting beside a pile of Christmas shopping. Where she'd found gifts worth giving, let alone the beautiful paper and ribbons, was something of a mystery, and half the passengers were staring at her with the same perplexed expression.

'Are you going to Hanna's family for Christmas?' Effi asked Thomas.

'I'm negotiating with the Russians. They think the works should only close for Christmas Day, and they don't believe anyone else is capable of running things if I'm away. But there are several who could – I just have to convince them.'

'You must miss Hanna terribly.'

'Of course.' He paused. 'It sounds ridiculous, I know, but when we're together there seems more of a point to life. To all of it, I mean. Eating, sleeping, anything.' He looked at her. 'You had more than three years apart.'

'We did. It was different, though. Or for me it was. The life I was used to just vanished, and normal feelings seemed almost beside the point. And then of course there was Ali – once we joined forces I was never alone.'

The tram was on the Ku'damm by this time, the sidewalks full of Germans scurrying home and soldiers in search of excitement. The Honey

Trap was already doing good business, but tables were still to be had. A six-piece band were pumping out American boogie music, and two GIs were teaching their German partners to jitterbug on the small dance floor, while a group of British soldiers offered loud disparaging comments. Most of those drinking at the tables and bar were Anglo-German couples, with the girls even younger than Effi remembered. There were, as yet, very few Russians.

After buying two beers, Thomas surveyed the scene with obvious disapproval.

'We don't have to stay long,' Effi said, looking at her watch. 'Irma should be here in ten minutes, and she'll be singing not long after.'

'I want to hear her,' Thomas said. 'And don't mind me, I'm just getting more conservative in my old age.' He grimaced. 'I'm afraid I look at all these young women...' He hesitated. 'I was going to say – this could have been my Lotte. But it's more than that. First we have the rapes – 80,000 of them, someone told me the other day – and now we have half the women in the city prostituting themselves. For the best of reasons, I understand that. But still. What will the outcome be? What is it doing to us all – to the women themselves, to the men in their lives? And it's not just sex – everything seems for sale. Everything has a price, and only a price.' He saw the look on Effi's face. 'I'm sorry, I'll shut up. Next thing you know I'll be feeling nostalgic for Hitler.'

'No,' Effi said. 'I know what you mean, but... who was it said you can still see the stars from the gutter?'

'It wasn't Goebbels, was it?'

Effi laughed, and caught sight of Irma slinking her way through the tables towards them.

The singer ordered them all complimentary drinks, and recounted a long talk she'd had the previous day with a visiting American film producer. 'They're worried that the Russians are making all the running,' she reported, 'and next year they're going to start making films here themselves. American money and German talent. He mentioned a couple of ideas for musicals, and said I'd be ideal. He was probably trying to get into my knickers, but that's okay. I told him to look me up again when he had a contract for me to sign. He wasn't bad looking. And neither is your friend,' she added, once Thomas had gone off to the toilet.

'He's married,' Effi told her. 'And he loves his wife,' she added in response to the raised eyebrow.

'No harm in asking,' Irma murmured.

'None at all.'

When Thomas came back she took her leave, and ten minutes later was up on stage, going through the familiar repertoire. As before, she finished with 'Berlin Will Rise Again', and Effi noticed a glint of tears in Thomas's eyes.

'I'll just use the bathroom before we go,' she told him when the performance was over, and worked her way through to the back of the club. Noticing Irma through the open door of her dressing room, Effi was just leaning in to say goodbye when a familiar voice sounded just down the passage. She stepped quickly over the threshold and pulled the door to.

'Oh it's you,' Irma said looking up.

'Shhh,' Effi told her, opening a narrow gap between door and jamb, and pressing one eye up against it. The youth from the canal basin rendezvous was standing outside another doorway, apparently waiting for someone to come out. He looked even younger than he had in the dark, and she noticed a long thin scar on the left side of his neck.

He turned to go, and the other man – the Gestapo thug from the station platform – emerged through the doorway. She had a fleeting glimpse of his face as he turned away, and followed his young partner out towards the back door. There had to be somewhere for parking, she realised – Geruschke didn't seem like a man who took buses.

She pushed the door shut.

'What are you doing?' Irma asked.

'Just someone I didn't want to see again.'

'A fan?'

'Not exactly.'

Irma worked it out. 'One of Geruschke's goons?'

'Yes.'

'Don't mess with him, Effi. He'd cut out his grandmother's heart and sell it for dog food.'

'Why do you work for the bastard?' Effi felt compelled to ask.

Irma gave her a sharp look. 'Same reason we both worked for Goebbels. Sometimes there's only one show in town.'

* * *

Albert's business with the Haganah people at Pontebba had used up most of Saturday, and persuading a local garage to supply him with a full tank of petrol took care of the rest. He had purchased the car, a black Lancia Augusta, from the widow of a long-vanished Fascist mayor in the Po valley, and was delivering it to a Haganah base outside Salzburg. According to the widow her husband had rarely used the car in peacetime, and had kept it locked in its garage throughout the war. Motoring smoothly up towards the frontier on that Sunday morning, it seemed eager to make up for lost miles.

As they neared the frontier Russell kept a lookout for Hirth's son, but saw no sign of the boy. The descending path from the guardhouse had indeed been easy to follow, and he hoped that hunger would eventually drive the boy down.

There were no problems at the border – Albert's papers were exquisite forgeries – and none at the subsequent checkpoints. They stopped for lunch at the Villach transit house, which had just received another shipment of orphans. They would be going south in the next few days, Lidovsky told Russell. And no, he added without being asked, there had been no sightings of the Hauptsturmführer's son. He felt it too, Russell thought. They had let themselves down.

Soon after one o'clock they set off again. Albert was eager for news of his mother and sisters. 'I can't believe I haven't seen them for so many years,' he said. Did Russell think they would eventually come to Palestine? 'I live on a kibbutz, but I can find them a flat in Tel Aviv.'

Russell told the truth as far as he knew it, that his mother was torn, that the girls were happy in England, at least for the moment. 'Of course, if you do get your state....'

'We will.'

'You're that certain?'

'Yes.'

'I have a journalist friend who agrees with you. He says the Zionists have the two things that matter – sympathy and money.'

Albert smiled at that. 'He's right.'

'The Arabs won't give up their home without a fight.'

'No, I'm sure they won't. But they will lose.'

'There are more of them.'

'That won't matter. Our men have learned a lot, first in our Palmach militia, then in the British Jewish Brigade – and we're better fighters than they are. And our morale will be better. We Jews are all in it together, but the Arabs with money treat the others like shit.'

Russell grunted his concurrence.

'And there's another thing. The Arabs in Palestine have other countries they can move to – Transjordan, Syria, Egypt, the Lebanon. We have nowhere else. We *have* to win. The British will try and stop us, but their hearts aren't in it, and in any case their day is over. The Americans are the ones that matter, and they support us.'

'Anti-Semitism is hardly unknown in the States,' Russell said mildly.

'No, but a third of our people now live there. That's a lot of money, a lot of sympathy. And a lot of voters that the politicians won't be able to ignore. Americans love an underdog.'

'That's the British. Americans love a winner.'

'Even better. We will win, believe me.'

'Oh, I do,' Russell said. And he did. In fact, only the British Government seemed otherwise inclined.

They drove up the Drau valley to Spittal, then turned onto the mountain road to Radstadt. There was snow on the slopes but rain in the air, and no fear of the road being blocked. It was around two

hundred kilometres from Villach to Salzburg, and by late afternoon
they had reached the first of the three Jewish DP camps that Albert
needed to visit. The first, a permanent affair, bore the unofficial name
of New Palestine; the others were purely for transients, and had less
to offer in terms of food and accommodation. The Haganah had an
arrangement with the American authorities not to increase the number of residents in their Austrian zone, Albert told Russell, so they
needed to keep people moving, shifting groups on across the Italian
or German borders to make room for new arrivals.

Having dropped off the car soon after dawn, they hitched a ride on a
lorry heading east to pick up another group of Jews travelling west. Cold
rain fell in sheets for most of the three-hour journey, and the River Enns,
when they reached it, looked almost too choppy to cross. But a small
boat heaved its way to their landing stage an hour or so later with thirty
Jews on board, and Russell watched several look round in wonderment
before climbing aboard the lorry. They had reached the relative safety of
the American zone.

Russell and Albert clambered aboard the boat, and watched with admiration as the captain worked his way up and across to the eastern shore.
It was a half hour walk from there to St Valentin, but they saw no sign
of Russian occupation forces until they reached the station, where a few
Red Army men were drinking tea in the platform cafeteria. They seemed
unusually subdued, Russell thought. Probably hung over.

Their train to Vienna only stopped once, and it was still early afternoon when they arrived at the Westbahnhof. Russell had expected an
overnight stop, but Albert was anxious to reach Bratislava that day. A
cab carried them across the city and over the Danube to the station in
Floridsdorf, where a local train was waiting, seemingly just for them. The
whistle blew the moment they were safely on board, and an hour or so
later they alighted at a desolate country halt. A ten-minute walk brought
them to the Austrian end of a long wooden footbridge, which extended
out across a wide expanse of marsh and river. The frontier was in there
somewhere, and two Red Army soldiers were guarding the Austrian end,

albeit with no great diligence. They waved the two men through without even checking their papers.

'How about coming the other way?' Russell asked once they were on the bridge. 'Do they just let your people through?'

'A small bribe is usually enough,' Albert replied. 'The only people they stop are their own.'

There were no guards on the Czech side, but a longer walk to transport. After twenty minutes or so they met a party of Jews heading in the opposite direction, around thirty in total, with the usual male majority. The luggage on display was remarkable, with everything from battered old suitcases to paper bags pushed into service. Spare pairs of shoes were laced together and hung around necks, and several umbrellas were vainly raised to ward off the mist. Many were carrying fresh loaves of bread, parting gifts from the refugee centre in Bratislava.

The two of them reached the city as darkness was falling, and walked down through rapidly emptying streets to a square at the heart of the old quarter. A domed Byzantine church loomed over one side; the other was dominated by the stone-built Hotel Jelen, where UNRRA and the Haganah shared quarters and responsibility for the Jewish emigrants. A small door cut in a larger gate led into a woebegone courtyard, overlooked by scum-covered windows and rusted iron balconies. They climbed the stone staircase to the first-floor reception, whose walls were plastered in writing. As Albert talked to the man at the desk, Russell skimmed through the messages in search of an Otto or Miriam. He found no trace of either, but the walls themselves seemed worthy of preservation. The wrong religion perhaps, but they brought back memories of reading *Pilgrim's Progress* at school; there was something both chaotic and intensely focussed about this migration, and a sense that nothing could deflect it.

The Jews he met that evening did nothing to shift this impression – even those intent on reaching America seemed committed to the Zionist idea. Albert gave a brief talk on current conditions in Palestine, and Russell sat at the back of the rearranged dining room, watching the eager faces of those all around him. He was impressed by Albert, who managed to enthuse and reassure his audience without minimising the obvious difficulties. When one man asked what their chances of reaching Palestine were, he said 'one hundred per cent' – some might have to accept British hospitality for a while, but everyone would get there eventually. When another man asked if their women would be safe, he didn't just say yes, he turned the question round. 'Where,' he asked his audience, 'could a Jew find greater safety than in a Jewish state?'

Afterwards, when Russell congratulated him, Albert thought he might have 'laid it on a little thick. But we need them,' he insisted. 'We need every Jew we can get.'

Russell said nothing to the contrary, but Albert must have detected some hint of ambivalence. 'You're not sure about it, are you?' he said later, as they lay in their parallel bunks. 'Our need for a homeland.'

Russell took the question seriously. 'I don't know. It's hard. I spent most of my life learning to hate nationalism, and all the other evils it gives rise to. And nationalisms built around race – as you and I know only too well – can be even more murderous. But putting all that to one side, and accepting that the Jews have the same rights to a homeland as anyone else, there's still the problem of the Arabs. Palestine already has a population. You're not moving into an empty house.'

'Jews have lived there for thousands of years.'

'So have Arabs.'

'God gave it to the Jews.'

'Says who? I didn't think you were religious.'

Albert grinned. 'I'm not.'

'I don't think you can use the Bible as a title deed,' Russell insisted.

'Some people do. Like the Europeans who conquered the Americas – being in touch with the right God made everything okay.'

'You don't believe that.'

'I think that's what will happen.'

Russell thought about that. 'Maybe it will,' he conceded. 'A friend of mine suggested emptying Cyprus – the Greeks to Greece, the Turks to

Turkey – and then giving it to the Jews. Lovely beaches, good soil, not that far from Jerusalem.'

Albert propped his head up on one arm and gave Russell a look. 'We already have our homeland.'

'Yes, I expect you do.'

'And I'll tell you something else,' Albert said. 'I understand why the Poles are expelling the Germans from their new territories. And I understand why they're making it impossible for the Jews to return. If my friends and I have our way, the Arabs will all be expelled from Palestine. Anything else is just storing up trouble for the future.'

'That will put a bit of a strain on the world's sympathy, don't you think?'

'Once we have the land, we can do without the sympathy.'

* * *

Since deducing the connections between her ex-Gestapo man, Geruschke and the Americans, Effi had been wondering what she should do. The sensible course, the one Seymour Exner had advised her to follow, was to wait for Russell's return. They could then ignore his threats together.

The fact that Exner had suggested waiting for Russell rather prejudiced her against the notion, but as long as working consumed most of her waking hours, and exhaustion ruled the rest, she had little choice in the matter. Then on Tuesday the film's leading man came down with a heavy cold, the cast was given the whole day off, and the chance arose to set something in motion.

But what? After giving the matter more thought, she still had no idea where to start with Geruschke, and reluctantly conceded that waiting for Russell might, in this one case, make sense. So what else could she do? Russell was dealing with Otto 3, Shchepkin, hopefully, with Otto 2. Kuzorra's sighting of Miriam had given them hope, but there were no more people to ask and no more places to check – all she could do was wait and hope for some response to their messages.

Once satisfied that logic, and not Seymour Exner, had ruled out anything else, she decided it was time to deal with her flat, and the people who were living there. It wasn't a prospect she was savouring, but she couldn't put it off for ever.

She and Thomas had discussed the situation again, and he'd more or less confirmed what she already knew. If abandoning the property and ejecting the occupants were equally unpalatable, then all that remained was negotiation – she would have to meet those concerned, and make it clear that she wanted the flat back at some not-too-distant point in the future. If the occupants were reasonable people, then they could all agree a timetable. If they weren't, Effi would just have to tell them she was starting legal proceedings.

All of which sounded fine, she thought, standing outside on the familiar street. And now for real people.

She climbed the communal staircase and knocked at the door. The woman who answered was thin and almost haggard, with pale blue eyes and straggly blonde hair.

'What do you want?' the woman asked, as Effi searched for the right thing to say.

She took a deep breath. 'There's no easy way to tell you this. My name's Effi Koenen, and this is my flat.'

'Yours?'

'Yes. My parents bought it in 1924, and gave it to me in 1931. I lived her for ten years, until 1941, when it was confiscated by the government.'

The woman looked bewildered. 'So how can it still be yours?'

'It was the Nazi Government that confiscated it. Their laws are no longer recognised,' she added, with less than complete honesty.

'Oh.' The woman seemed unsure what to do. 'Well you'd better come in.'

Effi accepted the invitation to examine her old home. Some of the furniture was hers, but the flat as a whole seemed like somebody else's, and for a few brief moments she experienced an acute sense of loss.

A child was sitting in the middle of the floor – a girl of about four with her mother's hair and eyes. 'What's your name?' Effi asked.

'Ute,' the girl said.

'I'm Effi. How long have you lived here?' she asked the mother.

'Since March. We were given the flat by the Housing Office – you can check with them. No one said anything about an owner.'

'Maybe the records were destroyed. Or they didn't realise I was still among the living.' The little girl was still staring at her, and Effi realised how cold it was in the flat. There were a few pieces of wood by the fireplace, but they were probably being saved for the evening. Noticing two rolled-up beds in the corner, she asked the woman where her other two children were.

'The boys are at school. Look... we came from Königsberg – my husband was killed by the Russians.' There was a dreadful weariness in her eyes as she looked around her. 'But if this is yours...'

Anger or resentment would have been easier. 'Please,' Effi said, 'I don't need the flat at the moment – I'm staying with friends. I shall want it back eventually, but I won't ask you to leave until you have somewhere else to live. And I'll help you find somewhere. In the new year, we can start looking.'

The woman was using a hand on the table to hold herself upright, Effi realised. Both mother and daughter were in desperate need of a decent meal.

'Look, I'm an actress,' Effi told her. 'For reasons best known to themselves, that means the authorities give me top-grade rations. More than I need. So please take these,' she said, searching through her bag for the relevant coupons. 'Give your children a good meal. And yourself.'

After only a slight hesitation the woman took them. She looked more bewildered than ever.

As well she might, Effi thought. A stranger arrives, claims the family home, and then dispenses gifts. 'I'll come and see you again after Christmas,' Effi said. 'And don't worry – you can stay as long as you need to.'

'Thank you,' the woman said.

'What's your name?' Effi asked her.

'Ilse. Ilse Reitermaier. Thank you.'

Effi went back down to the street. Sensing watching eyes, she turned to see mother and child looking out of the window. She waved and they waved back.

She wondered how many families Hitler had torn apart with his stupid war. And how many more Seymour Exner would destroy with the one that he was planning. Did men never learn?

Of course the war had been good to some. Men like Geruschke and his ex-Gestapo underling were thriving on the misery of other people's lives. She wondered how many other Nazis he was employing.

A sudden thought stopped her in her tracks. She could bring Jews to the Honey Trap, Jews from Schulstrasse and the survivor organisations, Jews that Ali and Fritz and Wilhelm Isendahl knew. They were bound to recognise some Nazis.

No, she thought. After what Exner had told her, it seemed clear that the authorities weren't interested, and without some guarantee of official protection she would be putting the Jews in danger. So no.

She had only walked ten metres when the solution presented itself. Photographs. If she obtained photographs of Geruschke's employees, she could show them around. The photographer would need an acceptable reason for popping off flashbulbs in the Honey Trap, but that shouldn't be too difficult. Some pictures for an article about something or other – how the soldiers enjoyed their leisure, the renaissance of cabaret, the rebirth of jazz in Berlin. Maybe Irma could pretend to commission some publicity photos.

First she needed a photographer. The one John used to use, the one Ströhm had told him was back from the dead. Zembski, that was his name. The Fat Silesian. John had said he was working at the KPD newspaper offices. She had no idea where they were, but they shouldn't be hard to find.

* * *

Next morning, Russell and Albert walked back up the hill to the station. Russell had vivid memories of catching a train there in August 1939 – his

American editor had sent him to Bratislava to report on a pogrom, before hustling him on to Warsaw to witness the countdown to war. Ambulance-chasing on a continental scale.

His fellow passengers on that train had included a family of Jews intent on reaching the safety of Poland. All dead, most probably. And if they weren't, they'd be fleeing in the opposite direction. In such circumstances, Zionism made perfect sense. A homeland in Palestine or shuttling to and fro across European borders, one step ahead of the knout. Put like that, it was no choice at all.

Their train headed north through the Czech countryside at a funereal pace, stopping at stations, on bridges, in the middle of dark, silent forests. Albert expressed no resentment over Russell's reservations – he was, Russell realised, sure enough of his own mind to forgive the doubts in others. They talked for a while about Otto Pappenheim, and the possible reasons for his disappearance. When Russell mentioned Effi's fear of handing Rosa back to a man who had abandoned her, Albert grew more serious, and warned them against pre-judgement. 'After what some of them went through,' he said sadly, 'you could forgive them almost anything.'

After Brno they had the compartment to themselves. Albert laid himself out across a row of seats and was soon asleep, but Russell sat by the window, watching the wintry Moravian countryside and thinking about the next few days. They would reach Náchod that night or the following morning, and after finishing their business would cross into Poland. There had been an atlas in the UNRRA office at the Hotel Jelen, and Russell, boning up on the local geography, had discovered that Glatz – or whatever the Poles were now calling it – was the nearest railway station. He could travel to Breslau from there, along the line he'd once used to visit the Rosenfeld farm. Breslau was now in Poland, and doubtless sporting a new name, but the tracks would still be leading west to Berlin. If the Poles were uncooperative, he'd find some friendly Russians.

Thinking about the Rosenfeld farm, a possibility occurred to him – one that he and Effi had somehow missed. If Miriam had had her baby, and somehow healed herself in the process, might she then have tried to go home? Kuzorra had seen her in January 1942, so it would have been after that. But if she'd gone home that year or the next, only ruins awaited her – by that time her parents had long since fled over the mountains. So what would she have done – gone back to Berlin?

There was only one source of sanctuary that Russell knew of – Torsten Resch, the gentile neighbours' boy who had always been sweet on her. He had worked in Breslau until his call-up in 1941. One or two years later, he was probably still in uniform, and Miriam would have sought him in vain. But the boy might have been invalided out; he might have been on leave when she came looking. It was the thinnest of chances, but she had to be somewhere. Alive or dead, she had to be somewhere. So why not Breslau? It shouldn't take him more than a few hours to find out.

The afternoon wore on, until darkness finally filled the valleys. Yellow lamps now glowed on the station platforms, and myriad wood fires crackled beside the frequent refuge sidings. At one such passing place, their train pulled up alongside another, and the sound of singing rose from the latter's lightless compartments, a young girl's voice both sweet and infinitely sad. It was, Albert said, a song about a Jewish mother who saves her daughter by placing her in a Christian orphanage.

Another song followed, this one sung by many voices and accompanied by mandolin. According to Albert it was a paean to the writer's home, a simple village somewhere in the Pale which he or she would never see again.

When their own train jerked into motion, and swallowed the voices up, Russell found himself feeling almost bereft. The emotions which flickered on Albert's face were the ones Russell remembered from 1939 – anger and bitterness.

They travelled on, eventually reaching the junction for Náchod too late for the last connection. After checking the time of the first morning train, they walked across the dung-strewn forecourt to the only available inn. The proprietor's initial suspicion of Albert was mollified by the false documentation, and Russell's American passport was enough to secure them a late supper. The latter was somewhat spoiled – for Russell at least

– by their host's insistence on regaling them with tales of Czech revenge against the local Germans. Albert seemed happy to hear them, but the proprietor's wife, who had served up their supper, looked even more disgusted than Russell. 'What an achievement,' she said sarcastically. 'We've become just like them.'

* * *

There turned out to be several Party offices, but the one where Miroslav Zembski worked was on Klosterstrasse, in a building that Effi remembered as once housing an art gallery. The size of Zembski's second floor office suggested a man of some importance.

He stared at Effi for several moments before recognition dawned. 'Fräulein Koenen,' he finally said, his face breaking into a smile. 'Or are you and Herr Russell married these days?'

'No, we still haven't got round to it,' Effi told him. Zembski was hardly wafer-thin, but it was difficult to believe that Russell had dubbed him 'the Fat Silesian'.

'I heard he was back. How is he?'

'He's all right. He's in Austria at the moment – at least I think he is. But I know he means to come and see you – he only just heard you're alive. When he turned up at your studio in 1941 and found that you'd been arrested... well, he feared the worst.'

'He wasn't the only one,' Zembski said drily. 'It would be good to see him again,' he added, 'but what can I do for you?'

She looked at him. Until that moment, she'd been planning on hiring him – or whoever he recommended – with some sort of cock-and-bull story, and without revealing her motives. But it made more sense to be straight with him. She would have a clearer conscience, and probably get better results. 'I need a photographer,' she began. 'I need someone to take pictures at the Honey Trap nightclub on the Ku'damm without arousing suspicion. Inside and outside. Inside, the photographer should look like he's concentrating on the singer Irma Wocz – she's an old friend, by the way – but catch as many people in the background as he can. Staff in particular, but customers too. The club is on a corner, and there's a back way out onto Leibniz Strasse which only employees use. The buildings across the street were destroyed, and there's plenty of rubble for a photographer to hide in. I need pictures of anyone using that exit.'

'Are you going to tell me what it's all about?' Zembski asked.

'The man who owns the club is a black marketeer who employs ex-Nazis. If I have photographs, I can get them identified.'

'Why not just go to the Americans?'

'That's a long story. John could tell you...'

'Ah, Mr Russell. Always in trouble with the authorities.'

'I'll tell him you said so. He'll be pleased.'

Zembski laughed.

'So do you still work as a photographer?'

'No, I don't.'

There was something in the way he said it that made her ask why.

'The camp I was in – the commandant saw the occupation on my arrest sheet, and made me his camp photographer. I won't go into what he had me photograph.'

'I understand. Can you recommend someone else?'

'Actually I can. He's the son of someone I knew in the camp – someone who died there. I let the boy use my old studio in Neukölln. His name's Horst Sattler. He's young, but he's good. Mostly he buys and sells cameras – there's not much demand for wedding pictures at the moment – but he knows how to use a camera. And I think he'd like your proposition.' Zembski looked at his watch. 'He's usually there until about six. Say that you talked to me about the job, and that I recommended him.'

She wrote down the address he dictated, promised to convey his good wishes to Russell, and walked to the nearest U-Bahn. Half an hour later she was in the studio, introducing herself to its young proprietor. Horst Sattler was skinny, with bushy black hair and glasses that made him look like a teenage Trotsky. Through the window behind him several young boys were playing football with a battered tin can.

Sattler's eyes lit up when Effi outlined what she wanted – which was hardly the reaction she expected. Did he realise who she was talking about, that there might be dangers involved?

'Of course,' he said with a grin, as if surreptitiously photographing black marketeers was something he did all the time.

'I haven't sorted out the inside part yet,' Effi told him; 'I have to talk to my singer friend.' Which was not only true, but would also give the boy a chance to prove his worth without actually sticking his head between Geruschke's jaws. 'If you could start outside...'

'Absolutely. I have the perfect lens.' He took it out to show her, and rattled on about stops and apertures and heaven knew what else.

'You must be careful,' she insisted. 'Don't let them see you.'

He raised both palms towards her. 'Don't worry about me. I'll have an escape route planned. And my assistants – he waved a hand in the direction of the boys outside – will be on the look-out. We've done this sort of thing before.'

She was astonished. 'When? Who else have you been taking pictures of?'

'Wives,' he said succinctly. 'Most husbands these days know not to ask where their food and fuel come from. But there's still some stupid enough not to make the connection. They think their wives are being unfaithful for the fun of it.' He shook his head, as if the antics of the adult world were too strange to credit. 'These days I'm more like a private detective than a photographer.'

Effi had to smile. 'So how much is this going to cost me?'

He considered. 'Given who the mark is, I'd almost do it for free. But I *am* running a business, and there are my "irregulars" to consider...'

'Your what?'

'The boys outside. Haven't you read Sherlock Holmes?'

'Never.' John's son Paul had tried to persuade her, but all she'd read in those days were scripts.

He tutted his disapproval, but otherwise let her failing pass. 'A pack for every face I capture?' he suggested, lingering almost lovingly on the final word.

'Okay,' Effi agreed. She had no idea whether that was a good deal, but was sure she could find more cigarettes from somewhere. And she didn't think he would cheat her.

She started to give him directions, but he interrupted her: 'I know where the Honey Trap is. Will you come here to see the pictures, or do you want them delivered?'

'Deliver them, if you can. I live in Dahlem, and I rarely get enough time off work to travel this far.'

'What do you do?'

'I'm an actress.'

He looked impressed. 'Should I have recognised your name?'

'Not these days,' she said. And not at your age, she thought.

'Do you have a telephone that works?'

'Sometimes.' She gave him the number and the Dahlem address. 'You can talk to me, John Russell or Thomas Schade – no one else. Okay?'

He nodded. 'I'll be in touch when I have something to show you.'

She was halfway to the door when another idea came to her. 'Your "irregulars" – do you ever use them to follow erring wives?'

'Sometimes.'

'Well some of the men leaving by the rear exit might go off on foot. I'd throw in another pack of cigarettes for each address that goes with a face.'

* * *

In the morning their one-coach train wheezed its way up through the snow-strewn foothills, arriving in Náchod soon after nine. The small town seemed unmarked by the war, but appearances were clearly deceptive – according to Albert, only twenty of its three hundred Jews had survived. And it was two of these – Moshe Rosman and Yehuda Lippmann – who had turned Náchod into a staging post for the Jews now fleeing Poland.

Both had been prominent businessmen before the Nazi takeover, and unlike most of their Polish counterparts had experienced little difficulty recovering their assets once the Germans were gone. Rosman's oak-pan-elled office near the station certainly seemed of long standing, and it was hard to believe that the man behind the desk had recently been in Auschwitz. Once Albert had introduced Russell, and told Rosman what his friend was writing, the Czech insisted they both have lunch with him and Lippmann.

Leaving Albert to conduct his Haganah business, Russell worked his way down the short list that Rosman had given him, of individuals and families who took in transient Jews. None had any that day, but more were expected soon, and no one seemed put out by the prospect. They weren't doing anything special, one woman told him – just providing food and lodging for a few nights.

At lunch he and Albert heard the full story from Rosman and Lippmann. Both seemed around forty, but were probably younger. Rosman's parents and only sibling had died in Auschwitz, as had Lippmann's wife, child and sisters. Soon after their return to Náchod a nearby camp had been liberated by the Russians, and they had done their best to feed and shelter the several hundred emaciated women who suddenly appeared on their doorsteps. They had approached their non-Jewish neighbours for help, and been almost overwhelmed by the response.

At first the townspeople were helping Jews find their way back to Poland, but since the summer the flow had reversed. Most returnees had searched in vain for the families left behind, and many had been given a hostile reception. The new Polish government had said all the right things, but fresh outbreaks of anti-Semitic violence were becoming an almost weekly occurrence, and those Jews that could had decided to cut their losses. They might have a future in Palestine or America, but none seemed on offer in Poland, and now several thousand were leaving each month. A figure likely to rise and rise over the coming year.

Russell asked Rosman and Lippmann how the government in Prague viewed their efforts.

'Oh, they seem to have realised that something not quite legal is going on,' Lippmann said. 'The police even arrested one man for sheltering an illegal immigrant. But there was an outcry straight away – everyone here supports us. I mean, it's not as if the Jews are planning to stay, either here or anywhere else in our country – we're just helping them get where they want to go. How could anyone in Prague object to that?'

How indeed, Russell asked himself that evening. He, Albert, Lippmann and around a dozen other locals were sharing a convivial time in one of the town's inns, and looking round the faces, Russell thought he detected an absence of the fear and resentment that still haunted most of Europe. Maybe he was imagining things, but Náchod seemed proof of the old adage that doing good was good for the doer.

* * *

Thursday was cold and clear, the line of mountains that marked the border stretching far into the distance. Jews travelling south were usually led along unwatched paths by friendly guides, but Russell and Albert had only to walk down the road and present their papers at the Czech and Polish frontier posts. They were soon parting company, and Albert was full of messages for his family in London, should Russell see them first. He also invited Russell and Effi to Palestine: 'Come and see what we're doing. It's not often you see a country built from scratch.'

Russell asked if he had any plans to visit England.

'If my letters won't persuade my family to join me, then I may have to do it in person. But not for a few years, I expect. Only when we have our homeland.'

They said their goodbyes in the small village just beyond the Polish frontier post, Albert walking off to see the local Haganah organiser, Russell engaging a decrepit-looking taxi to take him down to Glatz, or Kłodzko as the Poles had re-named it. He felt immensely pleased that his and Albert's paths had crossed again, and looked forward to telling Eva, Marthe and Ruth what an impressive young man their son and brother had become.

In Glatz he found a bank that was willing to sell him Polish currency for dollars. At the station he discovered that trains were still running to Breslau, or Wrocław as the ticket-seller testily insisted. And yes, the next one stopped at the former Wartha, or whatever he called it. He purchased a through ticket and walked out to the waiting carriages, which were German with Polish markings. A locomotive was huffing its way backwards to join them.

Soon they were off, and hurrying down the valley. Wartha Station looked unchanged, save for the Polish flag and stationmaster. There was even a Polish taxi, and with no little help from the stationmaster, Russell managed to explain his hoped-for destination. On his first visit here he had walked the six kilometres there and back, and the taxi ride seemed almost insultingly brief.

They stopped first at the neighbouring farm, which Torsten's parents had owned. They had once been friends of the Rosenfelds, but fear and the local Nazis had put an end to that. And now it was a Polish woman who answered the door, suspicious and slightly aggressive. '*Zniknął*,' she said several times. Gone. When Russell tried to asked her where, she shut the door in his face.

They drove on down the lane to the Rosenfeld farm. In September 1939 both house and barn had been blackened shells, but the house had at least had been partly rebuilt, and smoke was rising from a hole in the ramshackle roof.

The reception there was just as hostile. He wasn't at all sure that the man understood his questions, but there was no mistaking the answer. '*Polska*,' the man said, encompassing the landscape with sweeping waves of his arms, one hand to the right, the other to the left. '*Polska*,' he repeated angrily when Russell tried to speak. '*Polska*.'

He too slammed the door in his visitor's face.

Back at the station he read the chalked-up times and groaned – there were almost two hours to wait. After a while the stationmaster took pity on him, opening up the waiting room and even starting a fire in the small grate. A few shared smiles was the best they could manage when it came to communication, but by the time the train arrived the official had done more than he knew to salvage his nation's reputation.

The land seemed emptier than the last time Russell had made this journey, the fields more neglected, the skies clear of smoke. If the

Germans had all been driven out, not enough Poles had arrived to replace them.

As the train approached Breslau the residue of war grew commonplace – gapped rows of houses, the shattered trees and craters strewn across the fields, a cemetery of scorched and mangled rolling stock where the marshalling yard had been. The station was a functioning wreck, the city itself looked a lot like Berlin – the parallel lines of empty facades stretching north towards the Oder, and probably beyond. He should have known what to expect. Breslau, like all of Hitler's so-called 'fortress cities', had been promised eternal glory if it fought to the very last German. Refusal had not been an option.

And the Poles were inheriting the ruins. Their uniforms were everywhere, mingling with those of their Russian liberators. Too much history there, but appearances would be maintained, probably for decades. The men now ruling Poland were no less in thrall to the Soviets than Ulbricht and his gang. They'd all shared digs in Moscow, all learned to toe the collective line. National feelings would be repressed, at least for the conceivable future. The Moscow Poles would give great chunks of their country to the Russians, and the Moscow Germans would compensate the Poles with great chunks of theirs. All smiling as they did so. What their people felt was neither here nor there.

The only vehicle in the station forecourt was a horse-drawn cart piled high with scavenged bricks. No fire was visibly burning, no smoke curling up to the sky, but a faint smell of scorching hung in the air, reminding him of Berlin in the last days of the war. He started walking towards the city centre, down what he guessed was the old Taschenstrasse. The name itself had been whitewashed out, and replaced by something Polish.

As he crossed the old moat on a makeshift footbridge he began to wonder whether anything survived in the centre. The streets seemed desolate, particularly for the middle of the day. Whatever municipal offices there were – Russian, Polish, even German – must be out in the less damaged suburbs.

He turned left towards the Ring, and found himself walking toward a group of young men in uniform. They were Poles, he realised – some sort of militia. One held up a hand to stop him, while the others all looked at his suitcase.

The leader barked something incomprehensible in Polish.

Russell was about to ask if they spoke German, when he realised how mistaken that might be. 'Speak American?' he asked, with what he hoped was a winning smile.

This had them glancing at each other, uncertain how to proceed. Was the suitcase still fair game?

Disinclined to lose his notes, let alone his cigarettes and post-war wardrobe, Russell pushed his advantage. 'Do you speak Russian?' he asked in that language.

'A little,' the leader admitted.

'I'm looking for the Russian administrative headquarters. NKVD,' he added, enunciating each letter with a hint of relish.

'Ah, Russians,' the leader said sadly. He gestured down the road in the direction of the Ring, then passed on the bad news to his comrades, who couldn't resist a few rueful glances at the suitcase before resuming their patrol.

Russell watched them go. If he'd just been an ordinary German, there seemed a very good chance that they'd have stolen his suitcase and clothes, and left him lying in his own piss and blood. 'And the first shall be last, and the last first,' he murmured to himself.

He walked on to the ravaged Ring, and searched in vain for a building in use, let alone a working office. There were two Red Army officers sitting side by side on a salvaged bench, staring out across the rubble-ringed square with the air of experienced conquerors surveying their recent work. He approached them with suitable humility, and either that or his use of their language earned him a friendly response. The Soviet administrative HQ was in the big building behind the station, they told him in response to his question. As for the Germans, they had an office that dealt with their own affairs and made representations to the occupation authorities. It was housed in the cellars of the old Market Hall, up near the river.

Russell thanked the two of them, and headed north along another devastated street. Around a quarter of the old buildings were still standing, he reckoned, and many of those were badly damaged in one way or another. All for one man's addiction to death – the war had long been lost when all this happened to Breslau.

The market hall was a shell, the cellars beneath crowded with Germans. The relevant office was hidden away in one corner, a small oasis of quiet lit by several candles. Without being asked, the old man in charge told Russell that he wasn't leaving, that he'd worked for the city all his life, and intended to stay. When Russell told him what he actually wanted, the man looked almost aggrieved, but only for an instant. 'We have no lists of German residents,' he said, 'only of the dead.'

'Can I see those?' Russell asked.

The man reached for a ledger and hoisted it onto the table. It was a converted cash ledger, divided alphabetically with long lists of names underneath each letter.

There was three pages of 'R's. He started moving his finger down the column of names, conscious of the old man's wheezy breathing. There was no Rosenfeld on the first page, none on the second, and he was almost at the bottom of the third when he saw it. He had only been looking at surnames, but somehow the Miriam caught his attention. Not Rosenfeld but Resch.

No sign of Torsten, but it had to be her. Torsten marrying another Miriam would surely be too much of a coincidence.

Miriam Resch had died on the 3rd of May, while the city was still under siege. An address was written beside the name.

Russell went back through the 'R's, looking for a Resch he might have missed. There was none. Torsten might have died somewhere else, or he might still be alive. The child in Berlin might not have been Miriam's, or might be listed under the father's name.

'Where is Jahnstrasse?' Russell asked the old man.

It was a kilometre to the east, just beyond the Königsplatz.

The walk took him twenty minutes, first along the wreck-strewn Oder, then south through streets still choked with rubble and seemingly empty of life. Black flags hung from several balconies, but Russell had no idea why. He doubted whether anarchists lived there.

Miriam's address was a three-storey building which almost alone in the street remained whole. The Pole who answered the door was dressed in the same militia uniform as the four young men he'd met earlier, and was just as easily intimidated by Russell's aggressive Russian. When he understood that his inquisitor was looking for the former occupants, he led him down to the door of the neighbouring basement, and left him with a frightened-looking German woman. She, Russell saw, was wearing a white armband with the letter 'N' on it. 'N' for *Niemiec* – German – presumably. The Poles had watched and learned.

He asked about Miriam, but the name didn't ring any bells. The German inhabitants of the house next door had been evicted to make room for two Polish families from Lublin. '*Bauern*,' she murmured, peasants. She thought the Germans had moved out to Pöpelwitz. 'That is one of the German areas,' she told him, as if describing a ghetto.

'But you don't know which street?'

'No, but Frau Höschle will. She knew those people.'

'And where can I find her?'

'Ah, just across the street here.' She shepherded him up to the pavement. 'You see over there. But mind her steps – I almost fell the other day.'

'What are the black flags for?' he asked, catching sight of one further down.

'Typhus,' she said succinctly, and scuttled back down the steps.

He strode across the empty street and took care with his descent. Frau Höschle looked worn out and hungry, but her eyes flickered at the mention of Miriam, and after a moment's obvious hesitation, ushered him inside. The one habitable room contained an old rocking chair, several boxes of keepsakes and other possessions, and a ragged-looking mattress. A single candle was burning on an old-fashioned cake stand.

She lowered herself onto the rocking chair. 'What do you want to know?'

'What happened to Torsten Resch?'

'He's gone. They left several weeks ago. But why do you want to know – are you a relative?'

'Not exactly,' he said, standing up his suitcase and using it for a seat. 'I knew a Miriam Rosenfeld in Berlin, before the war even started. We lost touch, and I knew...'

'Rosenfeld,' the woman interjected. 'I always knew she was Jewish. Don't get me wrong,' she said to Russell. 'I've got nothing against the Jews, and Miriam was a lovely girl. But she never admitted to being Jewish. Why would she, I suppose. Torsten must have known.'

'He did.'

'You knew him too?'

'I met him once, here in Breslau. Before his call-up he worked at the Petersdorff department store.'

'He went back there.'

'When? Why did the Army release him?'

'He lost an arm at Stalingrad. Early on, before they were surrounded. Which was lucky in a way. He was in hospital for a long time, and then they discharged him. He went home for a while, then came back to his old job. That's when I met him – he took the room across the street.'

'And what about Miriam?'

'She arrived a few weeks later. He told people she was his cousin from Berlin, but eventually they dropped the pretence, at least with people they knew. And once it was clear she was pregnant... I was invited to the wedding. They got married at the Kreuzkirche, across the river. The 6th of June, 1944. That evening we heard that the English and Americans had landed in France.'

'The child – was it a boy or a girl?'

'A girl, which was nice. One of each.'

'She brought the boy with her?'

'Yes, and I don't think it can have been Torsten's. But it didn't seem to matter – he always treated Leon like a son, and a well-loved one at that.'

He showed her the photograph he'd been carrying for over six years. 'Just to be sure – is this her?'

'Yes. Yes it is.'

'How did she die?'

'In the siege. She was queuing for water at one of the street taps. A shell killed them all. At least it was quick – she wouldn't have known anything about it.' The woman looked up at Russell, and must have noticed the tears forming in his eyes. 'I'm sorry,' she said, 'we all loved Miriam. She was such a happy girl. They were such a happy couple.'

Russell found he was shaking his head. Of all the things he'd expected to find, the very last was Miriam's happiness. He wished that Leon and Esther were here with him now, that they might find some consolation for what had befallen their daughter, both before and after her year of joy.

He asked if the children were both still alive.

'They were ten days ago, when he came to say goodbye. But who knows. Hundreds are dying each day. For all I know they're still waiting at Freiburg Station. That's out in the western suburbs.'

'That's where they went?'

'That's where everyone goes who's allowed to leave. Torsten was high on the list, on account of his work on the anti-Fascist committee.'

'And he took the children with him?'

'Of course.'

'What's the girl's name?' Russell asked, already knowing the answer.

'Esther.'

'And you have no idea who Leon's father was? How old is he?'

She thought about that. 'He'll be six in April,' she said eventually. 'He was five just before his mother was killed. And no, if Torsten wasn't the father, then I've no idea who was.'

Neither, Russell suspected, had Miriam. He thanked Frau Höschle for her help and offered her a pack of cigarettes. The way she stared it might have been gold dust, but she made no move to take the gift. It was only when Russell insisted that she stowed it away in the pocket of her faded housecoat.

Outside the light was fading, and Russell felt disinclined to wander the streets after dark. He needed somewhere to stay, and hadn't yet seen a surviving hotel. The main station was probably his best bet – there had been enough Russians in evidence to inhibit the Poles, or so he hoped.

Walking south he felt strangely buoyed by what he had heard – strangely because Miriam was actually dead. Perhaps he had always known that, but he had never imagined that she would find happiness. Once the bad news had been taken for granted, the good news came into its own.

He wondered if Miriam's parents would feel that way. Would grandchildren named in their honour prove some consolation for the loss of their only child? They probably would. But first they had to survive the journey, and then they had to be found.

It took him twenty minutes to reach the station, which was much more crowded than it had been that morning. The reason for this soon became clear – trains were arriving but not departing, and the roofless concourse was packed with Poles newly arrived from the east, and uncertain where to go. Russell spent half an hour queuing for information, only to be told that none was available. The man behind the window would certainly sell him a ticket, but couldn't guarantee a journey. The next train west for ordinary mortals might run that evening, might run next week, and only the Russians could tell him which. If of course they knew.

At least there was food to be had. He bought himself some bread and sausage, and took it upstairs onto one of the platforms, which offered the same view of the stars, without the congestion. The appearance of a Berlin train would be tempting, but he knew that he couldn't leave Breslau without checking Freiburg Station. In the event, the only train rumbling in the right direction was made up of empty wagons, probably intent on collecting whatever was left of German industry.

It felt a lot longer than twelve hours since he'd said goodbye to Albert. He laid himself out on a platform bench with a sweater for a pillow, and finally found a use for the tie he'd been carrying, threading it through the suitcase handle and looping it around his wrist.

The night passed slowly by. There was no sign of the Polish militia, and hardly any traffic on the road outside, but distant cries and gunfire jerked him awake on several occasions. As soon as it began to grow light, he made his way back to the concourse and, picking his way through the sleeping bodies, found someone selling tea. Equally welcome, and much more surprising, the left luggage office was open for business. After dividing his last few packs of cigarettes between suitcase and coat, he deposited the former and started out for Freiburg Station.

The city was still waking up, and all he encountered on the half-hour walk were two mangy dogs and a swarm of bloated flies. Freiburg Station was a field of rubble, but a train was being loaded in the sidings beyond. A locomotive was backing onto the long line of cattle cars, leaking steam from every orifice and joint.

Russell held back for a moment, surveying the scene. There were several hundred people around the train. Most were German, but he could see small groups of Polish militia. The former were trying to get themselves and their meagre possessions aboard, the latter doing their best to separate the two, and the consequent struggles had already left several bodies on the asphalt. Some Red Army men were standing near the head of the train, apparently oblivious to the robberies going on all around them, but their mere presence probably explained the lack of gunfire or obvious bloodshed. They certainly made Russell feel safer.

He walked down the train, looking for Torsten. He felt sure he would know him, even without a lost arm to assist recognition, and young men in any case seemed thin on the ground. After drawing a blank, he sought out the dispatch office, where a couple of elderly Poles – old railwaymen, by the look of them – explained the situation. As none of the Germans were expected back, no records were being kept of their departures. And since the destinations were rarely known in advance, no records were kept of those either. The wretched Germans were leaving Poland, and where they ended up was of no interest to the Poles.

He walked back to the main line station, where more bad news was waiting. According to a friendly official, in two days time the Russians were planning on closing the Oder-Neisse border to all traffic but their own. When Russell asked how he might avoid permanent incarceration in the new Poland, no answer was forthcoming. Travel on scheduled trains to the border was restricted to those in possession of Soviet passes, and these, the official added with almost indecent relish, were never dished out to ordinary foreigners, only to fraternal Party officials or bosom friends of Uncle Joe.

Russell considered it unlikely that Stalin had bosom friends, but the rules seemed straightforward enough. So all that remained was to bend them. He walked through the pedestrian tunnel to the southern side of the station, and across to the old Reichsbahn building, which the two officers in the Ring had told him housed the Soviet HQ. The huge structure had taken several obvious hits – the six statues above the colonnaded entrance were down to three and a bit – but still seemed in working order. Inside the service was what he'd come to expect from the Soviets – slow verging on comatose.

Asking to see someone from the NKVD provoked the usual look – was the foreigner out of his mind? – but a representative was duly summoned from the lair upstairs. He was young, fair-haired and looked suitably paranoid. Russell led him gently away from the desk, offered up his American passport, and quietly revealed that they were working for the same organisation. Comrade Nemedin in Berlin could vouch for him. Or even Comrade Shchepkin.

The young man examined the passport again. What did Russell actually want?

'A rail pass. I have to be in Berlin by tomorrow morning. If you contact Comrade Nemedin he will confirm the importance of my work there.'

His companion visibly relaxed – distributing passes was obviously part of his remit. 'Wait here,' he said, 'I will talk to Berlin.'

Russell found himself a seat and prepared for a long wait, but only minutes had passed when the officer reappeared, clattering back down the staircase. He handed Russell his passport, open at the newly-stamped page. Phoning Berlin had obviously seemed too much of a chore.

He still needed a train, and one finally arrived at six in the evening. It was part-passenger, part-freight: three carriages half-full of Soviet soldiers, theatre directors, actors and Party apparatchiks; several boxcars full of who knew what. Russell sat with the thespians, who had plenty to drink, and were happy to share it with someone from the land of Shakespeare. They were doing *King Lear* in Berlin, which seemed, after several vodkas, astonishingly appropriate.

His new companions, whom he guessed had been drinking for days, passed out at regular intervals. Russell sat by the window of the barely-lit carriage, peering out at the darkened Silesian fields, wondering how many bottles he needed to drown out the taste of post-war Poland.

The Man I Shall Kill

The same young British soldier turned up at Thomas's house on Saturday morning with another letter from London. Effi insisted on making him tea, partly out of gratitude, partly for the pleasure of a few minutes' company. He talked about his girlfriend back in Birmingham and, rather more wistfully, about the vintage motorcycle he was restoring. Rommel, she remembered, had enjoyed the same pastime.

Once the soldier had gone she took the letter upstairs to read. There were two pages from Rosa about her schoolfriends and teacher, along with a folded drawing of a couple out walking on Parliament Hill, both wrapped up so warmly that only their eyes were visible. Somehow you could still tell that they were old.

Zarah's letter ran to several pages. She described two films she'd seen at the nearby cinema, both starring Ingrid Bergman. The one with her idol Bing Crosby was set in a Catholic school, and sounded far too schmaltzy for Effi's taste; the other, with Gregory Peck and dream sequences by Salvador Dalí, piqued her interest. Surrealism had been frowned upon in the Third Reich, at least where the arts were concerned.

Paul was still seeing a lot of Marisa, Lothar had taken up stamp collecting, and Rosa was again doing well at school. Again? Effi wondered. Her sister had never suggested anything else. And Rosa missed her, Zarah went on, before lamenting the poor selection of vegetables at Camden market.

There was no mention of Jens until the very last paragraph, and then nothing of Zarah's own feelings about his survival. 'I told Lothar his father was alive,' she wrote. 'I wasn't sure how he'd react, but I didn't expect him to be so angry. He said he'd write to his father, but he hasn't. I don't know whether to encourage him or not. What do you think? Anyway, I expect we'll be back in Berlin before long. I like England more than I thought I would, but it's not home. Perhaps we can all live together in Berlin. In a bigger house of course!'

Effi put down the letter, and wiped the tears from her cheeks. Rosa missed her. And she missed Rosa.

She walked to the window and looked out at the desolate garden. Over the last few years she'd grown happier with her own company, but today she felt the need of someone to talk to. Which was unfortunate. Thomas had left the previous day for his family Christmas in the country, and Annaliese was out in Spandau visiting Gerd's parents. Even Frau Niebel and her daughter had gone to relations, and the house felt almost deserted.

She wanted John back, but still hadn't heard a word. She hated not knowing where or how he was. When work had taken him away in the old days, there'd always been the telephone, but the occupying powers were still denying Germans any communications with the outside world. What was the point of that?

* * *

Russell's train terminated at Köpenick, the Berlin suburb where the Soviets had their military HQ, soon after seven that evening. The journey from Breslau had taken twenty-four hours, roughly four times the pre-war average, but he wasn't complaining. He had lost count of the number of motionless trains they had passed, either standing in stations or stabled in remote refuge sidings. Some had been surrounded by milling people, others just standing there, with all the appearance of being empty. And, in at least one case, only the appearance. Stopping alongside one line of cattle cars, Russell and his fellow passengers had heard frantic hammering and harrowing cries for release. The Russian thespians had looked appalled.

Had Torsten and the children been travelling in one of those trains? He had no way of knowing.

The Köpenick Station buffet was full of Russians, and appropriately stocked. After eating his first decent meal for twenty-four hours, Russell searched in a vain for a working telephone, then boarded the next train into the city.

It was almost ten when he reached Dahlem-Dorf. As he walked north through the mostly empty streets he felt a growing sense of anxiety about Effi. Anything could have happened in the last two weeks, and no one would have been able to reach him. When she opened the door, he let out an almost explosive sigh of relief.

They held each other for a long time.

'Is Esther here?' was the first thing he asked.

'Yes, but I think she's gone to bed. Why? What have you found out?'

He took her into the kitchen, shut the door behind them, and told her everything he'd discovered in Breslau. 'I'll tell her in the morning,' he decided. 'There's no point waking her now.'

'No,' Effi agreed. She was wondering, as Russell had, how Esther and Leon would take the news. 'But how did you end up in Breslau?' she asked. 'I thought you were going to Italy.'

'I did.' As Effi made them tea he took her through his journey – the meetings with Slaney and Mizrachi in Vienna, and with Otto 3 and Albert Wiesner in Pontebba; welcoming Náchod and unfriendly Breslau. The only thing he omitted was the encounter with Hirth and his son. That could wait.

'So Torsten and the children are somewhere between Breslau and here?'

'Probably. And the chances are good they'll pass through Berlin. I'll leave messages at all the reception centres tomorrow. But how are you? And where's Thomas?'

'He's gone to spend Christmas with Hanna and Lotte. And I've had some adventures of my own.'

'The flat?'

'Oh that. Yes, and you'll never guess who I ran into at the Schmargendorf Housing Office.' She told him about Jens. 'But that wasn't the adventure. Annaliese asked me for help – she had to collect some medicines from some black marketeers. I took your gun,' she added, seeing the look on his face.

Should that make him feel better or worse, he wondered. He considered admonishing her for taking such risks, but knew he'd be wasting his breath.

Effi described the meeting in Teltow, her recognising the man in the lorry, and the American invasion of her Babelsberg dressing room. She explained the connections she had made, and their confirmation during her and Thomas's Saturday night visit to the Honey Trap.

'Thomas went to the Honey Trap?'

'Only after I begged. He frowned a lot.'

'I'll bet he did.'

'You know, this has been our month for renewing acquaintances – Jens, Albert, that Gestapo officer. And I renewed another one on your behalf – your photographer friend Zembski.'

'You've seen him?'

'Yes, I saw him at his office.'

'By chance?'

'No, didn't I say? I thought it would be a good idea to get some pictures of Geruschke and his employees, ones we could show around. So I went to see him, and he recommended this boy – well, he's about seventeen, I should think.'

Russell knew he shouldn't be surprised, but he was anyway. 'Have you had time to do any filming?' he asked.

'We're nearly finished. I have to go in on Monday – they're having us work on Christmas Eve, would you believe? – but then not again until Thursday. Dufring's hoping to have it all wrapped up by the New Year, and then – I've decided – I'm going to England. To fetch Rosa,' she added, seeing the look on his face. 'And I think Zarah and Lothar will be coming back with us.' She told Russell what her sister had said in the letter.

'And Paul?'

'She didn't say. But what do you think?'

'About what?'

'About what I've been telling you. About Geruschke.'

'I've hardly had time to take it all in. It seems like we're in with a chance of getting something on the bastard, but only at the risk of enraging the Americans.'

'Do we care what they think?'

'I'm afraid we have to.' His and Shchepkin's future – in fact all of their futures – depended on it.

'So we just forget about him?'

'Of course not. We can still nail him, but we have to make damn sure we don't take the credit.'

* * *

Next morning was sunny and cold. Esther was on her way out when Russell caught up with her; he asked her to wait while he grabbed his own coat, and the two of them talked in the garden. She didn't cry when he told her that her daughter was dead, just lowered her head with the air of someone acknowledging an obvious truth.

'But there's good news too,' he told her.

Her look suggested he'd taken leave of his senses.

He told her about the children, about Torsten Resch, about the happiness Miriam had apparently known. He avoided the matter of the boy's parentage – he wanted to talk to Torsten before spelling out what he feared. 'The children's names are Leon and Esther,' he added, and that did bring tears to her eyes.

'Where are they?' she asked.

'I don't know. They left Breslau about ten days ago, heading west. Today I'll start checking the stations. We'll find them.'

'Will you come to the hospital and tell all this to Leon? And if Effi could come as well – she always seems to perk him up.'

Russell smiled. 'Of course.'

An hour later the three of them were gathered around Leon Rosenfeld's bed. He seemed better than he had a fortnight ago, and took the tidings of Miriam's death almost as stoically as his wife had done. By contrast, the news that he had grandchildren almost had him leaping from his bed. If no one had been there to restrain him, he would soon have been scouring eastern Germany and Poland for his namesake.

After a quarter of an hour, Russell and Effi said their goodbyes. On their way out, it occurred to Russell that Erich Luders might still be in the hospital, and a query at reception elicited directions to another ward. They found him sitting up in bed.

'They're letting me out tomorrow,' the young journalist told them. 'I've been lucky. Compared to some, at any rate.'

'Who do you mean?' Russell asked.

'Haven't you heard? Manfred Haferkamp was killed the other day. A suicide, according to the police in the Russian zone, but there are lots of rumours. Haferkamp hated the Russians and their German supporters – Ulbricht and his gang – and he wasn't afraid to say so.'

'Maybe he should have been,' Russell murmured. He felt sick inside. Had his report caused this? Hadn't Shchepkin implied that expulsion from the Party was the worst that could happen? Or had that been wishful thinking on his own part? He wanted to talk to the Russian.

'What's the matter?' Effi asked him, once they'd left the young man.

He told her.

She squeezed his arm, but didn't try to argue him out of feeling responsible. 'Is there anything you can do?'

'I can tell Shchepkin...' he began, but that was far as the thought went. What *could* he tell Shchepkin?

'Perhaps he was fooled too.'

'Perhaps,' Russell said doubtfully.

At the front entrance a public telephone was actually working. He dialled the emergency number that Shchepkin had given him, and left the agreed message. They would meet the next morning.

Effi took his place at the phone, called Lucie at home, and dictated a list of reception points for Russell to write down. All were stations or railway yards, and Russell remembered most of them from 1941, when they'd been used to ship Jews in the other direction. He supposed he should be pleased that Torsten and the children weren't headed for a Nazi death camp.

They went their separate ways, he to visit the railway locations, she to the local Housing Office. If the refugees reached Berlin they would need somewhere to live, preferably somewhere big enough to accommodate Esther and Leon as well. With grandparents and grandchildren both qualifying as Victims of Fascism, the man she spoke to seemed sanguine enough, though he noted that Torsten's status might prove problematic.

Effi felt like pointing out that Torsten was also a 'victim', but then so, she supposed, were half the people in Europe.

For Russell, the only difficulty was getting from place to place in anything approaching a reasonable time. It all seemed to take forever, but by the end of the afternoon he had left messages and contact details at all the relevant offices. He finally arrived home to find Effi ensconced in their bedroom with a bespectacled young man. The bed was covered with photographs, grainy blow-ups of faces and figures against the same desolate backdrop. 'That's my Gestapo killer,' Effi said, pointing out one face. 'And here's the American colonel we saw with Geruschke that night.'

There were two copies of each photograph. 'Here's our first Otto,' Russell said, noticing the accountant in the background of one picture. 'And this is the man who was going to shoot me in Kyritz Wood. I can't see his partner anywhere.'

Effi examined the face of the would-be killer, and shuddered. 'And we have three addresses,' she added. 'Including my Gestapo man's. Horst is a star.'

'It was the irregulars who followed them home,' the photographer admitted, but he still seemed pleased by the compliment. 'There are eleven faces,' he said, 'so that's fourteen packs.'

Russell pulled the suitcase from under the bed and counted out the cigarette packets. It was time he asked Dallin for more.

Sattler dropped them into a canvass holdall and zipped it up. 'Let me know if you need any inside shots,' he said. 'But please, I'd appreciate you not mentioning my name to anyone.'

'Geruschke makes a very bad enemy,' Russell agreed.

'It's my business I'm thinking of,' Sattler countered. 'I'm doing a lot of work for Americans – that's why I'm in Dahlem this afternoon – and I don't want to upset anyone.'

'What sort of work?' Russell asked out of curiosity.

'Nothing like this,' Sattler told him, gesturing towards the display on the bed. 'Mostly sex, but the Americans like to call it art. God knows how they won the war.'

Effi saw him downstairs to the door, then came back up. Russell was still scanning the photographs. 'That boy'll go far,' he observed.

'He will, won't he?'

'Germany's future,' Russell murmured, still looking at the pictures. 'Now what do we do with these?'

* * *

The Tiergarten black market seemed busier than usual, probably because it was Christmas Eve. Remembering he hadn't got a present for Effi, Russell took more interest than usual in the items for sale, but nothing leapt out at him. It was hard to take this Christmas seriously, even with a light coating of snow on the ground.

Shchepkin appeared at his shoulder with all the old magical abruptness, but seemed more agitated than usual. And when Russell started pouring out his indignation over Haferkamp's death, the Russian just told him to get a grip. 'We have a real problem,' he said. 'Nemedin is still furious with both of us. We have to fix him before he fixes us.'

'Why?' Russell asked. 'I mean, why's he furious?'

'The farce with Schreier, his guards getting killed. He had his knuckles rapped by Beria – if it weren't for his family connections he'd have been recalled. And he blames us. You in particular, but he's also suspicious of me.'

'Oh shit,' Russell murmured.

'Indeed.'

'So how do we fix him? Do you have any brilliant ideas?' Asking the question, he wondered what sort of answer he wanted to hear.

'I hope so. While you've been chasing Jews I've been digging up incriminating material. I now have access to Nemedin's NKVD personnel file, and such files – in case you don't know – are very comprehensive. Your own runs to forty-five pages, and Nemedin's is five times as long. He has, shall we say, a controversial history. He was responsible for the purging of several other communist parties during the time of the Pact, and he was involved in the execution of the Polish officer corps – almost ten thousand of them – in 1940.'

'So the Poles in London are telling the truth.'

'About that, yes, though not about much else. But can we concentrate on the matter in hand? There's enough in Nemedin's file to tell the Western allies who and what he really is, which is the first objective. I also have a photograph of Nemedin with a British agent. It was taken by our people in London, with a view to incriminating the Englishman, but we can use it the other way round, to cast doubt on Nemedin's loyalty. I want you to deliver the file and the photograph to a British journalist named Tristram Hadleigh – do you know him?'

'No.' Though judging by the name he knew the type.

'He has friends in your Secret Service, and I assume that he'll either get the story printed or pass it on to them. If the file and the photograph are published, Nemedin's ability to work outside the Soviet Union will be over. His face will be known, and there'll be a huge question mark over his loyalty. At worst, he'll be called back to Moscow; at best, Beria will have him shot for incompetence. Do I shock you? He'd like nothing better than to have me shot. And you too, after what happened with Schreier.'

'Why do I have to deliver these things? What's wrong with the post? Or some young German boy?'

'They'll be more credible coming from you. It mustn't look like one of our schemes. You're a journalist with a good track record here in Berlin, with ties to the old KPD. And that's where you say you got hold of the stuff – from a disgruntled German comrade.'

'Why not give it to the Americans? We can tell *them* the truth.'

'No, it has to be the British. If the journalist passes it to the British Secret Service, Beria will hear about it from his mole in London.'

'I'd forgotten about that. So how are you going to get the stuff to me? By post?'

'No. You'll have to collect it from a dead letter drop.'

'Why?'

'The post can't be trusted, and the fewer people who know about this the better. I'll be in Warsaw when you pick it up...'

'What?'

'Yes, I have to distance myself from this. Which will help you too – if they don't suspect me, they won't suspect you.'

That made a vague sort of sense, but...

'Look, you must collect the stuff on Friday, just before dark would be best. The drop-off is a shop at Roland Ufer 17. There's an overhead railway station just up the road. If you arrange to meet Hadleigh at the British Press Club you can take a train and hand the stuff over. As simple as that. And we'll be rid of Nemedin, which should save both our lives.'

Put like that...

'You'll do it?'

'I suppose so. How did you get hold of his personnel file?'

'I still have a few friends from the old days, most of them clinging on with their fingertips, just like me. We help each other when we can.'

'So what can go wrong?' Russell asked.

Shchepkin shrugged. 'There's always a risk, but we really have no choice. Take a good look around before you go in.'

'That doesn't really answer my question.'

'What could go wrong is your getting caught with the material, in which case we'll both be finished. But there's no reason why you should be. No one will know the material's missing until the next day.'

Russell gave him a suspicious look. 'If you're away in Warsaw, someone else has to be involved.'

'Of course, but you wouldn't expect me to give you a name. You wouldn't recognise it. And it wouldn't help you if you did.'

Russell sighed. As usual with Shchepkin, he felt as though he'd been led deep into a maze, and left to wonder where he was. Taking 'a good look around' was all very well, but the same thought had probably occurred to the fool who commanded the Light Brigade. 'Okay,' he said. 'But anything remotely suspicious, and I'm going home empty-handed. All right?'

'Of course,' Shchepkin said, sounding ever so slightly relieved. 'Now I have something for you. The Jew you wanted traced.'

'Otto Pappenheim.'

'Yes. He did receive a transit visa, and he did cross the new border between Germany and the Soviet Union.'

'Ah.'

'On June 21st, 1941.'

'The day before the invasion.'

'Exactly. His train was stopped at Baranovichi – eastward movements were halted so all available lines could be used to reinforce the frontier. And that's the last official trace of him. There's certainly no record of him reaching Moscow, or travelling on the Trans-Siberian. Either he was caught up in the early fighting, or he found refuge in one of the local Jewish communities. And you know what happened to them.'

Russell did. 'Could you find out his age?'

'Yes, I forgot. He was born in 1914, in Berlin. His documents claimed he was single, but many applicants lied about that. As much to themselves as to us. '

Russell grunted his agreement. If this was Rosa's father – and the age seemed about right – then a guilty lie was possible. But the chances of tracking him down seemed almost non-existent – if this Otto wasn't buried in an unmarked grave somewhere in western Russia, he could be more or less anywhere. If the man ever came back in search of his family, then he might well find them, but as things stood they would never find him. 'Thanks for that,' he told Shchepkin. As they got up to leave he remembered his original purpose. 'So why was Haferkamp killed?' he asked.

Shchepkin looked at him for a moment, then managed a wry smile. 'I don't know,' he said. 'Rumour says it was an accident – that some young idiot hit him once too often, and his superiors decided that a suicide was less likely to upset the German comrades. Then again, maybe someone thought they needed upsetting, and had him killed for that reason. I don't know.'

'So it wasn't just my report.'

'No,' Shchepkin said tiredly, as if he found Russell's concern to apportion personal responsibility more than a little exasperating. 'Your report didn't tell them anything new. Not about Haferkamp anyway. Now I must be off. If all goes well, we'll meet again in a fortnight.'

He strode off, briefly raising one arm in farewell. 'If all goes well,' Russell murmured to himself. He could imagine the riposte on his gravestone: 'If all had gone well, he wouldn't be here.'

But Friday was a long way off, and the Soviets far from his only problem. He had to come up with a plan for dealing with Geruschke, look out for Torsten and the children, and get his story off to Solly. He still hadn't fixed on an angle for the latter, and talking to Isendahl might jolt his thoughts into some sort of order. He could then find a café to write in, prior to joining Effi at Ali's.

He spent the long walk to Friedrichshain marshalling his thoughts, and was pleased to find Isendahl at home. His German friend was eager to hear how Russell had fared with the Haganah, and they ended up talking for over two hours about the options open to Europe's Jewish survivors, and the seriously mixed blessings that each seemed to offer. Neither man took to the idea of Israel, but both saw the need, and thought it inevitable. So what mattered was what kind of Israel – a racially exclusive state run by soldiers and rabbis, or an heir to European Jewry's socialist traditions that might, one day, share the land with the Arabs on more or less equal terms. Isendahl of course favoured the latter, but he wasn't hopeful.

'I was thinking about those options you listed,' he told Russell. 'And I asked myself: where would I – a German-Jewish socialist – feel most at home? And guess what answer I came up with? Not a Soviet-run Germany, not a Jewish Palestine, not the United States. It's almost the ultimate paradox – the place I know I'll feel most at home is a born-again bourgeois Germany. The same one that took such pleasure in murdering both socialists and Jews.'

Russell smiled, and found himself thinking of Albert Wiesner. He claimed to be a socialist, but his socialism didn't stretch to accommodating Arabs within the new state's borders. And when forced to choose between socialism and Israel, Russell had no doubt which way Albert would jump. The Nazis had given him his politics, and he would pass them on. There was still a price to pay.

But what was the alternative? Back in 1918 Russell had looked forward to a world in which anti-Semitism and other equally obnoxious prejudices would become increasingly unsustainable, but the Nazis had put paid to that dream, probably for at least another century. The old Jewish life in Germany and eastern Europe was gone for ever, and with it the hopes of a secular assimilation. It was Israel or the States, and Russell was inclined to favour the latter. It seemed better that the Americans profit from Europe's failings, than that the Arabs pay for them.

Not that it mattered what he thought. And he would not condemn those, like Albert, who thought differently. Or at least not yet.

Russell remembered something that Albert had said about the Nokmim, that he didn't agree with what they were doing, but would probably applaud their successes. He asked Isendahl whether they or the Ghosts of Treblinka had made the news in his absence.

'Only indirectly,' Wilhelm told him. He rummaged round for a newspaper, and pointed out an article. A man had been found dead in Neukölln, soon after a Jew identified him as an Auschwitz guard.

'Why wasn't he arrested?' Russell asked.

'Who knows? The Soviets may have had a use for him.'

'You think it was the Ghosts?'

'They left their mark on him. A Star of David cut into his forearm, where the Nazis used to tattoo their Jewish prisoners.'

'Wonderful,' Russell said drily.

'It is in a way. And dreadful too. Do you know that line by Yeats: "a terrible beauty is born"?'

'Uh-huh. High drama's addictive stuff, but right now I'd settle for a few years of peace and contrition.'

'Wrong place, wrong time.'

'Probably.'

Isendahl was improving with age, Russell thought, as he walked back down Neue Königstrasse in search of a café. He'd noticed a letter with US Army postal markings on the man's desk, so maybe Freya was in touch, or even coming back.

He eventually found a bar off Alexanderplatz, and spent a couple of hours sketching out a series of articles on 'The Jews after Hitler'. He reached the corner of Hufelandstrasse just in time to see Effi step down from the Soviet bus, and stopped her in mid stride with a long whistle. She hurried towards him, eager to hear the news from Shchepkin.

'It might have been Rosa's dad,' Russell told her, 'but we'll probably never know.' He explained the circumstances of Otto 2's disappearance.

Effi made a face. 'What more can we do?'

'Nothing more,' Russell told her, 'at least for the moment. I think we have to assume that Rosa's an orphan, and act accordingly.'

She took his arm as they walked back down to Ali's building. 'There's not much else we can do, is there? But she *so* needs to know, one way or another. She never says so, but I know that she does.'

And so do you, Russell thought.

They walked on up to the apartment, where another delicious-smelling meal was in preparation. Neither Ali nor Fritz had ever celebrated Christmas, but both confessed to a childhood fascination with the Christian festival and its rituals, particularly the one which involved taking a tree indoors and smothering it in trinkets. Fritz had been gifted a bottle of wine by a friend in the US forces, and they all drank a toast to the future.

'While I remember,' Effi said, 'the photographer I told you about has taken some pictures.' She took the sheaf from her bag and placed it on the table. 'If you could show these around. The more people get to see them, the more we'll identify.'

Ali leafed her way through them, Fritz looking over her shoulder. 'The stuff of nightmares,' he murmured. 'If you do get them identified, what then?'

'I'll take the names to someone in the US records office.' Russell replied. Luders had given him one contact, and there were bound to be others. 'From there – I don't know.' He knew he should talk to Dallin before taking the matter any further, but he didn't really want to.

'Like mopping up after a battle,' Fritz murmured.

Or clearing the decks for the next one, Russell thought sourly. He told himself to cheer the hell up. 1946 was bound to be better.

The women had gone into the kitchen, and he could see Effi leaning back against the wall, smiling at something. The world might be going even further to the dogs, but she was as wonderful as ever. How lucky was he?

It was a pre-war sort of evening, with good food and conversation, a wine that wasn't an insult, an enjoyable game of cards. It was snowing again when they left, large flakes floating out of the darkness and clinging to the riven walls. There weren't many roofs for Santa to land on, but several hopeful chimneys rose out of the empty shells.

It was, Effi decided, 'almost like a real Christmas'.

* * *

Christmas morning drew them to the Ku'damm, in hope of reprising their own pre-war ritual of coffee, cakes and a stroll in the wintry park. Rather to Russell's surprise, they did find an open café, its tables set out on the snowy sidewalk, the smell of real coffee strong in the air. The price was black-market steep, but the coffee seemed more than worth it, a suitable present for each to be giving the other. They sat outside and took their time, smiling at passers-by and imagining the boulevard re-built.

When a British jeep drove by garlanded in silver tinsel the patrons all clapped, causing the corporal next to the driver to stand up and bow.

The sound of a tram squealing its way round the truncated Memorial Church reminded Effi of what they had planned. 'So, Schulstrasse?' she asked.

'I suppose so. It doesn't feel very Christmassy.'

'Neither does sitting at home with no heat.'

'True. Well, let's hope we can get there.'

They walked down to Zoo Station, where both the Stadtbahn and U-Bahn were running some sort of service. The outdoor option seemed preferable, and not just to them – the high-level platforms were crowded with families, most of whom seemed in high spirits. A lot got off when they did, probably bound for the funfair in the Lustgarten. They walked down to the U-Bahn platform, where a train stood waiting to carry them northward. 'It's always like this for royalty,' Russell noted.

They reached the Jewish Hospital around one o'clock, and the crowded canteen seemed like a good place to start. With only the one set of photographs, they worked their way from table to table, trying to disarm what suspicions they encountered, as prepared as they could be for signs of anguish.

Effi's Gestapo officer was recognised almost straight away, first by one young man, and then by several women. All agreed his surname was Mechnig, and one of the women thought his first name was Ulrich. He had worked at the Columbiahaus 'wild concentration camp' before the war, and later at the Alex. He had no particular reputation as a sadist, but then the competition had been fierce.

An hour or so later, five other faces had been recognised. Russell noted the names on the backs of the photographs, along with the details of witnesses willing to testify.

Which was good, but less than they'd hoped for, and as they made their way out Effi insisted on interrupting a football kick-about in the ambulance bay. It was the third boy – a wary-eyed lad of around sixteen – who lingered over the picture of Geruschke. It *is* him,' he whispered eventually, and Effi thought for a moment that the boy was going to cry. But instead the eyes turned to stone. 'Standartenführer Fehse,' he said, and abruptly handed that picture back.

'Are you certain?' Effi asked, and received a pitying look. 'Where do you know him from?'

'He was in charge of the detention centre in Leipzig. He sent us to Auschwitz.'

'Who?'

'My mother, my father, my sisters. They all died.'

'How did you survive?' Effi asked.

The boy shrugged. 'I was a good worker.'

'What can you tell us about Fehse?'

'He was one of the worst. In Leipzig he took bribes to let people go – money, daughters, whatever they had – but later we found out that he'd just moved the girls to another building. They still ended up on the train.' The boy resumed his perusal of the pictures. 'And Fehse enjoyed watching beatings,' he added as an afterthought.

Two more men were picked out. The first he thought was named Schönhöft, the second he couldn't remember. Both had been jailers in Leipzig.

'Would you testify against these people?' Russell asked.

'Not in a German court.'

'An American one?'

'Perhaps.'

Russell asked the boy for his name.

'Daniel Eisenberg. But you'd better hurry – I plan to be in Palestine soon. We all do.'

* * *

'Did you mean it – about going to the Americans with what we've found out?' Effi asked Russell as they walked up Vogelsangstrasse. 'They've already warned us both to leave the man alone. Or are you hoping they don't know who he really is?'

'I'd be amazed if they didn't. And to answer your question, I really don't know. We have to tell someone, and maybe we can find some Americans who do want to listen. But first I think we might pay your Gestapo man a visit. We need more information, and we have his address. If we offer Herr Mechnig some money and a head start, he might tell us more about Geruschke's – Fehse's – operation. And particularly about the American that young Horst took the picture of. I'd like to know more about him before I go to Dallin. Or whoever it is we go to.'

'I don't like the idea of letting Mechnig go,' Effi protested. She could still see the boy on the U-Bahn platform.

'We won't,' Russell said. 'We'll take a leaf out of Fehse's book, and promise him something we have no intention of delivering.'

Effi thought about that. 'Okay,' she said eventually. 'He lives not far from Jens – we could walk over there this evening.'

'And wish him a Happy Christmas,' Russell added, as he opened Thomas's front gate.

In the event, Herr Mechnig had to wait. One of the residents had left a short note by the telephone: 'Message from Lucie – they've arrived.'

'Yes!' Russell exclaimed, clenching a fist in celebration. He re-read the message just to make sure. The 'they' was encouraging, though hardly definitive.

Effi already had the front door open. It was dark when they reached Kronprinzenallee again, and the buses had vanished with the light. After waiting almost an hour, Russell remembered the lot full of Press Club jeeps on nearby Argentinischeallee. They were used for taking visiting journalists on tours of the Berlin ruins, but such jaunts seemed unlikely on Christmas evening. And surely no one could object to one being used for the odd rescue mission.

The sergeant in charge was unimpressed by this argument, but proved susceptible to others – Effi's smile, an extortionate hire price in cigarettes, and Russell's surrender of his press accreditation as security. The deal done, he insisted on loaning Russell a US Army greatcoat and cap, 'just in case'.

Effi wanted to drive, but had to admit that might look suspicious, and once Russell got the hang of the gear-shift they made good progress through the dark and mostly empty streets. After all the frustrations of the last fortnight, moving through Berlin at this sort of speed seemed nothing short of miraculous. There were lights through windows and shell-holes, and the occasional sounds of Christmas revelry in the distance. As they drove past a roofless church in Moabit the bells began to toll, adding their own mournful commentary to the sea of broken homes.

The area around Lehrter Station was as crowded as the city was empty. Russell pulled the jeep up alongside others bearing the UNRRA initials, and was careful to take the key. Several trains stood in the station, and all seemed recent arrivals – the platforms were swarming with people, most turning this way and that for some notion of where to go. Other, earlier arrivals had given up wondering, and transformed the concourse into a field of small encampments, groups of prone bodies surrounded by suitcase perimeters. In one cordoned-off area stretchers were laid out in rows, some bodies twitching, others worryingly still. The strong smell of human waste hung in the air, and one line of cattle cars was being rinsed out by a chain of bucket carriers.

The only thing missing was noise. Apart from the tired hiss of engines and the odd cry of alarm, the crowd seemed subdued to the point of submission. They had reached Berlin and the safety of the newly shrunken Fatherland, but at the cost of their homes and most of their possessions. And now their lives had shrunk to this – a few square metres of concrete under a bomb-mangled roof.

They found Lucie bandaging a young boy's leg. 'They're in one of the offices,' she told them. 'Wait a few seconds and I'll take you.'

She tore and knotted the ends, smiled at the child and got to her feet. The child gazed back with empty eyes, then threw both arms around his mother's neck and tried to hide his face.

They worked their way along the crowded platform to an office near the end. Opening the door, Russell saw Torsten sitting on the opposite bench, his one arm securing the baby girl on his lap. He looked twenty years older than the young man Russell had met in 1939.

The girl had fair hair and Torsten's mouth and nose. The boy beside them had dark hair and the eyes from Miriam's photograph. He was about five, and looked like he hadn't slept for a week.

'Herr Russell,' Torsten said tiredly. It was almost a question.

'Do you remember me?' Russell asked.

'Of course.' He took a deep breath, as if trawling for energy. 'You came to Breslau looking for Miriam.'

Russell introduced Effi.

'And these must be Leon and Esther,' she said.

Torsten looked confused. 'How do you know that?'

'I saw Frau Höschle in Breslau,' Russell told him. 'She told me you where you'd gone.'

'Why? Why were you looking for me?'

'That's a long story, and I think you need rest and food first. Effi and I are living in the same house as Miriam's mother...'

'She's alive?' he asked, clearly astonished.

'And her father too, though he's in hospital. We'd like to take you home to Esther.'

'That's her name,' the boy said, pointing at his sister.

Torsten managed the faintest of smiles. 'That sounds like heaven.'

* * *

When Russell and Effi went out the next morning, the others were all still asleep. They had given up Thomas's bedroom to Torsten and the children, and colonised the one normally occupied by the Niebels. The mother would doubtless be livid when she found out, but Russell had unearthed a ready-made riposte while shamelessly rummaging through their possessions – a signed photograph of the *Reichsmarschal*, lovingly wrapped in velvet.

The Nazis lived on in so many ways, he thought, as he and Effi climbed aboard the unreturned jeep: in the devastation they had invited, in the *judenfrei* Germany which seemed irreversible; in bastards like Ulrich

Mechnig, whom the two of them were about to visit.

Russell glanced across at Effi, who gave him a joyous smile. In pre-war times her presence on such an outing would have crippled him with anxiety, but no longer. She had as much experience of dicing with danger as he had, perhaps even more. The thought crossed his mind that all their involuntary adventures of the last few years might have made them better people, but another thought running behind it suggested that the obverse was also true. Like travel, struggles with survival both broadened and narrowed the mind.

The address that Horst and his 'irregulars' had supplied was a corner house close to the Ringbahn. The street seemed relatively intact, the three boys who came to inspect the jeep almost healthy-looking. Russell promised them a cigarette each to mind the vehicle, and walked up the steps with Effi. The front door was hanging from one twisted hinge; they clambered through the opening and climbed the stairs to Apartment 4.

'I'll let you do the talking,' Effi told him.

'Okay,' Russell said, taking the gun from his pocket and rapping sharply on the door. 'You just look menacing.'

They heard footsteps inside, then a male voice demanding to know who it was.

'Housing Office,' Russell improvised.

'Come back another time.'

'If you make me come back, I'll have to report you.'

'Oh, what the...' Two bolts were thrown back, the door swung open, and Mechnig came into view. He was surprised to see Effi's face, alarmed by the gun in Russell's hand.

Russell prodded him back into the apartment, and heard Effi close the door behind them. A girl was sitting on a threadbare couch, a blanket wrapped around her, but otherwise seemingly naked. She looked about fourteen.

'Your daughter?' Russell asked sarcastically, drawing a short laugh from the girl. 'Go and get dressed,' he told her.

'I'll go with her,' Effi said, and followed her into the adjoining bedroom. The girl tossed the blanket aside and started putting her clothes on. She was all skin and bones, with bruises across her barely discernible breasts. Once dressed she took a pack of cigarettes from the row on the shelf and gave Effi a questioning look.

'Take them all,' Effi suggested, and the girl needed no second bidding.

In the living room Russell had ordered Mechnig onto the couch. 'Who do you Americans think you are?' he said sullenly, seemingly confused by Russell's greatcoat and hat.

It seemed churlish to disabuse him. 'What name are you using here?' Russell asked.

'My name is Meissner, Oskar Meissner, not that it is any of your business.'

'Your name is Ulrich Mechnig. SS Sturmscharführer Mechnig of the Berlin Gestapo. Or did you rise higher than that?'

Mechnig stared coldly back at him.

'You're a dead man,' Russell said mildly.

'You can't touch me. Not with the friends I've got.'

'Fehse and the others? They're finished. And I can not only touch you, I can shoot you here and now. I doubt anyone would come to investigate, but even if they did, I can't see them caring that much. The camps are full of scum like you, waiting for their trials. And their hangings.'

Mechnig opened his mouth to say something, but was distracted by the return of the women.

'I might have known,' the girl said, looking at him. She had obviously overheard their conversation. 'And I won't say anything,' she promised Russell on her way to the door. 'What a great companion you must be,' Russell observed after she'd left. 'But back to business. I want all you know about Fehse.'

'Or what?'

'Good question. Let me give you some options. If you won't talk, we'll drive you straight into the Russian sector, and hand you over to some NKVD friends of mine, along with your real identity, your false papers, and witness statements from several Jews who remember you all too well.

My friend here saw you kill a young boy on a U-Bahn platform and is more than willing to testify against you, should they ever bother with a trial. I think it's more likely that the Russians will just put you out with the rubbish.

'Ah, not so confident,' Russell noted. The look on Mechnig's face suggested that the NKVD still lay outside his boss's sphere of influence. 'But let's look on the positive side. If you do tell us all you know, we'll give you a free ride to Anhalter Station, and buy you a ticket to anywhere you like in the American zone. You can keep your papers and carry on being good old squeaky-clean Oskar Meissner. You can even join the rat-run to South America if you know how. This is your chance to live, Ulrich. Your only chance.'

Mechnig said nothing for a moment, but Effi could see he was weakening. If there were two things that Russell was good at, they were talking himself out of corners, and other people into them.

'He'll kill me,' Mechnig said tonelessly.

'Not if you leave while you can.'

Mechnig ran a hand through what was left of his hair. 'What do you want to know?'

'Nothing too dangerous. What's his first name, for a start?'

'Reinhard.'

'Tell me about his business – what he deals in, how he brings the stuff in.'

'That's easy. Everything. He deals in everything – drugs, booze, cigarettes, girls of course – we even brought in a lorry-load of bananas the other day. Anything you can move for a profit, we move it.'

It sounded like a company slogan. 'How is the stuff brought in? And where is it kept?'

Haulage was mostly by lorry, but Fehse also had men working on the railways. Mechnig listed several distribution centres, including the one out in Spandau where Russell's reprieve had been granted. 'We get stuff from everywhere – Denmark and Sweden, the American PX, all across the Reich.'

Russell felt like reminding him that the Reich was history, but concentrated on looking impressed. He could have guessed everything Mechnig had told them so far, but he didn't want the other man to know that. 'So Fehse has friends among the Americans?'

'Of course.'

'Anyone in particular?'

'What do you mean?'

Russell had brought four of Horst's photographs with him – the three still unidentified and the one of the uniformed American. 'I mean him,' he said, showing Mechnig the latter.

'His name's Crosby.'

'I thought it might be. What do he and Fehse do for each other?'

'We do jobs for him, and he keeps the occupation people off our backs.'

'What sort of jobs?'

'People mostly. He tells us which Germans he wants brought out of the Russian sector, and we go and get them.'

'What sort of people?'

'All sorts. Scientists, businessmen, patriots. These days the Americans are serious about fighting the Russians. It's a pity they didn't realise who their real enemy was a couple of years ago.'

'Isn't it just,' Russell said drily. 'So Fehse doesn't have any Russians on his payroll?'

'Only one that I know about. An army man out at Köpenick.'

'Name?'

'Sokolovsky.'

A shame it wasn't Nemedin, Russell thought to himself. One last question occurred to him: 'So why does Fehse hire so many Jews?'

Mechnig laughed for the first time. 'The man's a genius. None of them are really Jews, but he gets all the kudos for helping them. The Americans lap it up. A gangster with a real soft spot – that's what they think. A German Robin Hood.' He laughed again.

'Where does the genius live?'

'He has a villa out in Wannsee. It belonged to one of Heydrich's friends.'

'How apt.' Russell showed Mechnig the remaining photographs, and took down the names he gave. He had no way of knowing whether the other man was telling the truth, but instinct suggested he was. Mechnig seemed almost relieved that they knew about his past.

At that moment he was staring at Effi. 'When I saw you out in Teltow I knew I'd seen you at the club, but I had the feeling then that I'd seen your face before. And then the boss told me you were an actress.'

'I still am,' she told him shortly. 'But don't expect an autograph.'

He turned back to Russell. 'So can I pack a suitcase?'

Ten minutes later they were on their way, with Effi at the wheel and the others seated behind her. Russell didn't expect Mechnig to make a break for it – the promised train would carry him further and faster than his feet ever could – but he kept his hand on the gun, just in case the man had a brainstorm. When they reached Anhalter Station, he took Mechnig through to the ticket office. Frankfurt was the first available destination in the American Zone, which seemed to suit him well enough. Once Russell had purchased the ticket, Mechnig scowled his lack of gratitude, and promptly stalked away.

Behind the wheel of the jeep, Effi seemed excited. 'None of them are really Jews,' she repeated, as Russell climbed in beside her.

'So he's not a philanthropist after all.'

'No, you idiot. None of them. Including the first Otto.'

Russell gave her an admiring look. He'd been too busy intimidating Mechnig to notice.

'So why did he choose that name?' Effi asked.

Russell checked the petrol gauge. 'Let's go and ask him.'

They drove across the desolate Tiergarten to the house on Solinger Strasse. Russell's persistent hammering evoked no response, from either the phony Otto or any of his neighbours. 'He's probably at the Honey Trap,' Russell decided. 'And I think our welcome there may be less than effusive. We'll have to wait.'

'I'm working tomorrow and Friday,' Effi lamented.

'Then we'll wake him up on Saturday.'

He drove them to the Press Club in Dahlem, and returned the jeep to its owners.

While Effi made use of the pampered press corps' hot showers, he used one of the telephones to track down the number of a paper now printing in Frankfurt. 'There's a man on the train from Berlin,' he told the desk he eventually reached, 'the one that's supposed to arrive just after nine this evening. His papers say he's Oskar Meissner but his real name is Ulrich Mechnig. He was a Gestapo Sturmscharführer, and he has a lot of blood on his hands.'

'Who are you? How do you know about this?'

'I'm a journalist just like you,' Russell told him. 'And naturally I can't divulge my sources.' He hung up the phone, and stood there for a moment examining his conscience.

It was fine. What he'd done was hardly cricket, but who would invite the Nazis to Lord's?

* * *

That evening, they listened to Torsten recount Miriam's story. The children were sleeping; Esther, though she stayed with them in the dimly lit kitchen, had heard it all that morning.

After her rescue Miriam had, at Isendahl's instigation, been taken in by a Marthe and Franz Wilden. This Christian couple, who had no children of their own, had lavished the mute, traumatised and pregnant girl with care and attention. Frau Wilden, who had served as a nurse in the First War, had eventually helped deliver the baby, and her husband had paid a small fortune for the necessary documentation.

As Russell had guessed, the young Leon had been fathered by one of the SS rapists in the house on Eisenacher Strasse. But her son's birth had been Miriam's re-birth – according to Torsten she often said that having the child was like waking up again. And that, once a mother, she had become determined to survive the war.

It never mattered that Leon was the product of rape, or that the rapist was a killer of her people – she loved the child without reservation. She considered going home to Silesia but the risks seemed too high – her false papers were for a Berliner, and people would certainly recognise her in Wartha. She sent letters to her parents, but never received a reply – by this time, of course, the farm was in ruins, Leon and Esther long since gone. The lack of response upset her, but it still seemed wiser to stay where she was.

Then, in the autumn of 1942, the Wilden house had been bombed. She and Leon were in the cellar, but the Wildens were both killed, and her papers were destroyed in the subsequent fire. Risking everything, convinced that even a blind man could see she was Jewish, she went to apply for new ones, at the office which dealt with such eventualities. And the man she saw had flirted with her, ruffled Leon's hair, and provided the papers and home she needed without so much as a second thought. That afternoon she and the boy moved into a room of their own in Wedding, stunned by how easy the process had been.

As her confidence grew, the bombing got worse, and she eventually decided that the risks of staying outweighed those of going home. She realised that Wartha was still out of bounds, but Breslau would do until the war was over, and someone might have news of her parents. Something happened on the train – something she would never talk about – but they both arrived safely, and were allocated a room by the city authorities which a Jewish family had long since abandoned. She visited the Petersdorff store more in hope than expectation – Torsten was well past the age of call-up – but there he was.

And there she was. 'I couldn't believe it when I saw her,' Torsten said. 'I fell in love with her all over again. Or I would have, if I hadn't always loved her.'

He smiled at the memory. 'She came to stay with me, and, well' – he glanced across at Esther – 'soon we were living as husband and wife. No one troubled us, and we troubled no one. Little Esther was born, and it felt as though we had a complete family. The war was getting closer of course, but we never dreamt things would get as bad as they did. We were so happy. Until the day she died we were happy.' He raised his eyes. 'And she lives on in the children.'

'Yes,' Esther said quietly. 'Yes, she does.'

After the Soviet bus collected Effi next morning, Russell spent the pre-dawn hours working at Thomas's desk. By the time he set out for the Press Club it was fully light, but the canteen seemed emptier than usual, and most of the German staff looked bored to death. After satisfying his new addiction to pancakes and syrup, and downing two cups of the passable coffee, he retraced his steps as far as the American headquarters on Kronprinzenallee.

During their time together on Christmas Eve, Wilhelm Isendahl had given him the name of a sympathetic American in the Denazification section of the Public Safety division. According to Isendahl, David Franks was a New York Jew with a mission, and that was to nail as many Nazis to the wall as higher authority would allow.

His office was at the other end of the old Luftwaffe building, a good three hundred metres from Dallin's. Which was just as well – next week was quite soon enough for the resumption of his career as an American agent. Shchepkin had not said how much Russell should tell the Americans about Friday's scheme to torpedo Nemedin, and it seemed simpler to get that behind him before meeting Dallin.

Sometimes he thought he should write it all down as he went along. Like a paper trail in a maze.

David Franks, at least, conformed to expectations – he looked and acted like other New York Jews of Russell's acquaintance – dark and bespectacled, with a restless intelligence just on the cusp of neurotic. His office might well have been the fullest in Berlin, in terms of both paper and future prospects. Towers of completed *Fragebogen* rose from the floor like Franks' hometown skyscrapers.

Isendahl had already rung to introduce him, which saved a lot of explanation. It turned out the Nazi records he needed – the ones discovered in September and subsequently brought to Berlin – were held at a villa on the edge of the Grunewald. Franks commuted between the two, checking the *Fragebogen* against the official files, and as luck would have it he was on his way there. 'Wilhelm didn't give me any names, only the general idea,' he told Russell as they walked down to the jeep. 'But I'm happy to take all the help I can get. There are enough of our people who don't give a damn.'

'And why's that?'

'Two reasons. One, they've decided that fighting the Russians has top priority, and any enemy of theirs is a friend of ours. Two, anti-Semitism's not just a German disease.'

They drove down Argentinische Allee, passing the Onkel Toms Hütte U-Bahn station before turning west towards the forest. The villa was in Wasserkäfersteigstrasse, a cul-de-sac ending in trees. A shiny new barbed-wire fence surrounded the complex, and two sentries guarded the gate.

'Someone cares,' Russell murmured.

'So they should. The stuff in here will determine Germany's future.' He turned to Russell. 'Actually, they're pretty lax. They know me, so they probably won't even ask to see your papers, but if they do, I'll tell them you're helping me with some local knowledge. Okay?'

In the event, they were just waved through. Down in the over-stuffed vault, Franks collected the relevant file cards, and Russell transcribed any additional details that they contained. All the names they had gathered from their Jewish witnesses were there save one. There was no card for a Fehse, Reinhard or otherwise.

'Why would it be missing?' Russell asked.

'No reason. If it's not here, there isn't one.'

'Maybe someone just walked in and took it.'

'I doubt it. They may not always check papers at the gate, but they would if the face was unfamiliar.'

That, Russell thought, begged all sorts of questions.

* * *

He spent the afternoon writing, and was watching the street for the Soviet bus when Scott Dallin turned in through the gate. 'Let's walk,' were the American's first words. He was seething with anger.

Russell put on his coat, wrote a short note to Effi, and went out to join him. It hadn't snowed that day, but the temperature seemed about right, and the sky seemed to be slowly filling with the stuff. Dallin didn't say another word until they reached the corner, and started down Königin-Luise-Strasse in the direction of the Grunewald.

'You remember me saying that our two intelligence organisations would operate best if they maintained their separate identities?'

'Something along those lines.' This was obviously a rather big bee in Dallin's bonnet.

'But we do have to get on with each other.'

'I wish you luck.'

'It's nothing to do with luck. It's about not crapping in each other's garden.'

'I haven't got a clue what you're talking about,' Russell said, although a suspicion was growing.

'I've spent half the morning on the line to Washington, listening to some Ivy League asshole tick me off for messing with Sherman Crosby's plan to see off the Russians. Now do you know what I'm talking about?'

'Not exactly.'

They crossed Kronprinzenallee and started up the lane which led into the trees.

'The black marketeer who you thought was responsible for your friend Kuzorra's imprisonment...'

'And his death.'

'You're to leave him alone.'

'Why the hell should I?'

Dallin stopped and turned to face Russell. 'Because I goddamn tell you to,' he almost shouted. 'And if that's not enough, because he's working for us. In fact I'm reliably informed that he's one of our key people in this whole goddamn city.'

The American losing his temper helped Russell keep his. 'What does "reliably informed" mean? Who told you, and how do you know you can trust them? I can prove that Fehse – that's Geruschke's real name – ran the holding centre in Leipzig that shipped all the local Jews to Auschwitz, even those that bribed him not to with money or sexual favours. He's a drug-dealer and a pimp. He's been stockpiling insulin to push up the price while children are dying of diabetes. The Jews he supposedly helps are ex-Nazis with stolen Jewish identities...' He broke off to let a worried-looking German hurry by with his dog.

'Even if all that were true...'

'Why the hell would I make it up!?'

Now Russell's explosion calmed Dallin down. 'Even if all that were true, apparently we need him. You can't always choose your allies – we just fought a war with the Reds, for Chrissake. And I won't be telling you again. Leave the man alone, however big a bastard he is. Don't go near him, don't write about him, don't pass the story on – we'll know if you do, and nothing will make it into print. Forget about him. For your own sake as much as your country's.'

'For my own sake?'

'According to Crosby, Geruschke was ready to kill you once, but agreed to let you go when they told him you were working for us. Crosby had no need to do that, and I doubt he would again.'

'So if next time Geruschke really does kill me, he won't get so much as a slap on the wrist?'

'There won't be a next time. Get it into your head – he's off-limits. If he's as evil as you say he is, then he'll end up paying one way or another. Leave vengeance to God.'

'And if I don't?'

'Well, if Geruschke doesn't kill you, Crosby probably will. And if by some miracle you survive, you'll certainly be off my payroll. But I'm assuming you do want to serve your country. That's what you told Lindenberg in London.'

'Of course I do,' Russell said automatically. What would happen to him and Shchepkin if the Americans kicked him out? What would Nemedin do come to that? His use to the Soviets would be over, and he couldn't imagine their gratefully letting him go. A silver-plated bullet seemed likelier than a gold watch.

He needed to think. He needed to talk to Effi, although he guessed what she would say – that Kuzorra had saved his life, and wouldn't want him throwing it away over someone like Fehse. Which was probably true. But the detective deserved some sort of justice, and so did Fehse's other victims.

'It sticks in the throat,' he told Dallin, 'but you've made yourself clear. I'll let him be.'

* * *

Effi was still not back when Russell got home, but Thomas was ensconced in his study, having just returned from his family Christmas in the countryside. Hanna and Lotte were following on after the New Year, which seemed reason enough for a celebratory drink. 'I bought it from an American soldier on the platform at Erfurt,' Thomas explained, as he opened the bottle of bourbon. 'For a king's ransom, but I felt it would help me deal with the Russians.'

'You're not going to waste it on them?'

'No, of course not. Each time they almost drive me to distraction I shall remember that this little beauty is waiting at home.'

'It won't last long then.'

'Probably not.' He filled two short glasses that Russell recognised from pre-war days, and handed one over. '*Gesundheit!*'

'*Gesundheit,*' Russell echoed. The bourbon tasted wonderful. 'So you had a good Christmas?'

'Wonderful. For all the reasons you'd expect. And it was so good to get away from ruins for a while. How was your trip to Vienna?'

'That was just the beginning.' He filled Thomas in on what had happened since, concluding with the news that Miriam's husband and children were his latest lodgers.

'So Leon and Esther have grandchildren,' Thomas murmured. 'Which doesn't bring Miriam back, but...'

The way he said it drew Russell's eyes to the black-framed photograph of Joachim on the mantelpiece.

'He'd have been twenty-four in a few weeks' time,' Thomas said in an even voice. 'Now that the war's over, with all that we know of what happened in the East, his death seems... I don't know, even crueller, I suppose. I only hope he did nothing terrible. Nothing he had to take with him.'

'Joachim was a good boy,' Russell said, acutely conscious of how inadequate it sounded.

Thomas just nodded. 'Most of them were.' He managed a sad smile. 'I don't want to live in the past – that's not really life, is it? But sometimes... You know, when I got back to Berlin in August I borrowed one of the firm's Russian lorries and drove out to where Ilse and Matthias died. I don't know why really. I just felt like sharing the last things they'd seen. And it was such a beautiful stretch of road, especially in summer. I got out and walked around, and I started thinking about when we were young, Ilse and I, and all the good times we had growing up. She could drive me mad, but God I loved her. I remembered her bringing you home for the first time – an Englishman for heaven's sake, and an even more self-righteous communist than she was. But Ilse insisted that we get along, and in the end she had her way. And when the two of you split up, she was determined that it shouldn't affect our friendship, and she made damn sure that it didn't.'

'I never knew that.'

'Ilse was special.'

'That I did know.'

Thomas shook his head and reached for a refill. 'I wonder what she'd think of the family firm printing German schoolbooks written by the Soviets.'

'She'd appreciate the irony.'

Thomas grunted. 'I read today that Hitler was evil incarnate, but that Stalin is God's gift to the working man.'

'Well, 50% wasn't such a bad mark when I was at school.'

* * *

It started snowing around noon the next day, and persisted through the afternoon. By the time Russell stepped down onto the Jannowitzbrücke platform, several centimetres had fallen, and descending the outside staircase required considerable caution. That danger averted, he walked slowly westwards along the shell-gapped Spree promenade, eyes peering out through the curtain of snow for any lurking figures. There were none on either side of the yellow-lit shop that Shchepkin had specified, but having passed it on the other side of the road he hesitated before turning back. Shchepkin's reasoning had been clear enough, but that only mattered if his deductions were correct, and Russell wasn't even sure what they were. He had chosen to trust the Russian, but not with any great confidence. Even now, the impulse to walk away was only restrained by his complete lack of an alternative strategy.

He had told Effi only that he was picking something up. If things went wrong, she would know that he'd fallen foul of the Soviets, but not how or why. He should have told her the full story; his only reason for not doing so was his own awareness of how flimsy it all sounded.

There was no point in putting it off any longer. He patted the pocketed gun for reassurance, and crossed the empty Rolandufer. Through the door of the shop he could see the proprietor, an old man with wire-rimmed glasses perched on the end of his nose, sitting behind his threadbare counter. He looked up as Russell entered, and shook out the Soviet-sponsored newspaper that he was reading.

'Do you have a package for...' Russell began, then realised he'd forgotten the pre-arranged name. 'Liefke,' he suddenly remembered, and almost wished he hadn't.

The old man found this lapse amusing, but pulled a thickish envelope out from under the counter and held out both hands, one with the package, the other for payment. Russell gave him the cigarettes, stuffed the envelope inside his coat, and let himself back out into the snow. There was a couple walking past on the other side, but Rolandufer seemed otherwise empty.

He headed back towards the station, and gingerly climbed the slippery steps to the westbound platform. There were several other people waiting for a train, but none seemed to be watching him. He turned and looked out across the snow-shrouded Spree at the sparsely lit wasteland beyond. After dark this section of Berlin was about as welcoming as the Minotaur's cave.

But so far so good. No one had followed him up the steps, and a train was visible in the distance, its headlights gliding round the elevated curve. Another fifteen minutes and he would be at Zoo Station, and in the relative safety of the British sector.

The carriages that pulled in to the snow-covered platform were fuller than he expected. Stepping in through the sliding doors, Russell turned right in search of an empty seat, and found one near the end. As the train pulled out he glanced sideways through the window of the connecting doors, and there was Nemedin, shaking the snow from his hat.

Russell quickly looked away, cold sweat prickling on his back.

His first coherent thought was that he and Shchepkin were done for. His second was to search, like a guilty schoolboy, for some plausible excuse. Could he walk up to the NKVD man and hand him the papers? 'Oh, I was just looking for you; I got a tip-off that someone had stolen your personnel file and left it in a shop, and I knew you'd want it back.'

Ridiculous. And he was willing to bet that the envelope in his pocket was singularly devoid of personnel files. If Nemedin had known everything in advance, he'd had ample time to remove the incriminating material and replace it with scrap paper. Hadleigh was waiting in vain.

The train was pulling into Alexanderplatz Station, and when the doors opened it took all Russell's strength not to run howling into the snow. Think, he told himself. What could he do? There was no point in running – if Nemedin knew about Shchepkin's scheme, then he had enough on them both already. So why was the bastard stringing things out by following him? To find out where Russell was taking the package? Perhaps, although a penchant for sadism seemed just as likely.

The train jerked into motion once more. There had been no shared glances, so Nemedin was probably unaware that Russell had seen him.

But how did that help? What could? He and Shchepkin were finished. Unless.

It was him or Nemedin, and he did have the gun. Could he kill the Georgian in cold blood?

If he could manage it, he could live with it.

He would have to lure him somewhere. Away from people. Somewhere quiet, but not so secluded that Nemedin would smell a rat.

The train was pulling in to Börse Station. Where should he get off? He hadn't been near Börse since April, and all he could see from the window was ruins. Friedrichstrasse was next, and that was always crowded. But Lehrter Station... He could lead Nemedin up past the railway yards, along the streets he'd walked the other week to Hunder Zembski's garage. There had to be somewhere he could mount an ambush.

It sounded like a plan, but so had Schlieffen's. He resisted the urge to sneak a look at his pursuer, and tried not to convey the anxiety that was fluttering in his stomach. Perhaps Nemedin had got off. Perhaps his presence at Jannowitzbrücke had been the cruellest of coincidences.

No. He could feel the man's eyes on him.

The train stopped at Friedrichstrasse, where many got out and many got on. As the doors began to close he caught a glimpse of the snow streaming down through the shattered roof.

He was at the right end of the train for the Invalidenstrasse exit at Lehrter. As the Charité Hospital loomed on the right he got to his feet and went to the door, giving Nemedin plenty of warning.

Once on the platform, he strode rapidly towards the exit without looking back. The snow seemed heavier, a diaphanous curtain of small flakes. Even if Nemedin lost visual contact, he had only to follow the footsteps.

Russell consciously slowed his pace. He couldn't raise doubts – he needed the Georgian to feel safe, until he had him at his mercy. Not that any would be forthcoming.

He reached the Invalidenstrasse exit, and turning right caught a hint of movement behind him.

A couple of street lamps were burning, and the white flakes drifting past them reminded Russell of a snowglobe he'd once been given for Christmas. There were moving lights in the distance, and the sound of laughter closer at hand. A short way up on the other side, the silhouette of the district court building marked the entrance to Heidestrasse.

He angled his way across the wide boulevard and slipped round the corner. There was only darkness ahead, and he knew this had to be the place. Nemedin would be crazy to follow him further. The man I shall kill, he thought. The title of Effi's film.

He took the gun from his pocket, checked that it was ready, and stood there waiting in the falling snow.

One, two, three... he began to wonder if he'd imagined it all.

Four, five, six... would he soon be laughing at his own paranoia?

Seven...

Nemedin came round the corner. Slowly, cautiously, but without a gun in his hand. The faint smile vanished the moment he saw Russell, or more particularly his gun.

Russell pulled the trigger, aiming for the heart, and the echoing crash seemed, for an instant, to stop the snow from falling.

Nemedin fell backwards, a look of surprise on his face.

Russell stepped forward, steeled himself, and fired again. As he stood looking down, a snowflake landed on a glazed-over eye.

He was wondering what, if anything, he should do with the body when his ears picked up the sound of an approaching vehicle. Two headlights were growing brighter on Invalidenstrasse. It sounded like a jeep. The Red Army.

He began walking back towards the station, hugging the side of the buildings. Would the soldiers notice the body? And if so, would they bother to check who it was? He was about two hundred metres from the Stadtbahn station entrance, and he still had the wide and empty road to cross. The sector border was around here somewhere, but he was damned if he knew exactly where. And who would arrest the Soviets for trespassing?

He heard the jeep behind him start to slow, then suddenly rev up again. There was no time to cross the road. He had to get off it. As he ran towards the railway bridge, a turning appeared on his right, a road running down through the bomb-twisted gates to the distant yard and sheds. The road itself looked depressingly straight, so instead he plunged down the snow-covered embankment. Losing his footing, he rolled the rest of the way, and slammed into a post that was half-concealed by the snow. As he got painfully to his feet, he heard movement on the road above, a squealing of brakes and urgent voices. Somewhere behind him a bullet struck metal.

He was only a few metres from the road bridge, and Jesse Owens would have envied his sprint into the shadows that lay beneath it. A few hundred metres up the tracks several glowing fires were visible – the refugee camp around the main line station. He started running in that direction, and was daring to hope that the Russians had given up on him when another bullet hissed past his head. Glancing back through the veil of snow he could see two figures on the tracks, and two more on the bridge.

The next few shots were less accurate, and a line of empty cattle cars offered the chance to duck out of sight. He ran along behind the train, and as he neared the end, realised he had an audience – there were people living in the last few cars. He tossed his gun under one of them, and slowed to a walk as he passed under the elevated Stadtbahn and approached the main line platforms. Now there were lots of people, sitting or lying under the splintered canopies, or gathered round a line of makeshift braziers. As he walked up the platform he became conscious of a rising sound behind him, a strange blend of fear, surprise and loathing, as news spread among the German refugees that the hated Red Army had somehow caught up with them.

Russell walked on, past the room where he and Effi had found Torsten and the children, and out onto the old concourse, where UNRRA was serving watery soup to whoever wanted it. He took a bowl and sat with it, keeping one eye open for the Russians, waiting for the shock to subside. His heart was still drumming inside his chest, and it was all he could do not to burst into tears. When the thought crossed his mind that he wanted his mother, he almost laughed out loud.

Taking one life shouldn't feel so huge, not when a war had killed millions. But by God it did.

At least the Russians had thought better of invading the station, and after half an hour's wait he judged it safe to take his leave. After consigning the envelope to a convenient brazier he walked back up to the Stadtbahn platform which he'd left an hour and a killing before.

A train was pulling in as he reached the top of the steps, and he squeezed himself aboard. As it rattled along above Lüneburger Strasse he stood, face pressed against the window, his mind a foggy blank. At Zoo Station he sleepwalked his way down to the familiar buffet, and joined the queue before he realised that coffee was not what he needed. The first bar he came to supplied a ludicrously expensive schnapps which he downed in a single swallow. He felt like repeating the trick with the second, but carried it instead to a table, and sank wearily into a chair.

He had just killed a man in cold blood, and the most that he felt was a lack of surprise. It had been coming for years, he thought. Even the identity of the victim seemed part of the some strange logic – not a Nazi, but a high-ranking member of the NKVD, a guardian of the Revolution that had once so inspired him, that had changed his life, found him the mother of his son, brought him to Germany.

Shchepkin would understand the warped inevitability of it all, he thought. But no one else.

There was no use trying to explain this to Effi – she just didn't think that way. He would tell her he had killed Nemedin in self-defence. That if he hadn't, Nemedin would have killed him, and Shchepkin, and most likely Shchepkin's wife and daughter. And sooner rather than later.

A simpler story, and also true.

But there'd been so many other moments of choice. He found himself remembering his and Effi's day-trip to the Harz Mountains six summers earlier. That was when they'd decided that some sort of resistance to the Nazis was the least they could live with. Had they made the right decision? Would the world really have been that different if they'd put their consciences in hibernation for a few years? People now dead – like the Ottings in Stettin – might still be alive. He and Effi, he and Paul, would not have spent more than three years apart. He would never have met Nemedin, or stood above his corpse in the snow.

But good things had also flowed from that decision. If his own contribution had often felt marginal, he had no doubt that Effi had saved lives.

And Rosa, he thought. A random consequence of the path they had chosen, yet with more power to change their own lives than any twist of political fate. A fresh infusion of innocence to replenish their rapidly diminishing supply. And he missed the girl, much more than he'd expected he would.

* * *

'Are you sure you're all right?' Effi asked him, as they set out the following morning.

He had told her everything the night before, and she'd been less shocked, at least on the surface, than he'd expected. But he was still afraid of catching a new look in her eyes, one that said she saw him differently, that she was disappointed in him. 'I'm fine,' he told her.

She gave his arm an encouraging squeeze, but didn't pursue the matter. She was sure there were things she should say, but hadn't yet worked out what they were. Their business that morning seemed safer ground. 'What if Otto 1 – whatever his real name is – tells us to get lost, and goes straight to Fehse? Won't that bring the wrath of Dallin down on our heads?'

'It might, but what choice have we got? We'll just have to convince him that we're not after him. That talking is his best option.'

'Okay.'

They waited an age for a bus, and had to stand throughout the journey. Yesterday's snow was already melting, pools of water forming round the dust-choked drains on the Ku'damm. The only sign of life at the Honey Trap was the usual crowd of boys scouring the ground for cigarette stubs.

Alighting at the Memorial Church, they walked up past the ruined zoo, skirted the western end of the park, and crossed canal and river. It was only a few minutes past nine when they reached Solinger Strasse, and climbed the stairs to Otto 1's flat.

Their first two knocks met with no response, the third with an angry shout, the fourth with sounds of movement. 'Who is it?' the familiar voice shouted, whereupon Russell held a finger to his lips. When a second enquiry went unanswered, the door began to open, and Russell gave it a helping shove, throwing the opener backwards.

'We need to talk to you,' Russell said mildly, as Otto got angrily to his feet. Effi closed the door.

'Get the hell out of here,' Otto told them without much conviction.

'We're sorry to bust in on you like this,' Russell continued, 'but, like I said, we just need a short conversation.'

'I've got nothing to talk to you about.'

'Oh, but you have. We know that Otto Pappenheim is not your real name.'

'Of course it is.'

'And we know you're not Jewish.'

'Of course I am.'

Russell sighed. 'Look, we don't care what identity you use. If you like the name Otto Pappenheim, fine. We're not planning to tell anyone who you really are, but we do need to know what happened to the real Otto, the one whose papers you ended up with.'

'Why should I tell you anything?'

'Human decency ring a bell? A girl who wants to know what happened to her father?'

The man just shook his head.

'How about your own skin?' He took out the photograph which included the fake Otto, and held it up for inspection. 'If we show this round the Jewish DP camps someone will pick you out from somewhere, and you'll be finished. So why not just tell us what we want to know, and we'll just go away and leave you in peace.'

The man gave him a calculating look. 'How do I know you'll do that?'

Russell shook his head. 'You don't, but I will. Assuming you're not Josef Mengele.'

'Who's he? I was just a guard.'

'Ah, that's a start. Where?'

'At Grosse Hamburger Strasse. Just a guard,' he repeated. 'I was moved there from Moabit – I didn't have any choice in the matter.'

'Just obeying orders.'

'Exactly. And all these people nowadays who say we should have refused – I'd like to see what they would have done.'

'I know what you mean. So where did you get Otto Pappenheim's papers from?'

The man hesitated, then seemed to realise he'd gone too far to stop. 'He was just another Jew. The *Greifers* brought him in after one of them recognised him.'

'And then what?'

'The usual. They knew he had a wife and daughter, and they wanted him to give them up. They beat him for days but he wouldn't say a word. Not a single word. Some of them were like that. Not many, but some. '

'What happened to him?' Effi asked, speaking for the first time.

'He killed himself. Managed to cut his own throat somehow – they found him one morning in a pool of blood. No one could work out how he'd done it.'

'And how did you get his papers?'

'When the Russians got to the Oder everyone knew it was over, and we – all of us who worked there – we went through the papers of those who had died and picked a set with the right sort of age and physical details.' He saw the look on Russell's face. 'You said you would leave me in peace.'

'So I did. Where were they buried – the ones who died?'

'The first few were buried in a corner of the Prenzlauer Cemetery, but people objected, so they had to be dug up and burnt. After that they were all burnt.' He wrinkled his nose as if remembering the smell.

Russell gave Effi a questioning look, which she returned with a shake of her head. 'Then we'll be on our way. I won't say it's been a pleasure, but at least we don't have to meet again.'

They made their way back down the stairs, and walked to the bottom of Solinger Strasse. 'I shouldn't be happy,' Effi said slowly, breaking the silence. 'Not after what we've just heard. But I can't help it. I feel like... like I can stop holding my breath. Does that make me a terrible person?'

'Of course not. And Rosa will be proud of her father, when she finds out who he was. And if he knew about it, he'd be glad that his daughter found you.'

'Found us.'

'Yes.'

After skirting the park and walking down past the empty cages, they stopped off at the Zoo Station buffet. As Russell queued for their drinks he decided to honour his word, and not turn the fake Otto in. He knew it was ridiculous, but he felt almost grateful to the man, for preserving the real Otto's memory, for giving Effi the certainty she craved.

Fehse though was another matter, and hearing the story of the real Otto's death had helped Russell make up his mind. Carrying their coffees back to the table he knew what he would do.

As he put down Effi's cup, he realised she was crying. 'I thought I'd lost my chance,' she half sobbed. 'When I was alone in the war, I started regretting that I – that we – had never had a child, and with each year that went by it seemed less and less likely that we ever would. And then Rosa arrived and I couldn't believe my luck. I mean, I really couldn't believe it – I thought someone was bound to take her away.' She looked up at him, smiling through the tears. 'But there isn't anyone, is there? She's ours.'

Ghosts of Treblinka

With *The Man I Shall Kill* so close to completion Kuhnert had decided cast and crew would work on New Year's Day, and Effi had long disappeared on the Soviet bus when a dark-haired youth arrived at the door with a package for John Russell. Assured that he had the right person, the boy handed it over and walked away, ignoring Russell's query as to who it was from.

There were people in the kitchen, so Russell took the small parcel upstairs and unwrapped it on their bed. There was a stiff-backed ledger inside but no accompanying letter. Leafing through it, Russell understood why – the book spoke for itself. There was a page for each of Fehse's employees, stating their real names, and listing details of their past employ in various Nazi organizations.

Guessing what this meant, he stuffed the book under their mattress, and went downstairs to collect his coat. The sky was overcast, the air warm for the time of year, and his route to the American Press Club seemed unusually well-populated. Outside the Sector HQ the pavement was littered with New Year's Eve debris, and a large sign welcoming 1946 was draped across the front facade. Like everyone else, the Americans were hoping for something better than the year just ended.

As usual, all the local papers were available for perusal in the corner of the Press Club lounge, and it didn't take Russell long to find the item he was looking for. 'Night Club owner murdered,' the headline ran – Rudolf Geruschke had been found dead in his Wannsee villa, the latest victim of

Berlin's spiralling crime wave. There were two paragraphs lamenting the recent plague of robberies attributed to Russian and Polish DPs, but no specific connection was offered, let alone proven. The manner of death was not spelt out, and no mention was made of what had been stolen.

There had, Russell guessed, only been the one item – the book now hidden under his mattress.

He felt... what did he feel? After more than a little consideration, he had abandoned any idea of passing on all he knew about Geruschke-Fehse to another journalist. Dallin couldn't have stopped him, or even proved his guilt thereafter, but the American would have known. And the relationship between them – which he and Shchepkin needed to work – would be damaged beyond repair.

So he had done the next best thing. He had written down all he knew about Fehse, and persuaded Wilhelm Isendahl to fix up a meeting with the Ghosts of Treblinka. A young Jewish man had met him in Neukölln the next evening. He had skimmed through Russell's notes, raised his head, and offered a look of withering scorn. But he had taken the indictment with him.

And they hadn't wasted much time. There was no mention of a mark on the body, but Russell was willing to bet that there'd been one. Crosby would know about it, and that should let Russell out. As far as he knew, only the Ghosts could implicate him, and first they would have to be caught. And given the state of the Berlin police, that seemed less than likely.

Outside, the sun had broken through the clouds, and a stroll in the Grunewald seemed indicated. He was soon crossing the path that he and his Russian companions had traversed the previous April – only eight months ago, but it seemed like years.

He was glad that Fehse was gone, or grateful at least that someone had stopped him. He hadn't pulled the trigger himself, but felt responsible nevertheless. Which brought the number of men he had killed to a chilling six.

He had thought murdering Nemedin would haunt him, but it hadn't, not really. And neither would Fehse. If he was haunted by anything, it was leaving the boy on the mountain. Sometimes that awful cry of grief seemed to echo through the ruins.

There had been no repercussions over Nemedin, no public complaints from the Soviets, no desperate Shchepkin banging on his door. None of which had surprised him. Nemedin might conceivably have confided in someone, but it seemed unlikely – the man had been far too sure of himself.

He would be replaced of course. There would be another Nemedin looming over Shchepkin's shoulder, probably just as suspicious, and possibly not so careless. They would have to deal with whoever it was, and Russell would have to deal with Dallin, until Shchepkin found the magic spade that would dig them out of their hole.

He had hoped that the need for fancy footwork would vanish with the war, but life and the Soviets had had other ideas, and he would have to keep on dancing. Maybe he and Effi could emulate those winners of Depression-era dance marathons, and be the very last couple with their feet still twitching.

Dallin on Thursday, Shchepkin on Friday – what was it Eliot had said about measuring his life in coffee spoons? He seemed to be measuring his in espionage trysts.

But Miriam's father had decided to live, and the family had a flat of their own. Thomas was due back on Saturday with Hanna and Lotte, and Effi was leaving on Monday, intent on returning with Rosa, Zarah and Lothar. Only Paul seemed keen to stay in England, but at least his son seemed happy. A father could hardly ask for more.

Even his stock as a journalist seemed to be rising. According to Solly, his reporting of the Jewish exodus was the talk of Fleet Street.

And best of all, it seemed like he and Effi had found each other again, where it mattered, in the heart.

After walking through the trees for an hour or so, he turned for home. As he rounded the corner into Vogelsangstrasse a scrawny cat ran across the road and disappeared into the rubble.

It was the first he'd seen since their return, a fitting partner for the first bird, which had flown past their window that morning.

Maybe Berlin would rise again.

THE EXTRACT OVERLEAF IS FROM THE OPENING
CHAPTER OF **ZOO STATION**, THE FIRST 'STATION'
NOVEL, SET IN BERLIN IN 1939.

Into the blue

There were two hours left of 1938. In Danzig it had been snowing on and off all day, and a gang of children were enjoying a snowball fight in front of the grain warehouses which lined the old waterfront. John Russell paused to watch them for a few moments, then walked on up the cobbled street towards the blue and yellow lights.

The Sweden Bar was far from crowded, and those few faces that turned his way weren't exactly brimming over with festive spirit. In fact, most of them looked like they'd rather be somewhere else.

It was an easy thing to want. The Christmas decorations hadn't been removed, just allowed to drop, and now formed part of the flooring, along with patches of melting slush, floating cigarette ends and the odd broken bottle. The Bar was famous for the savagery of its international brawls, but on this particular night the various groups of Swedes, Finns and Letts seemed devoid of the energy needed to get one started. Usually a table or two of German naval ratings could be relied upon to provide the necessary spark, but the only Germans present were a couple of ageing prostitutes, and they were getting ready to leave.

Russell took a stool at the bar, bought himself a *Goldwasser* and glanced through the month-old copy of the *New York Herald Tribune* which, for some inexplicable reason, was lying there. One of his own articles was in it, a piece on German attitudes to their pets. It was accompanied by a cute-looking photograph of a Schnauser.

Seeing him reading, a solitary Swede two stools down asked him, in perfect English, if he spoke that language. Russell admitted that he did.

'You are English!' the Swede exclaimed, and shifted his consider-able bulk to the stool adjoining Russell's.

Their conversation went from friendly to sentimental, and sen-timental to maudlin, at what seemed like breakneck pace. Three *Goldwassers* later, the Swede was telling him that he, Lars, was not the true father of his children. Vibeke had never admitted it, but he knew it to be true.

Russell gave him an encouraging pat on the shoulder, and Lars sunk forward, his head making a dull clunk as it made contact with the polished surface of the bar. 'Happy New Year,' Russell murmured. He shifted the Swede's head slightly to ease his breathing, and got up to leave.

Outside, the sky was beginning to clear, the air almost cold enough to sober him up. An organ was playing in the Protestant Seaman's church, nothing hymnal, just a slow lament, as if the organist was saying a personal farewell to the year gone by. It was a quarter to midnight.

Russell walked back across the city, conscious of the moisture seep-ing in through the holes in his shoes. The Langermarkt was full of couples, laughing and squealing as they clutched each other for bal-ance on the slippery sidewalks.

He cut over the Breite Gasse and reached the Holzmarkt just as the bells began pealing in the New Year. The square was full of celebrat-ing people, and an insistent hand pulled him into a circle of revellers dancing and singing in the snow. When the song ended and the circle broke up, the Polish girl on his left reached up and brushed her lips against his, eyes shining with happiness. It was, he thought, a better than expected opening to 1939.

His hotel's reception area was deserted, and the sounds of celebra-tion emanating from the kitchen at the back suggested the night staff were enjoying their own private party. Russell thought about making himself a hot chocolate and drying his shoes in one of the ovens, but decided against. He took his key, clambered up the stairs to the third floor, and trundled down the corridor to his room. Closing the door behind him, he became painfully aware that the occupants of the neighbouring rooms were still welcoming in the new year, a singsong on one side, floor-shaking sex on the other. He took off his sodden shoes and socks, dried his wet feet with a towel and sank back onto the vibrating bed.

There was a discreet, barely audible tap on his door.

Cursing, he levered himself off the bed and prised the door open. A man in a crumpled suit and open shirt stared back at him.

'Mr John Russell,' the man said in English, as if he was introducing Russell to himself. The Russian accent was slight, but unmistakable. 'Could I talk with you for a few minutes?'

'It's a bit late...' Russell began. The man's face was vaguely familiar. 'But why not?' he continued, as the singers next door reached for a new and louder chorus. 'A journalist should never turn down a conversation,' he murmured, mostly to himself, as he let the man in. 'Take the chair,' he suggested.

His visitor sat back and crossed one leg over the other, hitching up his trouser leg as he did so. 'We have met before,' he said. 'A long time ago. My name is Shchepkin. Yevgeny Grigorovich Shchepkin. We...'

'Yes,' Russell interrupted, as the memory clicked into place. 'The discussion group on journalism at the fifth Congress. The summer of '24.'

Shchepkin nodded his acknowledgement. 'I remember your contributions,' he said. 'Full of passion,' he added, his eyes circling the room and resting, for a few seconds, on his host's dilapidated shoes.

Russell perched himself on the edge of the bed. 'As you said – a long time ago.' He and Ilse had met at that conference, and set in motion their ten-year cycle of marriage, parenthood, separation and divorce. Shchepkin's hair had been black and wavy in 1924; now it was a close-cropped grey. They were both a little older than the century, Russell guessed, and Shchepkin was wearing pretty well, considering what he'd probably been through the last fifteen years. He had a handsome face of indeterminate nationality, with deep brown eyes above prominent slanting cheekbones, an aquiline nose and lips just the full side of perfect. He could have passed for a citizen of most European countries, and probably had.

The Russian completed his survey of the room. 'This is a dreadful hotel,' he said.

Russell laughed. 'Is that what you wanted to talk about?'

'No. Of course not.'

'So what are you here for?'

'Ah.' Shchepkin hitched his trouser leg again. 'I am here to offer you work.'

Russell raised an eyebrow. 'You? Who exactly do you represent?'

The Russian shrugged. 'My country. The Writers' Union. It doesn't matter. You will be working for us. You know who we are.'

'No,' Russell said. 'I mean, no I'm not interested. I...'

'Don't be so hasty,' Shchepkin said. 'Hear me out. We aren't asking you to do anything which your German hosts could object to.' The Russian allowed himself a smile. 'Let me tell you exactly what we have in mind. We want a series of articles about positive aspects of the Nazi regime.' He paused for a few seconds, waiting in vain for Russell to demand an explanation. 'You are not German but you live in Berlin,' he went on. 'You once had a reputation as a journalist of the left, and though that reputation has, shall we say, faded, no one could accuse you of being an apologist for the Nazis...'

'But you want me to be just that.'

'No, no. We want positive aspects, not a positive picture overall. That would not be believable.'

Russell was curious in spite of himself. Or because of the *Goldwassers*. 'Do you just need my name on these articles?' he asked. 'Or do you want me to write them as well?'

'Oh, we want you to write them. We like your style – all that irony.'

Russell shook his head – Stalin and irony didn't seem like much of a match.

Shchepkin misread the gesture. 'Look,' he said, 'let me put all my cards on the table.'

Russell grinned.

Shchepkin offered a wry smile in return. 'Well, most of them anyway. Look, we are aware of your situation. You have a German son and a German lady-friend, and you want to stay in Germany if you possibly can. Of course if a war breaks out you will have to leave, or else they will intern you. But until that moment comes – and maybe it won't – miracles do happen – until it does you want to earn your living as a journalist without upsetting your hosts. What better way than this? You write nice things about the Nazis – not too nice, of course, the articles have to be credible... but you stress their good side.'

'Does shit have a good side?' Russell wondered out loud.

'Come, come,' Shchepkin insisted, 'you know better than that. Unemployment eliminated, a renewed sense of community, healthy children, cruises for workers, cars for the people...'

'You should work for Joe Goebbels.'

Shchepkin gave him a mock-reproachful look.

'Okay,' Russell said, 'I take your point. Let me ask you a question. There's only one reason you'd want that sort of article – you're softening up your own people for some sort of deal with the devil. Right?'

Shchepkin flexed his shoulders in an eloquent shrug.

'Why?'

The Russian grunted. 'Why deal with the devil? I don't know what the leadership is thinking. But I could make an educated guess, and so could you.'

Russell could. 'The western powers are trying to push Hitler east, so Stalin has to push him west? Are we talking about a non-aggression pact, or something more?'

Shchepkin looked almost affronted. 'What more could there be? Any deal with that man can only be temporary. We know what he is.'

Russell nodded. It made sense. He closed his eyes, as if it were possible to blank out the approaching calamity. On the other side of the opposite wall, his musical neighbours were intoning one of those Polish river songs which could reduce a statue to tears. Through the wall behind him silence had fallen, but his bed was still quivering like a tuning fork.

'We'd also like some information,' Shchepkin was saying, almost apologetically. 'Nothing military,' he added quickly, seeing the look on Russell's face. 'No armament statistics or those naval plans that Sherlock Holmes is always being asked to recover. Nothing of that sort. We just want a better idea of what ordinary Germans are thinking. How they are taking the changes in working conditions, how they are likely to react if war comes – that sort of thing. We don't want any secrets, just your opinions. And nothing on paper. You can deliver them in person, on a monthly basis.'

Russell looked sceptical.

Shchepkin ploughed on. 'You will be well paid – very well. In any currency, any bank, any country, that you choose. You can move into a better rooming house…'

'I like my rooming house.'

'You can buy things for your son, your girlfriend. You can have your shoes mended.'

'I don't…'

'The money is only an extra. You were with us once…'

'A long long time ago.'

'Yes, I know. But you cared about your fellow human beings. I heard you talk. That doesn't change. And if we go under there will be nothing left.'

'A cynic might say there's not much to choose between you.'

'The cynic would be wrong,' Shchepkin replied, exasperated and perhaps a little angry. 'We have spilt blood, yes. But reluctantly, and in faith of a better future. *They* enjoy it. Their idea of progress is a European slave-state.'

'I know.'

'One more thing. If money and politics don't persuade you, think of this. We will be grateful, and we have influence almost everywhere. And a man like you, in a situation like yours, is going to need influential friends.'

'No doubt about that.'

Shchepkin was on his feet. 'Think about it, Mr Russell,' he said, drawing an envelope from the inside pocket of his jacket and placing it on the nightstand. 'All the details are in here – how many words, delivery dates, fees, and so on. If you decide to do the articles, write to our press attaché in Berlin, telling him who you are, and that you've had the idea for them yourself. He will ask you to send him one in the post. The Gestapo will read it, and pass it on. You will then receive your first fee and suggestions for future stories. The last-but-one letters of the opening sentence will spell out the name of a city outside Germany which you can reach fairly easily. Prague, perhaps, or Cracow. You will spend the last weekend of the month in that city. And be sure to make your hotel reservation at least a week in advance. Once you are there, someone will contact you.'

'I'll think about it,' Russell said, mostly to avoid further argument. He wanted to spend his weekends with his son Paul and his girlfriend Effi, not the Shchepkins of this world.

The Russian nodded and let himself out. As if on cue, the Polish choir lapsed into silence.